Praise for The Curse

Billy Williams, Hall of Famer and former Cubs outfielder:
"This is a Hall-of-Fame book about curses, mysteries, doubt, and
hope. Dig your cleats in for one heck of an experience!"

Fergie Jenkins, Hall of Famer and former Cubs pitcher: "I have
dealt with The Curse for years. Andy and Rob may finally put it all
to rest!"

**Mike Murphy, long time Chicago sportscaster and Original
Bleacher Bum in 1967:** "My grandfather was a Cub fan born in
Chicago in 1909 and said until he died: 'Wait 'til next year'; my dad
was a Cub fan born in Chicago in 1927 and said until he died: 'Wait
'til next year'; I was born in Chicago in 1951 and FINALLY, I don't
have to say 'Wait 'til next year.'"!!!

Jay Johnstone, former Cubs outfielder and author of the book
Temporary Insanity: "I thought I knew about the insanity that
surrounds the Cubs, but now you're telling me they have a chance
to win the World Series? Now THAT'S insanity!"

Praise for The Curse

Joe Buck, Fox Sports broadcaster: "Andy Van Slyke and Rob Rains have combined to write a compelling book that will interest not only Cubs fans but all baseball fans everywhere."

Dutchie Caray, Harry Caray's widow: "The Cubs in the World Series? Harry would've been beside himself. There would not have been enough 'Holy Cows' to go around ... and believe me, he would have led the victory parade down Michigan Avenue."

Hall of Fame shortstop Ozzie Smith: "Andy Van Slyke and Rob Rains have written a book that will keep you entertained through every page."

Bob Ibach, former Cubs PR director and part owner of the Continental Baseball League: "I spent 10 years with the Cubs, watching, waiting, and wondering. Harry Caray once gave me a T-shirt that pretty much summed it all up. It read: 'Anyone Can Have A Bad Century.' Well, Harry was right - and now that long wait is over!"

Cubs Win! Cubs Win! ... Or Do They?

By
ANDY VAN SLYKE
with Rob Rains

www.ascendbooks.com

Requests for permission should be addressed to
Ascend Books, LLC, Attn: Rights and Permissions Department.

10 9 8 7 6 5 4 3 2 1

Printed in the United States of America

ISBN-13: 978-0-9841130-5-7
ISBN-10: 0-9841130-5-3

Library of Congress Control Number: 2010904861

Design: Lynette Ubel

Publisher's Note:
*This book is a work of fiction. References to real people, events,
establishments, organizations, and locales are intended solely to enhance
the fictional story, provide a historical perspective, and give the
book a sense of reality and authenticity.*

*All main characters, events, dialogue, and incidents in the novel are the
creation of the authors' imagination and their resemblance, if any, to actual
events or persons, living or dead, is entirely coincidental.*

www.ascendbooks.com

Additional Praise from Another Die-hard Cubs Fan

"**A**s a lifelong Cub fan I don't believe we're cursed, just due and hopeful. Which is why I don't give up, even on marriage.

"But as a lifelong Cubbie I know heartache. Rob and Andy's book captures metaphorically and literally the hopes and heartache of Cub Nation. It's an original, gripping story, which is only possible because it was written by men who intimately know 102 years of impossible stories and somehow found a way to make our 2003 collapse seem as trite as a goat in Wrigley. 'Oh, the humanity!'

"On the bright side, I know the publishing of this novel will undoubtedly be the catalyst that sends THIS YEAR'S CUBS into the World Series and beyond. Thanks guys!"

Actor, Tom Arnold

Prologue

Major league baseball charter flights are much different from commercial flights. They are more convenient and almost hassle-free. All of the normal aviation rules concerning passengers are ignored at will. Virtually nobody sits in his seat calmly wearing his seatbelt. Card games take over the back half of the plane. Players stand or sit on the backs of seats. Cups, cans of soda and beer, food and other trash are scattered throughout the plane.

"There's going to be a lot more stuff flying around here in a few minutes," Lisa thought to herself as her eyes darted around the noisy cabin.

She caught the attention of the other two flight attendants who were trying to control the mess, and quietly waved for them to come forward. Out of the corner of her eye she checked the passengers, but it didn't look as if anybody else was watching them.

Doris and Jane could tell by the look in Lisa's eyes that something was wrong.

"We've lost power in one engine," Lisa said, choosing to get straight to the point. "Jeff and Dave are looking for a place to land. Touchdown is going to be in about 15 minutes. We've got to prep for evac."

Doris and Jane were stunned. Both had worked on commercial flights for years, but the most serious incident either had experienced was a near-miss on a landing one time in Washington. They had of course trained for this, so in theory they knew what to do, but reality is far different.

Lisa reached for the microphone and cleared her throat. She didn't know exactly what she was going to say, so she quickly said a short prayer for God to give her the right words.

"If I could have everyone's attention for a minute," Lisa said. "I am sorry for the interruption, but this is very important. Could everyone quiet down for a moment? If somebody is sleeping near you, please give them a gentle nudge to wake them. I will wait until everyone is with us."

Doris and Jane were busy waking up a few sleeping players, getting others to remove their headphones and getting the rest to quiet down so they would be able to hear Lisa's instructions.

"Again, sorry to disrupt your evening, guys, but we've had a little situation come up that is going to change our plans. The captain has informed me that there is a mechanical problem with the plane and we are going to have to make an intermediate stop to see if we can get it corrected."

The moans and groans came from every row in the plane.

"Guys, I am afraid this is serious. We have lost power in one engine. We are about 15 minutes from landing. I will explain the procedures we will need everybody to use."

Lisa now had everyone's undivided attention. Professional sports teams fly hundreds of thousands of miles each year, and none had ever been involved in an accident. Everyone knew it was possible, but it was one of those realities that nobody wanted to discuss.

Now it was staring them right in the face. Some players reacted with shouts and curses, others began to cry. The Christians on the team closed their eyes and prayed. Lisa explained the brace position while Doris and Jane did a final walk through the cabin, then took their own seats and assumed the crash position.

An eerie silence filled the cabin.

Chapter 1

Ever since he was a young boy, T.J. had been in love with baseball. Even before he knew what the word meant, he loved the symmetry of the game. He loved walking into a ballpark and breathing the aroma. It didn't matter if it was a major league stadium, a minor league park or a Little League field. The smell of the hot dogs and brats on the grill almost always drew him to the concession stand. It was part of the ambiance of the game that he had loved for as long as he could remember, and today, as he walked into Hogland Ballpark, certainly was no different.

As he stood at the concession stand, ordering two hot dogs and a diet soda, he heard the familiar voice. "All right, let's go, and I want to see some hustle out there!" It took a second for the voice to register. When the recognition came, T.J. spun around, almost knocking over the young boy standing behind him in line. Too many people were in the way; he couldn't see the field. T.J. knew who he was looking for. It had been 13 years since he had heard the voice, but T.J. would recognize Mike Callan's voice anytime, anywhere.

As he tried to work his way though the crowd so he could see the field, T.J. remembered the first time he had heard Mike's voice. It was in spring training, 1983, after his dad bought the Chicago Cubs from the Wrigley family. In T.J.'s mind, it was the best thing his dad had ever done in his life. Tony Vitello had never loved baseball the way T.J. did. He loved making money, and buying the team was an investment that he thought would pay off over time. God, that was 27 years ago. There had been no kid anywhere in Chicago who was a bigger Cubs fan than T.J. Vitello, and now his dad owned the team. T.J. had posters of the players taped to the walls of his bedroom – Bill Buckner had the place of honor, directly above his bed. He had shoeboxes filled with baseball cards stored under his bed. He used 50 cents from his allowance each week to buy two new packs of cards at the drugstore on the corner. He hoped he would get a Cubs card but almost always was disappointed by the collection of Pirates, Indians, and Expos he found inside. When he opened the boxes to add the new cards to his collection, he paused for a moment to take in the smell of the gum residue on the cards. He didn't care for the gum, but he loved how it smelled.

It didn't matter that the Cubs were bad again in 1982 – at least they finished ahead of the Mets. The Cubs were his team, and this was next year.

He could recite every player's batting average. He screamed at the television when he didn't agree with the manager's strategy. T.J.'s love for sports, and for the Cubs in particular, was the only reason his dad started a subscription to that Republican rag, the *Tribune,* so he wouldn't have to fight his son for the sports section every morning at the breakfast table. Now there was a paper for each of them, the *Sun-Times* for Tony Vitello and the *Tribune* for T.J.

T.J. remembered the first time he stood on the field at HoHoKam Park in Mesa, Arizona, feeling so important. It was the first day of his two-week spring break. He didn't need a pass or a ticket; his dad owned the Cubs. He wore a badge of honor. For two weeks he went wherever he wanted. He could not believe he was this close to his heroes. The players thought he was just another pesky kid, the son of a clubhouse guy or something, and paid him no attention – except to tell him to get lost when he wandered into a coach's meeting or took a soda out of the refrigerator in the players' lunch room. T.J. didn't know the players viewed him as a pest, but he would not have cared anyway. He was in heaven.

On this memorable day, the sun was rising past the outfield bleachers, the start of another perfect 80-degree March day. T.J. had arrived at the stadium at the crack of dawn with his dad, who wished he was that easy to wake up every morning for school. His dad had arranged for T.J. to be the bat boy for that day's game against the Giants, and T.J. wasted no time putting on the team's uniform. He wore the smallest pair of pants the equipment manager had, but they were still three sizes too big. Standing alone near first base, tossing a baseball as high as he could and circling under it, pretending he was catching the final out of the seventh game of the World Series, T.J. was in his private dream world. He was oblivious to everything and everyone around him, which was why he didn't hear the sound of metal cleats walking across the concrete floor of the dugout.

The Voice shattered T.J.'s wall of silence, coming from somewhere behind him. In T.J.'s mind it sounded like the voice of God. It was so deep, so resonant, so distinctive. From interviews he had heard on radio and television, T.J. could recognize the voices of almost every player and coach on the Cubs. He knew he had never heard this voice before, but it was one he would never forget.

"Hey kid, you wanna play catch?" The Voice said.

T.J. quickly turned toward The Voice, which was coming from the Cubs' dugout. The only person there was Mike Callan, who T.J. recognized only because of his number, 18. T.J. had memorized the names and numbers of the players he didn't know on the spring training roster during the plane ride from Chicago to Phoenix last night. Mike was the team's No. 1 draft pick from two years ago, at 23 already labeled a can't-miss star, projected to be the Cubs' starting centerfielder by next year at the latest.

T.J. started toward the dugout as Mike sat his cup of steaming coffee down on the ledge and hopped over the railing onto the field. He walked toward T.J. with his outstretched hand.

"Mike Callan," he said. "What's your name?"

"T.J. Vitello," the boy said as his small hand was swallowed by Mike's large hand.

"Nice to meet ya. Hey, Vitello is kind of an important name around here, you know. Are you … ?"

T.J. nodded his head. "Tony's my dad."

"That's really cool. How about playing catch? I played 36 holes of golf yesterday and I'm kind of stiff. I need to loosen up and nobody else is around. It's too early."

The smile spread across T.J.'s face. "You want to play catch with me?"

Mike nodded. "First we have to jog a lap around the field. Nice and easy, we're not trying to win a race."

The two didn't talk as they jogged side by side past the advertisements on the outfield wall, but exchanged information as they walked back to the outfield.

T.J. told him that he was 10 years old, that he played shortstop on his Little League team, the Saints, and that he knew his dad would not have let the Cubs trade Bruce Sutter to the Cardinals if he had only bought the team earlier. He told him how his mom was really reluctant to let him come to spring training and hang out with the players for fear he would get hurt. She didn't even like him playing Little League for fear that he would get beaned or worse. He had to beg her to let him come on this trip. Mike just nodded and told him what it was like to be the Cubs' number one draft choice after his senior season at Oklahoma and how he was really looking forward to playing in the majors.

The two played catch for about 15 minutes. T.J. had to try really hard not to grimace on Mike's last few throws. He didn't know how hard he was throwing, seemingly without any effort at all, but they were the hardest throws T.J. had ever caught.

This early morning game of catch became a ritual for the next two weeks, before Mike was sent back to the minor league complex and T.J.'s spring break ended, sending him back to school in Chicago. In those two weeks, T.J. found himself looking at Mike not only as a friend but as a father figure. He had never played catch with his dad, not even on the birthday when he got his new glove. His dad never had time for him. T.J. now had a new favorite player, even if he was headed for Triple A Iowa and not the major leagues. T.J. followed his progress every week when *The Sporting News* came in the mail.

Mike never lived up to his potential of becoming a star, but T.J. never lost his fondness for him. He didn't know why Mike had been the only player who was nice to him that spring, but he had vowed to never forget it, or him. In those two weeks, T.J. found the friendship of an older man that he had been missing from his own father. He and Mike continued to have a good relationship during the years Mike played for the major league club. When Mike became a minor league manager, T.J. followed his progress as well. They kind of fell out of touch as T.J. went away to college, but he still was stunned when Mike was fired by the Cubs after a fight in the stands in Omaha. That had been 13 years ago, and Mike had dropped out of sight immediately after that incident. T.J. had written him a couple of letters, asking his dad to mail them, but there had never been a reply and T.J. didn't know if Mike had received them or not.

Why was Mike here? T.J. was at the championship game of this Fourth of July tournament in Lawrence, Kansas, to watch a high school pitcher the Cubs had selected in the fourth round of the amateur draft a couple of weeks ago. T.J. had gone to work for the team three years ago, after he earned his college degree in business, with an emphasis in accounting, and then had gone on and graduated from law school. His dad had given him a four-year assignment to learn every aspect of the team's operations. Every once in a while, T.J. caught himself thinking about what would happen when his father died. His dad had never said anything to him about his will, but as his only son, T.J. thought there was a good chance he might inherit the Cubs some day.

T.J.'s current assignment was working in the scouting department, his favorite job thus far because it meant going to baseball games. He grinned when he thought about the former owner of the Cincinnati Reds, Marge Schott, who wanted to know one time how come she was paying people – scouts – when all they did was watch baseball games.

The Cubs were going to meet with the lefthanded pitcher, Steve Barton, after the tournament to see if they could get him signed. T.J.

was there with the area scout, a veteran scout named Jay, so he could observe and better understand the process.

T.J. paid the girl for his hot dogs and soda and moved past the crowd where he could see the playing field. His eyes scanned the field, searching for Mike. It only took a moment before he recognized the familiar face, standing by third base, arms folded across his chest, watching his infielders go through their final warmups. Mike still had the same muscular, athletic build from his youth, except he had added some pounds around his waistline. T.J. looked at his lineup card for the game. The Lawrence team was playing a team called the Linn County All-Stars.

T.J. walked toward Mike, a little nervous. What would he say? "Hey, how's it going? What's new? Long time, no see?" Would Mike even recognize or remember him?

T.J. had changed a lot in 13 years. He was almost six feet tall, had put on a few extra pounds himself, and his blond hair was cut much shorter these days.

Mike started toward the dugout as T.J. walked toward the field. Mike looked up from the paper he had been reading just as he reached the edge of the dugout where T.J. was waiting.

T.J. called out to try to get his attention. Mike heard his name and looked up, scanning the crowd to see who had called his name.

"It's T.J., T.J. Vitello."

"Hey, T.J.," Mike said. "It's been a long time." As he reached up to shake hands, Mike found himself instead on the receiving end of a giant bear hug. Mike had never known the impact he had had on T.J's life.

When T.J. released his grip, Mike was able to catch his breath. "What are you doing here?" he said to T.J.

"I was going to ask you the same thing. You look good."

"Well, working with teenagers has given me a few more gray hairs under this hat, but I can't really complain. What are you doing?"

T.J. explained that he was there in his capacity working in the Cubs' scouting department, watching Steve Barton, the Lawrence pitcher. When he started to ask Mike what he was doing, Mike held up his hand, stopping T.J. in mid-question.

"Look, I will be glad to give you the nickel synopsis of my life's story, but I don't have time right now. I've got to get ready for the game. I'm coaching this team. Let me give you my phone number so you can call me later when I'll have time to talk."

"Sounds like a plan. Good luck," T.J. said. The two men shook hands, and T.J. headed back to his seat behind the plate while Mike jogged to the bullpen to watch his starting pitcher take his final warmup throws.

T.J. knew from the scouting reports – sitting in the war room on draft day had provided a real education – that Barton had been a dominating pitcher throughout his high school career. T.J. knew he should be focused entirely on Barton, but his mind and his eyes kept wandering to Mike, standing in the third base coach's box. He came away from the game reminded of why many people were projecting a dozen years ago that Mike would one day be a major league manager.

Mike really understood the game and it was evident he had passed on that knowledge to his players. T.J. could tell the players really respected and admired their coach. The All-Stars beat Barton, 3-1, despite getting only five hits. They played small ball, bunting guys over, perfectly executing two hit-and-runs, scoring two of their runs on a sacrifice fly and a groundout. Mike's team did all the little things a team has to do to beat a good pitcher.

T.J. would have loved to catch up with Mike after the game, but Jay had made reservations for dinner with Steve and his parents at the Eldridge Hotel. T.J. saw Mike slapping a couple of players on the back as they boarded a charter bus as T.J. walked toward his rental car. The conversation was casual over dinner, then the waiter cleared the table and Jay went to work. The negotiations went well, even though they took up most of the evening, and it was obvious to T.J. that Barton was going to sign.

T.J. got back to his hotel room in time to catch the last two innings of the Cubs' 4-2 win over the Giants on Sunday Night Baseball. As he got ready for bed, he replayed the conversation with Mike in his mind. He had learned from Jay during the game that the Linn County All-Stars was a team made up of players from three high schools in

Linn County, Kansas, about an hour and a half south of Lawrence. Mike had been the coach the last couple of years when Jay had seen the team play, but he didn't know any more details about what had happened in Mike's life or how he had come to coach there.

"I need to find out what happened to him," T.J. thought as he flipped off the TV and turned off the lamp on the table beside his bed. The Cubs' win, combined with the Cardinals' loss to Colorado, had increased the Cubs' division lead to five games a week before the All-Star break. Maybe this was going to finally be their year. T.J. was snoring within minutes.

Chapter 2

The Cubs had always been Kevin Andrews' favorite team, even before they chose him with their first-round pick in the 1996 draft, 14 years ago. Kevin, a left-handed pitcher and the only Northwestern University player ever selected in the first round of the baseball draft, couldn't believe it when the Cubs' GM, Tom McMurry, called him with the news.

It was one of the three most memorable phone calls he had ever received, and all of them combined illustrated his life story.

The call informing him he had been drafted by the Cubs came as a complete surprise. A 6'4", 185-pounder, Kevin had set the school strikeout record during his junior year at Northwestern as he became only the school's second first-team All-America selection, following infielder Mark Loretta in 1993. Blessed with good size, a 94-mph fastball, and a wicked curve that he threw with the same overhand delivery, Kevin expected to be selected fairly high in the draft, but it was a banner year for college pitchers and he was not convinced he would be a first-round choice. He knew scouts had raved about his curve ball and how it really made a hitter's knees buckle, especially left-handers, but still he didn't know what to expect. Waiting at home that day for the phone call had been one of the longest days of his life.

Kevin would have been overjoyed to go anywhere in the first round, but the news that the Cubs had taken him with the 17th pick in the draft stunned him. Kevin knew he was as good as some of the other college pitchers who were first-round selections, including Kris Benson of Clemson, the number one overall pick by the Pirates. He wasn't surprised that Braden Looper and Billy Koch went before him, and he was pleased that he was the first left-hander selected, three spots before the Yankees took Eric Milton. He practically said yes to the Cubs' offer of $1 million even before the scout told him how much the team was going to offer.

Kevin reported to the Cubs' rookie league team in Williamsport in the New York-Penn League and pitched well. Courtney Duncan was the team's pitching ace, but Kevin wasn't too far behind him, going 7-3 with a 2.84 ERA in 13 starts.

He was expecting to move up to Daytona in the Florida State League in 1997, but blew out his rotator cuff in spring training. Kevin underwent surgery, but stayed in Florida to begin his rehab. The doctors had told him the injury was one of the worst they had seen, but he still was not prepared for the medical reports that said he would never pitch again. That news brought about the second biggest phone call of his life, from his mother.

Kevin had called her from Florida and left her a message to call as soon as she got home. His mother had always been the one person in his life he could talk to, who believed he could do no wrong, and who always could see past the immediate problem to come up with what would no doubt turn out to be the perfect solution.

"Kevin, I got your message," he remembered her saying. "Is something wrong? You sounded upset."

"Well, I got some bad news today. I got the medical reports back on my arm. It's bad. The doctors said they don't think I'll ever pitch again."

There was a moment of dead air before his mom, Gloria, started to respond. Kevin interrupted her.

"I don't know what to do, Mom. Pitching is the only thing I have ever wanted to do in my life. I've got my signing bonus and all, but I can't just sit home and do nothing. I knew this was a possibility when they did the surgery, and I know my arm still hurts almost every day, but I really didn't think it was going to be this bad. My career can't be over. I'm only 22 years old. It hasn't even started yet."

"Oh, honey, I'm so sorry. Maybe the doctors are wrong."

"No, I don't think so. They have all of the test results, and I can just tell they are right. What am I going to do?"

"Well, you knew there was never a guarantee that you would make the big leagues, anyway. What did you tell me the percentages were of all the boys who were drafted who never made it, even the first-rounders? Remember we talked about this when you were deciding whether you wanted to sign if you got drafted out of high school or not, and how important it was going to be to get your college degree."

"I know, Mom, and I only have a year to go, but I just can't believe this happened."

"I know that, Kevin. I know how upset and disappointed you are. I'm so sorry for you. But you remember the advice Pastor Adams always gave at church – God has a plan for your life. You might not know what it is, but He does. God doesn't close any doors unless He opens another door at the same time. I believe you should walk through the door that leads you back to school and finish your degree."

That was what Kevin had done, of course. Even on the half dozen or so times he had disagreed with his mother, he knew in his heart she was right. He graduated from Northwestern, then was lucky enough to hook on with the *Tribune* right out of school, covering prep schools in the north Chicago zones.

Four years later, he moved to the paper's main section, assigned to cover the Northwestern beat. Two winters ago, he had received the third telephone call that defined his life, the call from his sports editor asking if he would be interested in the Cubs' beat. It had taken him approximately two seconds to answer yes.

Covering the team was not as good as pitching for the Cubs, of course. He knew other reporters at the paper had turned down the assignment, but Kevin didn't care. Other writers who didn't really understand the game thought baseball players, especially major leaguers, were the most difficult of any professional athletes to deal with. One of the reasons was that the schedule brought the players and reporters together every day. There really was no place for the players to go to get away from the media, and some resented watching reporters hanging around the locker room. There were exceptions, of course, but many were arrogant, spoiled brats who acted insulted if you asked any question tougher than "So what pitch did you hit for the home run?" Maybe because of his playing background, Kevin had a different viewpoint. There still were some jerks, but Kevin loved the game so much he just found ways to ignore them.

The other major drawback about the beat was the travel. The travel had become tougher since the Sept. 11, 2001, terrorist attacks created extra security checks, which was one of the reasons Kevin tried to fly on the Cubs' charter as often as possible. On the charter, you didn't have to go through the terminal, you received a first-class seat, you didn't have to worry about missing a connecting flight somewhere, and you were able to pick up your luggage in the lobby of the team hotel. Not a bad trade-off for giving up the frequent-flier miles.

The downside to flying on the charter was you had to file your stories quickly or you would miss the plane. Kevin never would forget the night he was in the press box at Dodger Stadium his first year on the beat. He was transmitting his story back to the newspaper as he watched the team bus pull away from the stadium. Luckily, he was able to hitch a ride to the airport on the equipment truck and made the red-eye flight back to Chicago.

Despite those obstacles, Kevin loved his job.

Kevin could have gone with the team tonight, headed for Los Angeles, but there really was no reason. He would have had only 30 minutes to write his story, then would have flown through the night and arrived in his hotel in L.A. about 3 o'clock in the morning and would have slept until noon. Instead, he was taking the American flight at 10 a.m. tomorrow, which gave him more time to write about tonight's game, would let him get a good night's sleep in his own bed, and would still get him to L.A. by noon, just when he would have been waking up.

As Kevin packed up his computer and notebook and got ready to leave the press box high above Wrigley Field, it was close to midnight. He was glad the team would be on the road for the next week; he always had fewer distractions away from home. His editor had assigned him to write a major profile of Tony Vitello, the Cubs' owner who had just celebrated the anniversary of his group buying the team from the Wrigley family. He wanted to run it on the front page next Sunday. Kevin was scheduled to interview Tony on Tuesday in Los Angeles, then would have a couple of days to write the story.

The interview had originally been scheduled for a couple of days ago, on Friday, but Kevin got an email early that morning from the team's PR director that something had come up and Tony had to re-schedule. He had decided to go on the trip this week, so could they meet for breakfast at the hotel on Tuesday? That was fine with Kevin – it gave him time on Monday's flight to re-read all of the clips he had pulled out of the *Tribune* archives about Tony.

When he had read the clips the first time, Kevin had been amazed at how much he didn't know about the Cubs' owner.

What he had known, both from the years he had been covering the team and even before that just as a Cubs' fan, was that Tony was not the kind of owner who sought out the headlines or worried about what the press said about him. He would never be confused with George Steinbrenner. Kevin knew players who had been with the Cubs for years and their only conversations with Tony had been when they signed with the team and when they were released.

He had the research assistant at the *Trib* pull all of the stories that even included Tony's name for the past 40 years. He was amazed at how few stories there were and what little personal information they contained. Many of the stories had no information that was helpful to Kevin at all.

The one that was the most intriguing to Kevin was the obituary for Tony's first wife, Melissa, who had drowned in Lake Michigan in 1970, apparently after falling overboard. The story had appeared on the front page for two days, then disappeared. There never seemed to be any follow-ups on what had caused her death. The police report said that Melissa and Tony had been out with some friends for an overnight cruise on their yacht. It wasn't a big boat, but it had sleeping accommodations for six people, which is how many people were onboard. They apparently had a big party during the evening, then everyone went to bed. Tony told the police that when he woke up in the morning, Melissa was gone.

He got dressed and went up on the deck, expecting to find her sitting in her favorite chair. A couple of the guests were there, but not Melissa. They told Tony they had been up for an hour or so and had not seen her. Tony awakened the other couple and searched the boat, but Melissa was not there.

The guests told reporters that Tony was frantic as he used the radio to call the Coast Guard, which arrived minutes later. Nobody had heard anything unusual overnight. Tony said he didn't realize she had gotten out of bed until he woke up and found her gone. Divers were called in, and since the boat had been anchored overnight, the search area was pretty well confined. Melissa's body was found about six hours later.

The autopsy revealed she had drowned, and there were no apparent signs of foul play. The obituary said it would be several weeks before the results of all the toxicology tests were complete. Kevin made a note to himself to see if he could find out more about Melissa's death. The couple had been married for seven years, but had no children.

Another clip from the *Trib*, from the society page, revealed that Tony had remarried just six months later. His new wife, Katherine, was 15 years younger than Tony and was from one of Chicago's more prominent families.

Another society page notice, in 1972, announced the birth of a boy, Thomas Jefferson Vitello, known as T.J., to Tony and Katherine Vitello.

Kevin knew T.J. well enough to say hello, having seen him around the ballpark once in a while the last couple of years. He didn't remember seeing him since draft day, a couple of weeks ago. "I wonder if he would talk to me about his dad?" Kevin thought, making a note to try to call him on Monday. He could not recall ever seeing Tony with T.J.

Kevin had always believed the advice one of his professors at Northwestern had given him about writing profiles. You almost always got better information from people other than the person you were profiling. The professor said that most people are reluctant to talk about themselves, while their friends and associates are much more apt to provide good anecdotes and background information. The biggest problem with this story was there didn't seem to be a lot of people Tony was close to, at least that Kevin had been able to find out about.

Much of Kevin's information about Tony came from the only major profile he could find about him, which ran in the *Tribune* a couple of days after the group he had put together bought the team from the Wrigley family in 1981 for $20.5 million. The story had been written by one of the business writers at the *Trib*, Roy Singer.

"I wonder if he is still around," Kevin said. He put in a call to the research department, and the assistant took down his request. Five minutes later, Kevin's phone rang. Singer was retired but still lived on the west side of Chicago. He gave Kevin his phone number.

The reporter had been retired for a dozen years, but still seemed sharp and with it when Kevin called him and told him what he wanted. Singer said he was coming to the game the next afternoon with his grandson and agreed to meet him for a burger and beer at the Cubby Bear, across the street from Wrigley. Kevin was coming to the game, but didn't have to write the game story. Singer told him to look for a guy about 5'5", bald on top, with white hair around the ears. They exchanged cell phone numbers just in case a problem came up. After he hung up, Kevin thought to himself, "That guy has the deepest voice I have ever heard in my life."

Kevin recognized Singer by his description as soon as he entered the bar. Singer had already grabbed a table near the window.

After saying hello, Kevin said, "I thought you were bringing your grandson to the game."

Singer took the giant cigar out of his mouth and blew a big puff of smoke. "I did, but his mother works not too far from here, so when

I agreed to meet you I asked her to come by after work and pick him up. I didn't think he should be hanging around here with all these drunk Cubs fans, or hear what I might have to say."

Each ordered a cheeseburger and a beer, then Kevin took out his notebook and fired his first question at Singer.

"When you were working on the profile, did you ever come up with more information about Melissa's death? Did you ever find out about the toxicology reports? I never saw a followup story in the paper."

Singer sipped his beer as he thought about the question, and his response. He scratched the back of his head before he finally spoke.

"I always wondered that myself. Her death seem awfully suspicious to me. You know his new wife had worked as a paralegal at the same firm. One of Tony's partners told me off-the-record he was convinced they were having an affair before Melissa died. Once Melissa's death was ruled an accidental drowning, it just seemed the police never had any more to say about it. I wondered if Tony had gotten to somebody and made sure the reports were kept sealed."

"Did you ever talk to the police about it?"

"Yeah, but I didn't get anywhere. You have to remember I wasn't the police reporter. I worked on the business desk. The only way I got involved with the story was when Vitello bought the Cubs. We had an editor then who thought every story that involved a lot of money had to be written by a business reporter. I drew the short straw and had to do the story. I had never talked to Vitello before, and all I knew about him was the tidbits I picked up from some of the other writers."

"What did the cops say when you asked them about it?"

"One detective, his name was Frank Malone, told me he had his doubts that it was an accident but they did not have any evidence to prove it wasn't," Singer said. "He told me he couldn't figure out how a guy could be sleeping next to somebody in a very small double bed and not wake up if she got up, or realize that she was missing. And if he did realize it earlier, why did he wait until morning to start looking for her and report her missing? He thought Tony might have had something to do with her death, but couldn't prove it. They didn't have all the DNA tests they have today. Since it was just

Malone's opinion, and he told me off the record, I couldn't write that in the paper.

"I did say something to Tony about it during our interview, but he just called it a terrible accident and quickly changed the subject to the Cubs. You know him, he can be pretty slick when he wants to be. He had all of his charm working then because he was all proud of himself for buying the Cubs."

"Tell me what else you found out about Tony that you didn't put in the story."

Singer described how Tony had grown up in a poor working class neighborhood on Chicago's north side. He had been born right after the depression, the son of a man who ran an automobile parts store and was a mechanic on the side when he was sober, which apparently was only part of the time.

Tony had gone through the public schools and earned an academic scholarship to Notre Dame, where he graduated in 1953. He was a pretty good prep athlete and had some offers from smaller colleges, but he had his heart set on going to Notre Dame. He was accepted into law school at the University of Chicago, and earned his degree in 1956. After passing the Illinois bar exam, he went to work for one of the city's leading firms, Howe, Duwe and Chesney. He had always been fascinated by planes, and joined the Air National Guard after law school. He earned his private pilot's license, and flew himself to meetings and conferences as often as possible through the years.

"He earned a reputation as being a good lawyer, but an even better negotiator," Singer said. "I talked to a few of his clients who didn't want to be quoted, and they said he was a perfect lawyer – the guy you wanted on your side, a guy you would hate if he was on the other side of the table.

"One thing I found kind of strange was that he represented both large corporations and individuals who were suing large corporations, mainly insurance companies. Not at the same time, of course. You rarely found a guy who would work both sides of the table like that."

Almost none of his cases went to court, Singer said, because Tony was able to negotiate settlements between the two sides. On some of the cases that did go to trial, there were accusations that Tony had tried to use some force to "assure" there was a settlement, but those charges were never proven.

"I heard the rumors, but I couldn't prove it, and quite honestly I didn't try. When Tony was promoted to partnership in the firm in 1967, he continued to attract bigger corporations and more high-profile individuals as clients.

"You know the story about how he came to buy the Cubs, don't you?"

Kevin had to admit the answer was no.

"Tony was retained by the families of two very wealthy women who became violently ill a day apart from each other. The women did not know each other, and their only apparent connection before they showed up at the same hospital was that they both had shopped in a local grocery store a few days before they became ill. Investigators went to both of their homes and actually found the receipts in their purses for the groceries they had bought at the store. They were both long lists, but the only item they had in common was each had bought a pack of chewing gum."

"The police found some of the unwrapped gum in their purses. When they ran the tests on the gum, they found out it had been poisoned. The families hired Tony with the intention of suing Wrigley's."

"How come I never heard about that or read it in the paper?"

"That's what I am in the process of telling you. Because Tony was such a good negotiator, he went to the Wrigley people first before he filed the lawsuit. They knew how terrible it would be if the lawsuit became public, so they were willing to do almost anything to settle the cases quietly and keep the story out of the media.

"While he was negotiating the settlement with Wrigley, Tony found out about the bad tax problems Bill Wrigley was having. He had inherited the Cubs when his dad, Phil Wrigley, died in 1977, four years earlier. He was going to have to pay the IRS $40 million. Even though he was a billionaire, that was still a lot of money.

"Tony's timing was incredibly lucky because Bill Wrigley didn't like the way baseball was going. He thought the game was headed for economic catastrophe. Free agency was just beginning, and Nolan Ryan became the first player in history to sign a $1 million a year contract in 1979. Bill Wrigley almost had a heart attack when he heard that. He told everybody there was no way a baseball player was ever going to be worth that kind of money and he for damn sure was never going to pay it. Total team payrolls in those days weren't much more than a million bucks. Hell, only four years earlier, in 1977, the Cubs' highest paid player was Bobby Murcer, making $250,000 a year.

"It had been four years since the Andy Messersmith and Dave McNally cases had brought about free agency. Some of the maverick owners like Steinbrenner and Ted Turner saw this as a chance to try to buy a pennant. It made Wrigley sick. He was an old-school guy, brought up that way by his father, thinking the only way to win was to develop prospects, then make trades to try to get something you needed. Of course that had not really worked out too well for the Cubs, now had it?"

Kevin tried to hold back a snicker.

"Wrigley thought baseball was headed for a strike, and of course he was right. He really thought the game was going to hell. Bill was looking for a way out. Tony came up with a plan that Wrigley bought in to – Tony would head up a group that would buy the Cubs for a fair market price, Wrigley would settle the two lawsuits out of court, and the cases would never be made public."

"Wow," Kevin said. "I never knew that."

"Most people don't. It's like I said earlier, if I knew all of that today and was writing the story, I would be fired if I didn't use it. Back then, the paper kind of looked the other way. So did I."

Kevin looked up from the notes he had been taking. "Did the women ever talk about the lawsuits?"

"Nobody knew who they were. Their names were never made public because the lawsuits were never filed. The hospital had a privacy code, and wouldn't release any information except to the police. Everything was alleged this and alleged that. It really showed what kind of negotiator Tony was that he was able to ram that deal through."

"What about Wrigley? If the gum was poisoned, somebody should have gotten in trouble."

"Oh, they did. Wrigley launched its own investigation within the company and traced it back to one of their plants. A couple of employees were pissed because they had been passed over for a promotion, and were trying to get back at the company. It turned out they admitted injecting poison into a few packs of gum. They thought it would be a big public scandal and the Wrigley stock would plummet. It was their way of getting back at the company, but it didn't happen that way.

"They got fired, of course. Some people in the company wanted to press criminal charges against them but Wrigley said no, again because he thought the publicity would be bad for the company."

"I still don't see how the case never got into the papers," Kevin said. "Wouldn't the hospital have called the police when there was a suspected case of poison?"

"They did, but that again was where Wrigley and Tony's influence came into play. You know Tony was always closely aligned with the Daley family, and he had a lot of political pull. He was well connected politically in addition to financial connections. He and Wrigley's pull combined was enough to keep the police reports locked up."

It had been headline news when Vitello's group bought the Cubs, which had been in the Wrigley family for 60 years, dating back to 1921. Nobody ever delved too deeply into the circumstances that led to the sale, however. The reporters either didn't know, or they didn't care. The only people who knew the true story, Singer said, had been sworn to secrecy.

"Tony had no trouble putting together a group of his well-to-do clients to serve as minority partners. The sale of the Cubs was signed and announced before many people even knew Wrigley was think-ing about selling. Tony resigned from the law firm and relocated to Wrigley Field. That's it in a nutshell. You know the history from there."

Kevin did indeed. Unfortunately, the Cubs under Tony Vitello's leadership had not been much more successful than they were in all the years the Wrigley family had owned the team. They came close to winning the pennant a few times – most notably in 1984, when the ball went through Leon Durham's legs in San Diego. The Cubs had been ahead in the series two games to none and needed only one win in three games in San Diego to win their first pennant since 1945. Instead, they lost games three and four to force the decisive fifth game. Even then the Cubs were ahead 3-2 going into the seventh inning, and had one out, leaving them eight outs away from the pennant, but Durham's error opened the door to a four-run inning. The Padres won the game and the pennant.

There had been more disappointments – in 1989, when they won the division but lost to the Giants in the playoffs; and in 2003, the year a fan named Steve Bartman tried to catch a ball down the left field line that Moises Alou might otherwise have caught for a key out in the sixth game of the playoff loss to the Marlins. The Cubs were cruising, ahead 3-0 in the top of the seventh, before that play. Even then, they could have gotten out of the inning except for Alex Gonzalez kicking a would-be double-play ball. Instead, Florida scored eight runs and won, 8-3. The Cubs could have won the series the next night in game seven, but lost a 5-3 lead in the fifth when Florida scored three times and went on to a 9-6 win.

The brutal reality was the Cubs had not won a pennant since 1945 and had not won the World Series since 1908, no matter who owned the team. A lot of people actually believed the team was cursed.

Singer stood up, signaling the end of their conversation. He took a final swig of his third beer, wiped his mouth with the back of his hand, inhaled his cigar deeply, then said to Kevin, "Good luck with your story. And for what it's worth, I think the SOB killed his first wife."

With that, Singer and Kevin shook hands, and Singer headed out the door.

Kevin had replayed his conversation with Singer in his mind over the past couple of days, wondering how he was going to bring all of that up during his interview with Tony. He knew that Tony, who was now 79 years old, likely would not want to talk about it, but maybe he would. Maybe this would be his chance to come clean and tell what he knew about Melissa's death. Maybe it had always tugged at his conscience. There is no statute of limitations for murder, Kevin knew, but maybe Tony knew what had happened. Maybe he would talk about how he came to buy the Cubs. That was the thing about interviews, you never knew what direction they were going to go because you never knew what the person was going to say.

Kevin knew one thing: if Tony was willing to discuss everything, Kevin was sitting on one hell of a story, probably the most important one he would ever write in his career.

If he thinks this is going to be the Cubs' year, maybe he will talk, Kevin thought, mentally planning out how he wanted to structure the interview – get him relaxed, talking about this year's team, how good things are going, then start hitting him with the hard questions.

Kevin knew the All-Star break was still a week away, but he had to agree this was the best Cubs' team he had seen. He knew one other thing – if the Red Sox could win the World Series, and so could the White Sox, why not the Cubs?

Chapter 3

The team bus began to pull away from Wrigley Field as Kevin walked down the ramp from the press box. He probably would not even have noticed if the cheers had not drawn his attention.

Fans were standing outside the stadium, clapping, cheering, and waving as the bus headed toward O'Hare. There were grown men and women, as well as little kids, wearing Cubs' T-shirts and jerseys. Fathers and sons were there, united by blood but also by their love of the Cubs. These people were the heart and soul of this franchise, Kevin knew, through good times and bad. The players came and went, but the fans remained.

A lot of people said St. Louis had the best fans in America, but Kevin didn't buy it. Sure, the Cardinals had great fans, and they had moved into a swank new ballpark a few years ago. The reason Kevin didn't think their fans were so great was that the team had enjoyed a lot more success than the Cubs. It's easy to cheer for a winning team. Try coming to games and finding a reason to cheer when the team is 30 games out in August. Let's see who has the best fans then.

Kevin's uncle, Frank, was the most die-hard Cubs' fan he knew. He planned his vacations around going to see the Cubs play on the road, usually trying to go see new stadiums or inter-league games in the American League parks and cities he had never visited. Kevin knew there were a lot of fans like Frank. He saw them in spring training every year. He saw them in every city on the road. It really mattered in these people's daily lives whether the Cubs won or lost a particular game. Win and they were happy for an entire day. Lose and you had better stay away from them.

Kevin didn't think the players understood that, at least not very many of them. They lived in their own little world, uneffected by almost everything that happened outside their environment. He knew some players who could not tell you who the President was, not just Cubs' players, but players from every team. He knew players who had no idea who Jackie Robinson or Roberto Clemente were, and how important they were to the history and success of the game. Forget asking them about Marvin Miller or Curt Flood. They would have no clue.

Only a very few players in the game today had any appreciation for the struggles the players of past generations had experienced and the fact that Miller, the head of the players' union, and Flood, through his legal challenge of the reserve clause, had changed the future of the game forever. Miller was such a shrewd negotiator that he agreed to the arbitration system requested by the owners, knowing it was going to turn out to be more beneficial for the players, and acted as if he were doing the owners a favor.

What the players did appreciate was the support of the fans. It is always much more enjoyable to have somebody cheering for you rather than booing you. Nobody likes to be booed. That was one of the big reasons players liked to play in cities like St. Louis and Chicago, and not in New York, Boston, or Philadelphia.

People always speculated what it would be like if the Cubs actually won the pennant and then won the World Series. Kevin couldn't imagine it. He had seen World Series parades in other cities, and had participated first-hand in the parade in 2005 when the White Sox won, but he still knew that would pale in comparison to what the scene on Michigan Avenue would be if the Cubs won. The whole city of Chicago would be there, not just the folks from the South Side. It would be the biggest celebration in the history of the city.

Just look at these people now, Kevin thought. Here it is, midnight, a week before the All-Star game, and they are still here outside the ballpark, waving and cheering as their heroes climbed onto the bus. The Cubs were in first place. Life on the North Side of Chicago could not get much better.

⚜

Life was pretty good for the players, too. Team buses and charter flights can be pretty confining when a team is doing bad, when the silence can be deafening, but when the team is winning, it can be the most carefree, relaxed, fun-filled environment in the world. It's grown men, acting like 10-year-olds.

Kevin didn't have to be on the bus to know the target for most of the abuse tonight would be Sam Johnson, the left-handed reliever who had allowed the home run to the Giants' Johnny Anderson in the ninth inning that tied the game. Since the Cubs had won it in the 12th, the players could rip him and nobody would care.

"Hey, Sam, nice gopher ball, you prick," was one of the insults that came flying as Sam got on the bus. "Way to make us wait an extra hour to win the game, you asshole."

Johnson, always one of the leading pranksters on the club, took it in stride and fired insults right back. That's the way it went on a winning club.

"I just wanted to give you a chance to get a hit for the first time this week, since you couldn't do it the first four times you came up to bat," Johnson fired back. "If you had gotten a hit, I wouldn't have had to pitch."

"Hey, Jonesy, where's the 400 bucks you owe me from the last trip?"

"I got your $400 right here," came Jones' response, as his hand reached down to the zipper of his trousers.

The bus pulled up next to the charter terminal at O'Hare, and the traveling party quickly climbed onto the waiting 737. Many of the players couldn't wait to get to the back of the plane to get the card game going. Others had a DVD playing on their laptop before the plane taxied away and headed toward the runway. They viewed the four-hour flight to LA as merely an excuse to either win or lose money, get drunk, or both.

As he took his customary front-row window seat, manager Buck Williams had to fight to prevent a smile.

In all the years Williams had spent in baseball, 37 now, counting his years in the minors, he had won only one pennant as either a player or a manager. He was starting to believe that maybe this team could be the second.

Williams had managed in the majors for too many years to normally let himself think that way or get caught up in that kind of talk, especially so early in the season. He just had a feeling, however, that something was going to happen with this team. Sure, he didn't really care much for any of the players individually, on or off the field, but he really hadn't ever liked many of the players he had managed.

Williams was not a friendly guy. He had no time for idle chat. He was all business. If you could abide by his rules and accept that, then you got along fine. If you were the kind of guy who liked to have a lot of fun and not take the game very seriously, then the two of you were going to have problems.

He was always trying to get an edge over the next guy, whatever that edge might be. He was one of the first managers to use computers to compile data about pitcher vs. hitter statistics, or other more complicated statistical analyses. The beat writers often joked that he wouldn't know when it was time to take a crap if he didn't check the computer printout first. Nobody worked harder at the job, though. Even his critics had to give him his due for that.

This team was playing so well that Williams' critics said they were winning in spite of him. Even Williams knew that was partially correct. His influence on the games was the lowest it had ever been, because there simply were very few late-game strategic decisions that had to be made. The team was kind of on auto pilot.

On the nights when he did have to make a move, it just seemed to be shaping up as one of those years when even if it was a decision no other manager in the game would have made, it worked.

As the plane taxied away from the gate, Williams closed his eyes for a moment, thinking back to all of those long, uncomfortable bus rides he had taken as a player, coach, and manager in the minor leagues. Was he ever glad those days were over. There was a lot of fun along the way, but nothing beat traveling in major league style, first class, with a never-ending supply of drinks handed to you by a cute young flight attendant. You had to put up with a lot as a major league manager, all of the million-dollar babies complaining and whining and bitching about something. Williams just tuned them out. This was one of the perks of the job, and he enjoyed it immensely.

His focus was never far from the next game, but right now that was 21 hours away. He was going to have a couple of drinks, eat a steak, and light up his favorite cigar – another advantage to a charter plane – nobody telling him he couldn't smoke.

Williams wanted to read the scouting reports on the Dodgers and catch up on the latest minor league reports, but he would get to that in a little while. He also knew that with the owner on the trip, part of his time was going to have to be spent bullshitting with him. He liked Tony, probably better than he had liked most of the owners he had worked for, but he still didn't like him coming around very much. Williams didn't know why Tony was on the trip, and he didn't really care.

❦

The players don't normally pay attention to all of the support people around them, those who perform the tasks that make their lives so comfortable. Players never even give a second thought to what happens to their luggage, for example, between the time they drop it off in the clubhouse and it shows up in their hotel room in another city hours later.

There always are several people working around the team's plane when the bus pulls alongside and the players, coaches, manager, and others get off. The people servicing the plane, making sure it is fueled and ready to go. The mechanics who make certain everything is in working order. The baggage handlers. The folks who work for the catering company that delivers the food for the flight – something more than a bag of peanuts and a warm beer.

In a scene similar to the one the players had just witnessed at the ballpark, however, this night was different. When the bus pulled up to the plane, the players were greeted by all of these folks cheering and clapping as they got off the bus and climbed the stairs.

None of the players paid any attention to the short, pudgy man in blue overalls standing on top of the wing of the plane. He had a small container in his hand, and was screwing the cap back to the end of the gas line .

While the players weren't watching him, he was looking intently at them. "Those poor bastards." Looking down, he froze when he saw the long black limo pull up next to the plane. He watched silently as Tony Vitello, the owner of the Cubs, got out and started to climb the steps to board the plane.

"What is he doing?" Eddie thought, recalling the only other time he had seen him.

The instructions had been very explicit.

"I am the only one who knows the number for this beeper," the man wearing the dark suit said as he handed Eddie the small black device, along with a bundle of cash. "When it goes off, that will be your signal. You know what to do."

Eddie had done what he was paid to do, but suddenly he had a great feeling of guilt. Was it too late to do anything? What could he do? He contemplated trying to warn Tony, but could only stare as Tony ducked through the door and disappeared inside the plane.

❧

The wisecracks between the players continued as the plane picked up speed down the runway and lifted into the quiet Chicago night. The third baseman, Bobby Scott, was always one of the quietest guys on the plane, sitting closer to the front than most of his team-mates. Scott had only confessed to one person that he was deathly afraid of flying. He knew he didn't have any choice if he was going to play major league baseball. It wasn't like he could become the next John Madden and get his own personalized bus and drive to all of his games.

The one exception to Scott's fear of flying was leaving Chicago at night because he loved to look at the city from the air. The lights were breathtaking when the plane takes off to the east, as it did tonight. The city has a remarkable beauty during the day, Scott knew, but it is even better at night. As the plane climbed through the clear sky, Scott stared out his window, looking at the downtown buildings below, and then Lake Michigan as it came into view when the pilots banked the plane to the left, climbing over the lake as they began their turn to the north, then west, headed for Los Angeles.

In the cockpit, pilots Jeff Jackson and Dave Curtis relaxed. Flying a plane these days is a breeze, both knew, because once you got the big bird in the air the autopilot takes over for most of the trip. If you are going to have a problem, it almost certainly will happen during takeoff or landing. The time in between gave Jackson and Curtis a chance to walk back into the cabin and mingle with the players for a few minutes. They were as caught up in the team's success as the rest of the fans. In years past, the team had played so poorly neither pilot wanted to go back to the cabin.

Both Jackson and Curtis had much more difficult assignments on their resumes. Each had been a military pilot, Jackson in the Navy and Curtis in the Air Force. Each had flown commercial jets for years before being lucky enough to land jobs with the Cubs when owner Tony Vitello decided to buy his own plane for the team about five years ago.

Vitello had the plane reconfigured with all first-class seats, and he went into the sports charter business himself. When the plane wasn't being used to fly the Cubs, Jackson and Curtis flew college or other pro teams all over the country. Both men were huge sports fans, and they were thrilled they got to be this close to the stars, plus go to a lot of games for free.

Both were aware that Vitello was on this flight. He did not routinely accompany the team on the road, but Jackson had seen him as he was getting settled in the cockpit when the bus arrived. Vitello showed up at the same time in his big black stretch limo, wearing his $3,000 custom-designed suit. Jackson had only met the man once, after he was hired, and that was fine with him. One of the reasons he was glad to be out of the commercial airline business was not having to put up with corporate politics. He found the richer somebody was, the more involved in that shit they were. "Just leave me alone to fly the plane," Jackson had often said to himself and he had to give Vitello credit for doing that.

The plane completed its turn to the west after flying north over Lake Michigan and the autopilot came on as the air traffic controller advised the plane that it was cleared to climb to its cruising altitude of 35,000 feet.

Jackson and Curtis both relaxed in their seats. It was a quiet night, at least here, but the forecast was that they might run into some thunderstorms just before they reached the Rockies. They should be above them, however, so neither pilot expected anything other than a smooth, routine flight.

※

About an hour into the flight, Jackson reclined his seat, loosened his seatbelt, and turned to stare out the captain's side window. It was a beautiful night, the kind a pilot was lucky to see once a summer. The moonlight reflected off the thin cloud layer thousands of feet below. From his vantage point, Jackson thought it looked like a thin bed sheet floating above the earth. The lights from the small towns and big cities broke through the clouds to illuminate the underside of the sheet.

As he looked toward the south, Jackson saw large white columns of cumulous clouds rising toward the heavens. The amazing light show of the thunderstorms a hundred or more miles away captivated him. Curtis' voice brought him back to reality.

"Fuel looks good over Sioux City," Curtis said. "You are 200 pounds up on gas and right on time."

"OK, thanks. Look at those storms down to the south. I'm glad we took the northern route."

Both pilots watched the lightning, which Curtis said reminded him of his high school prom date.

"From a hundred miles away she was real pretty to look at, but once you got up close, she got ugly in a hurry."

Jackson laughed, but grew serious when he noticed the left fuel tank aft boost pump light was illuminated. "Dave, look at that, I don't think I've ever lost a boost pump before. Have you?"

"Not that I can remember. Must be a faulty pump."

"Look behind your seat, maybe we popped a circuit breaker for some reason. It should be on the P6-3 panel."

Curtis took a pen flashlight out of his pocket as he moved his seat forward so he could inspect the panel.

"Sure enough, there it is. You want me to reset it?"

"Better check the manual first. See if you can find a checklist for low boost pump pressure."

Curtis pulled his flight bag from the right side of his seat and took out the Boeing 737 flight handbook. He turned to the section for irregular checklists.

"What's it say?" Jackson said.

"Well, it says, 'Warning, do not reset a tripped fuel pump circuit breaker.'"

"OK, that takes care of that. I guess they think if the pump is screwed up it might overheat. Even I know a hot pump in a fuel tank is not a good combination. Is there any other information?"

"Let's see ... Yeah, it says, 'If only one main tank low pressure light is illuminated, sufficient fuel pressure is available for normal operations.'"

"That sounds good to me," Jackson said. "Let's just remember to tell the maintenance folks about it so they can check it out in L.A."

As Curtis settled back into his seat, he said, "You want a cup of coffee?"

"Sounds good, with cream and sugar."

Curtis reached up and punched the flight attendant call button as he picked up the service interphone handset. "Hi guys, this is Lisa at door 1 left."

"Hey," Curtis said. "The temperature OK back there?"

"No complaints."

"Could we trouble you for a couple cups of coffee?"

"Sure, I'll make a fresh pot. How do you want it?"

"One black, one with cream and sugar."

"How about a sandwich? You guys hungry?"

Curtis glanced over at Jackson who was shaking his head yes.

"Yeah, sounds good. Thanks, Lisa."

About five minutes later, Lisa knocked on the cockpit door and delivered the coffee and sandwiches. "Let me know if you need anything else," she said, closing the door behind her.

Curtis and Jackson were both silent for a moment before Curtis finally said, "OK, admit it, that's another one of the great perks of this job. Most airlines hire professional flight attendants, we hire professional strippers."

Both men were trying not to smile when the air traffic controller interrupted the silence.

"Charter 1908, Kansas City center, contact Denver center on frequency 128.2. Good night."

"Charter 1908, Denver center on 128.2. Have a good night," Curtis said.

"Denver center, Charter 1908, checking on flight level 350," Curtis said after he switched to the new radio frequency.

"Charter 1908, roger,"

Just as Jackson took a sip of his coffee, a second warning light illuminated a small glow on the overhead panel.

"What the hell," he said, setting his coffee back in the cup holder. "Now we've got a warning light for low pressure in another fuel pump. It's the right forward boost pump."

Curtis stared at the light, then at Jackson. "Wow, that's strange. What do you think?"

"I don't know. I'm not sure. It could be several things. Could be metal shavings on the electric bus, faulty pumps, maybe fuel contamination. You got any ideas?"

"No, but I would think if it was a fuel contamination problem we would have some other indications. All the engine parameters are normal."

"Yeah, you're right. Get the book out and let's go over the checklist again. I have never heard of two separate boost pumps losing pressure in two separate tanks."

Curtis re-read the section that warned the pilots not to try to re-set a tripped circuit breaker.

"Hold it right there," Jackson said. "Is the right circuit-breaker popped, too?

"Let me check." Curtis pulled his seat forward and again took out his pen light to inspect the panel. "Yep, sure is."

"OK, let's see what else the book says," Jackson said.

Curtis read, "Fuel pump low pressure lights may flicker when tank quantity is low and the airplane is in turbulent air or during climb and descent."

Jackson shook his head. "That doesn't apply to us. We know we have plenty of gas and we are flying straight and level."

"I agree," Curtis said, pausing for a moment as he continued to read through the checklist. "We went over this before, but it says 'if only one low pressure light is illuminated then sufficient fuel pressure is available for normal operations.'"

"So we still have one operable fuel boost pump in each tank providing sufficient pressure."

"That's what I think."

Curtis continued to read. "There's a caution note at the bottom of the page. It says 'Fuel pump pressure should be supplied to the engines at all times. Above 30,000 feet, thrust deterioration or engine flameout may occur. If required, descend to maintain positive fuel feed.'"

"So we are OK for now, but if we lose another pump in either tank we would not be able to maintain fuel pressure in that tank without cross-feeding, which would create an imbalance," Jackson said.

Curtis nodded his head in agreement.

"Why don't we play it safe and drop down to 28,000 feet," Jackson said. "It should still be a smooth ride. Go ahead and call ATC."

"Denver center, Charter 1908. We would like to request flight level 280."

"Charter 1908, Denver center. Descend and maintain flight level 280."

Curtis adjusted the altitude window in the mode control panel. "Denver center, Charter 1908, descending to flight level 280."

While the plane was descending, Jackson studied the instrument panel above his head, then glanced over to the circuit breaker panel behind Curtis' seat. Curtis could tell Jackson was concerned.

"I know this is strange, but it doesn't seem like a big deal," Curtis said. "We still have positive fuel pressure in each tank, and below 30,000 feet the engines will suction feed without boost pump pressure. All engine parameters are still normal."

"You're right. It just pisses me off that I can't figure out what is wrong. There should be some kind of explanation."

"Well if you really think something is wrong, why don't we see if we can land short in Denver and get maintenance to check it out."

"You know how the folks in the back would react to that. We might as well stay off the plane if we do that. Those pampered bozos would scream and holler so much Vitello would fire us on the spot."

"We'll make sure to get it checked in L.A. It's probably just a couple of old pumps that suddenly went out at the same time. Who knows how old they are."

Curtis reached into his flight bag and pulled out a giant candy bar and began to unwrap it.

"How can you eat that junk?" Jackson said. "I thought you told me you were going to try that low-carb diet?"

"I did. I have never been hungrier in my life. I decided I would rather be fat and happy than skinny and hungry. You should try it sometime. If you get any skinnier you are going to fall through your ass and hang yourself."

Jackson had to laugh, but immediately stopped when a third boost pump light illuminated, followed in quick succession by a fuel filter bypass light and a master caution light.

"What the hell."

"OK, I got the aircraft and ATC. You've got the book. Get it out and let's go over all this again. Something is definitely wrong. Read through the fuel boost pump checklist one more time, then look for a fuel filter bypass checklist."

Curtis read, "If both low pressure lights for a main tank are illuminated, place the start switch for the affected side to continuous."

Jackson reached above his head and placed both start switches in the continuous position and the ignition switch to the both position.

"OK. Now what?"

"It says, 'If fuel filter bypass light is on, degraded engine operation may result due to a contaminated filter. Place the start switch to continuous.'"

Curtis continued, "There's a note. It says, 'If contaminated fuel is a possibility, use an alternate fuel tank as source of fuel for the affected engine(s). Consider landing at a suitable airport before excessive fuel imbalance occurs.'"

Before Jackson could respond, the fuel filter bypass light for the right engine was illuminated. Curtis and Jackson looked at each other but didn't need to speak. Each now knew they were likely dealing with a fuel contamination issue.

"Where are we?" Jackson asked.

"Just passing Hayden, Colorado. We've got to get this thing down in Denver. We don't have a choice."

"Denver center, Charter 1908. We are declaring an emergency. Suspect fuel contamination."

"Roger, Charter 1908, Denver center. Say souls on board and fuel remaining."

Jackson looked at the gauge. "We have three hours, 30 minutes of contaminated fuel remaining and 51 souls on board. Request weather conditions for Denver, Cheyenne, and Scottsbluff."

Curtis had pulled out his low altitude enroute chart, anticipating Jackson's next question.

"While ATC is checking on the weather, let's see what our options are. Where are we in relation to the airports?"

"About 100 miles to Denver, looks like about 90 miles to Cheyenne, and a little farther to Scottsbluff."

"Charter 1908, Denver center. Weather at Denver is ceiling 800 broken, thunderstorms in the vicinity. Visibility 2 miles in light rain, winds variable at 12 knots. Low level wind shear advisories in effect. Cheyenne is better, 5000 thin overcast, 10 miles visibility, wind 10 degrees at 10 knots. Scottsbluff reporting about the same."

"Roger Denver, Charter 1908, standby."

Jackson looked at Curtis but didn't have to ask the question. "Cheyenne," Curtis said. Jackson nodded his head. "Denver center,

Charter 1908. Request direct clearance to Cheyenne."

Even though it meant turning the plane around, both Jackson and Curtis knew it was the most accessible airport. There wasn't time to be picky.

"Charter 1908, Denver center. Turn right to a heading of 070 degrees. At your discretion descend and maintain 14,000. Cheyenne altimeter is 30.01. Do you request emergency equipment?"

"Denver center, Charter 1908, negative, not at this time." Jackson said.

Jackson turned the aircraft to a heading of 070. "OK, Dave, you have ATC. We have to let our friends in the back know what is going on." He punched the flight attendant call button.

"Hi guys, it's Lisa. Do you need something else?"

Jackson said, in a firm, unwavering voice, "Lisa, we need you to come to the cockpit immediately."

Lisa had noticed the plane was turning to the right. "I'll be right up."

Just as she knocked on the door and entered the cockpit, another warning light illuminated, this time informing the pilots the left engine had failed.

"SHIT," Jackson yelled. Lisa was caught off balance and had to catch herself to keep from falling. The A autopilot kicked off, but Jackson quickly gained control of the plane. He set the speed to 220 knots and set it for maximum continuous thrust on the operating engine. Jackson then reset the autopilot.

Jackson looked directly at Lisa. "Lisa, this is very serious. We have a possible fuel contamination issue and are now flying on a single engine. I don't know if we are going to lose the right engine or not. We need you and the other girls to prepare for an emergency landing and evacuation of the aircraft. We have about 15 minutes before landing. You know what to do. I will give a 'brace, brace, brace' warning over the intercom 30 seconds before landing."

Jackson could see the fear in Lisa's eyes. He reached out and took her hand.

"We're going to be OK," he said in a reassuring voice. "You can do this. Let me know when the cabin is ready."

Lisa was fighting back tears but nodded her head bravely. "OK."

Curtis already was on the radio with ATC. "Denver center, Charter 1908. We have lost the number one engine. We now are requesting that emergency equipment be standing by in Cheyenne."

"Charter 1908, Denver center. Roger. I am contacting Cheyenne now."

Curtis told Jackson to take over the ATC contact while he took out the manual to go over the flight engine start checklist.

While Curtis was looking for that page, the right engine sputtered and flamed out. The autopilot again kicked off and Jackson regained the controls.

Jackson realized the plane also had lost all hydraulics, making it very hard to move the flight controls. He barked to Curtis, "Start the APU."

Both pilots knew the APU, or auxiliary power unit, is an engine generator in the tail section of the plane that is used primarily for electrical power while the plane is on the ground. The APU generator was capable of powering at least one generator bus, and thus one electric hydraulic pump.

"I'm already on it. I can't get it started."

The cockpit had been plunged into darkness when the second engine failed. The only light was a single fluorescent background light, powered by the hot battery bus, and the glow of the instrument gauges.

"Read me the checklist on loss of all engines, it's in the emergency section," Jackson said.

"Got it."

He read off all the items on the list and nothing worked. The APU would not start, either.

"Screw it Jeff. I am going to reset all of the fuel boost pump breakers."

"Do it."

Curtis made several attempts to restart both engines with no success.

"Whatever has contaminated the fuel has blocked every pump,

every bypass valve, and has even blocked the fuel pickup for the APU. Nothing is going to help. We're going to have to take this thing in with no power," Jackson said.

Curtis got back on the radio.

"Denver center, Charter 1908. Be advised we have now lost both engines. We have no hydraulics, battery power only for electrics. We are flying with manual reversion only. Need vectors to the nearest runway regardless of winds with minimum turns please."

"Charter 1908. You are 30 miles southwest of Cheyenne. If you can turn to a heading of 050 you will be on a 30-degree intercept heading for runway 8 in Cheyenne."

"Denver center, Charter 1908. Roger. Attempting to turn to a heading of 050."

Without any power, flying a 737 was similar to driving an 18-wheeler down the highway with no power steering. It was doable, but it wasn't very much fun. The powerless plane had become a 120,000 pound glider, which was going to be descending about 2,000 feet a minute whether the pilots wanted it to or not.

Jackson struggled to turn the aircraft. It takes up to 80 pounds of pressure on the control wheel just to turn the aircraft. His arms were tired, his muscles ached. He maneuvered the plane to the proper heading.

"Denver center, Charter 1908. We are now on a heading of 050. Be advised we have limited breaking and landing with no landing flaps. We are going to need all of the pavement you guys got."

"Roger Charter 1908, Denver center. Cheyenne is aware of your situation and is standing by."

Jackson turned to Curtis. "Read me the list of inoperative components."

"Stand by trim, auto pilots, rudder trim, yaw damper, flap position indicator, flap asymmetry protection, alternate flap operation, aileron trim, outboard anti-skid, and a few other minor bullshit items."

"OK, now do the same with the loss of hydraulics checklist."

"Here we are," Curtis said. "Flight spoilers, ground spoilers, autoslats, normal flaps, normal brakes, alternate brakes, nose wheel steering."

"Shit. What do we have?"

"You've got me, babe."

Despite the tenseness of the situation, Jackson had to smile. He really liked Curtis, and was glad he was in the seat next to him. He would not have said that about many of the people he had flown with over the years.

"We're going to need both of us, too," Jackson said. "We're going to have to drop the landing gear manually. We need to wait until the last possible moment, though. I want to make sure we are going to make the runway."

The intercom chime indicated that Lisa was calling from the cabin. "We're all ready back here."

"We're going into Cheyenne," Jackson said. "Remind everybody I will give a 'brace, brace, brace' signal 30 seconds before landing. That should be in about five minutes."

"Right," Lisa said. "Everybody is ready."

"I bet those guys almost shit when Lisa told them we had an emergency," Jackson said.

※

Major league baseball charter flights are much different from commercial flights. They are more convenient and almost hassle-free. All of the normal aviation rules concerning passengers are ignored at will. Virtually nobody sits in his seat calmly wearing his seatbelt. Card games take over the back half of the plane. Players stand or sit on the backs of seats. Cups, cans of soda and beer, food and other trash are scattered throughout the plane.

"There's going to be a lot more stuff flying around here in a few minutes," Lisa thought to herself.

She caught the attention of the other two flight attendants who were trying to control this mess, and quietly waved for them to come forward. Out of the corner of her eye she checked the passengers, but it didn't look as if anybody else was watching them.

Doris and Jane could tell by the look in Lisa's eyes that something was wrong.

"We've lost power in one engine," Lisa said, choosing to get straight to the point. "Jeff and Dave are looking for a place to land. Touchdown is going to be in about 15 minutes. We've got to prep for evac."

Doris and Jane were stunned. Both had worked on commercial airlines for years, but the most serious incident either had experienced was a near-miss on a landing one time in Washington. They had of course trained for this, so in theory they knew what to do, but reality is far different.

"Doris, you go about halfway back and Jane, you take the rear of the cabin. I'm going to make the announcement, then I will deal with the folks up front. Any questions?" Both Doris and Jane shook their heads no. Each knew the only question they had was one neither Lisa nor anybody else could answer – were they going to die?

Lisa reached for the microphone and cleared her throat. She didn't know exactly what she was going to say, so she quickly said a short prayer for God to give her the right words.

"If I could have everyone's attention for a minute," Lisa said. "I am sorry for the interruption, but this is very important. If everyone could quiet down for a moment. If somebody is sleeping near you, please give them a gentle nudge to wake them. I will wait until everyone is with us."

Doris and Jane were busy waking up a few sleeping players, getting others to remove their headphones, and getting the rest to quiet down so they would be able to hear Lisa's instructions.

"Again, sorry to disrupt your evening, guys, but we've had a little situation come up that is going to change our plans. The captain has informed me that there is a mechanical problem with the plane and we are going to have to make an intermediate stop to see if we can get it corrected."

The moans and groans came from the first row and the last row of the plane, and from every row in between.

Some of the wisecracking players found a target for their humor, Tony Vitello, who owned both the team and the plane.

"What's the matter, Tony, did you forget to pay for the fuel?"

"Trying to cut costs again, Tony?" came another shout.

Lisa and the other flight attendants motioned for quiet.

"Guys, I am afraid this is serious. We have lost power in one engine. We are about 15 minutes from landing. I will explain the procedures that we will need everybody to use."

Lisa now had everyone's undivided attention. Professional sports teams fly hundreds of thousands of miles each year, but none had ever been involved in an accident. Everyone knew it was possible, but it was one of those realities that nobody wanted to discuss.

Now it was staring them right in the face. Some players reacted with shouts and curses; others began to cry. The Christians on the team closed their eyes and prayed.

Bobby Scott reached out from his seat and grabbed Doris by the arm. Tears were streaming down his face. Doris remembered that Scott had told her how afraid he was of flying last year.

"Tell me we're going to be OK," Scott blurted out. "I don't want to die."

Up in the third row of the plane, Vitello was not saying a word. He looked stunned, almost as if he were in shock. Lisa thought maybe he had passed out, but then she saw him take a big gulp from the bottle of Scotch he held in his right hand.

The scene quickly erupted in chaos. Players, broadcasters, and coaches were standing, waving their arms, crying. All appeared hysterical. The Christians were the only ones who appeared somewhat calm, praying silently.

"Hey, Jonesy, I wish I had listened to you more about Jesus when you tried to tell me about him," Sam Johnson said. "I'm sorry I didn't pay more attention."

"Jonesy, can you say a prayer for the rest of us?" Bobby Randall asked. "I know God will listen to you."

Jones was sitting calmly in his seat, with a peace about him that the non-Christians on the team could not understand. Tears were forming in his eyes.

Sam Johnson was sitting across the aisle. "Hey, Jonesy, are you afraid?" Johnson asked.

"No, I am not afraid of anything happening to me," Jones said in a very calm, moderate voice. "I am crying for you, and the other guys on this team who don't know Jesus. I am sorry for my wife and kids. I know whatever happens, I will be taken care of."

Barry Williams heard the conversation and turned around from his seat in front of Jones. He was crying, too, but for a different reason.

"Is it too late for us?" he asked. "I know you tried to get us to go to chapel and Bible study, but we were always too busy or didn't think we needed Him. Can you say a prayer for us, too?"

Jones nodded and all three men closed their eyes and bowed their heads in silence. Jones started to pray out loud, and told Williams and Johnson to join him.

By this time the flight attendants had gotten the rest of the passengers into their seats with their seatbelts fastened. Looking at her watch, Lisa saw they were about two minutes from touchdown.

She got on the microphone again and explained the brace position while Doris and Jane did a final walk through the cabin, then took their own seats, and assumed the crash position.

An eerie silence filled the cabin.

"Charter 1908, contact Cheyenne approach on 118.7. The rescue coordinator is monitoring the frequency. You can contact him directly if you like. Good luck."

"Denver center, Charter 1908. 118.7 for Cheyenne approach. Before we go, what's your name?" Curtis said.

" It's Brian. Brian Florence, sir."

"Brian, thanks for your help. Good night."

"Good luck guys, and God bless," Florence said.

The plane was descending rapidly, too rapidly, Jackson thought. In the distance he could see the lights of runway 8.

"It's going to be close," he told Curtis. "Do you think we're going to make it?"

"We're going to make it. We have to make it. When are we going to drop the gear?"

"At 300 feet. Any sooner than that would slow us down too much. We need all the speed we can get at this point."

"We are below glide slope," Curtis said. "I can just make out the VASIs on the left side of the runway. You are low."

Both pilots knew without saying it that even if the plane reached the runway before touching down, there was a good chance Jackson would not be able to hold it on the runway. It was long enough, but without hydraulics, he was going to have only six brake applications and would not have any reverse thrust to slow down the plane. They were going to hit the ground doing about 200 miles an hour, about 70 miles an hour faster than normal.

The runway had been foamed and the emergency equipment was standing by.

Jackson was doing his best to hold the plane steady as Curtis watched the altimeter. He saw it reach 1,000 feet, then 750. He glanced up and saw the runway lights straight in front of them.

"500 feet."

"300 feet, here comes the gear." Curtis reached for the floor and pulled all three manual gear extension handles. "Brace, brace, brace," he yelled over the P.A.

"We're going to be short!" Jackson screamed. "We're not going to make it! We're screwed!"

"Hold it off, hold it off, hold it off," Curtis pleaded.

The plane hit the ground just at the start of the runway lights, about 150 yards short of the runway with a force of about 12g's, 12 times the force of gravity. The gear collapsed under the pressure, breaking the wing spar on impact.

Sparks were flying everywhere as Jackson tried desperately to keep it together, The plane was on its belly, sliding toward the side of the runway.

The plane began to break apart. Pieces of metal ruptured the fuel tank, and the explosion and fire could be heard for miles.

The last thing Jackson heard before passing out was the wail of sirens.

Chapter 4

T.J. Vitello heard the telephone ringing, but he was having difficulty transferring that information from his brain to his hand to pick up the receiver.

As he slowly came to, he remembered he was in Lawrence. He glanced at the alarm clock on the nightstand – 3:23 a.m. Who in the world would be calling him at this hour?

"Hello," T.J. groggily said into the receiver. All he heard in return was a dial tone, but a phone was still ringing. Looking through the dark room, he realized it was his cell phone that was ringing. It was plugged into the charger on the dresser, next to the television.

T.J. hung up the hotel phone and stumbled out of bed and followed the glow of his phone, reaching it on the last ring before it would have switched over to voice mail.

"Yeah," he said in a gruff voice, angry now that he was fully awake.

"T.J., it's Paul Wendel in Chicago. Sorry to bother you at this hour."

"I'm sorry, too," T.J. said to Wendel, the Cubs' director of player development and technically T.J.'s boss while he was working in the scouting department.

"I wish I had another reason for calling," Paul said as his voice began to break.

"What is it?" T.J. answered quickly.

T.J. could tell Paul was fighting back tears. His mind was racing about what could have happened.

"I just got a call from Tim Jenkins, in the P.R. department," Paul said in a choking voice. "There's been an accident. Our plane went down."

T.J. paused for a moment, more confused than panicked. "What did you say?" he asked.

Wendel was trying to compose himself. "T.J., our plane, with the team on board, crashed an hour or so ago in Cheyenne, Wyoming. I don't know what happened. A reporter from the A.P. office called Tim and woke him up as soon as they got word from out there that it was our plane. He called me. God, how could this happen?" Wendel broke down again in tears.

By now the basic information had registered in T.J.'s brain. The Cubs' charter flight had crashed. He was too stunned and in shock to cry. He had to get his brain to think.

"What did the reporter tell Tim? He had to know something else if they had confirmed it was our plane."

"He was calling to try to get more information from Tim," Wendel said. "He said they had a reporter at the scene, but he was still getting the information. T.J., I know everybody was on the plane. Harry Johnson (the general manager) was on the trip."

Wendel was crying again, sobbing into the phone.

"T.J., your dad was on the plane."

The news almost knocked T.J. over. He reached down with his right hand, bracing himself on the top of the television. "Are you sure? Why was he going on that trip?"

"I don't know, but I saw him before the game last night and he told me he was going with the team to L.A. after the game. T.J., I am so sorry. I cannot believe this happened."

"Did the reporter say if there were survivors?"

"The only thing Tim told me was that they believe there were some survivors because the plane broke apart when it crashed. I'm sure it's on CNN but I wanted to call you before some stupid reporter reached you. What are we going to do?"

T.J.'s mind was racing. His dad might be dead. Certainly there were fatalities, but who? Nothing like this had ever happened to a professional sports team. There had been close calls before, and college teams had been killed in crashes, but never a professional team. T.J. wondered if baseball had a plan for dealing with something like this.

"I don't know Paul, this is such a shock. What else did Tim say?"

"He was going to see what else he could find out, mainly from CNN, I guess. I told him I would try to get in contact with you. The only other guy I know who wasn't on the trip is Jack Reynolds (the assistant GM). He was in Des Moines watching the Triple A team this weekend. Tim was going to call him. God, T.J., how could this happen? What are we going to do?"

"We've got to try to stay calm," T.J. said. "Since nobody really has much information yet we can't be jumping to conclusions. Maybe it wasn't as bad as they think it was. Call Tim back and see if he reached Jack. Tell him I will catch the first plane from Kansas City back to Chicago. There has to be a plane leaving by 6:30 or so. Get him to have Jack get back to the office as soon as he can. You and Tim try to get there as soon as you can. The main thing we are going to have to deal with right away is all the press. Try to hold off making any statements. Tell them we just don't have enough information yet to comment but we are looking into the reports. Tell them we will have a statement and probably have a news conference later this morning."

Wendel couldn't believe how calm and under control T.J. was. T.J. was helping calm him down. Everything he said made perfect sense.

"OK, T.J., we'll do that. I should be able to get to Wrigley in about an hour. Call me on the private line as soon as you know your plans. If I hear anything before that I will let you know."

The two men hung up the phone, and T.J. let out a deep breath. He rubbed his face with his right hand, squeezing his nose as he glanced again at the clock – 3:34 a.m. He did the quick math in his head – he was about an hour away from the Kansas City airport, and he knew there would not be any planes leaving before 6 a.m. He had about 30 minutes before he would need to leave the hotel.

He took a quick shower, then turned on CNN as he was getting dressed. The term "breaking news" was displayed across the top of the screen. A reporter was doing a live standup from the scene of the crash, the Cheyenne airport. T.J. turned up the volume.

" … so we really don't have much additional information. We have confirmed that a charter plane carrying the Chicago Cubs baseball team reported it was having an unidentified problem and tried to make an emergency landing here in Cheyenne. The plane was headed from Chicago to Los Angeles. The plane went down about 150 yards short of the runway and broke apart. The local police have confirmed there have been fatalities but we also understand some survivors have been taken to area hospitals. We are expecting a briefing by the airport police within the next hour, at which time we anticipate additional details. Tom, back to you in Atlanta."

The news anchor reappeared on the screen, and T.J. flipped off the television, grabbed his suitcase, and left the room.

On his way to the airport, T.J. dialed information and got the 800 numbers for Southwest and American Airlines. As he had suspected, both had flights out of K.C. within minutes of each other at 6:25. He booked the Southwest flight, knowing he could get from Midway to Wrigley quicker than he could from O'Hare, fighting rush hour traffic.

The next call he made was to Tim Jenkins, the assistant P.R. director. He needed to find out if there was more information that had not been released to the media. Tim answered on the first ring.

"Tim, it's T.J. Vitello. Thanks for being so prompt this morning. This is going to be a rough day for all of us and I wanted to let you know I appreciate everything you are doing."

"Hi, T.J. Paul told me he reached you. I think everybody is in shock. I only called Paul and Jack, yet by the time I got to the office about 20 minutes ago, we had about five people here. A couple of the secretaries came in to work the phones. I don't even know how they found out about the crash."

"We're going to need everybody's help," T.J. said. "I know Paul told you I am in Kansas. I'm on a 6:25 flight to Midway, so barring delays I ought to be in the office by 8:30. Did you reach Jack?"

"Yeah, he was in Des Moines. He will catch the first flight out this morning, too, but I don't know what time it will be. He was going to call me back as soon as he got the information."

"Good. As soon as Jack and I get there, let's get you and Paul and get together and come up with an idea of what we've got to do. See what you can find out about the crash. Do we know any more about how many were killed or who survived?"

"Not really. We know most of the fatalities were in the rear of the plane." Jenkins paused. "T.J., did Paul tell you your dad was on the plane?"

"Yes, he did. Do we know … "

"No, we don't. I've got a couple of our assistants on the phone to the Cheyenne hospitals trying to get a list of who has been brought in. So far they haven't given us any names. I'm sorry."

"You don't have anything to apologize for," T.J. said. "You're doing a great job under some unbelievable circumstances. Is the media driving you crazy?"

"It's just starting to build as the word spreads. The last time I sent somebody out to look we had about six cameras and some other people on the sidewalk. We're keeping them there by the ticket windows. I know it is going to get crazier in the next couple of hours."

"Try to hold off making any statements for the time being," T.J. said. "Tell them we are trying to find out exactly what the situation is the same as they are, and when we have more confirmed information we will be releasing a statement. Tell them we will have a news conference later this morning."

"Got it. Thanks, T.J. See you in a few hours."

T.J. hung up and called Wendel, and the two exchanged basically the same information. Wendel was watching CNN in the office, but there had been no further developments since T.J. had left the hotel.

T.J. pulled in the rental car lot at the Kansas City airport just as he hung up with Wendel. He quickly turned in his car and hopped on the waiting shuttle to the terminal. Luckily, the airport was nearly deserted and he breezed through the ticket counter and security, grabbed a donut and a cup of coffee, and reached the gate just as the plane was beginning to board.

The flight was only about half full, so T.J. had no trouble getting a row to himself and sat silently, alone in his own thoughts, for the 75-minute flight.

As the plane landed and taxied toward the gate, T.J. flipped on his cell phone. He had two new voice mails.

The first was from Jenkins, 10 minutes ago.

"T.J., it's Tim, I know you are on the plane but I wanted you to get this as soon as you landed. We got our first report from the hospital in Cheyenne. Your dad is there. He is in critical condition, but he is alive. The nurse didn't know the extent of his injuries. She said they should have more information in the next hour or so. Also, Jack called and said he is on the 7:30 American flight to O'Hare. It's supposed to land about 8:40 and he said he will be here as quick as he can. I'll let you know if we find out anything more before you get here. See you soon."

The second message was from Wendel, five minutes ago.

"T.J., it's Paul. It's not been confirmed, but CNN is reporting there were eight survivors out of the 51 people on board, including the flight crew, but they don't have ID's on all of them yet. They said your dad was one of them. He's at the hospital. They didn't say anything about his condition. I don't know about any of the players yet, but CNN said it had been told Buck Williams and Harry Johnson were among the fatalities. I am sorry to tell you this through a voice mail, but I knew you would want to know. Be careful and we'll see you in a few minutes."

T.J. jumped in a waiting taxi as his head spun with the latest news. His dad was alive, but the manager, Buck Williams, and general manager, Harry Johnson, were dead. If the CNN report was correct and there were eight survivors, that meant most of the players were dead, too.

"Wrigley Field," he told the cab driver.

The driver spun around, as if he was questioning the request. "Did you hear about the Cubs' plane? Do you work for the Cubs?"

"Yeah," T.J. said, aware that even the most die-hard Cubs' fan would not be able to recognize him, a fact he enjoyed. "It's a shame. I'm sorry but I don't feel up to having a conversation right now."

The driver nodded, turned back around and headed for Wrigley. The all-news station, WBBM, was delivering the latest headlines. The announcer basically repeated the same information T.J. had received in his two voice mails.

As the cab got within about a block of Wrigley, the driver spoke again for the first time since leaving the airport. "I don't think I'm going to be able to get you any closer. The place is crawling with TV people and cops. You want to just get out here and walk? I think it will be quicker."

T.J. paid the fare and got out, and was once again thankful he was fairly anonymous as he approached the door to the Cubs' offices, which was blocked by a Chicago policeman.

"I'm sorry sir, the offices are closed," he said before T.J. could pull out his wallet and show the officer his Cubs' ID.

"I'm T.J. Vitello, I work here."

"Yes sir, I'm sorry," the officer said, opening the door.

T.J. couldn't believe the scene. A crowd of employees, mostly women, were gathered around the television in the lobby watching CNN. All were crying, some more hysterically than others. He knew everyone was in shock.

Because he was rarely at Wrigley, T.J. did not have his own office. On the cab ride from the airport, he had thought about where he was going to go. He still hadn't decided, but without thinking, found himself walking into his dad's office.

The secretary, Nikki Williamson, was sitting at her desk, staring at the wall. She had only worked for T.J.'s dad for a couple of years and T.J. did not know her very well. She looked over when she heard T.J. enter the office.

"T.J., I'm so sorry," she said as she broke down in tears, burying her face in her hands. Mascara was running down her cheeks, but she made no attempt to stop it. T.J. reached out and tried to pat her on the shoulder, which was covered by her long, curly blond hair.

"It's going to be OK, Nikki, we don't know all the details yet. We just have to remain strong and stay together and we will get through this. I'm going to work out of dad's office if it is OK with you, since I don't have my own office here."

Nikki nodded her approval, trying to choke back the tears. T.J. dropped off his suitcase and briefcase, then left to track down Tim Jenkins and Paul Wendel.

He found both men in their offices, each on the phone. He motioned for them to join him in his dad's office as soon as they were free. They walked in together about five minutes later.

"I got both your messages. Do we know anything else yet?"

Jenkins and Wendel shook their heads no. "Apparently, most of the fatalities were in the rear of the plane, which caught fire after the crash," Jenkins said. "Anybody sitting from the wings back didn't stand a chance."

All three men were silent, because they all had been on enough baseball charters to know that the rear of the plane was almost always the exclusive domain of the players. That meant very few players had likely survived.

"Any word on the other survivors?" T.J. asked.

"We know one of the pilots survived. He is at the hospital," Paul said. "Your dad is there, too. Brady Lee, the hitting coach, and Ron and Barry, the radio guys. They are pretty banged up but they are hanging in there. The others were taken to a different hospital and they haven't given us their ID's yet."

T.J. nodded.

"T.J., the press is really starting to get antsy," Tim said. "They know we don't really know anything yet, but they want something, anything. We've got to come up with a plan on how we are going to deal with them."

"Yeah I know," T.J. said as he looked at the clock on the wall – 8:15 a.m. "Jack should be here in about an hour. Why don't you tell them we anticipate having a news conference at 10:30. That will give us time to talk to Jack and maybe get a little more information. If they are still hounding you after that, let me know. I'm going to see if the hospital out there will tell me anything more about my dad. Be on the lookout for Jack and when he gets here, let's get back together again and see where we are."

The last time T.J. could remember sitting in his dad's black leather chair behind the big desk was when he was 10 years old, soon after his dad had bought the Cubs. The chair had swallowed him, and his little eyes could barely see across the top of the desk. Was this really happening, or was this all a bad dream, he thought as he asked Nikki to get the number for the hospital in Cheyenne.

The person he had been thinking of while enroute to Chicago was his mother, Katherine. She was traveling in Europe with her best friend. T.J. had no idea where she was or how to reach her. He knew she would hear the news somehow. He knew she would call as soon as she heard about the crash.

Nikki had the hospital administrator on the phone. The man's name was Ron Allen. He confirmed that Tony was at the hospital, but he was unsure of his exact condition. He transferred the call to the nurse's station in the emergency room.

The nurse at first said she was not allowed to give out that information on the phone, but when T.J. persisted, she told him to hold on and she would get her supervisor.

T.J. could tell something was wrong by the tone of the supervisor's voice. "Yes, Mr. Vitello, your dad was brought here after the accident. He kept trying to say something to the nurses, but his voice was very weak. They could not make out what he was trying to say. I'm sorry to be the one who has to tell you this, but your dad passed away about 10 minutes ago. There really was nothing we could do. His injuries were just too severe. I'm sorry."

T.J. hung up the phone without speaking. Nikki could tell what had happened by the look in T.J.'s eyes. She burst into tears again and ran from the office.

For the first time since Wendel's call had awakened him five hours earlier, T.J. could not hold back the tears. They came in a flood as he buried his face in his hands and rocked back and forth in his dad's chair.

What really was the most upsetting to T.J. is that he knew why he was crying. He wasn't crying because his dad was dead ... he was crying because he knew he would not get a chance to become better friends with his dad. His dad was always working, and never had time for T.J. when he was growing up. T.J. really hoped they would have a chance to spend more time together now as his dad was growing older, and that had just been taken away from them.

Tony's life was driven by his love for power, status, and money. In essence, he was married to himself and was not a parent. T.J. was sitting in his dad's chair, crying uncontrollably, not because his father was dead, but because he could not remember ever having sat on his father's lap in this chair when he was a young boy. His relationship with his father was broken almost from the time he was born. T.J. was crying because of that, crying out of anger and resentment for the relationship they had never had, and now never would have.

T.J. had friends who had lost their fathers to cancer, or in car accidents, and he had visited them at the funeral home. The sadness was evident because of the love his friends had had for their fathers. As T.J. cried, he knew it was for an entirely different reason.

T.J. wanted what every son wants from his dad, in addition to his love and companionship. He wanted his approval. He wanted his dad to tell him he had done a good job. He wanted his dad to say he was proud of him. He honestly could never remember his father saying any of those words to him.

As he sat in his dad's chair, T.J. realized, he could not even remember the last time he had talked with his dad, either in person or on the phone. The tears continued to flow.

T.J. also knew he was crying for the entire Cubs franchise. This was going to be their year, he could just tell. Now, in one sudden moment, that was all gone.

T.J. looked up when he heard a noise. Jenkins and Wendel were there, joined by Jack Reynolds. They all looked like this was the last place on earth they wanted to be, but T.J. waved them over to the desk as he tried to compose himself.

"I just got off the phone with the hospital," he said. "My dad passed away 10 minutes ago."

Jenkins was the first to speak. "T.J., we are so sorry. We can come back … "

"No, you guys stay right here. This is going to be tough on all of us, and we've got to stick together. I'll be OK in a minute."

The room was silent for a couple of minutes, each man alone in his own thoughts. They heard a phone ringing in the outer office. Nikki had come back from the restroom and she answered it, then poked her head in the door.

"T.J., I'm sorry to interrupt, but it's the Commissioner on the phone."

"OK, I'll take it."

Commissioner Douglas White and Tony Vitello had never been the best of friends, but they had a decent, professional relationship. T.J. had only met the man a couple of times.

"T.J., I know this is a tough day for everybody there and for everybody in baseball. We are going to do everything we can to help you and the Cubs. Let us know what you need from us and you will have it."

"Thanks, Commissioner, but I really don't know yet. We are still trying to figure out everything ourselves. This is all such a shock."

"I know," the Commissioner said. "All major league games are going to be canceled for at least the next four days. Later today I will have Sam Lawson call you. He is going to research the rules on our disaster plan this morning. To be honest with you, I know we have a plan, but I don't know what it is."

T.J. again thanked the Commissioner for calling and hung up. He turned to the three men sitting in the office and relayed the Commissioner's information.

"This all seems so wrong," Jack said. "We shouldn't be sitting here worrying about this. This kind of thing doesn't happen here."

"I remember watching news like this on television and feeling sorry for the people involved and wondering how they could get through it and go on and live their lives," T.J. said. "We're about to find out because that is exactly what we have to do.

"Let's start at the beginning and figure out what we know. Then we can figure out what we don't know and start looking for those answers. Tim, you go first. Start with the first report of trouble. What happened to the plane?"

"All we know is the pilots radioed the flight controllers in Denver that they thought they had fuel contamination and were declaring an emergency. The weather conditions were better in Cheyenne then Denver so that was where they attempted to land. They came up just a little short. The NTSB folks are due into Cheyenne this morning and will take charge of the investigation. Joe Pearse, the MLB security guy, is going out there as well and will be there early this afternoon."

"Is there any indication of sabotage or terrorism?"

"Not that we know of. Of course, if there was contaminated fuel we don't know where that came from. We will know more about that as the investigation gets started. They have to find the flight data recorder and the cockpit voice recorder and that will tell us a lot."

"OK, what about survivors and fatalities?" asked T.J.

Paul spoke up. "We know eight people were taken to the hospital. Unfortunately, two of them, including your dad, died at the hospital. The other was Randy Barnes, our TV announcer. The hitting coach, Brady Lee, looks like he will be OK. Both our radio guys, Ron and Barry, are in critical condition. The pilot, Jeff Jackson, survived, as did two players, Bobby Scott, and Sam Johnson. It looks like everyone else didn't make it. The reports from the scene said that anybody sitting behind the wings never had a chance because when the plane broke apart, it caught fire and exploded. They said they don't think they will be able to make definite identification on some of the victims because they were burned beyond recognition."

"And we know that Harry and Buck were killed," added Jack. "They were sitting in the front of the plane, but apparently died instantly when the plane broke apart. I just can't comprehend this whole thing."

All four men were wiping tears out of their eyes again. T.J. was the first to speak.

"And we know from the Commissioner that all games have been canceled for four days. We also know there is a disaster plan in place for something like this, but nobody knows what that plan is."

"We also know we have about 200 media people milling around

outside waiting for us to say something," Jenkins said. "They really have been remarkably patient, but I can't keep telling them to wait forever. We've got to give them something."

"OK, here's what I think we ought to do," said T.J., who proceeded to outline an area of responsibility for each man. All agreed they would each play a role in a press conference that would begin in about 30 minutes.

Jenkins, Wendel and Reynolds were just standing up to return to their own offices when Nikki knocked on the door and poked her head inside. "I'm sorry to interrupt, but Mr. Donnelly is here and said he needed to see you," she said to T.J.

Phil Donnelly had been Tony Vitello's personal attorney for as long as T.J. could remember. They had gone to Notre Dame together and even though Tony was an attorney himself, he liked to have Phil involved in almost all of his affairs. The three members of the Cubs' staff exchanged greetings with Donnelly as they left the room and he entered.

"I can't begin to tell you how terribly sorry I am about the accident," Donnelly said. "I know you are going to be hearing that a lot today and for a long time to come, but I couldn't believe it when I heard it on the radio this morning. I almost passed out.

"As soon as I got to the office I heard it confirmed that Tony did not survive. You may or may not know this, but I drew up his will several years ago." For the first time, T.J. noticed Donnelly had a large brown manila envelope in his hand.

"I hadn't really had time to think about it."

"Well, I know you don't know this, and I know it is going to come as another shock. Your dad told me a couple of months ago he was thinking about selling the Cubs. He wanted me to draw up a new will, which did not mention the team. I have a copy of both wills here. He never signed the new will, so it is not legal. Plus, as far as I know, he never completed the negotiations for the sale of the team. So, his old will is still the legally binding document. And that will leaves the Cubs to you."

Donnelly was right. T.J. was almost as shocked as he had been with Wendel's initial phone call earlier that morning. He hadn't known any of this was going on. His dad wanted to sell the Cubs? Why? To whom? What had happened to turning the team over to him?

T.J. realized that had just happened, even if it had occurred in a far different and more tragic manner than he had ever imagined. He knew he was staring at Donnelly, but he couldn't help himself.

"What about my mom? I would have thought Dad would have left everything to her."

"You know your mother doesn't understand or care anything about baseball. Your dad and I had this conversation when we were drawing up the will. He left the rest of his estate to her, but the ball club is yours. I'm so sorry it happened under these circumstances, but you are the new owner of the Cubs."

Donnelly continued, "Speaking of your mother, have you been able to reach her? I know she was going to spend the summer in Europe."

"No, I have no idea where she is. I was hoping when I got a chance I could poke around on dad's desk and see if I could find a phone number or a name of a hotel or something. Since I've been on the road for most of the last couple of months myself, I really don't have a clue where she is. I am sure she will hear about the accident and contact me, but I hate for her to find out that way."

"Well, when you talk to her, pass along my deepest condolences as well. You and I both know there were a lot of people who didn't particularly like your father, but we always were great friends. I can't believe he is gone."

With that, Donnelly stood up, extended his hand, patted T.J. on the shoulder and left the office.

T.J. was alone, standing in silence, more alone than he had ever been in his life. He slowly crossed the office and slumped into the desk chair. He leaned back, closed his eyes, and let out a deep breath. He thought about how dramatically his world had changed in the last six hours. It would have been understandable for his emotions to overtake him, but as he sat in his father's chair, the statement that kept coming back to him was something he had heard Tony say more than once. "You're a Vitello. We don't show our emotions." T.J. pinched his nose with his right hand, and made a silent promise to his father that he would carry out that family trait.

What Donnelly had told him was slowly starting to sink in. He was the new owner of the Cubs. He knew that would have to be approved by the other major league owners, of course, but that was only a formality. The Cubs, the team he had loved all of his life, were his. Despite the sadness, he almost felt a smile crossing his lips. He was glad there was no one in the office to see it.

Outside, in the hallway, T.J. heard a great deal of commotion. Looking at the clock on the wall, he knew Jenkins had let the reporters and TV people in the office so they could get ready for the news conference. They had decided to do it on the field, because there really was no room inside the stadium to accommodate so many media people and cameras. They had set up a podium and microphone between home plate and the pitcher's mound, and folding chairs filled the foul territory behind the plate, spreading toward the dugouts.

T.J. picked up the phone to call Jenkins, wanting to let him know they had something else to announce to the media.

Despite their frustration for wanting to know everything and know it 10 minutes ago, the press had been pretty accommodating. They knew the Cubs' personnel were suffering, and they were more compassionate than sometimes is the case with media members.

The Chicago reporters knew the basic information from what they had seen on the networks from the crash scene, and had read on the wires, so they were more interested in what was happening inside the Cubs' offices. The briefing included the report on survivors and fatalities, the report from the Commissioner about the cancellation of games, and the fact there was a disaster plan to deal with tragedies such as this. The Cubs also announced the plans to stage a giant memorial service at Wrigley later in the week, with the details to be announced.

Jenkins then made the final announcement, that as dictated in Tony Vitello's will, the new owner of the Cubs was his son, T.J. Vitello.

T.J. stood up and walked to the podium. He was still dressed in the same blue polo shirt and khaki slacks he had put on in his hotel room in Lawrence several hours earlier. "I would like to read a short statement, and I appreciate your cooperation in not asking any additional questions at this time."

T.J. then read from the sheet of paper he had taken out of his pocket.

"This is an extremely sad day for the Cubs' organization, the city of Chicago, Major League Baseball, for baseball fans everywhere, and for me personally. No one could ever imagine what happened early this morning. Yet, I am here today to pledge that this organization will come back from this. We will recover, and we will be better and stronger than ever before. We ask for your prayers for the victims of this tragedy, and we ask for God's guidance for all of us in the days and weeks ahead. Thank you."

Kevin Andrews and the other reporters just looked at each other. They could not believe how robotic T.J. had sounded as he read the statement. There was no emotion in his voice, no hint of sadness. His voice didn't break or crack; it was strong and steady. He did not act like a man who had just lost his father, who had just become the owner of a major league baseball franchise, and who had just had virtually his entire team and organization wiped out. He read the statement as if it were a list of items he needed to get at the grocery store on his way home.

As the media filed back through the stands, T.J. noticed one reporter standing near the dugout whom he thought he recognized. The man saw T.J. looking at him, and slowly moved in his direction.

"T.J.," he said, extending his hand. "Kevin Andrews from the *Tribune*. I can't believe everything that has happened this morning. It is just incomprehensible."

"I know what you mean. Nothing has really sunk in yet."

T.J. and Kevin walked together down to Tony's old office, now T.J.'s office, and T.J. agreed to call him if the team had any major announcements later in the day.

When they separated, Kevin walked up the ramp to the press box, where he would write his story. He had covered a lot of accidents during his early reporting days, and had written terribly sad stories about coaches battling cancer, but nothing had ever come close to a story of this magnitude. He could have been on that plane. He could be dead. His friends, people he was laughing and joking with just 14 hours ago, were dead. He knew it would only be a matter of time before he came out of shock and began to cry. He kept telling himself he could do this, he could write this story, but only one word kept coming to Kevin as he flipped open his computer, saying a silent prayer that God would take over and tell him what to write. Kevin typed the word. "Why?"

T.J. had given Reynolds, an expert on computers and the guy in the organization with the best knowledge of other teams' players, the task of setting up a system to evaluate players who might be available to the Cubs. Even though nobody knew the exact details of the disaster plan, they knew it would basically work like the last expansion draft a few years back, and that the Cubs would be permitted to select a certain number of players off the rosters of the other teams.

Wendel had the best knowledge of the minor league players already in the Cubs' system, so he was assigned to come up with the list of players the Cubs ought to think about promoting to the majors.

Jenkins had his hands full working with the media, and trying to begin the task of planning the memorial service. T.J. had not assigned himself a specific task when the other men left his office, but ever since then, he kept finding himself thinking about one person, and it was clear to him now what his next task should be.

He asked Nikki if his dad still had his private jet at O'Hare. When she said yes, he asked her to phone the charter services company to see if they had somebody who could take him on a quick trip. "Where to?" she said.

"I have an old friend I need to go talk to. I don't know exactly where the nearest airport is. It is somewhere in Kansas. We can look it up on a map when I get to the airport."

As he left the office, T.J. asked Nikki to tell Jenkins, Wendel, and Reynolds to plan to meet back in his office at 8 p.m.

"What do I tell them about where you went?"

Chapter 5

On his way to the airport, T.J. reached into his pocket to make certain he had Mike Callan's phone number. He had already called information, found out Callan lived in Mound City, Kansas, and gotten his address. When he arrived at the charter terminal at O'Hare, he found a state atlas so he could figure out where the closest airport was to Mound City. That turned out to be the Johnson County Executive Airport near Olathe, a little more than an hour north of Mound City, population 815, the county seat and third largest town in Linn County. Somewhere in the back of his mind, T.J. remembered that was Mike Callan's hometown.

He gave the information to the pilot of the Falcon 900, the corporate jet Tony Vitello had purchased a few years earlier, and they headed west.

Once they were in the air, T.J. tried to remember everything he could about Mike Callan. It had been 13 years since Mike had been fired as the manager of the Cubs' Triple A team, and as far as T.J. knew, Mike had not worked in professional baseball since.

Prior to that moment, many people projected that Mike might one day be the manager of the Cubs, or some other major league team. He had won at every level he had managed in the minors and had a great rapport with his players.

Mike, of course, had been a can't-miss prospect when he was drafted out of Oklahoma. An outfielder, he had all the tools – he could hit, hit for power, had great speed, was a terrific defensive player, and had a great arm. At 6' 2", 195 pounds, he was the perfect pro prospect. The Cubs thought he would be a fixture at Wrigley for years.

Instead, Mike never was able to make the adjustment to the professional game. He made it to the majors, and hung around for a few years, but never became a star. When he was 29 years old, in 1989, the Class A manager suffered a heart attack in spring training and had to retire. The Cubs offered Mike the job and he said yes.

He moved up through the system over the next eight years, earning Manager of the Year awards and championships, and was once again labeled a can't-miss prospect, this time as a manager. Then came the night in Omaha, in July of 1997.

T.J. remembered the story from the newspapers, but some of the details were hazy. Mike had gone into the stands during the game after one of his players went after a heckling fan. Somebody had punched him, Mike had fought back and there was a near riot. The police threatened to file charges but never did.

The Cubs, however, said they could not have somebody with that kind of a temper working for them and fired Mike two days later. Until he saw him yesterday, T.J. had not seen or heard anything about him since.

T.J. knew he was managing the all-star high school team, but he knew Mike had to be doing something else. He was about to find out what it was, and he hoped Mike was ready for another job change, and the biggest challenge of his life.

❧

After renting a car at the small corporate airport, T.J. headed south on Highway 69. He made the turn onto Highway 52, and in a few minutes found himself driving through Mound City.

T.J. didn't think he had ever been in a town this small. He hoped to find Mike without calling first. He wanted this to be a surprise, because he thought he would get a more natural reaction that way.

He pulled into the parking lot of the Food Fair grocery store and went inside. A teenager was working the cash register.

"Excuse me, I was wondering if you could help me with some directions," T.J. said. "I'm looking for Dement Street."

"Dement Street? You passed it coming into town. It's back up the road about a mile," the teenager said. "What's the address?"

T.J. glanced down at his piece of paper. "232 Dement."

"232?" the teenager said, his eyes widening. "That's Coach Callan's house. Are you looking for Coach Callan? Everybody in town knows where he lives. I played for him the last three years before I graduated last month. He is a great guy. I think I spent as much time at his house the last two years as I did at home. Why are you trying to find him?"

T.J. didn't feel like going into great detail, so he simply said, "He's an old friend. He told me to stop by if I was ever passing through town, and I am, so that's what I am doing."

The explanation seemed to satisfy the teenager, who proceeded to tell T.J. how to get to Callan's house. T.J. thanked the young man, bought a soda, and got back in his rental car.

T.J. had no trouble finding the house, a neat, two-story house with a huge wraparound porch. There was an older model Ford Mustang, red, parked in the driveway. T.J. guessed it was from the early 1990s. T.J. assumed it was Mike's car, which meant he was home. That was the only part of his plan he hadn't thought of: what would he do if Mike wasn't there?

T.J. walked up the six steps to the front door and rang the doorbell. He had not been this nervous since Sally Jones stuck her hand down his pants on their first date in high school. When there was no answer on the first ring, T.J. punched the bell again. Still no answer.

He walked across the porch, where he could see around the house to the back yard. There was a garden out by the garage, and T.J. saw Mike picking weeds out of the tomatoes, wearing blue jeans, tennis shoes, and a well-worn Oklahoma Sooners t-shirt. He climbed down from the porch and headed toward him.

Mike must have heard the noise because he stood up and turned around, starting to say "Can I help you?" before he recognized that it was T.J.

"Hey, T.J." Mike said, walking toward him and extending his hand. "I don't see you for 13 years and now I see you twice in two days. What in the hell are you doing here? God, that was an awful thing about the Cubs' plane going down last night. I heard it on the news when I got up this morning. All of those times I flew on those planes I was never scared, but you always knew something like that could happen. A couple of those guys had played for me in the minors. I can't believe it happened. Why aren't you in Chicago?"

"I was, earlier this morning. I left because I had something else I needed to do."

"What was that?" Mike had a puzzled look on his face. The two men walked back to the rocking chairs on the porch and sat down. "To come see you," T.J. said.

Mike looked even more confused. "What did you say?" thinking he had misunderstood.

"I needed to come see you."

"Why?"

"You already know about the crash. All but two of the players were killed. Our manager, Buck Williams, and the general manager, Harry Johnson, were killed, too. So was my dad."

"God, T.J., I didn't know about your dad. I'm really sorry. I didn't know … "

T.J. held up his right hand to stop Mike. "That's OK, I have accepted it. I know I am probably still in shock, but I will grieve later. That can wait. I've got more important things to do right now."

Mike just nodded. The two sat in silence for a moment. Then T.J. began to speak, in a strong, steady voice.

"I need you to come back to Chicago with me. We can talk on the way. Please do this for me. I need you."

Now it was Mike's turn to think before he spoke.

"Why me?"

"I just need you. You're the one guy in baseball I know I can trust. I looked up to you. I admired you. Now I need you. Please do this for me."

Mike could tell by the look in T.J.'s eyes that there was no way he was going to turn this man down. "What about my team? We've got a game at 4 o'clock."

"Don't you have an assistant coach?"

"Yeah."

"Well, call him and tell him something came up and you've got to go out of town. He can handle the team. I'm going to take you to dinner tonight, so make sure you grab a sport coat and tie."

"Give me a few minutes to grab a quick shower, get a change of clothes and my shaving kit, and tell Mom where I am going."

As he went upstairs, T.J. glanced around the living room. He guessed Mike must have been an only child, because his were the only pictures spread around the room. T.J. could never remember Mike talking about having any brothers or sisters. There Mike was in his Little League uniform, then in high school, graduating from high school, and at Oklahoma, and finally with the Cubs. T.J. sat down on the couch, and noticed the stack of magazines on the coffee table. There were the current issues of *The Sporting News, Sports Illustrated* and *Baseball America*. A smile formed on T.J.'s lips.

Mike came back downstairs about 15 minutes later. "OK, ready to go."

The two men rode in silence until they got out of town and were back on Highway 69, headed north, when T.J. finally spoke.

"So how long have you been back in Mound City?"

"Ever since I left the Cubs, in '97. My dad died about three weeks after I got fired, and I came home for the funeral and to help Mom out and I never left. I really had nowhere else to go. Chelsea, my wife, and I were having problems. She and I had been together since high school, and I think the baseball lifestyle was finally wearing on her. She was pregnant with our child, and that kept her pretty tied down. When I got fired, she said that was it. She moved back to Chicago, near where her sister was living. I couldn't really blame her. I thought maybe she would come back to Mound City, but her parents had moved to Florida and there really wasn't any reason for her to come back except for me. And I guess that wasn't a good enough reason.

She had said she never wanted to come back here.

"Nobody was hiring coaches or managers at that point in the season. I thought I would stay here over the winter, get a job, and leave for spring training. I called every club and nobody wanted me.

"Then Mom got sick, and was in the hospital for a little while, and I knew she wouldn't last long if I didn't stay, so I did. I moved back in the house where I grew up, the house we just left, and I've been there ever since."

"Did you try to get back in baseball after that?"

"I made a few calls for a couple of years, but then I settled down here and never really thought too much about it."

"What happened with Chelsea? Weren't you expecting?"

"She had the baby. It was a boy. She named it Charlie, after her dad. She sent me pictures every year. I asked about coming up there to see him or have him come to Mound City but Chelsea thought it might screw him up. She said it would be easier on him if she just raised him as a single mom. I know I have missed being part of his life, but there wasn't anything I could do about it."

"She never remarried?"

"No, it's just been her and Charlie the past 13 years."

Both men were silent for a few seconds before T.J. tried to change the subject.

"So what have you been doing all this time? I know you haven't just been sitting around weeding the tomato plants."

"Oh no, that first winter I was here, my old coach at the high school retired," Mike said. "A buddy I had gone to school with had taken over a couple of years earlier as principal, and he offered me the job of coaching and teaching the boy's PE classes. My dad had always insisted that I should finish college and get my degree and teaching certificate just because 'you never know.' That was the biggest reason I didn't sign after my junior year, when the Orioles took me in the third round. My dad said no, and I don't think I ever did anything my dad told me not to do. He was my mentor, my coach, my best friend. The day he died I cried harder than I have ever cried in my life. I knew it was coming because he had been so sick, but I still wasn't prepared for it."

T.J. could see the tears forming in Mike's eyes as he spoke about his father. Mike's dad had been dead for 13 years and he missed him so much he was crying just thinking about him. T.J.'s dad had been dead less than 13 hours and he was not as sad about it as Mike was about his dad's death. T.J. realized he was developing an ability he never knew he had, to turn off his emotions.

"Do you like the job?" T.J. asked.

"I love it, I really do. It's funny, when I left Mound City to go to Oklahoma, and then when I got drafted by the Cubs, I could never imagine myself coming back here. I missed my folks, but I was glad to get out of here. Then, when I came back, I had an entirely different feeling about being here. The people around town accepted me back, and treated me great. All of the kids on the team are always coming by the house, just for a soda or to talk, and it gives me a real special feeling.

"It's kind of the same way I felt about my players in the minor leagues. Not that I was trying to replace their own dads or anything, but I enjoyed them asking for my opinion or advice. It really made me feel needed."

"I noticed on your coffee table at your house that you still get all the current baseball magazines. You still keep up with the game pretty well?"

"Oh yeah, plus I watch all the Cubs games on WGN and as many games as I can on ESPN when we're not playing. They may have taken my body out of professional baseball, but nobody can ever take away my passion for the game."

T.J. and Mike continued their conversation as they reached the small airport near Mound City. Walking onto the plane, Mike just stood in awe.

"This is your plane?" Mike said.

"Well, it was my dad's, so I guess technically it belongs to my mother now. My dad left everything to her in the will, except for one thing."

"What was that?"

"The Cubs."

"You're the new owner of the Cubs? That's awesome." Realizing immediately that T.J. had inherited the team only because of the death of his father, Mike quickly apologized.

"That's OK. My dad and I were not that close. I'm sorry he died, but I am really more upset that I don't seem that upset by his death. Right now I want to focus on the club and what we have to do as an organization."

The plane taxied down the runway and headed toward Chicago.

"And that's why you wanted to talk to me," Mike said.

"Exactly."

T.J. decided to be very direct and see what reaction he got out of Mike.

"I want you to be the new manager of the Cubs."

Mike sat in silence for a couple of minutes. "I haven't been able to get a job in baseball for the last 13 years and now you want me to manage the Cubs. I don't get it. Why me? Why now? I don't understand."

"Let me explain it to you."

T.J. began with the first time he met Mike in spring training, and how Mike had been the only player who had been nice to him. He went through Mike's entire career, both as a player and minor league manager, and ended with his observations of watching Mike interact with his players during the tournament championship game in Lawrence yesterday.

"Plus, when we started talking today, one of the first things you told me was how much you cared about your players. This is not going to be an easy time for any of us. Nobody in baseball has ever had this kind of challenge before. It will be the most difficult job in the history of the game. None of us knows what is going to happen.

"I want people with me that I can trust, and I know I can trust you. I know you are a man of high character and principle. I know you can motivate players. I know you know the game as well as anybody I have ever met. You should have been the manager of the Cubs a long time ago. Now is my chance to make that happen.

"I don't know what happened that night in Omaha, and I don't care. All that matters to me is that you were coming to the defense of one of your players. We are going to have a lot of battles to fight. We need a team that isn't scared, that won't back away from the challenge. We are still in first place. The standings don't change just because we are getting a new team. We are still the Chicago Cubs. We are still going to be in a pennant race. This team needs a manager who can lead these players and get the most out of whatever talent we can put together. I think you are the guy to do that."

When T.J. finished his monologue, he let Mike sit quietly for a couple of minutes, letting the news digest. He started talking again as the plane began its approach to O'Hare.

"I know this a major surprise. Twenty-four hours ago we lived in a different world. Our world has changed. We have to change. When this plane lands I am getting off and heading to Wrigley and going to work to build the new Chicago Cubs. I want you to come with me. I want you to be the new manager of the Cubs. I need you to be the new manager of the Cubs. If you don't want the job, stay on the plane and the pilot has instructions to fly you back home. I will understand and I will never bother you again."

The plane taxied to a stop, and T.J. got off. He hesitated for a moment at the bottom of the steps, wondering if he should turn around and see if Mike was following him. He finally decided not to look and walked straight toward his car in the parking lot.

Reaching his car, he noticed a reflection in the window. Mike was behind him, headed his way. T.J. opened the back door and tossed his briefcase on the seat. Mike walked around to the passenger door.

"Hop in," T.J. said. "We've got to go to work."

Chapter 6

The media frenzy had calmed down somewhat by the time T.J. and Mike pulled up and parked in the employees' lot at Wrigley. All of the evening newscasts were over, and only a couple of television vans remained on the street. Most of the front office employees had left as well, after experiencing the longest, saddest, and worst day of their lives.

As they walked toward the door to the team's offices, T.J. noticed the makeshift memorial of flowers and memorabilia piled in front of the stadium entrance. Fans had been coming by all day, dropping off items, and the display was now five feet high and just as wide.

Several people were there now, including a man and a boy, probably about 10 years old, who was carefully placing a baseball glove on the growing pile. Both the man and boy were crying. Silently, except for the tears, they turned and the man placed his arm around the boy's shoulders as they headed to the El station located behind right field.

T.J. was reminded of his missing father once more. He didn't want to become emotional again. The pain was too great; he didn't want to let himself go there. He wanted to just ignore it, to block it out, rather than have to deal with it.

"The place is kind of quiet," Mike said.

"Yeah, it's almost like the stadium itself is in mourning," T.J. said.

"You know, there are people who really believe the Cubs are cursed," Mike said. "I heard about it when I played here, all about the billy goat, and the ball going through Durham's legs. Now it's going to start all over again with the plane crash. How many teams were going somewhere by plane last night? Half of them. Whose plane crashed? The Cubs. Why do things always happen to the Cubs?"

"I don't know. I have never believed in curses, not against the Cubs or against anything. I don't believe the Cubs are cursed."

During their ride to Wrigley, T.J. had gone over the other key people Mike would be meeting tonight and their various roles on the team. He explained how he had asked Jack Reynolds to do an analysis of players from other organizations who might be available to them in the disaster plan draft, and to find out the details of how that draft would work. Paul Wendel had been assigned to prepare reports on players already in the Cubs' system who might be ready for the majors. The PR guy, Tim Jenkins, was going to report on the plans for the memorial service and what else had been learned about the crash.

The three men already were waiting in Tony, now T.J.'s, office, when T.J. and Mike walked in. "I hope you didn't mind us waiting in here, but you had the couch and the chairs and we just didn't feel like sitting behind a desk anymore," Jenkins said.

"Not a problem. Guys I want you to say hello to Mike Callan."

Only Wendel, who had been with the organization the longest, five years, seemed to recognize the name as Callan made the rounds of shaking hands. "You used to play here, didn't you?" "Yeah, I had a cup of coffee," Callan answered.

"Guys, I know this has been an incredibly long day for each of us and I don't want to keep us here any longer than we have to," T.J. said. "I need to know what you found out while I was doing my little errand so we can see what needs to be done before tomorrow.

"Jack, let's start with you. What did you find out about the disaster plan?"

"The Commissioner's office is still working on the details. They might even call tonight. I told them you would be back and we would be meeting here at 8. Sam Lawson, the guy who used to work in player development here, is putting all of it together for the Commissioner. I talked to him a couple of hours ago and he said he would try to call tonight."

Nobody noticed Callan shiver when Lawson's name was mentioned.

"They have to know something," T.J. said.

"Yeah, they know the basics. It is going to essentially be set up the same way the last expansion draft worked, when the Diamondbacks and Rays came into the majors, only we will be the only team drafting. Every club gets to protect 20 players off its 40-man roster. We can only select players who are eligible for the 40-man. Teams can only protect eight pitchers. Once we select a player from an organization, they can pull back five more players, only two of whom can be pitchers. We can't take more than two players from any one organization."

"How many players do we get to pick total?"

"That's one of the things Lawson is still trying to figure out. We had 23 players killed, but we are not sure when or if Scott and Johnson are going to be able to play. We don't know if we get to draft 23 or the full 25."

"And once we draft them, they are our property, and we can do what we want with them, right, like either send them back down to the minors or even trade them off somewhere else, right?" T.J. said.

"That is my understanding, with all of the normal roster provisions. We can't send a guy to the minors who has more than three years of experience unless he agrees to it. And the normal option rules all apply."

"When do we get the lists of the protected players?" T.J. asked.

"They are still working out the timetable. The Commissioner's office has given each club 48 hours to get its list together. The order went out today about noon our time, giving them until noon on Wednesday to turn them in. I think the Commissioner wants to review those lists and make certain there are no mistakes. All the five-and-10 guys, for example, plus those with no-trade clauses, have to be protected unless they waive that right. Once all of the lists are verified I think they will email or fax them to us, I would guess sometime Wednesday night or first thing Thursday morning. They tentatively would like us to make our picks on Friday."

"OK, now did you run some projected lists as to how we are going to rank the players we might get?" T.J. said.

"Yeah, I tried to work on that but I didn't get too far. Right after you left, our server crashed. It seemed we were getting so many emails about the crash the server couldn't handle it."

Jenkins interrupted Reynolds.

"You wouldn't believe it," Jenkins said. "All our computers are still down and the IT guys are hoping to have them back up and working, even if on a backup system, by tomorrow morning. I had one of the girls in the office trying to go through some of the emails before the system crashed. She was in tears reading them, they were so sad.

"People were saying they were crying harder than when one of their parents died. They were talking about games they saw here. The phones were swamped, too, and overloaded the switchboard. Our cell phones were the only things that were working. I finally sent our staff home because there wasn't anything they could do."

T.J. just nodded his head.

"Anything else come down from the Commissioner?" he asked Jack.

"Yeah, a couple of things. I know the Commissioner told you this morning they had called off the games for four days. They decided to go ahead and cancel them for all week. They also will announce tomorrow that they are canceling the All-Star game next week in Anaheim. The union balked at that at first, but finally agreed. The season, including us, is going to resume on Thursday, July 15. They are going to tack all of the missed games onto the end of the season, just like they did when they missed the games for 9-11, if they can't fit in some doubleheaders. They are working out all of those details."

"They really canceled the All-Star game?" T.J. said.

The other men nodded silently.

"So what is our plan, assuming we get to select the players in the draft on Friday?" T.J. asked.

Wendel answered. "We thought we would try to get as many people in here Friday night as possible, the rest on Saturday. That includes the guys we want to bring up from Des Moines and maybe Double A. We could do meetings and some light practice on Saturday, then a full-scale practice on Sunday, Monday, and Tuesday. We need to have the team picked by Wednesday because we start play Thursday in Houston.

"And somewhere in there we have to get a new manager, a new coaching staff, a new trainer, new broadcasters, and the equipment guys. Even the guys who survived the crash aren't going to be returning to work anytime soon.

"I tried to pull together some info on possible manager and coaching candidates out of the system … "

T.J. held up his right hand, motioning Wendel to stop.

"That's good for the coaching guys. Don't worry about a manager."

Reynolds, Wendel, and Jenkins all just stared at T.J., then diverted their gaze to Callan, sitting quietly on the couch. He had been taking notes on a yellow legal pad, but the three had kind of forgotten he was there because he had not said a word.

"You already met our new manager," said T.J., pointing his finger at Mike.

Mike could tell he was in the middle of a firestorm that was not of his doing. T.J. quickly came to his defense.

"I know this might be kind of a shock, but I want Mike to be the manager of the Cubs. You guys are going to be in charge when it comes to picking the players and all that, but Mike is the manager. Trust me on this. He is the best guy we could possibly hire. I would bet my life on it. You guys don't know him, but you will get to know him very soon."

The three men said nothing, because there really was nothing to say.

"Tim, what kind of schedule do we have for tomorrow as far as the press is concerned?"

"We told them we would have a briefing at 10 a.m. just updating them on what was going on. We didn't say anything specific because I didn't know if we would have all of the information set up about the memorial service, or about the draft or what. We can change it if you want … "

"No, 10 a.m is fine," T.J. said. "We just have to add the fact we will be introducing our new manager, as well. You don't have to announce that ahead of time, just after we get started.

"What is set up about the memorial service?"

"It will be at 1 p.m. on Thursday," Jenkins said. "We don't have many of the details as far as who will be speaking, etc. I wanted to talk to you about that first. Maybe in the morning, before the news conference."

"That will be good. Let me give that some thought tonight. Why don't we all meet here again about 8:30 a.m. and see if we know anything else or if anything has changed.

"Jack, when we get the computers back up and running I want you to pull all of the reports you can find on the players we might be getting. Look for the most likely guys. We know there will be some surprises when we get the lists, but if we have prepared for the obvious guys then we will be that far ahead of the game. Call our scouts in the field as well and see if they have seen some of these guys in the last few weeks and can give us a fresh opinion on them.

"Paul, you get with the minor league guys and give us a list of who is the most ready for the big club. I would guess we're mostly looking at pitchers from Triple A and Double A, but let's see what we've got. We can always bring them up for the camp this weekend and let Mike see them, then send them back if he doesn't think they are ready.

"Mike, I want you to focus on some candidates for your coaching staff. Take a look at the lists that Paul has prepared, plus I know you have your own ideas. By the way, I reserved a room for you at the Westin. I will drop you off after dinner."

The men all stood up, shook hands, and said good night. Callan stayed behind as T.J. slumped down in the cushions of the couch.

"Just think, a little over 24 hours ago you were coaching a high school All-Star team in Kansas and tomorrow morning you will be introduced as the manager of the Cubs."

Callan started to answer but was stopped by T.J.'s ringing cell phone.

T.J. answered. It was Sam Lawson from the Commissioner's office.

"T.J., sorry to call on the cell phone, but Jack Reynolds gave me the number when we talked this afternoon because he said your switchboard was overloaded."

"No problem, but Jack and everybody just left. Our meeting ended a little early."

"Well, I will go ahead and tell you what I have found out here researching the disaster plan and you can pass it on if that's OK," Lawson said.

"Sure, let me grab a pen."

"I gave most of this info to Jack earlier, but the one big thing we had to check out was the number of players you get to select. It's 23, one for each player who was killed."

"OK, got it. Anything else?"

"Well, I put together a list of managerial candidates for you, especially the minority guys ... "

T.J. interrupted Lawson. "That won't be necessary Sam. We already hired our new manager. We're going to have a news conference in the morning."

"Oh, OK," Lawson said, a bit taken aback by that news, and by the speed of the Cubs' decision. "Mind if I ask who it is?"

"Actually you may know him. He managed in the minors for the Cubs when you were here. Mike Callan. He's an old friend of mine, a guy I trust and the perfect man for the job."

There were several seconds of dead air before Lawson responded. T.J. was puzzled by the silence before he finally heard Lawson say, "Did you say Mike Callan?"

"Yep, do you remember him? He's sitting right here if you want to say hello."

Callan almost fell out of his chair at that comment, but T.J. didn't notice.

"No, that won't be necessary. I really would strongly urge you to reconsider that choice, T.J. I think you are making a big mistake."

"Why do you say that?"

"He was blackballed from baseball. Did you know that?"

"I knew he hadn't been in baseball for 13 years after he got fired following the fight in Omaha, but I don't know any details, and quite frankly, I don't care. He is our new manager. Thanks for the information about the draft. I will pass it along to Jack."

Lawson said, "I'm going to have to talk this over with the Commissioner."

"You go ahead and do that Sam, and call me back."

T.J. hung up the phone and sat down on the couch. Callan was still sitting in the chair opposite him.

"Mike, we've got to talk some more. That was Sam Lawson from the Commissioner's office. He said I was making a big mistake by hiring you and tried to talk me out of it. He said you were blackballed. That's why no club offered you a job all these years. Do you have any idea why he said that, what he was talking about?

"I've got to know the truth, Mike, because if you don't tell me, the press will find out about it and the organization could be embarrassed. Remember that happened a few years ago when the Diamondbacks tried to hire Wally Backman? He had a couple of ghosts in his closet that he didn't disclose, and the press had a field day with it. He got fired four days later. We can't have that happen to us."

"OK, I will tell you what I know. You can decide if you still want me as the manager. Lawson used to work here, he had Wendel's job, I think you know that. He came the year after I was promoted to Triple A, in '94. He never liked me. He had one player that he was very high on and he kept bugging me to play him. He had brought him in from the Yankees, where he was before. T.J., the guy couldn't play. You could play better than him. If it had been A ball, yeah, I could have played him a little bit just to keep Lawson off my butt, but not in Triple A. We were playing to win, not to keep some suits in the front office happy.

"Lawson was looking for a reason to get rid of me. I knew I was going to be fired at the end of the year. That was one of the reasons I was stressed out, which probably explains why I went into the stands that night. I know he also thought I was having an affair with his wife, which wasn't true. She had a pretty good reputation around the clubhouse, if you know what I mean. She accused me to try to deflect the attention away from my players that she was sleeping with. Lawson knew his wife was cheating on him, but he thought it was with me.

"A few weeks after I got fired, Lawson left the Cubs to go to the Commissioner's office. He was the one who blackballed me. He sent the word out to all the other teams not to hire me. A friend of mine who worked for the Cardinals told me. That was why I gave up and never tried to get another job."

"That's it?" T.J. said.

"I swear that's it. That's all I know."

"Well, I'm not going to let some donkey in the Commissioner's office tell me what to do, not now, not ever. Let me call him back and then we can grab something to eat and I'll drop you off at the hotel."

Lawson answered on the first ring. "Lawson, it's Vitello."

"Did you reconsider?"

"No, I didn't."

"The Commissioner wasn't happy with the news. He has several minority candidates and he thinks this would be the perfect time ..."

T.J. interrupted him. "Save your breath, Lawson. I've made my decision. We have our manager. I would advise you to worry about your own problems from now on, not ours."

When Mike was alone in his hotel room, he opened the dresser drawer and pulled out the white telephone book. Turning to the residence pages, he quickly found the entry for C Clark on Bucknell Drive. Chelsea had their baby, a boy she named Charlie, four months after they separated. She had never remarried since the divorce. She had not asked for alimony in the divorce, just monthly child support, and Mike had been grateful for that. Charlie was 13 now.

Mike missed being a father, but that wasn't his choice. He wished his life would have turned out differently and he could have had the same relationship with his son that his dad had had with him. Maybe that was one reason he cared so deeply about his players in high school, treating them as if they were his own kids.

As Mike stared at the phone number, he glanced at the clock on the nightstand and thought about calling his ex-wife, to let her know he was coming to town. The two didn't talk very often, but she had kept him informed about what was happening in her life with Charlie over the years. So much had happened to him today, however, that he just couldn't yet bring himself to pick up the phone and call her. If she paid attention to the news, she would know tomorrow that he was here.

🐝

The next morning, the introduction of Mike Callan as the Cubs' new manager landed with a huge thud. The columnist in the *Tribune* was the harshest critic. "First the Cubs lost their team, now they've lost their mind and named a high school coach as their new manager," he wrote.

"Welcome to Chicago," T.J. told Mike.

Chapter 7

Adam Mathis had been a lead investigator for the National Transportation and Safety Board for six years. Luckily, there had been only one serious commercial airline accident in that time, so most of his time was spent working smaller crashes, usually caused by inexperienced pilots making a mistake in poor weather conditions.

When his phone rang at 5 a.m. in his home in Falls Church, Virginia, Adam knew he would be going some place. The initial reports were very sketchy, but were detailed enough that he knew it would be the most important investigation of his career.

His wife could tell from the tone of his conversation on the phone that there had been a serious accident. She propped herself up on her pillow and turned on the lamp on the nightstand. Adam hung up the phone and turned his attention to her. She could tell the phone call had shaken him.

"A charter flight carrying the Chicago Cubs baseball team crashed trying to make an emergency landing in Cheyenne," he said. "There are only a few survivors."

Barb Mathis' hand covered her mouth when her husband was speaking. "Oh my God … is there any … "

"Not really. There was a report that the pilots told the ATC they suspected their fuel was contaminated, but that's all we know. Weather was fine. The pilots had a lot of experience. We won't know anything else until we get there."

Barb grabbed her robe and headed to the kitchen to make a pot of coffee while her husband showered and dressed. She flipped on CNN on the kitchen TV. A reporter was giving a live update from Cheyenne, but didn't say anything more than what her husband already knew.

Adam came into the kitchen and poured himself a cup of coffee, glancing at the television. He hoped the airport cops and fire department had been able to preserve the crash scene. He saw that much of the wreckage had burned, destroying what evidence was probably there.

He downed a quick cup, grabbed his briefcase and flight bag, kissed Barb, and headed for his car and Dulles Airport.

❧

Because of the nature of this tragedy, Mathis knew, he was going to be under more pressure and scrutiny than all of his previous investigations combined. The government would want to make certain this was not a terrorist attack. Major League Baseball, and the other professional sports teams, would want to be assured it was pilot error or some other simple explanation. The media demands also would be intense. Everybody involved would want answers today, and that would only make finding the actual cause of the crash that much more difficult.

The sun was just beginning to appear on the horizon as he parked his car in the government lot at Dulles and headed for the small government jet. An initial team of 10 investigators was headed to Cheyenne, to be joined by other federal agents from the field. The mood when this group assembled in the early morning like this was always somber, but Mathis could tell this crash had shaken even the most senior members of his team.

When the plane was airborne, Mathis pulled out his legal pad to make some initial notes. Joe Clark, his top assistant, was on the phone with the Cheyenne authorities to see what other information was becoming available.

"I have never heard of a professional sports team being involved in a crash before," said Susan Thomas, one of two female investigators.

"There have been some close calls, usually because of bad weather," Mathis said. "When the Lakers were still in Minneapolis back in the early 1960s their plane went down in an Iowa cornfield, but nobody was hurt. A couple of hockey teams have had near misses, again usually weather-related. There have been the college disasters – the Wichita State and Marshall University football teams back in the 1970s, the Evansville University basketball team, and those few guys from Oklahoma State a few years back in Colorado."

Clark hung up the phone, and the others interrupted their conversations to listen to what he had learned.

"Nothing much new. There were eight survivors out of 51 people on board, including the crew. Two of those died at the hospital. It looks like the others are going to pull through, including the pilot. There were reports the pilots told ATC they thought they had a fuel contamination issue. They lost both engines and tried to glide the plane in and came up about 150 yards short of the runway. The plane broke apart on contact. The fuel tanks ignited and everything from the wings back was torched. All of the survivors were in the front of the plane.

"It looks like they have done a pretty good job of securing the scene. The emergency crews knew they were coming so they were prepared. Other than trying to pull out the survivors and put out the fire, they are waiting until daybreak and for us to get there."

Mathis nodded his head, then leaned his seat back and closed his eyes. He knew sleep would be impossible, but he had to try. Once he got to the crash scene, he knew, he could forget about resting for a long time. The other investigators did the same thing.

Mathis could see the wreckage as their flight landed in Cheyenne. The debris field was not too spread out, which would make the investigation somewhat simpler. The first goal of any investigator was to find the two items considered most crucial to determining the cause of the crash: the flight data recorder and the cockpit voice recorder, the so-called "black boxes."

The investigators had a little head start over some crashes because of the opinion of the pilots that they suspected fuel contamination. On the flight west, he had already requested the maintenance records of the company that had serviced the plane at O'Hare before departure. Crews already were en route to seize those records and check the fuel supply at the company. If they could find any fuel at the crash site, that also would be tested for contaminants.

Mathis wanted to believe this was just an accident, but unless there really was a problem with the fuel, he couldn't think of any other reason for this plane to crash. If it had been an act of terrorism, there should have been a bomb on board somewhere, but at least from what he knew so far, there was no indication of that. The pilots would have had no warning; the plane would have just blown up. The pilots obviously knew there was a problem of some sort and tried to land; they just didn't quite make it.

The two black boxes would help the investigators, at least to give them an idea of what they were looking for, other than the question about the fuel. The flight data recorder monitors the parameters such as time, altitude, airspeed, and heading. It also keeps a record of the in-flight characteristics such as fuel flow, rudder position, center of gravity, electrical systems, hydraulics, and the position of the throttles.

The cockpit voice recorder would let the investigators know what had been happening in the moments leading up to the crash. If any warning alarms had gone off, they would hear them. The conversations of the crew, and how they talked, would be major keys. Were they talking about a suspected problem? Were they calm or suddenly surprised? All those clues would help in the investigation.

Mathis' cell phone rang about a minute after the plane landed. The caller introduced himself as Douglas White, the Commissioner of baseball.

"I understand you will be heading up the crash investigation?" he said.

"Yes sir."

"In the best interests of both baseball and the entire country, I hope you can put this investigation on the fast track," the Commissioner said. "We all need to know what happened as soon as possible."

"Yes sir, we will do our best," Mathis said as he hung up the phone.

Eddie Marshall already knew about the Cubs' crash when he arrived for work at Charter Air Services at O'Hare late Monday morning. Since he had worked late the previous night, he didn't have to be in today until noon. He knew the cops and feds would be all over the place as soon as they learned where the Cubs' plane had been serviced, so he wasn't surprised by all the commotion as he walked into the office.

Until today, the biggest items of discussion around the office had been the rash of apartment break-ins that had been occurring in Schiller Park and Norridge, near where Marshall and some other company employees lived. The cops thought it was some teenagers trying to steal items they could sell to get money to buy drugs. Marshall wasn't too worried, but some of the women who worked in the office admitted to being a little spooked.

Marshall knew he would be interviewed, since he was the fuel man on duty last night. He also knew they would take samples from the fuel trucks and tanks, thinking the crash might have been caused by contaminated fuel. He also knew they would not find any evidence that the fuel was contaminated.

His boss was waiting for him after he clocked in. "Eddie, these men are from the National Transportation and Safety Board. They want to ask you a few questions about last night."

"Sure," he said, trying to act as nonchalant as possible even though he was more nervous than he had ever been in his life.

The investigators motioned Eddie into the boss's office, followed him in, and closed the door.

"Did you see anything unusual last night while the Cubs' plane was being serviced?" Eddie was asked.

"No. It all seemed routine to me."

"Nothing out of the ordinary? No extra people you didn't recognize, nothing strange about the plane, even if it didn't seem significant at the time?"

"No," Eddie said. "Honestly, it all looked the same as always." As he talked, his right leg could not stop twitching, moving up and down as he if were running a race even though he was trying to sit still.

"Are you OK? You seem a little nervous."

"I'm fine, just shook up about what happened last night and the crash. That's the first time a plane I've worked on has left here and crashed. Just kind of hits you in the gut a little."

"Take us through your job last night ... you were the person who fueled the plane, correct?"

"Yeah, that's usually my job. The only thing last night was we couldn't use the high pressure system. It wasn't working for some reason, but that happens all the time. It didn't work for any of the planes we serviced yesterday."

"So how did you fuel the plane?"

"We pulled the fuel truck up to the plane and began fueling through the gravity feed on the top of each wing. It's really not an unusual procedure, it just takes a little longer, that's all. You just have to be sure when you are done that the caps are securely tightened so you don't have a problem with fuel siphoning out of the tank when the plane is in the air."

"And you did that?"

"Yeah, I went back and double-checked the caps on both wings, right before takeoff. Everything was fine. Did you check the fuel in the truck?"

"It was clean, and so were the reserve tanks. It doesn't look like there was any problem with the fuel here, if you didn't notice any problem."

"No, I told you everything looked OK and normal to me. I know it's a terrible accident and I am really sorry about what happened. It shook me up when I heard it on the radio this morning, but I honestly think everything was done right before the plane left here. I don't know what could have happened."

The investigators thanked Marshall for his time. Until they had a chance back at the office to examine the plane's maintenance records, there really didn't seem to be anything unusual that had occurred before the plane left O'Hare.

Marshall finished his shift at the normal time of 9 p.m., then decided to stop by the local club on his way home, as he frequently did. He really intended to just have a sandwich and a couple of beers, calming himself down so he could sleep. The bartender, who knew Eddie's routine well, asked if he wanted the usual and he said, "Skip the sandwich." A couple of beers turned into four or five, and it was close to midnight by the time he pulled into his apartment complex.

Even in his inebriated condition, Marshall could tell something was wrong as soon as he reached his front door. The key wouldn't go in the lock, but as he turned the knob, the door opened. Walking into the living room, he could see it had been ransacked. "Shit! The money," he mumbled to himself.

Just as Eddie reached for the light switch, a man wearing a ski mask and carrying a revolver appeared in the hallway, only a few feet in front of him. Eddie was so stunned he couldn't speak, and even though he opened his mouth, no words came out.

"You Eddie Marshall?"

Before Eddie could answer, his voice still frozen in his throat, the slug hit him right in the middle of his forehead.

Chapter 8

After the news conference announcing his hiring as the new manager, Callan and T.J. went back to T.J.'s office, trying to collect their thoughts about what needed to be done next. Nikki knocked on the door and peaked in.

"Sorry to interrupt, but Kevin Andrews of the *Tribune* was wondering if he could have a word with you."

"Sure, send him in," T.J. said.

"I know you guys are busy and I don't mean to intrude, but I just had a couple of things I wanted to ask that I didn't want to bring up out there," Andrews said as he entered the room.

T.J. motioned for him to have a seat on the couch, and he and Callan sat in the adjacent chairs.

"You guys are going to be spending a lot of time together, so it is only fair that you get to know each other better," T.J. said. "What's up?"

"Well, I know you explained your connection to Mike from the past, and I honestly do remember when you were managing in the minors, but I don't mind telling you this whole hiring has me a little confused. I mean, we haven't even had the memorial service, everybody is still in shock, and you have hired a manager and are acting like it is business as usual. I don't really get it."

T.J. took a moment before answering.

"I knew people would be in shock, but since I had my mind made up, I didn't see any reason to wait. I said at the news conference how important Mike is to me personally, and he's the guy I want in charge. With him already in place, he can help us as we organize our thoughts as far as selecting the players in the draft, putting a coaching staff together, with everything we have to do."

"But don't you think it is all happening too quick?" Kevin asked.

"As soon as I heard about the crash, and then found out I had inherited the team, I made a decision that as an organization we were going to focus on the future. We are not going to ignore the past, and we are going to remember and honor the past, but we are not going to spend the rest of this season or the rest of our lives in mourning. We are simply not going to do it."

"Your own dad was killed," Kevin said. "I don't see how you can be so callous about the crash and about everyone who died."

"Look, there is something you need to understand," T.J. said, getting a little agitated, the volume of his voice rising as he talked. "This is for your information only and is not to ever be reported any-where. My dad and I were not close. I think you know that. He and I rarely spoke. I can't remember the last time we talked. I am sorry that he died, and I know my mother is going to be devastated when we finally find her in Europe and she gets the news. I am not going to allow myself to be drawn into a pity party. I had hoped that I could get closer to my dad before he died, but that didn't happen, and I am not going to lose any sleep over it.

"Let me ask you something, again off the record. Did you know my dad was talking about selling the Cubs?"

Now it was Kevin's turn to be stunned.

"What are you talking about?"

"When Phil Donnelly came to the office yesterday to tell me that I had inherited the team in my dad's will, he also told me that my dad had asked him to draw up a new will that did not include the Cubs, because he was planning to sell the team. He never signed it, and obviously never sold the team, so the old will is the one that is valid and will be filed with the probate court. I didn't know anything about it, and I can tell by the look on your face that this is news to you, too."

"I didn't know your dad that well, as you know, T.J., but I had never heard talk anywhere among other GMs, front office folks, anybody, that the Cubs were for sale. Why would he want to sell the team?"

"I have no idea," T.J. said. "I guess we will never know, because the team is now definitely not for sale."

That news derailed Kevin's attempts to learn more about Mike Callan and his background, but he recovered in time to get a couple of phone numbers for people in Mound City that he could call for background interviews. He thanked T.J. and Callan for their time as he left the office.

"He seemed about as shocked that your dad was thinking about selling the team as he did that you hired me as the manager," Callan said. "You honestly didn't know what your dad was up to?"

"I had no clue about anything until Phil Donnelly told it to me yesterday. It makes no sense. I'm just glad he had not gotten further along in the process."

T.J. had delegated Tim Jenkins in the PR office to direct all planning for the memorial service on Thursday. He knew he would have to speak, but the crowd and press would understand his desire to keep his remarks short. He really wanted to focus his energies on building the new Cubs, which was why he was glad to see Paul Wendel and Jack Reynolds walking into the office. T.J. knew some people would question how he and the rest of the front office staff could focus their energies so quickly and not be in mourning for all of those who were killed, but he just refused to let himself think about it. He really had not had all that much contact with those players, and while he was sad for their families, he was not as close to them as some people might have thought.

It would be another day, at least, before they would see the lists of protected players from the other clubs, but maybe they at least had an idea of candidates, and certainly would know better who was worth considering in their own organization, T.J. thought.

"We've come up with a list of guys at Des Moines and Tennessee that we would recommend at least bringing in for Mike to see over the weekend," Wendel said. "We have to be a little careful because both clubs are still playing through Sunday. They have the same three-day All-Star break we have next week. We can bring in some of the pitchers who aren't scheduled to pitch, but we have to leave them enough position guys to field a team."

Wendel handed T.J. and Callan a sheet of paper that included the names and pertinent statistics for the players they were recommending. T.J. noticed there were six players from Des Moines, including three pitchers, and four from Double A, two of them pitchers.

"In a normal situation there is really only one guy who I think is definitely ready to get a shot in the big leagues," Wendel said. "But we know this is not a normal situation."

"Who's that?" Callan asked.

"An outfielder at Des Moines, Billy Slagle. You can tell by the numbers that he is having a pretty good year. No offense Mike, but some people in the organization said he kind of reminds them of you."

"You mean he's a stiff?" Callan joked.

"No, and don't take this wrong, but when he was signed everybody thought he would be a major league player. He has all the tools, runs well, understands the game well, but for some reason he just hasn't had a year when he has put it all together. This is his third year at Des Moines, and it looks like he might finally be getting it."

Callan noted that Slagle was a switch-hitter and was hitting .319 with 12 homers and 38 RBI in 77 games. He also had stolen 17 bases in 21 attempts.

"How old is he?"

"28," Wendel said. "He's been in big league camp the last two years but got sent back pretty early. We actually came close to releasing him this year, but Harry (Johnson, the late general manager) was such a softy that he couldn't bring himself to do it. He wanted to give him one more chance."

"Well, it looks like Harry might have been right," T.J. said. "What do we know about his makeup? Will he be able to handle the situation if he comes up here?"

"I think so. He's a college kid, went to Georgia somewhere, I think. He's a little older, so he's not as wild as some of the kids. Obviously, he knew a lot of the players who were killed, so I am sure he is upset, but I think he'll be OK."

The four men went over the rest of the names on the list, deciding to bring eight of the 10 in on Friday night to begin the workouts on Saturday. They decided to hold off on the other two for now until they saw what kind of players they were going to be able to select in the draft.

Reynolds had been working on some notes about that, thankfully having been able to get back on the computer this morning.

"I ran some charts," he said. "I figured we really wouldn't want to look at many older guys, but we also didn't want a lot of guys who weren't ready to play. We know this is more than a one-shot thing for the rest of the year. We have to get guys that can help now, but we need to think a couple of more years down the line as well.

"I know there are going to be some surprises on the list, but we can deal with that easier if we have some basic information out of the way. I ran the list of every club's roster and pulled out the players between 25 and 32. I figured if they were younger than 25 and already in the majors, chances are they will be protected. If they are older than 32, chances are we don't want them, or we will be able to look at them separately.

"I then looked at each organization's prospects on their 40-man roster and tried to project who they would want to protect, given the age of their big league players, length of contracts, etc. Then I went back to the big league rosters and added in all of the 5-and-10 and no-trade guys. What it all boils down to is these two lists."

Reynolds had a bundle of pages in each hand, stapled together.

"This is the list of players I believe each organization will protect, at least for our first selections. Remember they get to pull back five more players after we make a choice, and we can't take more than two from any one organization."

Reynolds dropped that stack of papers on the conference table.

"This other sheet lists what I, and our friendly computer, believe to be the top players from each organization who could be available to us. We know there will be some surprises, but it will be fairly easy to update these lists when we get the official protected lists tomorrow."

"That's terrific work Jack," T.J. said as he picked up the first pile and began to glance through it.

"This lists all the stuff I think we need to know," Reynolds said. "If they are on the 25-man roster, I have their contract terms included. I've got their age, their current stats, stats from last year. If we need to find the individual reports from the scouts on each guy, that is easy to do.

"There is one major advantage we have in this draft. We are the only club drafting."

T.J. looked up from the list of possible unprotected players he had been studying.

"I know we can do all of the computer analysis and come up with some good selections, but the one thing that is not reflected on any of these pages is the size of the man's heart. You just mentioned it. This is not a normal situation. I know we can't go out and interview these guys before we take them to ask how they feel about becoming a Cub under these circumstances. But we have to know a little bit about their character.

"What we are doing is unprecedented. Hopefully, no club will ever have to go through it again. We don't get a second chance here. We basically have to replace an entire roster, not just the one-third or so turnover you have in a normal year. I think we need to get guys who are hungry, who want to play, who might not have a chip on their shoulder but will look at this as both a challenge and an opportunity. Strong character guys. Guys like Slagle. Those are the kinds of guys I think we need to get."

The room was quiet for a minute before Callan spoke.

"One thing to keep in mind here," he said, "because I think it has kind of been lost because of the situation. Whoever we pick up and bring in here is joining a first-place ball club. I know the roster might be entirely different, but the jersey will still say Cubs on the front, and the standings still say Chicago is in first place in the NL Central with a five-game lead. You said it yesterday to me T.J., on the plane coming here. I don't want any players on my team who don't want to be here. I want players with moxie. I want to test them and see what they are made of.

"This is not an expansion team. We are going to have one goal, and it will be the focus of my speech when this new team gets together. We are going to go out there and do our damnedest to pay tribute to everyone who died the best way we possibly can, and that's by realizing they have inherited first place. I want players who are determined to hold onto that and go beyond it, bringing a world championship to the people of Chicago. We are going to settle for nothing less."

If the press and fans had heard that short speech, T.J. knew, there would be no doubt in anyone's mind why he wanted Mike Callan as his manager.

Chapter 9

As much as he enjoyed covering the games, Kevin Andrews considered that the "ordinary" part of his job. After all, there wasn't a lot of extremely creative ways to report that Bobby Scott's three-run homer in the eighth inning had lifted the Cubs to a 4-1 victory over the Cardinals. Most of the people he knew who cared about the game at all were either at the game, watched it on television, or listened to it on the radio. They didn't need to read his story in the *Tribune* the next morning to find out what had happened.

What Kevin considered the "fun" part of his job was the in-depth profiles, the stories where he had time to write and the extra space needed to really bring his readers inside the subject's life. That was the kind of story he had been planning to write about Tony Vitello, and the one he now was preparing on Mike Callan.

As he had done with Vitello, Kevin had the research department pull all of the stories they could find from the *Trib's* archives on Callan. He didn't care so much about the game accounts, about how Callan had won a game with a hit here or lost a game with a base running error there. He wanted to learn more about the type of person Callan was; he wanted to find out more about the circumstances when he was fired as the Triple A manager, and most important to him, what he had been doing in Mound City, Kansas, for the past 13 years.

Kevin knew there would be no stories about those years in the *Trib's* files. In normal circumstances, for a story of this magnitude, he would have taken a few days off the daily beat and gone to Mound City to do his background interviews and research in person. These were far from ordinary times, however, and Kevin wanted to get this story completed and in the paper before anybody from the *Sun-Times* or the Arlington Heights paper beat him to it.

That was why he was working the phones, trying to call the numbers that Callan had given him a couple of hours ago in T.J.'s office. One was the main number to Jayhawk-Linn High School, where he asked to speak to the principal, Jerry Luebbert.

Luebbert was quite willing to talk about his former high school teammate, even though he was a bit in awe that he was talking to a reporter from the *Chicago Tribune.* The only reporter he knew was from the weekly *Linn County News,* published in Pleasanton. He explained to Kevin that he and Mike Callan had gone to the school all four years together, graduating in 1977. They had been freshmen the year after the school opened, in 1973, after the school district closed the separate Mound City, Prescott, and Blue Mound high schools and started sending all of the kids to one school. Luebbert lived in Prescott, 12 miles southeast of Mound City.

The consolidation was not well received, and one student from Mound City actually refused to participate in the first graduation ceremony because he was so upset "his" school had been closed, Luebbert said. The move made sense, however, for financial reasons, and it also gave the school much more competitive athletic teams.

The biggest reason for the success, Luebbert said, was Callan. He was the best athlete ever to come out of Mound City and made all-state in football, basketball, and baseball. Luebbert was his teammate in basketball and baseball.

The two men went their separate ways for college, with Luebbert heading to the University of Kansas and Callan to Oklahoma on a baseball scholarship. When Luebbert graduated, he came back to Mound City and started teaching history at his alma mater. A few years later, he became a vice principal, and then moved up to the principal's job in 1992.

"So you were the one who hired Callan to become the baseball coach and a gym teacher after he got fired by the Cubs?" Kevin said.

"That's correct," Luebbert said. "He had been back in town for a few months, after his dad died, and I could tell he was really depressed. I hate to say this, but I think he was developing a pretty bad drinking problem. I caught him a few times leaving Everybody's, our local bar, and he was in pretty bad shape."

The sudden knowledge that Callan's friend was telling a reporter that the new manager had a drinking problem caught Andrews off guard. He had not expected this interview to produce that kind of information.

"You mean he was an alcoholic?" Kevin said.

"No, I wouldn't go that far. I think he was just depressed by all of the bad things going on in his life. He got fired by the Cubs, his dad died, his pregnant wife took off and left him, he didn't know what he was going to do for a job. He had a lot of issues he was trying to deal with and sometimes it was just easier to drink until you forgot about all that."

"So you decided to try to help him?"

"That's right. He and I had been good friends and I felt sorry for what he was going through. I could see why he was depressed. It just so happened that coincided with our former coach retiring, so we had an opening for a coach and a gym teacher. I knew he had his teaching certificate, so I thought maybe giving him a new job would take his focus away from his problems and might help stop his drinking."

"Did it?"

"I think so. I think there were still some rough nights the first couple of years, as he realized that he wasn't going back to pro ball or that he and Chelsea were not going to get back together. He had a lot of free time on his hands without much to do. This town isn't exactly a rival to Chicago, you know. We had a few heart-to-heart talks and I told him I stuck my neck out hiring him when some people didn't think he was qualified for the job, and I was not going to be able to defend him if he got caught drinking. I think he had a few games that first season where he had a few pops before the game started, just to calm his nerves.

"I smelled alcohol on his breath one time at school. I sent him home and told him if I ever suspected he had been drinking at school or was drunk around any of the kids, he was gone. I think that sobered him up."

Kevin made a note to talk to T.J. and Mike about Mike's drinking problem. He asked a few more questions about Mike's relationships with his players, style of coaching, the success the team had over the years, then thanked Luebbert for his time and hung up.

Both men were still thinking about Mike after the call ended. Luebbert suddenly realized he had just told a Chicago reporter that the new manager of the Cubs had a problem with alcohol in his past. "I hope I didn't screw him," Luebbert said to himself. "I probably shouldn't have said that."

Kevin was thinking, "I wonder if he had been drinking when he got into the fight in Omaha?"

There were several stories in the *Trib's* clips about the fight, and Callan's dismissal as the team's manager. None of them made any reference to Callan being drunk or having a problem with alcohol.

Sam Lawson, at the time the Cubs' director of player development, explained in one story that Callan had been dismissed because the team management did not believe he was setting a good example for the organization's young players, losing his temper in such a manner. The media seemed to accept that explanation. Callan's view of what happened was never reported. After a story a couple of days later about Callan's replacement being hired, his name disappeared from the *Tribune.*

The last thing Kevin wanted to do was bring up an old story if Callan had solved his drinking problem. That had been more than 10 years ago, and Luebbert had said as far as he knew, Callan had not had any reported problems since then. He had never been arrested or accused of any other wrongdoings. Still, Kevin knew he would not be doing his job if he did not investigate this side of Callan's personality as thoroughly as possible.

As he thought about how to bring up the topic with Callan,

Kevin's mind drifted back to his brief meeting with Callan and T.J. in T.J.'s office a few hours ago. Something T.J. had said bugged him – that Tony Vitello had been working on a plan to sell the Cubs. Andrews had been around the team every day for the past two years and he had never heard anything about that possibility and that bothered him,

Kevin considered himself a good reporter and a good judge of people's character. He always thought there was a somewhat shady side to Tony, even before he read all of the background clips on him, before Singer told him his opinion that maybe Tony had been involved in the death of his first wife, and before he heard this rumor about him possibly wanting to sell the team. Now, he knew, he needed to dig a little deeper into what had been going on in Vitello's life the past few months as soon as he had a little extra time.

Kevin wandered back from the press room into the Cubs' front office. One thing he did appreciate about the Cubs, at least under the old regime, was they were not like a lot of teams in various sports that kept their offices locked up like they were Fort Knox. He had the freedom to go from the PR office to the general manager's office or even the owner's office without an escort, and without somebody questioning where he was going or what he was doing there.

Nikki was on the phone when he came into T.J.'s outer office. She motioned him to take a seat, indicating she would be done with the call in just a minute.

When she hung up the phone, Kevin smiled at her.

"Been pretty crazy here the last couple of days ... how are you holding up?"

"OK, I guess," she said. "It helps to stay busy, kind of keeps your mind off what happened. Every time I have a minute to think about it, I still can't believe it. It has not sunk in."

"I know what you mean," Kevin replied. "I feel the same way. I think we're all going to be like that for quite a while."

Kevin had really never noticed how attractive Nikki was. She had an engaging smile, a great figure, and long, curly blond hair. Kevin guessed she was a few years younger than him. He had always been in a hurry, seeing her as just the go-between when he needed an interview. He made a note to stop by her office more often, even when he didn't need to talk to T.J.

"So are they in?" he said, pointing his finger at T.J.'s closed door.

"They should be back in a few minutes. They just went across the street for lunch. You're welcome to wait."

Kevin didn't think that was a bad idea, spending a few more minutes with Nikki. He was about to ask another question when her phone rang.

He could only hear Nikki's side of the conversation, but it was obvious the caller was not happy. He or she certainly was not calling to offer condolences about the people who had died in the plane crash.

"Well, I'm sorry, sir ... I really don't know what to tell you ... What was this for ... I don't know ... Yes, Mr. Vitello's son has taken over as the team's owner ... I don't have any idea if they talked about it or not, sir ... No, I'm sorry, he is not in the office ... If you would like to leave me your name and number, I would be happy to give him the message ... I really don't know, sir ... I'm afraid I don't know ... Mr. Vitello never told me anything about that, sir ... I'm sorry."

She looked at Kevin as she hung up the phone, a confused look on her face.

"What was that all about?" Kevin said.

"I have no idea. He said he was calling because Mr. Vitello – Tony, not T.J. – had failed to send him a package he had promised him. He wouldn't tell me what it was about, said it was a private matter.

"That's about the third or fourth strange call I've had since the crash. Most of the callers want to talk to T.J. because they were friends of Mr. Vitello's, and want to offer their condolences, but these calls have been weird. I wonder if he was up to something. Come to think of it, he was acting kind of strange the past couple of weeks. He usually had me make all of his calls and do all of his emails, but he had been doing a lot of them himself. I asked him about it and he said he was just trying to take some of the work off my shoulders.

"Now that I think about it, that was really out of character for him."

Kevin's reportorial instincts had been raised about six notches while Nikki was talking. He wondered if any of Vitello's unusual activity had anything to do with the possibility that T.J. had told him that his dad was planning on selling the team. He was about to quiz her to see if she knew anything about that when T.J. and Callan walked into the office.

"Hey Kevin, long time, no see," T.J. said. "What's up?"

"Not too much. I just had a couple of more questions for you and Mike for that story I am working on, if you have a minute."

T.J. motioned Kevin to follow them into his office as he focused on Nikki. "Anything I need to know?" he said.

"Mostly the normal condolence calls, but I just had a weird one a couple of minutes ago. A guy said your dad had promised to send him something last week and he never got it. I have no idea what he was talking about and he would not be more specific. Said he had to talk to you, but wouldn't give me his name or number. It came up as an unknown caller on caller ID. The guy sounded kind of creepy. He didn't sound threatening, really, but he came off like he was really unhappy with your dad about something."

"Don't worry about it," T.J. said. "If he calls back put him through and we'll try to find out what he's upset about. If you didn't know anything about it, I don't think it could be anything very important."

When Kevin, T.J. and Callan were inside the office, Kevin took out his notebook as he sat down on the couch.

"I just had an interesting phone interview with Jerry Luebbert," Kevin said. The name didn't mean anything to T.J., but it obviously did to Callan. "He had a lot of great things to say about you, but he also told me there was a period after you got back to Mound City when you had a drinking problem. Is there anything you can say about that?"

Even though the question was directed at Callan, T.J. looked as if he had been slugged in the gut. Callan was quiet for a second, then was calm as he answered.

"That was a long time ago. It's in the past and I prefer to leave it in the past. I don't know what Jerry told you, but I really don't want to make any further comment about that."

Kevin tried to rephrase the question a couple of times, but got the same no comment answer. He finally gave up, thanked Callan and T.J. for their time, and left.

The door had been closed for maybe a second when T.J. sprang toward Callan, pumping his outstretched arm into his chest.

"What the hell was that all about? What did he mean about you having a drinking problem? I asked you last night if there was anything in your background that could cause us problems and you told me no. I believed you. Now it's going to be in the paper that we hired a damned alcoholic as our new manager? What the hell was that all about? You better have some answers and they had better be good."

Callan had never seen T.J. act like this before. He took a step back, raised both his hands, and motioned for T.J. to calm down.

"OK, OK, settle down for a minute. It's no big deal, really. I'll tell you about it.

"I started drinking right before I got fired in Des Moines in '97. I told you I was all stressed out. Chelsea and I were having trouble, Lawson was on my butt and I knew I was going to get fired. The only thing that made me relax a little was a couple of drinks. I never drank in public, just in private.

"Then when I got fired, and then when my dad died, it seemed I started drinking a little more. Jerry was my buddy from high school and the principal I told you who hired me. He saw me drunk a couple of times, but it really wasn't a big deal. I think it was caused by my depression with everything that was going on. It went for six, maybe eight months, and then I stopped."

T.J. had calmed down as Callan was talking.

"OK, I'll buy that, it makes sense. But why didn't you tell me that last night when I asked you if there was anything else we needed to know? I warned you I didn't want anything to come up that would embarrass the organization, and that's exactly what this does. Why didn't you tell me?"

"Because I thought it was in the past and I wanted to keep it in the past. How did I know Jerry was going to blab like that to a reporter? It kind of pisses me off that he said that. I wanted everything here to be focused on the future, not dredging up old shit from my past. It's like you have said since the first time we talked … we are going to have enough problems focusing on what we have to do that we can't get caught up or worry about the past. We can't keep thinking and feeling sorry for the guys that died, and I kind of viewed my drinking problem the same way. I didn't think about it because I was thinking only about the future."

"Well, we've got to think of some way to soften the blow when it comes out in the paper. Kevin is a good reporter and he is fair, but you know he is going to use that in his story. What can we think of that will divert some of the attention away from that?"

"What about if we name the coaches, and announce our plans for the practices this week? That would at least be stuff that is new and not 10 years old."

"That might help," T.J. agreed. "Do you think we can do that? I know you have been making a lot of calls."

"Give me a couple more hours to check on a few things, and then we can go over it and see what you think. If it all looks good to you, we can announce it later this afternoon or first thing in the morning, right before the memorial service."

T.J. agreed that sounded like a good idea. He moved over to his desk to return his stack of phone messages while Callan began to make his calls from his temporary office on the couch.

Two hours passed, then Callan looked up as T.J. hung up from another call.

"I think we're all set," he said. "Here's what we've got."

As T.J. listened, he had to admit he was impressed. Callan had put together what seemed like an impressive staff, especially on such short notice and under such incredible conditions.

"For the third base coach, I would like to promote Alex Thompson from Des Moines. He has managed there for three years, and I know from experience he would like a shot. He knows his players we are going to bring up, and he has seen the Double A guys in spring training and in Instructional League. I think he will be a big help.

"For first base coach, I would like to bring in Luis Melendez. He's been the roving base running and defensive instructor in the minors. We are going to put a lot of emphasis on speed and defense and I think he'll do a good job."

"I want to bring in a couple of my own guys to be the pitching coach and hitting coach. Steve Grimm pitched for me in the minors and has been coaching in the Twins' system. He is the most knowledgeable guy about pitching I know. He is a real enthusiastic guy, a non-stop talker, and will do a great job. I would like to hire Vince McGee as the hitting coach. You remember him from his days here. He was real popular with the press and the fans and I think he will provide that link to the past that we want to maintain. The only Cubs' players I know who were more popular than him over the years were Ernie Banks, Billy Williams, and Ron Santo."

T.J. nodded his head in approval. "You've already talked to all those guys and they all said yes?"

"Yep. Obviously, they are waiting for me to call them back and tell them everything is set before they say anything to their own teams, but they all said they can be here on Friday ready to go."

"What about a bench coach and the bullpen guy?"

Callan told him his choices for both those jobs, two of his ex-players who had coached in the majors for years before being let go from their previous jobs last year.

"It all sounds good to me," T.J. said. "Go ahead and make the arrangements. I will get Tim Jenkins over here to prepare the press release. Hopefully, that news will push your profile story out of the top spot in the *Trib* tomorrow. I know we are still going to hear about the drinking problem, but maybe it will be softened a little."

❀

It didn't take the announcement of the new coaching staff to prompt Kevin to downplay the history of Callan's drinking problem. The more he worked on the story, and the more people he talked to, the further and further removed Callan seemed to be from those days. Kevin did include a couple of paragraphs, toward the bottom of the 35-inch story, but it was not nearly big enough news to create a media or fan uproar.

Another story in the newspaper received even less attention, buried with a one-column headline on page 12 of the Metro section. Police said the body of Eddie Marshall, 46, of Schiller Park, had been found inside his apartment. Apparently, Marshall had been shot and killed when he interrupted a robbery.

Chapter 10

The Cubs had roped off a section of the seats behind home plate at Wrigley for the media's use during the memorial service. Kevin Andrews could have sat there, but decided he would get a better feel for the emotions of the crowd if he sat in the unreserved seats. He opted for a spot on the aisle in the first row above the walkway.

He was scanning the packed stadium, noticing that almost everyone was already wiping away tears, when he saw Nikki Williamson standing right in front of him.

"Is anybody sitting there?" she said, pointing to the open seat next to Kevin.

"No, come on up."

Kevin had to admit he was starting to develop a fondness for Nikki. She certainly was better looking than most of the female reporters he knew, and she seemed to be smart at the same time. Good looks and brains didn't often go hand-in-hand. His mother always said timing was one of Kevin's strong suits, but he was a little uncertain about how to play his cards in this relationship. He could count on one hand the number of times he had talked to Nikki before the last two days, and he didn't want to appear insensitive to what was happening. He opted for a casual approach.

"I will certainly be glad when this service is over," he said. "I have been dreading this since Monday."

"I know exactly what you mean," said Nikki, dabbing her eyes with a tissue. "Everyone in the office was crying all morning. We had been so busy with everything that you are forced to put what really happened out of your mind, but this makes it all too real."

The two sat in silence, staring at the field. A podium was set up directly between home plate and the pitcher's mound, and there were several white folding chairs in two rows on each side of the podium. Kevin guessed that was for the speakers at the service as well as the other front office and Major League Baseball personnel.

He saw another section of reserved seats, just to the right of the Cubs' third-base dugout, which he knew were reserved for the families of the victims. Nikki told him some of them had come into the office this morning and were waiting until the last minute before taking their seats.

"T.J. seems to be holding up pretty well," Kevin said.

"I had only met him a couple of times," Nikki said, "but I could tell even then that he and his dad were not very close. His dad never asked about him or said where he was or what he was doing. It's a shame. I don't know what I would do if something happened to my dad. I feel closer to him than I do my mom, really. He was the one who pushed me to take this job, even though he thought I was over-qualified for it. I think it was his way of making sure he could get playoff tickets if the Cubs ever got there."

"It looked like this might have been the year, too," Kevin said. "I wouldn't think he'd have to worry about that now."

The speakers and other dignitaries were making their way from the dugout to the seats on the field. At the same time, the family members of those killed in the crash began to take their seats. There didn't appear to be an empty seat in the ballpark, not even in the bleachers, and the place was completely silent. It was really an eerie feeling.

For the next 45 minutes, the only sounds were occasional clapping when one of the speakers remarked about somebody who had died, and the steady, constant sobs of everyone in the ballpark. Kevin had been to a lot of funerals in his life, for his grandparents, for parents of friends, even for a fraternity brother killed in a car accident, but he had never experienced anything like this.

He glanced at Nikki and saw she was not attempting to hide the tears. Neither was anyone around them.

When it was over, the two continued to sit in their seats as the crowd silently filed out of the ballpark. Kevin decided to make his move.

"This may seem kind of out of place, and I hope you don't get offended, but I really would like to get to know you better, on a personal level. When everything kind of calms down in a few days, would you like to go out to dinner or something?"

Nikki brushed back another tear and took a deep breath. "I would like that. I think I need to do something to get my mind off all of this. I don't know when I can go, though. T.J. told me he wants me to work all weekend because of the new players coming in for the meetings and practices."

"I've got to work, too," Kevin said, "so I will just see you in the office and we can set something up. There's no big rush."

Nikki nodded.

"Speaking of the office, I need to get back there. I'm sure I've got another 20 voice messages to check."

"Any more strange calls like the one you had when I was waiting for T.J.?"

"Not really. Katherine, T.J.'s mom, finally called this morning. She was in a villa in the south of France. Said she hadn't turned on the TV for two days, then finally caught the CNN International feed this morning. I am sure she was in shock. I just talked to her for a minute, then put the call through to T.J."

"Have they said if they are going to have a separate funeral for Tony?"

"I am sure they are waiting to decide that until she gets back. I heard T.J. say she would be home in a couple of days. … I need to go. I'll see you later." Kevin sat and watched her walk down the aisle to where the ramp disappeared beneath the seats. It was not a bad view.

⋏⊩

As soon as the service was over, T.J., Jack Reynolds, Paul Wendel, and Mike Callan assembled in T.J.'s office. The protected lists for the draft had been sent from the Commissioner's office earlier in the morning. Each had a chance to look at them quickly, but they had not had time to get together and start discussing their strategy and response to the lists.

"Any surprises?" T.J. asked as they all sat down.

"We were really pretty close," Reynolds said. "The one thing Paul and I were just talking about was if we knew anything yet regarding the insurance policies on the contracts of the guys who were killed."

T.J. had asked Phil Donnelly to look into the legal question of what happened to the contracts of the deceased players. Was the club still responsible for paying the balance of the contracts, or did insurance protection take over those payments? Determining whether the club was still responsible for paying the contracts would be a big factor in deciding which players the Cubs could select in the draft.

The player payroll this year was $130 million, the highest in team history. T.J. did remember his dad complaining about a couple of the players who won their arbitration cases back in February, and wishing he had a way to get out of some of those contracts.

"I just talked to Phil as we were leaving the field," T.J. said. "He was heading back to the office. He is waiting for a call back from the lawyer for the Player's Association and the legal guy in the Commissioner's office. If the contracts were guaranteed, they have to be paid. Phil is almost positive the insurance policy will cover the costs of the contracts, just as they would if the player was hurt and couldn't play. He just wants to make sure. He will call as soon as he hears something."

"Well, until we know that we can't really complete our strategy," Reynolds said. "There are a couple of guys left available to us because I am sure their clubs didn't think we would want to take on the salary, but if we can, they would be great players for us and I think would help make our team a little more credible to the fans, too."

"Who are they?" Callan said.

"Keith Orlando from the Dodgers, for one," Reynolds said.

Orlando was a former runner-up in the league MVP voting, a

hard-hitting first baseman. Now 34, the Dodgers had overpaid "the Big O," as he was affectionately known during his years in Cincinnati, when he became a free agent two years ago. They signed him to a five-year deal and he so far had been a major disappointment. He was making $15 million this year, with $50 million more due him over the next three years.

"Can he still play?" asked T.J.

"That's the $50 million question," Reynolds replied. "I talked to Marty McDonald, our advance scout. He just spent the last week watching the Dodgers since we were supposed to play them this week. He thinks he has some injuries he has tried to play through and that caused the hitch in his swing. For the first time in the past year, he saw some signs this week that he was coming around."

Orlando had hit three homers in the past eight games, as many as he had hit in the first two and a half months of the season.

"God, that's a lot of money," T.J. said.

Wendel spoke up.

"But really, when you think back, we went almost that high with our offer when he was a free agent. He already is a year and a half into the deal, so the total burden of the package is less that we were offering two years ago."

"The contract doesn't really bother me if we know he can still play," T.J. said. "I know he is popular with the fans, and the fact that he grew up in northern Indiana wouldn't hurt. Anybody know how he would feel about coming to us now?"

"McDonald got the feeling from the Dodgers' people that he would love to get out of L.A.," Reynolds said. "Of course he was talking about the possibility of making a trade last week, but I think he would be OK. It's not like he really has any roots there. For my two cents worth, I really think we need to pick up a couple of veteran guys who can give us some leadership and experience and not rely solely on backups and younger players. I think we should take the chance."

"Mike, what do you think?" T.J. asked.

"You guys have to decide if we can afford him, but if that answer is yes, I would like to have him. His older brother, Sam, was in the minors when I was managing and I always liked his attitude. He didn't have the physical talent his brother has, but if Keith is anything like Sam in makeup, he would be a good guy on the club."

"OK, so we put him in column A, at least for now," T.J. said. "Who else is out there in that category?"

"Steve Watson of the Braves," said Reynolds, a shy grin forming on his face.

The other three men all spoke as if in unison.

"What? The Braves didn't protect Watson? What the hell are they smoking down there?" T.J. said.

Watson was a left-handed pitcher who had led the NL in wins the previous year but had gotten off to a slow start this season, with a 3-7 record in his first 13 starts. At 29, he was in the prime of his career.

"I can't answer that," Reynolds said, "but I can tell you what I think and what the rumor mill says."

When nobody interrupted him, Reynolds continued.

"You know he can be a free agent at the end of the year. The Braves were trying to get him locked up to a long-term deal over the winter but didn't get it done. Rumor was he wanted the kind of deal Zito got from the Giants, seven years and close to $120 million. The Braves said no, thinking they could open talks again during the year.

"Watson supposedly was ticked off and didn't work as hard in the spring as he should have. Some of the scouts, including ours, think he has a sore arm. Others just think he is pitching bad because he is ticked off at the Braves and knows he is going to be a free agent so he doesn't give a shit."

"So if we take him we don't know if he has a sore arm or not, and he could still be a free agent at the end of the year?" T.J. said.

"Which is good in one sense, because then if he doesn't pitch well or is hurt, we only have to pay him for three months," Reynolds said. "If he is OK and pitches well, we can try to sign him. Harry really liked him. We already had talked about trying to make a big push for him this winter if he became available."

"I think he is worth taking a shot on," Wendel said. "We know what he can do if he is healthy, and it is worth three months salary to find out if he is hurt or just pissed off at the Braves. At least we know he won't be upset to leave them."

"Two down, 21 to go," T.J. said.

"Those were the two guys who really jumped out at me," Reynolds said. "I'm glad you guys feel the same way about them as I do. I am excited about both of them."

"Do we have to take somebody from every organization?" Mike asked.

"No, we can't," Reynolds said. "We only get 23 picks and there are 29 other clubs."

"And we get to pick a second player from an organization if we want, right?"

"Yes, but they first get to pull back five more players, so we would only be getting their 27th best player. I don't know if many organizations are that deep in prospects that their 27th player would be better than somebody else's 21st best player, but that is the rule.

"I think we should go through all of the clubs, identify who we think is the best player available to us, and then figure out where that would leave us at the end. That would give us 29 guys, and we only get 23. Then we can decide if a second player in an organization is better than some of those we have on the list. We already know who we would take from Atlanta and Los Angeles, so let's just start at the top of the list and go from there."

"It doesn't make any difference if it is AL or NL?" T.J. said.

"No difference," Reynolds said.

The men spent the rest of the afternoon going over every club's available players. It was almost like a fantasy draft, except this was real life. At about 6:30, they admitted they were getting hungry but were too energized to stop. T.J. picked up the phone to buzz Nikki, somewhat surprised she was still at her desk when he realized what time it was.

"Nikki, why didn't you go home?"

"Because you didn't tell me I could leave."

"Well, go home, as soon as you call Luigi's and get us three large pizzas, two deluxe and one cheese, for delivery. Just tell the security guard on your way out to buzz me when they get here and I will come out."

"Who's the healthy one in the bunch?" she said.

"That would be Wendel, you know him."

The men returned to their work, devouring the pizzas when they arrived, and finally about 9 p.m. had settled on a preliminary list of players.

"We don't have to notify the Commissioner's office until tomorrow, so let's all sleep on it and come back and take a fresh look at it in the morning," T.J. said. "Then we can decide if it still looks good or if we want to make any changes."

"I just had a thought," Callan said. "Obviously, the club knows its own protected list, but do they get to see the lists from the other clubs? I remember back to the expansion draft because I was still in the minors, and there were some trades made, kind of back door deals really."

T.J. sat back down, intrigued by this idea.

"So if the Dodgers, for example, knew that the Cardinals had left a player they really liked unprotected, they might be willing to trade us one of the guys they had protected if we took that guy from the Cardinals, then traded him," he said.

"Yeah, basically. But the Dodgers wouldn't know the Cardinals left the guy unprotected if they didn't see the list."

"Jack, can you see if you can get a hold of Sam Lawson in the Commissioner's office and get an answer to that question?" T.J. said. "Either that, or just call one of the other GMs. You know all those guys. We're not asking for them to release a government secret here. I would think they would be interested in knowing who the other teams protected."

"Got it."

"Let's see what Jack finds out about that, then that might dictate our strategy in the morning," T.J. said. "We can maybe add a couple of players we didn't expect to get if we could work out a deal or two."

Reynolds said he would be glad to drop Callan off at the Westin, and he, Callan and Wendel stood up to leave as T.J. crossed the office and sat down behind the desk.

"Aren't you leaving?" Wendel said.

"You guys go ahead, I want to just try to get a little better organized here. There has been so much going on I haven't even had a chance to clear off the desk or see who is in this stack of calls that Nikki took today. I'll get out of here soon. Go have a good night's sleep and I'll see you in the morning."

T.J. couldn't believe the clutter and number of piles that had grown on top of the desk. One quality he did admire about his father was that he was extremely organized; not to the point that he was a neat freak, but at least he could find anything he was looking for. T.J. guessed that came from being a lawyer, where even if his dad spent 30 minutes clearing off his desk and putting papers in files he could find some client to bill for the time.

The two biggest piles on the desk were the stack of phone messages that T.J. had not returned over the past three days, and the mail. T.J. went through the phone messages first; most of them were simply calls of condolence. He could not take the time to return all of them, so he put them in a stack and would have Nikki write a note to all of them tomorrow. The calls that looked important, that he thought he should return, he put in another stack to get to when he had time.

T.J. then moved to the pile of mail. It was all for his father, not surprisingly. Most of it he disposed of quickly in the trash can. He also had received a bank statement and a statement from his investment company.

Going through the mail, T.J. realized he had not even thought about checking his emails for the past four days. Knowing the Cubs' server had crashed the day of the accident because of all the emails coming in, he wondered if any emails to him had been lost in cyber-space or were all stacked up in the system. He made a note to have Nikki check on that tomorrow, as well as his dad's emails, and figure out how to send the auto-reply to redirect those emails to him or Nikki.

This had been a long day and he was beat. For the first time since Sunday night, he honestly felt he would be able to sleep tonight. He turned off the light, said good night to the security guard, and headed home.

Chapter 11

Billy Slagle and the rest of the Iowa Cubs watched the memorial service on television in their hotel rooms in Memphis. Slagle did not cry easily, but he was in tears throughout most of the ceremony.

He had been stunned when he was awakened early Monday morning by a teammate yelling at him on the phone to "turn on CNN. The Cubs' plane crashed."

That kind of bulletin would be alarming enough if you were wide awake, but when you were still groggy, it took a few extra moments for the words to register in the brain. Ever since, he could not get his mind to think about anything else. He knew many of the people who had died, of course, having played with them for the past couple of years.

Slagle felt bad for the families of the victims, and he also felt a little guilty. He knew if he had played as well as he was supposed to have played last year, and even in spring training this year, he would have made the major-league roster. He could have been on the plane. He could have died.

The thought that kept coming into Slagle's head was this: Was there a reason he wasn't on the plane? Was there a reason that God had kept him out of the major leagues, knowing that plane was going to crash, and knowing that He had another plan for Slagle's life? If so, what was it? Slagle wanted to know.

Slagle had never really questioned God before. The son of a Southern Baptist minister, he had been brought up to trust God and not to question God's timing. Slagle was not one of those players who, if he hit into a double play to end a game, said that it was "God's will." By the same token, he never hit a home run to win a game and then opened his post-game comments praising God.

To Slagle, religion was very personal. His dad could go out and talk openly about God and his beliefs, but Slagle couldn't do that. He had a different personality from his dad, and found his release through sports. To his dad's credit, he had never pressured him to follow in his footsteps and had always found time to attend his Little League and high school games and to support him through college, as well. Their relationship today was as solid as it had ever been, talking to each other at least two or three times a week either by phone or on the buddy chat on the Internet.

Even though he was a college graduate, from Georgia Tech, Slagle didn't consider himself gifted intellectually. Even though he was the son of a minister, he knew he didn't know everything there was to know about God. He had gone to school on a baseball scholarship, not academic, and had passed the classes he needed to pass to remain eligible to play baseball and to graduate.

Since the crash, Slagle and his dad had talked at least twice a day on the phone. Slagle was questioning his dad as if he were God. "How could God let something like this happen?" he asked. His dad didn't have an answer. He said it was an accident, pure and simple.

"I thought God had a plan for everything!" Slagle said. "Why did He let this happen?"

"I can't answer that," his dad told him. "Only God knows the answer. The answer will be revealed to us in time."

Slagle was thinking about that as the memorial service ended, and he and his teammates got on the bus for the ball park. Walking into the clubhouse, he almost bumped into Alex Thompson, the team's manager.

"Billy, I was going to come looking for you. Come into my office for a minute," he said.

Usually it is not good news when a manager calls you into his office. It means you have most likely been traded, or worse, released. Slagle's head was scrambling to recall how he had been playing and if he had done anything wrong as he crossed the clubhouse and followed Thompson into the office.

Thompson shut the door, went behind his desk, and motioned for Slagle to sit down. "What's up, Skip, am I in trouble for something?" Slagle asked.

"No, not at all," Thompson said. "I've just got something I need to tell you."

When Slagle did not make an attempt to interrupt him, Thompson continued. "I got a phone call early this morning from Mike Callan. I'm sure you saw in the paper he's going to be the new manager of the Cubs. He wants me to come to Chicago and coach third base for him for the rest of the season."

"That's great, Skip," Slagle said. "Congratulations. You've earned it. You will do a great job."

Slagle's unspoken comment was, "What does that have to do with me?" Thompson knew that, so he continued.

"As you know, they also have to replace all of the players who were killed. They will select players from other organizations tomorrow, but they are also going to bring up some guys from our system, at least to look them over in practices this weekend, and then decide if they will keep them in Chicago or send them back."

Thompson paused for a moment, then continued, "They want you to come to Chicago for the weekend."

Slagle's eyes almost popped out of his head. "I'm going to the big leagues?"

"Hold on, not exactly," Thompson said. "I just told you that they are bringing up guys to work out this weekend, then will make a final decision on the roster that will stay up there when the games start. If you do a good job and impress Mike and the front office guys, I think you can make the team. But it's not guaranteed so I don't want you taking anything for granted."

"Oh, I understand. Thank you, Skip, thank you. I can't believe it. The day I have been praying for is here. I've got to call my dad."

Thompson gave him the details of their flight arrangements for Friday, congratulated him, and left him alone in his office so he could use the phone in private.

Slagle's dad was almost as excited as his son. "I know how hard you have worked for this opportunity, Billy, and I am so proud of you. Just relax and do everything you are supposed to do to impress the coaches this weekend and I'm sure it will work out. Your mom and I love you and know you will make it. Keep us posted on how it's going."

Slagle promised to call as soon as he got to Chicago and found out more information.

※

Finding out information, of a different sort, was what Adam Mathis and his team of NTSB investigators were doing as well. When they took a break for lunch and went into the small cafeteria near the Cheyenne airport, the television was on, covering the memorial service from Wrigley Field.

Even though it had no bearing on his investigation, Mathis watched the service and felt the sadness coming through the television screen. The crash had been seemingly the only news on television all week, and he knew people were going to look at his investigation for some kind of an explanation about what had happened.

Luckily, nobody was banging on his door yet. Even the people who wanted answers yesterday realized these investigations took time. Many times the cause was not known for a year or longer. The biggest factor in determining how fast the investigation could come to a conclusion was the evidence that was collected at the scene, and the interviews with witnesses or the workers who had serviced the plane.

Mathis took a few minutes to take stock of where the investigation stood. Both black boxes, the flight data recorder and the cockpit voice recorder, had been found and sent to Washington for analysis.

He should know some preliminary information from both sources when he got back to the office in Washington, probably next week.

The investigators had talked with the air traffic control personnel who had been involved in communications with the plane for the last hour or so of its flight. They knew from those conversations the pilots suspected they had a fuel contamination problem. Unfortunately, all the excess fuel on the plane had burned in the fire after the crash, so there was nothing left to test at the site. The fuel trucks and reserve tanks at the charter services company at O'Hare had been tested and were found to be clean. The interviews with the employees there also didn't indicate that anything was out of order Sunday night, so they were back at square one on that part of the investigation.

Mathis glanced at his watch as he finished his second cup of coffee. The doctors at the hospital thought the pilot who had survived the crash, Jeff Jackson, might be awake enough for Mathis to interview him for a few minutes. They had told Mathis to come by around 2 p.m.

Jackson had been lucky. He had been knocked unconscious, and he had a broken leg and broken wrist, but otherwise had come out of the crash pretty well. The co-pilot, Dave Curtis, had been killed, as had the three flight attendants. There was no special reason Jackson had lived and Curtis had died that Mathis could find – it just wasn't his time to go.

Mathis got up from the table, left a tip, and headed for the hospital. The other investigators were going back to the airport, trying to wrap up that portion of the investigation. All of the crash debris had been cleared, and moved into an unused hangar. Workers were attempting to piece the plane back together as best they could, even though much of it had been burned beyond salvage.

When he got to the hospital, the lead doctor was waiting for him. He said Jackson was awake enough to talk, but he cautioned Mathis that because of the concussion, he wasn't sure how much Jackson would remember about the accident.

"Don't worry, I'll take it easy," Mathis said.

The nurses had propped Jackson up with an extra pillow and he was waiting when Mathis came into the room and introduced himself. Jackson's head was covered with a thick bandage, his left leg was in a cast and hung from a bar above the bed, and his arm was in a cast just past his elbow.

"I don't want to take up much of your time, but we are trying to find out why the plane crashed and I was hoping you felt up to answering some questions," Mathis said.

"I don't know how many answers I can give you, but I will do the best I can," Jackson said.

"You told the ATC you thought there was a fuel contamination problem. What was happening that made you suspect that?"

"The first sign of trouble was when we lost a fuel tank boost pump. I had never had that happen before. Neither had Dave. We thought it was just a faulty pump. Then we had a second one go out, and we knew that had to be more than a coincidence."

"So what happened was the fuel wasn't getting to the engines, and that made them eventually stall out," Mathis said.

"It appeared that way to me. The biggest thing we couldn't figure out was what was keeping the fuel from going through the pumps to the engine. The gauges told us we still had plenty of fuel."

"And even if the fuel was contaminated somehow, it still should have been getting to the engine, it just wouldn't have been burning correctly," Mathis said. "So the big question is what was keeping the fuel from getting to the engine."

"That's what it seemed like to us."

"So when you lost the second engine, you planned a dead stick landing at Cheyenne airport," Mathis said.

"Yeah, we just came up short. We were so close."

"Don't blame yourself, Jeff, it wasn't your fault. You did the best job you could. We'll figure out what happened. Do you think somebody tampered with the plane somehow?"

"I don't know. I've been trying to ask myself the same question. Everything appeared OK Sunday night. I didn't see anything out of the ordinary, nothing that made either Dave or I suspicious."

"We talked to the people at O'Hare and they said all of the activity there was normal," Mathis said. "We tested all of the fuel supplies and they all came back clean."

"So something happened to the fuel between the time it was put into the plane and when we got about an hour and a half or so into the flight."

"It looks that way," said Mathis, "but what?"

Mathis thanked Jackson for his time and left, knowing he had to find out what could have happened to that fuel supply.

Chapter 12

Ever since he was a youngster, T.J Vitello had hated waking up in the morning. His parents practically had to drag him out of bed to get him to school on time. When he didn't have to get up, usually on Saturdays, the kid could sleep until noon, no matter what time he went to bed.

The dislike of hearing an alarm clock ringing before 9 a.m. had never left T.J., even after he went to college and law school. He still hated waking up early, and early was any time before 9 a.m.

This week had been different. T.J. wasn't sure if it was all of the adrenalin taking over, or anxiety, or a combination, but he had more energy and felt more alive than he had ever felt in his life. He didn't even have to set an alarm clock. As soon as the sunlight came through the windows of his bedroom, he was awake and eager to get the day started.

By 7:30 a.m., he was back in his office, looking at the list of players he, Reynolds, Wendel, and Callan had put together the previous night, as of now the players they intended to select to re-stock the Cubs. He had to admit, as much as he loved and followed baseball, he was not familiar with many of the names. He was relying on Reynolds' and Wendel's recommendations, and the suggestions of the team's scouts, and he had faith in their opinions.

T.J. liked the idea of picking up Keith Orlando from the Dodgers and Steve Watson of the Braves because they were names their fans could identify with. They had played in the big leagues, and had success in the big leagues. As loyal as the Cubs' fans were, and even though he knew those fans would be even more tolerant given the circumstances of the crash, he still wanted the new Cubs to be competitive and give the fans their money's worth when they came to Wrigley or watched a game on television.

T.J. also realized that perhaps nobody in baseball history had experienced this opportunity to put his personal stamp on a franchise that now belonged to him. All other franchises that basically started from scratch were expansion teams. They didn't have the history that a franchise like the Cubs had. If he could put together a team that could somehow win the pennant, he and his franchise would be on top of the baseball world for years to come.

He was so absorbed in his own thoughts that he didn't hear Reynolds, Wendel, and Callan come into the office.

"Mornin', guys, sorry I was just day-dreaming a little there. How's everybody this morning? Ready for a big day?"

All nodded their heads as they took turns filling their cups from the coffee pot on the table in the corner of the office.

"We have one big question to decide," Reynolds said, "and that is how seriously we want to pursue trying to make some deals before we make our choices. Lawson called me last night on my way home and said all of the other clubs will get the protected lists this morning, so I suspect we will be getting some calls.

"The other clubs, especially those that are struggling a little, may want to try to scoop up some of the younger prospects that were left unprotected. I suspect they might be willing to part with some people off their current roster, knowing they won't have another opportunity like this to get those younger players. We have to decide if we want to do that."

As they sat down, T.J. spoke first.

"I think we have one goal, and one goal only here, and that is to get the best players we can get for the Cubs. This isn't like an expansion draft in that we are looking to stock an entire franchise. We still have our minor league talent. We still have our own prospects. What we don't have is major league players. I don't mind us trying to pick up some younger players if we think they are great prospects, and can help us in a year or two, but not at the expense of a guy who can help us now, and maybe still help us in a year or two, too. Let's see what calls come in, and then we can evaluate each possible deal on a case-by-case basis."

Wendel had been studying the top 23 names the group had settled on last night, listed on a giant bulletin board lining one wall of T.J.'s office.

"I think this is a very good group of players," he said. "When you add the five or six guys we are bringing up from our system to look at this weekend with them, I think we will come out of that with 25 very good major-league players. We had more talent to choose from then I thought we would get. We've got pitchers who have big league experience, and have won in the big leagues. Luis Roman is a quality defensive catcher. We've got some guys who can hit, and they aren't slouches defensively. I think our fans and the media are going to be pretty surprised by this list."

"It's one thing to look at these names on the wall and it's another to see them on the field," Callan said. "I just want to get them here and see what we've got before I start making any predictions. I was thinking about it last night. I have two areas of concern. I really don't see anybody on our list of potential pitchers who I consider a bonafide closer. I know we have some guys with some career saves, but only as the second or third guy in the pen. It's natural clubs want to protect those guys, but I think maybe that would be one area we should look at trying to improve through a trade.

"My other concern is something we can't do anything about until we get the players in here. That's to evaluate their heart and their desire. If I have to choose between a great player with a lousy attitude and a good player with a great attitude, I'm going to take the good player every time. That's an intangible skill that you can't measure with statistics, and even the best scouts in the world can't really judge it because so much of that isn't visible except to the people within the team. I just hope we are getting those types of guys."

"Do we know if there are any closers who might be available in a deal?" T.J. asked.

"There are three or four clubs that might be in a position to deal, because they are out of the race or because their closer can walk at the end of the year," Reynolds said. "I will have to find out what they are looking for, and if there is anybody who wasn't protected that they are interested in. Let me go make some calls. I'll be back in a few minutes."

Reynolds had just left the room when T.J.'s private line rang.

"Morning, T.J., it's Phil Donnelly. Sorry I didn't get back to you last night. I just got the final details worked out. The team's insurance policy will cover the costs of the contracts. Each of the players also had an individual life insurance policy issued through the Players' Association. They selected the beneficiary for that policy. Our understanding is that the balance of the contract will be paid to the person listed as the beneficiary on the life insurance policy. I suspect most if not all of the players also had private life insurance policies, or at least accidental death policies, but we wouldn't have any of the information about that."

"So we don't have any financial obligation in terms of the contracts for any of the players who were killed," T.J. said.

"The club still has to pay the contracts, but we will be getting the money we need to do that from the insurance company."

"OK, that helps us figure out what we can do here. Thanks a lot, Phil, I appreciate it."

Callan and Wendel had heard T.J.'s part of the conversation but waited for him to tell them what he had found out.

"That was Phil Donnelly. He said insurance will cover what we owe on the contracts of the players who were killed. So we can build our new team without regard to payroll."

T.J. thought for a second after he had said that and then added, "Well, we do have to be concerned with payroll, but you know what I meant."

T.J. walked over to the coffee pot and refilled his cup.

"Hey, Mike, while we are waiting for Jack, have you got everything figured out with your coaches and a plan to run this kind of mini-camp for the next four days?"

"Pretty close," Mike said. "The coaches are all coming in this afternoon and we are going to meet at the hotel tonight. Tomorrow is going to be kind of loose since we don't know who all will be able to get here in time for the workout. We're going to have three pretty intense days Sunday through Tuesday. We're going to fly to Houston Wednesday morning and work out in the afternoon at Minute Maid Park, right?"

Wendel had picked up the additional duties of working as the interim traveling secretary, and he had made all of those plans.

"Yeah, Mike, that's all set. We've got a United charter, planning to leave O'Hare at 10 a.m. That will get us to Houston a little after noon, bus to the hotel, let the guys grab some lunch, bus back to the park at 2:30 and work out starting at 4."

Callan nodded his approval of the plan just as Reynolds walked back in the office.

"Well, I got a match," he said. "Of course it's not official because we have to go through the draft first. But if we draft Jay Cooper, the Double A outfielder from Toronto, the Pirates will trade us Tom Tippett for him. He was one of the guys I thought we might get. Pittsburgh is going nowhere, and he can be a free agent at the end of the year."

"Is he the best guy we can get?" Mike asked.

"I can't say for sure, but I think so," Reynolds said. "He is 31 years old, righthanded, throws about 92 and has converted 19 of 21 save chances so far this year. He has a good strikeout to walk ratio. It's hard to say what he will do here, because his chances were pretty limited with the Pirates. I like him, and we have solid reports on him.

"Oh, yeah," he said, directing his attention to T.J. "There's one more part of the deal. I told them we would throw in $500,000."

"You did, did you?" T.J. said. "Your salary will cover that, won't it?"

Reynolds could not immediately tell if T.J. was kidding, before his boss started laughing. "I'm kidding, Jack, that's not a problem if everybody agrees it's a good deal."

Wendel stared at the board. "We were going to draft Cooper anyway because he was the best guy Toronto had, but we thought he would probably end up in Iowa. If we think Slagle can start in center, I like the corner guys we've got up there, McKenzie, Peterson, and Zach Adams."

Everybody in the room nodded.

"OK, Jack, call the Pirates back and tell them as long as nothing gets screwed up during the draft and we get to take Cooper and the other outfielders we want, we have a deal."

"Yes, sir."

"One more time before we call Lawson and tell them we are going to send him our list, is everybody OK with all of these guys?" T.J. asked. "Let's go through them one more time, one by one."

Thirty-five minutes later, the list was final. T.J. had Nikki type it up and fax it to the Commissioner's office.

"They have to go over it and make sure there are no mistakes," Reynolds said. "Then they will notify all of the clubs who have lost a player. They want a couple of hours to do that, so they can notify the players. We can announce the players at 4 p.m. our time.

"The current clubs all have been told that we would like those players to report to Wrigley no later than noon tomorrow. We are holding rooms for everybody at the Westin tonight in case they can make it in. They are going to make the individual flight arrangements, send us the information, and we will reimburse the old clubs. That seemed like the simplest way to do it, since they only have to make arrangements for one player and we would have to make them for 25 guys."

"What do you think all of these guys are going to think about coming here?" T.J. said.

"It will be mixed," Reynolds said. "Some guys will be glad to move, others will be upset, just like happens with any trade. I suspect most will look at it as a good opportunity. After all, they are joining a first-place club."

"Everybody is going to be sad about what happened, and the circumstances," Wendel said, "but I think they will realize pretty quickly this will be good for them. I don't think we will have any problems."

"I hope not," Callan said.

The list of players was approved by the Commissioner's office with no problems. The media reaction was mostly positive. The *Tribune* ran the list the following morning, adding that the three players from the Cubs' system who looked as if they had the best chance of making the club were Billy Slagle, an outfielder, backup catcher Jared Horton, and left-handed relief pitcher Jerry Doyle.

There was some surprise that Orlando and Watson had been left unprotected, and their agents were making noise about trying to block the deals. The Dodgers and Braves were catching a lot of heat from their local media, T.J. read on the Internet, and that was fine with him. He didn't particularly care for either organization.

The trade for Tom Tippett with the Pirates had been well received. Kevin Andrews, in his analysis, gave the Cubs an overall grade of B+ for their moves.

"For a team that had less than a week to make their selections, and with most of the top front-office personnel killed in the crash, the Cubs did an admirable job of re-stocking the team," Andrews wrote. "New manager Mike Callan has more talent to work with than many had expected, and it will be interesting to see how he molds this group into a team, and whether it will be one which can be competitive."

Callan was curious to see how many of the new players would show up for the "unofficial" workout at 2 p.m. Because of the travel questions, he had decided to make the first day optional, knowing all of the Cubs' own personnel would be there, and hopefully some of the others. None of the new players were required to show up before 10 a.m. on Sunday.

He got to the ball park early, as he always did, anticipating today as if it was the first day of spring training or the first day of tryouts back at Jayhawk-Linn. The fact this was the major leagues probably contributed to his excitement, but only marginally. He was excited to be managing a baseball team, regardless of the level of competition.

Callan also was relieved that he had taken care of the last piece of personal business he needed to attend to, finding an in-home nursing service that would be able to stay with his mother during the day and make sure she was OK when she went to bed at night. The service wasn't cheap, but his new salary would easily let him handle the cost. Now he could devote all of his attention to baseball.

All he wanted to do today was let the players find their way around the clubhouse and the field, play catch and loosen up, and meet some of their new teammates and staff. A couple of the coaches were ready to throw batting practice if anybody wanted to hit, but it wasn't mandatory.

If enough of the guys showed up, he planned to have a short talk, but if there weren't enough, he would wait until tomorrow. The message he wanted to convey was to keep the focus off the tragedy. He wanted the players to think about something else. The best way he knew to do that was to schedule a grueling workout, so maybe the players would focus on him, and be mad at him, instead of why they were there.

About noon, the first players started to arrive. The Iowa and Tennessee guys were all there, and they were joined by half a dozen of the new arrivals. More came in during the day, and even though some of them didn't work out, Callan was pleased to see that more than half of the new players had made it to Wrigley. He told all of them to get a good night's sleep and be back at 10 a.m. He hoped the rest of the players would be there then, too.

❧

T.J. wanted Callan to be in charge of the players, so he did not intend to speak to the team, at least not yet. He did want to meet them, so he came down from his office about 9:45 a.m. Sunday, just as many of them were finishing getting dressed and headed down the steps through the dugout and onto the field.

He was not surprised the mood was pretty quiet. He would have been surprised if it had been otherwise. Virtually none of the players knew each other, and they were still reeling from the circumstances that had brought them together.

At precisely 10 a.m., Callan blew a whistle and yelled for the players to assemble in front of the dugout. A couple of the veteran players looked at each other but nobody said a word.

"Good morning. For those of you I haven't met yet, I'm Mike Callan, the new manager. We all understand that we have been brought here because of a terrible accident, but that is not going to be our focus. We are here to play baseball, and win games, and what has happened in the past will not affect how we go about our jobs. We have three days to make our final selections for the major-league club, so I want you to consider this a shortened, intensified version of spring training. We have a very strict timetable we are going to be following, so we will need everybody paying close attention. This is not a time to be lazy. I hope I am making myself clear.

"Everybody take a lap, get good and loose, then line up at home plate."

As the team pulled up near home plate after the jog around the perimeter of the field, Jim Baker, the third baseman picked up from Oakland, saw one of the coaches with a clipboard and another with a stopwatch standing beyond first base. Callan was near the plate, waiting for the last runner to finish his jog around the field.

"OK, get in a single file line, and when I say go, take off for first base like you are trying to beat out an infield hit in the ninth inning of game seven of the World Series," Callan ordered.

More than a couple of the players looked at each other with a questioning twitch, but nobody said a word. All ran their sprints, then walked back to the plate. Next, Callan had them try to leg out a double, then a triple, and eventually an inside-the-park home run. Less than an hour into the practice, most of the players had their hands on their knees, gasping for air.

"What the hell is this shit?" Baker said to no one in particular. "I feel like I'm trying to make the damn American Legion team. I'm a major leaguer. I don't need to put up with this bullshit."

"Who does this guy think he is?" said Lee Thomas, expected to be the second baseman. "I read the stories about him having coached high school the last several years, but I thought they were kidding."

"He isn't going to have any players to manage," huffed Orlando, more out of breath than the rest of his teammates. "They're going to have to plan another memorial service because we're all going to keel over with heart attacks."

Callan seemed oblivious to all of the comments and bickering, standing several feet away from the players, conversing with his coaches. Finally, their little huddle broke up.

"OK, now I want everybody to take their positions in the field. All of the pitchers stay here. We're going to work on cutoffs and run-downs."

"What?" screamed more than one player. "This really is like spring training all over again. You've got to be kidding me."

Callan wasn't kidding. For the next 45 minutes, the new Cubs worked on cutoffs and rundowns, then he finally told everybody to take a 30-minute break before reassembling on the field. Next, they would work on bunts, bunt defense, and pitchers covering first.

Scott McKenzie, the new left fielder, threw up his arms in a sign of protest. The players were all grumbling and shaking their heads as they took a seat next to the dugout and grabbed a bottle of water.

"Is this what the next three months are going to be like?" McKenzie said. "I don't think I can put up with this genius running the show. I haven't been treated like this since high school."

The others agreed, but were too tired to voice their opinion.

The afternoon consisted of more of the same – drills, more drills, and more running. The practice most players were used to – take some swings in the batting cage, shag some fly balls, go home – was a distant memory. At the end of the day, they all dragged themselves into the locker room and plopped down, too tired to take a shower and change clothes.

"I don't know the last time I felt this tired," Baker said. "Does anybody know any of these coaches? We've got to talk to somebody. We can't go on like this. This guy has no clue about how to manage a major-league team. I would do it but I'm too damn tired. All I want to do is sleep."

The next morning, the players were just as upset when Callan addressed them on the field before the start of practice.

"I heard there were some players who were upset with our practice routine yesterday," he said. "I'm sorry to hear that. I want you all to understand something here. I don't give a damn about where you came from or what you did when you were there. You're on the Cubs now, and I'm the manager, and as long as that is the case, we are going to do things my way.

"The coaches and I have three days to watch you practice, and then we have to select the players who are going to go with us to Houston and start the rest of the season. We have more players here than we can take. Some of you will be going back to the minor leagues, some of you might be released. The coaches and I have these three days to watch you and find out what you can and can't do.

"The most important thing to me is your attitude. We are in a situation that none of us asked for, but since we are, my advice to you is to try your damnedest. I don't want prima donnas on my team. I want players who are going to bust their ass on every play and do whatever they have to do to win. I'm sure some of you have already made up your minds that I can't manage, that I don't know what I am doing and that I am in over my head.

"I can assure you nothing could be farther from the truth. I have more confidence in my ability now than I have ever had. I have a lot more confidence in my ability to manage than you do. I can do this job and I can do it well. The coaches and I have three days to evaluate all of you and figure out who is going to be with us for the next three months. I am going to take 25 players with me who can do their jobs and do them well. If that means we get rid of all of you and get 25 more guys in here who will do what I say, then that's exactly what we will do. Have I made myself clear?"

None of the players said a word or moved a muscle.

Callan sent them on the field for another pre-practice lap, then put them through a second grueling workout. All were drooping when it was over.

As Callan sat in the coach's office, nursing a bottle of water, Thompson, who had been the Triple A manager, spoke up.

"Hey, Skip," he said, "don't you think you might be pushing these guys a little too hard? I know what you are trying to do and all, but these guys aren't used to this. They might pull a muscle or something. I don't care about the bitching, I heard that every day in Des Moines. I'm just worried about somebody getting hurt."

"If they are not in shape now, and they don't get into shape, then they have a better chance of getting hurt," Callan said. "These were the two hardest days. Tomorrow we are going to hit and work on some situational drills. It won't be as hard physically, but we've still got to find out what these guys can and can't do."

Callan held true to his word. The morning practice on Tuesday was more of a traditional batting practice, and he had to admit he was impressed with several of the players' performances. It really looked like Reynolds and Wendel had done an amazing job putting this team together.

In the afternoon, Callan had the players go through simulated drills – what they would do with a runner on first and second and one out; trying to hit a fly ball with a runner on third and less than one out; hitting behind the runner; drills that every major leaguer knew but rarely practiced.

Even those players who had been the most vocal in their criticism of Callan the previous couple of days had to admit this had been an effective day of practice.

Afterward, Callan called everybody over.

"OK, the coaches and I are going to meet tonight. Those of you who don't get a phone call in your room, be here at 8:45 a.m. The bus for the airport leaves at 9, and I don't mean 9:01. If you are on this team, you will be here by 8:45 in a coat and tie and slacks. No jeans. We will call those of you who will be going back to Des Moines or some place else and talk to you later tonight.

"I want to say one more thing, fellas. I really appreciate how hard everybody worked the past three days. I know it wasn't easy. I know it was more than you were used to. But we're going to do things differently here. The work we did was important for me and the coaches to evaluate what we have to work with. Some of our decisions about the moves we make during the games, and our strategy during the games, is going to be determined by what we think you guys can do. My job as a manager is to win games. I win games by putting my players in a position where they have the greatest chance of being successful. That is all I am trying to do.

"I have no idea what you guys can do. That's the reason we are doing this. I know you have doubts about what I can do. I know I can manage in the major leagues. Believe me when I tell you that I am not just trying to be a hard ass. You will understand later why we are doing this.

"Everybody get a good night's sleep and we'll see you tomorrow morning."

Chapter 13

T.J. loved watching baseball, but he didn't consider watching pitchers fielding bunts or covering first base to be real baseball. After a couple of hours of watching his new players participating in those and other drills, he retreated to his office.

Nikki had a new stack of phone messages for him. He returned the ones he considered most important, then resumed his task of trying to clear off the desk and figure out what other jobs needed to be completed.

He had given Tim Jenkins the authority to hire radio and television broadcasters for the rest of the season. There had been some thought given to trying to pull John Rooney away from the Cardinals and bring him back to Chicago, where he had worked for the White Sox, but they instead had hired a guy from New York, Ed Randall. Wendel and Reynolds, working together, had filled the trainer positions. Luckily, they were able to talk Yosh Kawano out of retirement to come back and be the equipment manager for the rest of the year. They had shuffled people through the minors to make sure all the positions where somebody had been promoted to the majors were covered.

As T.J. sorted through the papers on his desk, he noticed he had never opened the latest statements from the bank and his dad's financial investment firm that he had found the other night. He opened the bank statement, not really knowing what to expect. His dad had always been pretty tight-lipped about his personal finances.

The statement showed a balance of just over $20,000 in the checking account at Bank One and about $200,000 in savings. "That's it?" T.J. said out loud. He noticed two cash withdrawals in the last month – one for $8,000 and one for $9,000, from two separate branches, two days apart, one in Evanston and one in Northbrook. "That doesn't make sense," he said.

"Maybe he had a new stock he wanted to buy," he said as he opened the investment statement. There were no new transactions listed for the previous month, but T.J. saw the net worth of his dad's portfolio had decreased by 4 percent over the previous month.

"What in the world was he withdrawing that money for?" T.J. thought.

"I wonder if Phil Donnelly knows anything about this?" Donnelly had always been his dad's closest confidant. Tony would have confided in him. As T.J. picked up the phone to call Donnelly, he was reminded of Donnelly's first comments to him after the crash that his dad was working on a plan to sell the Cubs. Was this all connected somehow?

"Hey, Phil, it's T.J." he said when Donnelly came on the line. "I'm just curious about a couple of things and wanted to see if you could shed any light on the situation."

"Sure, T.J., I will if I can. What's up?"

"I was thinking about what you said about my dad working on trying to sell the Cubs, and I got to thinking – was he in any kind of financial trouble?"

"No, I don't think so, at least he didn't indicate to me that there were any problems. Why do you think that?"

"I just opened up his last statement from Bank One and the statement from the investment company. In the last month he had two cash withdrawals of $8,000 and $9,000 at different branches two days apart, one in Evanston and one in Northbrook. Do you have any idea why he would do that?"

"That does seem out of character for Tony, but he had been doing some strange things in the last year," Donnelly said. "There's no record of where the money went?"

"Not that I can tell."

"You know he included me in most of his business affairs, especially the larger deals, but I don't know anything about that."

"What was going on with the ball club?" T.J. asked. "Why was he trying to sell the club?"

"T.J., I don't know that it … "

"No, I want to know," T.J. said. "I want to know what he told you about why he was going to sell the team."

"He didn't really tell me any of the specifics. He was my client, so when he asked me to do something, I did it. All he had me do was call a couple of the large investment banks, putting some feelers out that if they had any clients who might be interested in buying a baseball team it might be coming up for sale. Nothing official, nothing definitive."

"He didn't tell you that he needed to sell the team because he was in financial trouble?"

"No, he never told me that."

"And you have no idea why he would withdraw that money or what he did with it?"

"No, I don't, I'm sorry."

"OK, well, if you think of something please let me know. I just have a feeling this is all connected somehow, but I don't know how, and more importantly, I don't know why."

After hanging up the phone, T.J. said, "I'll bet Donnelly knows more than he is letting on."

Kevin Andrews was about as excited to watch the new Cubs going through their three-day workouts as T.J. had been. One of the reasons he liked covering spring training was that it allowed him time to write features and opinion pieces about the team, merely so he wouldn't have to spend hours sitting there watching pitchers covering first. He couldn't believe fans, including his Uncle Frank, actually spent their vacations coming to Arizona to do just that. Did these people need to get a life or what?

Kevin's mind tended to wander when he was not writing, or interviewing somebody, or actually covering a game that counted. That was why even as he sat in the press box, or in the dugout, or stood behind the batting cage, he found himself thinking more and more about Nikki Williamson.

She had actually said she would go on a date with him. Kevin needed to pick the right setting, but he had to decide what he was looking for in the date. Was he still so upset about the plane crash that he just wanted companionship, and a friendly face to talk to, or was this possibly more serious than that? He didn't want to overwhelm her by taking her to a four-star restaurant, but he didn't want to look cheap and take her to a bar, either. He needed someplace in the middle, maybe a place like Harry Caray's. It was a good atmosphere and they had good food. Yeah, that would be a good choice.

Now he had to figure out when they could go. He had to leave with the team on Wednesday. His boss wanted him to fly on the charter, so he could write a piece on the "mood" of the team as it flew for the first time since the accident. He had to admit he was a little nervous about that; just getting on any plane for the first time probably would give him the willies. But he knew everything on this plane would be double and triple-checked to make sure there were no problems. There probably is no safer time to fly than right after an accident.

The trip was for 10 days, four games in Houston, three in Cincinnati, and three in St. Louis, the longest trip of the year. He didn't want to wait that long to ask Nikki out. Kevin knew she had to work this weekend, so maybe he would give her the choice of either Sunday night or Monday. Either would be fine with him; he could get his stories filed early and be able to enjoy the rest of the evening.

Now all he had to do was work up the nerve to actually ask her.

Kevin left his seat in the press box and walked down the ramp to the street level and into the Cubs' front office. He wandered into the PR office, just so it wouldn't look so obvious, and asked a couple of generic questions about tomorrow's schedule. Then he ducked into

Nikki's office. She looked up from her computer with a big smile. Her lipstick was the same shade of pink as her blouse.

"Hi," she said. "Sorry, but T.J. is out on the field right now. He should be right back ... "

"That's OK. I was coming to talk to you."

Nikki's smile grew even bigger.

"I was just thinking, hoping actually, that we could set up that dinner we talked about a couple of days ago. I was thinking we could go either Sunday night or Monday night, whichever is better for you."

Nikki was still smiling.

"T.J. did ask me to come in for a little while on Saturday and Sunday, mainly to keep up with the voicemails and the emails. He just doesn't want to get too far behind answering them. But I will probably leave here middle of the afternoon on Sunday, so if you wanted to go Sunday night, that would be OK with me."

"Great, Sunday night. I thought we would go to Harry Caray's if that was OK with you. I thought it would be kind of fitting."

"Sounds great to me. Let me write down the directions to my apartment. It's pretty easy. It's in Evanston, not too far from the university." She wrote it on a piece of paper and handed it to Kevin.

"I know exactly where this is. How about I get you about 6:30."

"That will be great."

Kevin smiled and left, feeling better than he had for a week.

※

Kevin managed to keep most of the shop talk out of his conversation over dinner. He asked Nikki about her background, how she had come to work for the Cubs, what her goals were for the future, all the normal "get to know you better" type questions. Finally, just as they ordered a second cup of coffee, he asked about her new boss.

"So, how do you like T.J.?"

"He is different than anybody I've ever known," Nikki said. "I couldn't believe how calm he was right after the accident. I mean his dad died, and I only saw him cry once for just a few minutes. It almost was like he had no feelings, no emotions. Everybody else in the office has been crying for a week. I know he was trying to be strong, and bear the burden for everybody else, but it's almost like he isn't human.

"The last couple of days he has acted a little different. I don't know if he has some more problems or what's going on. I think there were some problems with his dad's money that he wasn't aware of."

Kevin was too good of a reporter not to pick up on Nikki's comments.

"What did he say about it? What kind of problems?"

"I don't know, he didn't say specifically. I think there was some money withdrawn from his accounts and he couldn't figure out why his dad would do that. I know he asked Phil Donnelly about it, but I don't think he knew anything about it, either, or at least wasn't saying. You know, the whole attorney-client privilege thing."

"Yeah, but I don't know how much that applies after the client is dead," Kevin said. "Any more strange phone calls come in?"

"No, they have all been the pretty standard stuff," Nikki said as she slid her cardigan off her shoulders. Kevin leaned over to help her, and noticed a small diamond necklace dangling precariously close to the top of her low-cut blouse.

"T.J. asked me if I had any records of calls his dad might have gotten the previous couple of weeks that were out of character, but I looked back through my log and couldn't find any. Sometimes if I was at lunch or in another office and the calls came in on Tony's private line he would take them directly and I wouldn't know anything about it."

"T.J. asked me a couple of days ago if I had heard any rumblings that his dad was thinking about selling the team," Kevin said. "That really caught me off guard. I had heard nothing like that, and usually that's something that isn't much of a secret."

"He asked me that, too," Nikki said. "It was news to me."

"Do you think all of this is connected somehow? Tony is thinking about selling the team, he apparently is having some kind of money problems and he withdraws a lot of money out of his accounts. That seems like a lot of stuff to just be a coincidence."

"And there's one more thing, since all this started," Nikki said. "He's dead."

Chapter 14

Adam Mathis kept replaying his conversation with Jeff Jackson in his mind as he left the hospital and headed for the site where investigators had reconstructed as much of the plane as possible.

He knew finding at least part of the answer to why the plane had crashed lay in the fuel tanks. He knew that the fuel boost pumps in both tanks had failed, but he didn't know why. Like Jackson, he found it hard to believe both pumps could have failed at the same time without something having caused them to fail.

All of the fuel had burned in the fire, but maybe there was something left that could be tested. He needed to check the lines and the filters, anywhere some fuel could have survived. The tanks themselves had not burned; maybe he could find some clues with a more extensive examination.

Mathis tried to remember if he had ever been involved in any similar cases, but kept coming up empty. Usually if a crash involved fuel contamination, the problem was found when they traced the source of the fuel. They had done that here, and all of the fuel had been clean.

No, he was convinced something had happened to the fuel after it had been loaded into the plane's fuel tanks. He just didn't know what it could be.

Luckily, the investigators had been able to rebuild most of the plane. He arrived in the hangar at the Cheyenne airport and immediately began to take a closer look at the fuel tanks.

"What did you find out from the pilot?" Susan Thomas asked.

"We know the engines failed because the fuel was somehow blocked from getting to the engines," Mathis said. "We have to find out why. We also know the fuel was clean when it was loaded into the tanks. Either something was already in the tanks that contaminated the fuel, or it was contaminated in some other way once it was loaded into the tanks.

"Did we find enough fuel that didn't burn at the site that we could test it?"

"Only in the fuel lines," she said. "Everything that was in the tanks burned."

"Did we test the soil near where the fire occurred? Maybe some seeped into the ground and didn't burn because it got mixed with the dirt. I know we would have to eliminate the dirt as a contaminate, but that's easy enough to separate."

"I don't think we checked that," Thomas said. "We'll get on it right away."

"I also want us to look at the fuel pumps and the filters. Let's take them apart and see if we can find something that might indicate why they stopped working."

Mathis also wanted to get a look at the maintenance records from the charter services company at O'Hare. He knew the fuel had been tested and was clean, but this might just be a simple case of poor maintenance, and maybe they were looking for something they weren't going to find.

Mathis felt he was getting closer to a possible answer, but he still had no idea what it was going to be.

Chapter 15

The headline in the Tribune read "Cubs Set to Resume Season." On one side of the paper was the roster of the new Cubs, listing their former teams, along with the projected starting lineup.

PITCHERS	43	Dave Cochran	Philadelphia
	32	Jerry Doyle	Iowa (Triple A)
	39	Mark Hacker	New York (AL)
	49	Jake Lewis	New York (NL)
	46	Ray Robinson	Baltimore
	38	Pedro Romero	Minnesota
	36	Jason Smith	Anaheim
	29	Tom Tippett	Pittsburgh
	30	Steve Watson	Atlanta
	48	Charlie Wolford	Arizona
CATCHERS	22	Gary Goodwin	Houston
	25	Jared Horton	Iowa (Triple A)
	33	Luis Roman	St. Louis

INFIELDERS	2	Jim Baker	Oakland
	7	Chico Gonzalez	Florida
	17	Randy O'Connor	Cincinnati
	5	Keith Orlando	Los Angeles
	11	Frank Rodriguez	Kansas City
	12	Lee Thomas	Colorado
OUTFIELDERS	4	Richie Edwards	Seattle
	16	Willie Kelly	San Diego
	20	Matt Kennedy	San Francisco
	19	Scott McKenzie	Cleveland
	18	Billy Slagle	Iowa (Triple A)
	9	Junior Peterson	Boston

PROJECTED STARTING		
LINEUP	1. Chico Gonzalez	SS
	2. Billy Slagle	CF
	3. Keith Orlando	1B
	4. Jim Baker	3B
	5. Scott McKenzie	LF
	6. Junior Peterson	RF
	7. Lee Thomas	2B
	8. Luis Roman	C
	9. Steve Watson	P

Mike Callan was as glad as the players were that the process of selecting the team was over. The challenge now was for this group of players to blend into a team, and the sooner the better. The team was beginning play inheriting a 49-41 record and a five-game lead over the Cardinals. There were 72 games to play.

He knew the players, especially some of the older guys, would be the hardest to win over. You would think Frank Rodriguez, for example, would be happy to be out of Kansas City and thrust into the middle of a pennant race. The only thing Royals players can look forward to every September is the leaves changing color. Still, Frank had made more than his share of negative comments the past three days.

Willie Kelly was another player who had surprised Callan. Sure, he was leaving beautiful weather and a beautiful new park in San Diego for the old, cramped locker room at Wrigley, but he was going to get more of a chance to play here than he was getting with the Padres, who looked as if they were heading nowhere again this season.

Callan could see in the attitude of some of the other players that they really didn't want to be there, either. He had decided to give them some space and not try to smother them with attention and demands. He had made the bold statement during the workouts that if none of them worked out the Cubs would get rid of them and get 25 more players, but he knew that was impossible.

One player who he had thought would be getting on the plane this morning for the flight to Houston, however, wasn't there. A couple of hours after the workout ended yesterday, Callan stopped by the front office as he was leaving the ball park. Jack Reynolds was in T.J.'s office and the two waved him in.

"We just got a call from Zach Adams' agent," Reynolds said. The Cubs had drafted Adams, a 31-year-old outfielder, from Texas.

"Yeah, so?" Callan said.

"He wants to be traded. He doesn't want to be here."

"You're shittin' me," Callan said. "We're giving him a chance to get out of Texas and become our starting rightfielder and he wants to be traded. He hasn't played one game and he already wants out? Give me a freakin' break.

"What did you tell him?"

"That we would get back to him. I just was telling T.J. about it. What do you think?"

"I say we release him. Don't give him the benefit of trading him, unless you can send him to Pittsburgh. We don't want players and their agents telling us what to do. We don't need him. I liked what I saw of Peterson the last three days and he's four years younger than Adams. He can do the job for us.

"Keep Horton instead. I was a little uncomfortable going with two catchers, and since he's a left-handed hitter he will give us another bat off the bench. That's fine with me. The one thing we can't have on this team is players bitching and moaning about not wanting to be here. I knew we would have some of that, and I was prepared for it, but I can't believe he wanted out of here before we even played one game."

Reynolds and T.J. looked at each other. "I was telling T.J. that I really think we should ignore the agent and keep him on the team," Reynolds said. "I think we're sending a bad message if we grant his wish. It's going to look like the agent is telling us what to do."

"I kind of agree with Jack," T.J. said. "We're all so new in this we don't want to give the impression that agents or other teams can push us around. Why can't we keep him, at least for the time being, and see if he comes around?"

"Because I don't want anybody here who doesn't want to be here. That kind of attitude rubs off on other guys, and we can't have a cancer like that spreading through the club. Look, you told me I got the final say on which players were going to be on the team. That's my decision. If he doesn't want to be here, I want him out of here. I don't care how you do it, that's up to you guys. But if he is on the plane to Houston tomorrow morning, I won't be. It's pretty simple. It doesn't matter to me. You make that call."

"Mike, don't you think you've over-reacting a little bit?" T.J. said. "I mean, this isn't an All-Star that we are talking about. We just don't want to send the wrong message to the rest of baseball."

"Screw baseball," Callan said. "I'm not worried about anybody except my 25 players. I don't want to have 24 who want to be here and one who doesn't. That doesn't add up to 25. We need 25 who want to be here."

Reynolds and T.J. slumped back in their seats. "I did tell you that you can control the players," T.J. said, "so Jack, you call the agent back and tell him we are going to release Adams."

Reynolds stood up, but Mike stuck out his hand and pushed Jack back down into his chair. "If you don't mind, would it be OK if I called him? I would like to give him a piece of my mind."

Reynolds and T.J. looked at each other. Both said at the same time, "Sure, go ahead. You can use the phone out in Nikki's office if you want." Reynolds left and went back to his office.

When the agent, Scott Sarob, answered, Mike was very calm. He also was very sarcastic.

"I understand that your client, Zach Adams, has expressed his desire to be traded. He said he does not want to be a Cub. I want to know if you are advising him to make that request?"

Sarob said, "That is what he wants, yes. He's my client and he's not happy, so I am acting upon his wishes."

"Well, let me tell you something," Callan said. "You're giving your client some bad advice, because I will tell you exactly what is going to happen. Your client is no longer employed by the Chicago Cubs. We just released him. That means he no longer has a job in Major League Baseball. We only want players on our team who want to be here. If your client doesn't want to be here, fine, we don't want him. We don't need him. And we are going to tell every other team in baseball why he is no longer on the Cubs. Good luck trying to get him another job." Callan hung up without saying goodbye.

Callan walked back in T.J.'s office with a smile on his face. "That was fun," he said. "I haven't gotten to tell an agent off before. I kind of liked it."

T.J. grinned back. "Well, mister manager, tell me what you think about your team."

"I like it, I really do. It is going to take some time for the team to come together, but hopefully not very long. I know we have guys who still are feeling emotional about being here, and the reason they are here. They will think even more about it when we hit the field wearing the black arm bands and have the moment of silence. It is going to be tough for all of us, you included, and nobody is going to deny that.

"I plan to have a little talk when we get on the plane tomorrow. Hopefully, it will set a positive tone. I know I didn't make any friends working them as hard as I did the past three days, but honestly I did it for a reason. We can't have them feeling sorry for themselves because they are here, or feeling sorry for the players and others who died. If that is the case we might as well forfeit the rest of the schedule and start planning for next year. I'm not going to do that, and I'm not going to let them do that."

"Good," T.J. said. "Just do me a favor and don't try to overdo it. I know you are right, and you know you are right, but they may not know you are right. You need the players working together, but not all ganging up against you. Most of these guys have already been playing in the majors, so they know the basic routine. Let's let them get their feet on the ground and see what happens."

Callan had thought about that conversation as he planned his remarks to the players. When everyone had boarded the plane, he asked the pilot to give him 10 minutes before they pulled away from the gate. Callan got the flight attendant to give him the intercom microphone and asked for all of the players to take a seat in the last 15 rows of the plane.

"I know I have probably talked to you more in the last few days than some of your former managers talked to you in a year," Callan began. "That's OK. You will learn as we go through the rest of this season I really am not that big on making speeches. I am big on communication, and the best communication is the kind that goes both ways. I am going to talk to you, and I want you to talk to me.

"I know a lot of you are nervous getting on the plane this morning. That's understandable. You know if you are going to be in the major leagues you have to fly to the road games. None of us can change the fact that a plane carrying a Major League Baseball team crashed last week. It happened. It was a terrible accident. But a lot of other teams were on a plane that night, and the rest of them arrived safely. We're all sorry it happened, but there is nothing we can do to bring any of those people back. We can't think about the accident every time we get on a plane for the rest of the year.

"We also can't think about the accident every time we step on the field. We are going to be swarmed by the media, especially the first couple of games. We were able to control it the last few days in Chicago, but we can't prevent the media from covering these games. They are going to be all over every one of you. You each will have to deal with it in your own way. I just ask that you be respectful and considerate, the same request we are going to make of the media. If you don't feel like talking, or don't want to answer a question, just say it politely. Baseball, and baseball fans, are going to be watching how we handle this. Our reaction is going to set the tone for how all baseball reacts.

"I know there are a lot of you who still don't know how you feel about being here. You know you always liked coming to Chicago, and your wives liked it, too, when they got to spend the weekend hitting all the stores on Michigan Avenue. Now that you are on the Cubs, however, it might be different. I know you are all coming from different organizations. You will have to develop new relationships. You're going to have to find out who you want as your bridge partner. I know that is tough. Nobody is saying this is going to be easy, for any of us.

"I know some of you were bitching about me behind my back, and complaining about the situation. I can assure you the last four days I was testing you. You passed, that's why you are here. Now we can focus on one thing, playing baseball or, more accurately, playing winning baseball. No one ever said life was going to be fair. We are all here and a week ago none of us could have predicted that. Certainly not me. But now that we are here, the question is what are we going to do about it? Are we going to complain about our situation, throw up our hands and say 'woe is me' and not try? I'm not going to lie to you fellas. What we are about to do is not going to be easy. It is going to be the hardest thing any of us have ever done in our lives and the hardest thing we may ever do in our lives.

"There was one player I thought would be with us this morning, but I found out last night that he didn't want to be here. I couldn't believe he called his agent and asked him to get him traded … before we had played one game. He's not here. We're better off without him.

"I'm only asking you one thing … give it a chance. Don't get caught up on all of the negatives of the situation. Approach it as the opportunity of a lifetime. Approach it as a baseball player, as a baseball team, as an organization. Look at the possibility of what we can do. We can make history. You have to decide if you are up to the task. I can't do it for you.

"If you have the same attitude as the player who called his agent and wanted out of here yesterday, show me some balls and walk off this plane right now. I will have more respect for you than if you stay and maintain that attitude for the rest of the season."

Nobody moved.

"Fellas, you may think this is easy for me. It is beyond my comprehension that I am in this position. Since I am here, I can promise you that I am going to do everything in my power to help you. This is not about me. It's about the opportunity that you guys are being given, starting tomorrow. You guys are going to be the ones who decide if this works or not. I have no ego to fulfill, believe me when I say that. We're all starting from the same place. You are no longer a Dodger or a Cardinal or a Brave. You are a member of the Chicago Cubs. You have to think that way. This is a new beginning for all of us. I have my own fears. I don't know what's going to happen any better than any of you. But how we handle this situation, how we approach the challenge, is going to say more about us and our character than how many home runs you hit or how many strikeouts you get. I don't want anybody who is going to duck that responsibility. You are going to have to be perfect.

"I'm not talking about making an error in the field or missing the cutoff man. Those things are going to happen. I am talking about being perfect in our approach to the game and being perfect in our effort. When our game is over, I want each of us to think 'What did I learn today that can make me better prepared for tomorrow?' That's all I ask. I don't want to read or hear one negative comment about your situation or the Cubs' situation. If I do, you will have to answer to me.

"Congratulations on being a member of the Chicago Cubs. I am proud to be your manager. Good luck to you."

Callan walked back to the front of the plane, told the captain the team was ready to go, and sat down in the first row next to T.J.

Luckily, it was a perfectly clear day and the flight to Houston was routine. As the plane began its final approach to Hobby Airport, Yoshi stopped by Callan's seat after going to the restroom.

"I just want you to know," he said, "that in my 60 years in

baseball, I have never heard a plane flight of silence. It has got to be some kind of record, Skip. You must have really gotten to them."

Callan was right about the media frenzy. There were camera crews waiting at the airport when the plane landed. There were more reporters at the team hotel, and even more when the team bus arrived at Minute Maid Park for their workout. He had agreed to hold a news conference when the team arrived at the stadium in hopes of diverting some of the attention away from the players.

The questions, like the answers, were predictable. Callan understood the media's role and knew the reporters were just doing their job, but he would be glad when a couple of weeks had passed and he and the team could fall into a more normal routine.

He was pleased with the spirit of the team during the workout, perhaps because the boot camp was over and they were able to practice as they were accustomed. Callan almost laughed a couple of times when Slagle tried to go back on fly balls to center and fell while running up Tal's Hill, the stupid tribute that Astros' President Tal Smith had created to Crosley Field in Cincinnati.

"If that happens in the game tomorrow night, I won't be laughing," Callan told Slagle after the workout.

The first game was scheduled to be nationally televised by ESPN, a fact that didn't surprise Callan but made him a little more nervous than usual. As he arrived at the ball park six hours before game time Thursday afternoon, his mind drifted back to his first game as a player with the Cubs.

It was in St. Louis, at old Busch Stadium. The Cardinals and Cubs always were intense rivals, so the stadium was packed. His first at-bat came as a pinch-hitter in the ninth inning of a game the Cubs were losing, 3-2. Bruce Sutter was on the mound for the Cardinals.

In all his years playing the game, in high school, college, and the minors, Callan had never seen a pitch like Sutter's split-finger fastball. When the pitch was working, the ball just dropped as it reached the plate. It looked as if somebody had rolled it on a table and it had reached the edge and fallen straight down.

The first pitch, Callan stood and watched as the umpire called strike one. "There's no way in hell I can hit that thing," he thought to himself. "If everybody in the major leagues pitches like that I might as well go back to Iowa right now."

By the time he had stepped out of the batter's box to collect his thoughts and stepped back in, Sutter had thrown a second strike.

"I cannot take three straight pitches and strike out in my first at-bat in the major leagues," Callan said to himself.

So, he swung when Sutter brought his third pitch to the plate, and realized immediately he had been had. Sutter had thrown a changeup instead of a split-finger, and Callan had completed his swing before the ball came close to the plate. He lowered his head and walked back to the dugout, trying not to look as embarrassed as he felt.

Callan knew the emotions his players would be going through today as they got ready for the game. The advantage most of them had over him was this was not their first game in the big leagues. Slagle was the only player who fell into that category, at least among those in the starting lineup.

Callan made a special point of talking to Slagle during batting practice.

"How you feelin'?"

"Hey, Skip, excited, nervous ... I don't know how you would de-scribe it. I have dreamed of this day for so long. I just hope I don't screw up. I haven't figured out that goofy hill out there, you know."

"Don't worry about it, you'll be fine. Are your folks here?"

"Yeah, they flew in today. My dad wouldn't miss this for the world. Thankfully, it's not a Saturday or a Sunday or he would have had a tough decision to make. He's a minister, you know, and I have never known him to miss giving a sermon just because he wanted to be at a game. They are staying for tonight and tomorrow then going home Saturday."

"Well, I know they are awfully proud of you. You've worked hard and earned this chance. Just relax and have fun out there. Remember this is a team game. You can do your part and let your teammates take care of their end of things. This is the same game you have been playing all of your life. The pitcher's mound is still 60 feet 6 inches away from home plate, the bases are still 90 feet apart, we still get three outs in an inning. It's all the same. Play the same way and give the same effort as you did in Iowa and things will work out fine."

"Thanks, Skip, I appreciate that. Thanks for giving me a chance."

Callan made it through the required pre-game radio and television interviews, and another press conference with the print media, and at last was where he wanted to be, in the comfort of the dugout. After a moment of silence was observed, it was finally game time.

As he thought back about it later that night, Callan realized he was probably like his players, expecting too much too quickly. The Cubs lost, 4-2, and he knew he had probably screwed up by leaving Watson in the game an inning too long.

Watson had pitched great, holding the Astros to two runs through seven innings, and the game was tied, 2-2. Watson was scheduled to bat fourth in the top of the ninth, so instead of bringing in a reliever to pitch the eighth, Callan tried to get Watson through the inning, knowing he would pinch-hit if his spot came up in the ninth.

Instead, Watson got knocked around and gave up the two go-ahead runs and Callan had to pull him with two outs and two more runners on base. The reliever got out of the jam, but the Cubs didn't score in the ninth and lost.

They lost the second night, 3-1. Callan was second-guessed by the media after the game. He let Keith Orlando bat in the ninth against Roy Oswalt with runners on second and third and two outs, even though he knew Orlando was 1-for-16 lifetime against Oswalt. He flew out to center to end the game.

After the reporters had left his office, Callan saw Orlando walk by on his way back to his locker from the shower. "Hey, O," he said. "Come in here a minute."

Orlando came in the office. "Yeah, Mike?"

"I just want you to know that I knew you were 1-for-16 lifetime against Oswalt. I don't care about that. I knew you could get the job done. You just missed that pitch. You'll get him next time. That's all I wanted to say. Go get 'em tomorrow."

The Cubs lost their third game in a row the following night, before finally winning the finale of the series on Sunday, 6-2. The win did a lot to lift everyone's spirits as they headed to Cincinnati.

Over the course of the four days, even though the team lost three of the four games and three games off its division lead, the players had come to realize Mike Callan was different from other managers they had played for.

Orlando was one of the first guys to bring it up, sitting in the training room after the game Saturday night.

"Maybe we were wrong about this guy," he said. "The way he is treating us is different than any other manager I have ever played for."

"You know what it is," Thomas said, "he's still treating us like we're in high school, only in a good sense, the way he is patting us on the back and encouraging us. We've lost three straight and I haven't heard him say a negative thing all week. He told us that was how he was going to act, and how he wanted us to act, and so far he looks like a man of his word."

Orlando spoke up again.

"I have never had a manager say something positive to me after I made an out to end the game before. Usually they are so pissed off they turn their back when you walk by. They only want to talk to you when you are the star of the game or hitting .360. This guy almost acts like he doesn't care what you did in the game, and we know that isn't the case. Maybe this isn't going to be so bad after all."

The series in Cincinnati went about the same as the first four games in Houston. The Cubs lost two of three, and found themselves moving on to St. Louis clinging to a half-game division lead over the Cardinals.

Despite the poor won-lost results, Callan was encouraged. He was starting to see a bond forming among the players that he knew was necessary for the team to be successful. There were still a lot of games to play.

Chapter 16

The Cubs lost two of three in St. Louis, and nobody was surprised the "new" Cubs had gotten off to a slow start. Now the long 10-game trip was over and the team was coming home, set to play its first game at Wrigley, and the atmosphere was a curious mix of somber and electric.

Mike Callan knew one thing had to change for his team to be successful. He could already tell, in just over a week, that his players were pressing. They were trying too hard to get the big hit, or make the key defensive play, and as a result they were too stiff in their movements, too disciplined. Nobody was having any fun, and the biggest reason it seemed to Mike, was they were afraid to act like they were having fun.

The players, he could tell, were worried that if they laughed or even smiled, somebody would think they were being disrespectful to the players who had died. He knew these guys had feelings and compassion for the victims of the accident, but they were playing as if they had no feelings and no compassion for themselves. They were remorseful, and that was the way they were playing, too.

When an umpire made a bad call in Cincinnati a few days ago, only the first base coach reacted. None of the players involved – the runner, the batter, or the hitter standing on deck – said a word in protest. It made the coach feel silly because he was the only one protesting, until Mike could get out on the field. Players were striking out with the game on the line and walking back to the dugout and calmly placing their bat back in the rack. Before, the same player would have heaved the bat toward the dugout, and maybe tossed all of the other bats out of the rack as well.

Callan wanted to see that emotion, that passion. He knew these guys had it in them and were afraid to let it out.

Today wasn't the day for that speech, however. Because this was the first game at Wrigley since the accident, there was going to be another pre-game memorial and a moment of silence. Mike was going to let the players have one more game, and then he was going to hit them with a speech tomorrow.

Luckily, the Cubs played well. Dave Cochran stopped the Mets on six hits through eight innings, Orlando hit a home run, Tom Tippett closed it out in the ninth, and the Cubs won, 5-2. Everybody seemed to be in a better mood after the game. Maybe now this team could start doing what Callan knew it was capable of doing.

҉

One player who had gotten off to a decent, but not blazing, start was Billy Slagle. As Kevin Andrews was trying to learn as much as he could about all of the new Cubs' players, a task normally reserved for the off-season or spring training, he made an interesting discovery – Slagle was the great-great grandson of Jimmy Slagle, who had played for the Cubs in the 1900s. He was the centerfielder on the Cubs from 1902 through 1908. He was the starter through 1907 and was a reserve on the Cubs' last World Championship team in 1908.

"I wonder how much he knows about him," Kevin thought, as he waited for Slagle to come out of the shower. Kevin had introduced himself to Slagle earlier in the week and they had chatted a couple of times, but Slagle had made no mention of his relative. "Maybe he doesn't even know it," Kevin wondered.

Slagle was using the towel to dry his hair as he approached his locker.

"Hey, hope you weren't waiting for me," he said as Kevin stuck out his hand.

"No problem, I don't have to write today," Kevin said. "I just wondered if you had a few minutes. I was doing a little research and found out something I thought was pretty interesting."

"What's that?" Slagle answered.

"About your great-great grandfather."

"Ol' Shorty?" Slagle said. "You figured out he played for the Cubs, didn't you? I've got to give you some credit. I thought somebody might figure that out sooner or later, but you did it a lot quicker than I would have guessed. I didn't think anybody would have had that much time on their hands to dig that out."

"Well, it helps to have been a big Cubs' fan all of my life. For some reason I knew your name registered in my brain and when I went back and looked through the record book I found it.

"Do you know much about him?"

"Yeah, my dad has told me some stuff and then I went back and read some of the old books and newspaper stories in the library. I'm kind of a history buff. That was my major at college. We had one class where we had to research our family history for a paper, so I found out a lot about him then. He was a pretty interesting guy."

"You called him Shorty," Kevin said, "Was that his nickname?"

"That was one of them. The reason was pretty obvious. He was only 5'7" and weighed 144 pounds. He also was called The Human Mosquito because of his height, and he was called Rabbit because of his speed. He had 40 stolen bases in 1902, which was his best year for the Cubs, and he stole six bases in the 1907 World Series against Detroit. That was the record for one World Series until Lou Brock broke it in 1967.

"He was at the end of his career when he came to the Cubs. He made it to the majors in 1899 when he was 26 years old and also played for Philadelphia and Boston before he came here. He moved around a lot, but as far as I know wasn't ever traded for two uniforms and a bat like Joe Tinker was.

"If Jimmy wasn't my great-great grandfather I probably wouldn't know so much about him. There were a lot more famous people on those Cubs' teams, you know. That was where the Tinker to Evers to Chance poem came from."

"I knew that," Kevin said, "but none of them have a relative on this Cubs' team."

Slagle just smiled, and continued.

"He grew up in Pennsylvania and moved back there after his career was over. He died in 1956, a year after my dad was born, but my dad heard a lot about him from his father. One of the things my dad told me was that when Jimmy played he was said to be one of the 'thriftiest' players in the majors."

"Guys had to be thrifty back then, didn't they?" Kevin said. "I don't think they made much money playing baseball."

"No, but they didn't have to spend much, either," Slagle said.

"One of the funny things about those teams, and I know this because I looked it up, was that everybody remembers Joe Tinker, Johnny Evers, and Frank Chance because of the poem, but none of them was ever that great a player. I mean, I know they went to four World Series in the early 1900s, but they never led the league in double plays or hit for much power. Only Chance came close to being a .300 hitter. The other thing is, I think they hated each other off the field.

"Chance was the player manager, and my dad said Jimmy told stories about how hard he was on the other players; he just rode them like crazy. He supposedly fought "Gentleman" Jim Corbett one time. Supposedly the three of them fought in the clubhouse all the time. After a while, I don't think Tinker and Evers even talked to each other, and they were the second baseman and shortstop.

"Harry Steinfeldt, who is the answer to the trivia question because he was the third baseman, once went after Tinker in the clubhouse with a pair of trainer's shears. Evers one time tried to cut Tinker with his spikes."

"How do you know all of this stuff?" Kevin asked.

"I told you, I kind of got into it when I realized I was related to one of the players on those teams. It was kind of hard to ignore when you found out everything that was going on with those guys, and of course none of it was ever reported in the newspaper. It was a different era back then. It was like when they said Babe Ruth was suffering from stomach pains when he really was hung over or worse. The reporters couldn't write that stuff back then."

"No, you are right about that," Kevin said. "They were too afraid they would lose their job if they didn't write all positive things."

"All three of those guys were voted into the Hall of Fame together by the old-timers committee in 1946, but I don't think that ever would have happened without that poem," Slagle said. "You know the true history of it, don't you?"

Kevin shook his head no, even though he knew it was probably the second most famous poem in baseball history, trailing only Casey at the Bat.

"It was written by a man named Franklin P. Adams in 1910," Slagle said. "He was a reporter for the *New York Evening Mail* at the time. The foreman of the composing room said he had eight lines to fill, and that was what he wrote. He didn't think it would ever be famous, and really didn't consider it very good."

"You're kidding," Kevin said.

"No, see, what you write in the *Tribune* tomorrow might become famous some day."

"I seriously doubt that," Kevin said, "but I do think you have given me a pretty good story."

Kevin's story was headlined "History Buff Making History for Cubs" and was the featured story on the sports page. He was pleased with how it turned out, and knew he had uncovered an angle that nobody else had touched. He knew there had to be more good stories with all of these news guys on the team; he just had to find out what they were.

Mike Callan enjoyed reading the story, and he wondered if he could somehow use this knowledge, plus Slagle's enthusiasm, to light the fire he knew needed to be lit under this team. Maybe giving them a little more background on Cubs' history would allow them to focus on the big picture of what it would mean to bring a pennant and World Championship to Chicago instead of thinking about the short-term history, the plane crash. At least it was worth a shot.

A couple of players, Junior Peterson and Matt Kennedy, were looking at the story while sitting on the clubhouse couch when Slagle walked through the door.

"Hey, Billy," Peterson yelled out, "how did you know all this shit? The Cubs really have not won a World Series since 1908?"

Slagle was nodding his head as he walked toward the couch.

"God, that's over 100 years ago," Kennedy said.

"I'm glad to see that you could still pass third-grade math," Slagle said. "You know they only got into the Series that year on a fluke."

When both players stared at him like they had no idea what he was talking about, Slagle continued.

"Haven't you heard of Fred Merkle and Merkle's boner?" Peterson and Kennedy still sat stone-faced.

"OK, you guys do need a history lesson. The Cubs were playing in New York against the Giants …"

Kennedy interrupted. "What do you mean New York? The Giants play in San Francisco."

Slagle just shook his head. "You guys are unbelievable. Just listen, OK. The Giants didn't move to San Francisco until 1958. They were the New York Giants and they played at the Polo Grounds. It was a key game in September with both teams fighting for the pennant.

"It was 1-1 in the ninth and the Giants had runners on first and third with two outs. Merkle was on first. He was only 19 and was starting his first game of the year because the Giants' regular first baseman was sick. He still should have known better. The next New York hitter singled to center, and the winning run looked like it scored. Merkle saw the runner cross the plate, and he thought the game was over. Instead of tagging second, he stopped and went straight to the clubhouse.

"Johnny Evers was the Cubs' second baseman, and legend had it that he slept with the rule book under his pillow. He knew it inside and out. He knew that they could force Merkle out at second and the run would not count. He got the ball and tagged the base and the umpire called Merkle out.

"By this time, the fans had all stormed the field so there was no way for the game to resume. They called it a tie, and when the Cubs and Giants were tied at the end of the regular season, they had to have a playoff game. It must have been an incredible scene. They said two hours before the game the stadium was packed, close to 40,000 people. People were scaling a 15-foot fence at the back of the bleachers to try to get high enough to see.

"People were climbing over the elevated railroad tracks station outside the stadium. One man fell off the tower and was killed. I read *The New York Times* and it said 'his vacant place was quickly filled.' The estimate was close to 100,000 people were either inside the stadium or outside, trying to find a spot to watch the game.

"The Cubs won, 4-2, and get this, the game lasted only 1 hour, 40 minutes, and they won their third pennant in a row. They didn't have any other playoffs back then, so they went straight to the World Series, where they beat Detroit in five games to win the Series for the second consecutive year."

As Slagle was telling the story, more players had gathered around the couch. Callan walked through the clubhouse on his way to the training room and saw the players standing in a group. He came up behind them, close enough to hear Slagle and immediately he knew what he was talking about. He didn't stay, but turned and walked away with a smile on his face. He had gotten what he wanted without even having to ask.

Kevin Andrews had also walked in on the group. He respected the players' privacy as much as possible in the clubhouse so he waited on the other side of the locker room until the players broke up.

Slagle saw him and came toward him.

"Thanks for writing a great story," he said. "I told you you were going to be famous."

"I still doubt that, but you were the one who made the story. I just reported what you told me. What was going on over there?" pointing to where the players had been gathered around him.

"Oh, I was just giving the guys a little more history. There actually were some players who didn't know what Merkle's Boner was, and one guy was surprised to learn the Giants had not always been in San Francisco. I don't know if they crawled out from under a rock or what."

"That doesn't surprise me one bit," Kevin said. "That was why I enjoyed our conversation yesterday so much. It was one of the most intelligent interviews I have ever had."

"There's one thing I meant to ask you," Slagle said. "You knew all the stuff I was saying yesterday – how did you became such a baseball and history buff? Did all that come from your dad like it did mine?"

"No, it didn't," said Kevin, a sad look forming on his face.

"I never knew my dad. He was a career Army officer and was one of the last soldiers out of Vietnam in 1973. He came home and worked in the states for a couple of years and I was born. He really missed the international job, though, so he was sent back to Japan for another tour of duty. Since I was so young, my mom thought it would be better if we stayed in Chicago until I was a little older. We were going to move to Japan when I was three, but about six months before we were going to leave, my dad was killed in a car accident."

"Oh, God, I'm sorry to bring that up," Slagle said. "I had no idea."

"That's OK. I have learned to live with it. I always wondered what it would have been like to have a dad, especially when it came to playing and talking about baseball. My grandpa helped out as much as he could before he died, and my Uncle Frank. My mom tried. She became a fan and made sure I played Little League and all that stuff, but I kind of grew into it on my own.

"I envied all of my friends who had close relationships with their dads, and some of those dads took me under their wing a little bit, too. Luckily, I've got a great relationship with my mom and we had a lot of fun together. I had cousins and uncles and a lot of male figures in my life. Don't feel sorry for me.

"The only times I have really missed my dad were when I got drafted by the Cubs, because he wasn't there to share that moment with me, and when I got this job covering the team for the *Trib*. He was a huge Cubs' fan, and I know he would have been busting his buttons. He would have been bragging to everybody in town."

One of the clubhouse attendants had been waiting patiently for Kevin to finish his conversation with Slagle. "Excuse me. Mr. Callan wants to close the clubhouse for a meeting."

"Got it," Kevin said, turning back to Slagle. "Thanks again for your help with the story. We can talk more later." He left the room and headed to the dugout. "Wonder what Mike wants to talk to them about?" making a mental note to ask him as soon as the players hit the field for batting practice.

"Gather round guys, this won't take long. I've just got a couple of things I want to say before we head to the field," Callan said.

"I just want to say that I appreciate how hard everybody has been working. I know we haven't won as many games as we would like, but we still have a lot of the season to go and I am encouraged by what I've seen.

"I also know this has been a really tough couple of weeks for everybody emotionally. We knew it was going to be rough, but nobody knew exactly what it would be like. It has been hard, and we are never going to change the fact that a plane crashed and a lot of great men, players and others, died. That is never going to go away.

"But I want you guys to know that I am officially giving you permission to forget about it. When you go on the field today I want you to play baseball the way you have played it all your life. I want you to smile. I want you to laugh. I want you to have fun. If somebody says you're not supposed to be acting that way, I will handle it. You tell them to talk to me.

"You have one job for the rest of the season and that's to relax and play the game the way I know you know how to play it. People, including some of our opponents, might be feeling sorry for us now, but I guarantee you if we get up by four or five runs they are not going to let us win because they feel sorry for us. They are going to try to crush us. The 'feeling sorry' stuff by ourselves and against us ends today. What happened, happened. We can't change it. But we can change the way we act, and the way we play, and that's what we are going to do. If you feel like throwing your helmet, throw your helmet. If an umpire's bad call makes you feel like throwing your bat, throw your bat. It's OK with me.

"Everybody got it? OK, let's go."

Chapter 17

The 10 days out of the office had been good for T.J. It had let him watch baseball, and think only about baseball. He had never wanted to work in an office, and now that he knew it was going to be his future, he already had decided to travel with the team as much as possible. He didn't really need an excuse, since he was the owner, but he was glad to have that opportunity.

Of course, working in an office in Wrigley Field as the owner of the Cubs was not exactly like working on the 50th floor of the downtown highrise. He could get up and wander out to the ivy-covered walls whenever he wanted, or take a seat behind home plate and soak up the sun and the still-ageless beauty of the ball park. He couldn't believe some people thought the Cubs would abandon Wrigley some day, just like people thought the Red Sox might build a new Fenway. That would never happen with him in charge.

As soon as T.J. walked into his office and flipped on the light, he saw a package, about the size of a shoe box, sitting on his desk. The return address was the United Medical Center in Cheyenne, Wyoming. T.J. immediately recognized the name. That was the hospital where his father had died.

"Nikki, what's this?" he yelled into the outer office.

"I don't know, it came one day last week in the mail. Sorry I forgot to mention it to you."

T.J. began to open the package and immediately realized what it was – his dad's personal belongings. In the box were his wallet, his watch, his key ring, and his wedding ring. T.J. had forgotten he had told the emergency room supervisor to send all of those items to him.

"I'll have to look at this later," he said, leaving everything in the box and moving it to the corner of his desk.

Nikki filled him in on what had transpired while he was out of the office, even though they had talked everyday on the phone and T.J. had kept up with his emails. He was still receiving mostly condolence calls from people who were having a difficult time coming to grips with the tragedy.

"It is so sad talking to them on the phone," Nikki said. "All they do is cry and it is hard to understand what they are saying. There was one lady who said she was more upset by this than when her husband died of cancer last year. She said 'I'm so glad he was already dead, because this would have killed him.' She honestly said that.

"Then we get the usual assortment of nut cases calling, people saying they can't believe we didn't cancel the rest of the season out of respect for the players and others who died. They vow never to watch another Cubs' game because of our 'insensitivity.'"

"Well, no matter what we do about anything, we're never going to please everybody," T.J. said. "I honestly believe there are some very loyal Cubs' fans out there who don't want us to win, because it would change our image as the 'lovable losers.' Nobody would be able to talk about 'the curse' anymore."

"Do you really believe the Cubs are cursed?" Nikki said.

"No, of course not, not anymore than the Red Sox were. You can't tell me selling Babe Ruth to the Yankees was the one single reason they went from 1918 to 2004 without winning a World Series. I know there are people who believe that, and there are people who believe the Cubs are cursed, but it's not true and we're going to prove it.

"So, how are you doing with all this? I know none of us asked to be dumped in the middle of this mess, and you've done a great job. You seemed a little more upbeat on the phone last week. Is everything OK with you?"

Nikki had to try to not break into a shy grin. "Yeah, I've been a little happier lately, but we'll just have to see what happens. I've started dating somebody, and it seems to be going along pretty well."

"Well, as long as it isn't one of my players or a reporter, I'm happy for you. I think anyone in either of those categories would be bad news."

Nikki tried not to react but suddenly a million thoughts were racing through her head. She had never thought going out with Kevin might compromise her job. She knew enough not to date a player, and she never had met any she would want to date anyway, but she had no second thoughts about dating Kevin. How could that possibly create a conflict of interest? At least T.J. didn't know about their relationship, and she was going to have to keep it that way, at least until she had a better idea where that relationship was going.

"Good to have you back in the office," she said. "I've got to get back to work."

T.J. had a steady stream of visitors the rest of the morning. Wendel needed to talk to him about a couple of issues in the minor leagues, Reynolds needed to give him an update on his activities, and the marketing and public relations folks had some reports to go over with him. He also had to approve the schedule for the pre-game moment of silence before today's game.

"I really hope this is the last moment of silence we have to have," T.J. said to Tim Jenkins. "We have got to move on."

"I know how you feel," Jenkins said. "But we've got to do it today because this is the first home game since the accident."

"I'm not questioning or disputing that," T.J. said, "I'm merely saying that I will be glad when all this is over."

The ceremony went off as well as could be expected, and as T.J. hoped, the game quickly became the focus. He was able to sit in his private box suspended from the upper deck, where the old press box used to be, and watch the Cubs beat the Mets. He was in a better mood when he got back to the office, intending just to make certain there were no calls or emails he had to answer and then head for home.

He saw the box sitting on his desk. He had forgotten about it during the game.

T.J. sat down in the chair, his dad's chair, and picked up the wallet. He really felt kind of creepy, like he was invading his dad's privacy. It wasn't as bad as the time he searched through the dresser in his parents' bedroom looking for where they kept their extra cash one night when he was in high school, but it wasn't very far behind. If his parents ever knew he had taken $40 that night, they never let on.

T.J. pulled out the cash first, actually surprised and pleased that somebody at the hospital had not helped themselves to it. There wasn't much, $133, but nobody would have known if that money had disappeared. Tony Vitello never carried much cash, preferring to charge almost every expense so he would have a record of it when it came time to work on his income taxes each year.

T.J. set aside the cash, the driver's license, the American Express card, the Visa debit card, the Cubs identification card, the ID card issued to all employees by Major League Baseball, and the car insurance card. He put all of that in a pile to give to his mother, along with his dad's watch, car keys, and wedding ring.

Tony had a few pictures in his wallet, including, surprisingly, T.J.'s high school graduation picture that had been taken 19 years ago. "Must have gotten stuck," T.J. said.

Also in the wallet were a couple of receipts, and a yellow folded Post-It note. As T.J. opened it, he saw a handwritten number, which he quickly determined was a Chicago phone number: 312-606-7963. Under the number was a name, "Eddie." There were no other identifying comments. T.J. played the number over in his head a couple of times, trying to see if it jogged his memory. He came up empty. He also couldn't think off-hand of anybody he knew named Eddie.

He set the note aside and examined the receipts. They were from Bank One, for withdrawals from his dad's checking account. One was dated July 1, the day before the plane crash. His dad had withdrawn $7,000 from the branch at 1048 Lake St. in Oak Park.

"God, this is weird," T.J. said as he quickly looked at the second bank receipt – another cash withdrawal, this time for $8,000, from the branch bank at 504 Broadway in Gary, Indiana. It was dated June 30.

"What the hell … what was going on with Dad and this account?" In the pile of papers on the corner of his desk, T.J. found the bank statement he had received in the mail a week ago. He took the pages out of the envelope and went immediately to the list of transactions. The information was the same as he remembered it – a cash withdrawal of $8,000 from the branch bank in Evanston on June 10, and a cash withdrawal of $9,000 two days later from the branch in Northbrook.

T.J. did the quick calculation – in three weeks' time, his dad had made four cash withdrawals from four different branch banks totaling $32,000. And he had no idea what he had done with the money.

He thought about calling his mom to see if she could offer any suggestions, but remembered she had been in Europe all that time. T.J. knew his dad wasn't withdrawing money to send to her. His parents really had a marriage of convenience more than of love. His mom had her own money – she would not need Tony to be taking money out of his account for her.

T.J. thought of possibilities that could explain the withdrawals. Was somebody blackmailing Tony? That seemed like a stretch. Who, and for what reason? Phil Donnelly definitely would have known if that was the case because they certainly would have called in the cops. What about drugs? T.J. could not imagine his dad on drugs. He liked good cigars and an expensive bottle of Scotch, but he could not imagine him with any other abuse problem. Not at his age. No, it couldn't be drugs.

What did that leave? Gambling? His dad always liked going to the horse track and the dog track when he was in Florida, but those were all little bets, $10 and $20. He had never known his dad to bet more than $50 on a race. He didn't think that was the answer, either. There was nothing else. T.J.'s brain was more muddled than the day before he took the bar exam.

As T.J. was trying to think of other possibilities, his eyes focused on the Post-It note and the mysterious phone number, apparently belonging to Eddie, whoever Eddie was. Acting on impulse, he punched in the number. All he got was a tone, like he had called an answering machine or a fax machine – or a beeper. He hung up without putting in his number.

T.J. scratched the back of his head. Something was going on, and he had a feeling it was bad. He also had no idea what it was – or how long it had been going on.

"I wonder if the old bank statements are here somewhere?" he said out loud.

The third drawer T.J. opened revealed the answer. The statements for the first five months of the year were in a stack, tied together with a rubber band. T.J. was as nervous as a burglar as he removed the rubber band and started to open the envelopes.

By the time he had finished looking at all five statements, all of the color had gone out of his face and he had broken out in a cold sweat. T.J. took out a legal pad and a calculator and transferred all of the relevant information from the bank statements. When he was done, having included the statement in last week's mail and the two receipts from his dad's wallet, he just stared at the numbers on the paper.

Between January 10 and July 1, Tony Vitello had made 15 cash withdrawals, each from a different branch of Bank One, in Chicago and various suburbs, totaling $125,000. There had been eight withdrawals of $9,000 each, four withdrawals for $8,000 each, and three withdrawals of $7,000 each. All were just small enough to stay under the $10,000 mark, which would have had to have been reported by the bank to the federal government.

What the hell was his dad doing?

T.J. thought again about Tony making inferences to Donnelly that he was thinking about selling the Cubs. He could not separate the two – the only possible reason for him to want to sell the Cubs was if he needed the money. And if he needed money, why had he withdrawn $125,000 in cash in six months, in such small amounts? Why hadn't he gone to his normal bank officer, Tom Wilkinson, and just transferred it from one of his other investment accounts and withdrawn the money? This was not like his dad at all.

"I wonder if Tom knows anything about this?" T.J. said out loud.

On the same sheet of paper, T.J. wrote down the names of everyone he could think of who were close enough to his dad to maybe have some idea what was going on – Phil Donnelly; his wife; his secretary; Tom Wilkinson. That was it. That was all of the people that T.J. knew who he thought his dad would trust with such private information.

"Tomorrow I am going to see what I can find out," he said. He also wrote another name on the bottom of his list – Eddie ?

The first call T.J. made the following morning was to Donnelly. "Phil, it's T.J. I wonder if you have some time today that I could come see you. I've got a couple of things I want to ask you about."

"Sure, T.J., about 11 o'clock OK for you?"

"That would be great. See you then."

T.J. then called Nikki into his office.

"I want to ask you a couple of questions. Don't worry, you are not in any trouble. We have kind of had this conversation before, but yesterday I found out some more information about my dad's finances that has me concerned. Did he say anything to you over the past six months or so that made you think he was having money troubles?"

"No, not that I can think of," she said. "You know he usually didn't confide in me about things like that. Have you talked to Phil Donnelly?"

"We are meeting at 11 o'clock. How about how dad was acting? Did you notice any changes in his behavior or activities over the past six months? Did he act nervous, or confused, any change in his schedule, anything like that?"

Nikki was quiet for a moment, thinking. "Not that I can think of at the moment."

"How about his phone calls and emails, letters, that kind of thing? I know you said there were a couple of strange phone calls recently. Do you remember when those calls started, and if it was always the same person calling or if there was any pattern to the calls? Did the caller say anything about my dad paying him money for something?"

"There were just a few calls, like I told you, and they were always vague … just questions like when Tony would be back in the office, did I know where he was, there was kind of an implication like he was supposed to have met someone and had not shown up, or was late. At least that was the way I took it."

"Did you mention those calls to Tony?"

"Yes, but he didn't seem too concerned about it. It seemed like he must have known who was calling and why, because he never quizzed me about it. He just said it was OK, he would take care of it … Do you think your dad was in some kind of trouble?"

"I don't know, it's just weird and not like him at all. He made a lot of large cash withdrawals out of his bank the past six months and I have no idea why or what he did with the money. Did you see him walking around with more cash than usual, or did he say anything about needing to go to the bank, or anything that would give us any kind of a lead at all?"

"I'm sorry I can't be of any help, T.J. I really didn't notice anything out of the ordinary."

"Did he say anything at all about wanting to sell the club, or give any indications that he was thinking about it?"

"Not to me. I don't know if he said anything to anybody else, but I doubt it. You know your dad. He wasn't very big on communication."

T.J. nodded his head, thanked Nikki for her help, and let her go back to her office. At 10:30, he picked up the bank statements, placed them in his briefcase and left to go see what he could find out from Donnelly.

❦

Kevin had called Nikki just a few minutes after she had talked to T.J. and asked if she was busy for lunch. Today's game was not until 7:05 p.m., so he was free until about 2:30 or 3. He could come to the park a little early, they could meet for lunch, and then he could go to work. She agreed to meet him at 1 p.m. at Murphy's.

As she walked down the sidewalk, she kept thinking about T.J. and the problems with Tony. She wanted to say something to Kevin about it, but kept coming back to T.J.'s comment yesterday that he hoped she was not dating a reporter. Was this a conflict of interest? The problem was she wanted to help T.J., and she trusted Kevin. She also knew with his reporting background, he might have some ideas about how to find out what had been going on with Tony.

T.J. wants the answer to what was going on, and if Kevin can help us get an answer, I think that's a good thing, she finally decided.

The two had just sat down and started looking at the menu when Nikki found herself pouring out her guts to Kevin about everything T.J. had said that morning.

"Whoa, whoa, calm down a little bit," Kevin said. "I can tell you're excited, but you're going to have to go a little slower if I'm going to be able to play along."

Nikki caught her breath and proceeded to tell Kevin everything she knew, including the bank withdrawals, and that T.J. had no idea what Tony had been doing with the money.

"There's no indication of what happened to the money?" Kevin said. "Wow, that's strange."

"Yeah, the other thing T.J. told me yesterday, by the way, was that he hoped I was not dating a reporter."

"He actually said that?"

"Yeah, I think he was joking, because I know he doesn't have a clue that we are going out, but I'm really kind of nervous about this whole deal. If his dad was in some kind of trouble, whoever was on the other side might come looking for T.J. He could be in trouble, too. And, if he finds out that I told all of this to you, I could be in trouble.

"I really think you can help, though. I've read your stories in the newspaper. I know reporters can get answers to questions that normal people can't get. Just make me a promise, OK. If you find out something bad, please tell me first so I can figure out how to tell T.J. I don't want him reading something in the newspaper first and then figuring out I was the one who told you about it. Can you do that for me?"

"Of course I can. I don't know what I can find out, but I certainly will look into it. It sounds like Tony was really in some kind of trouble. I don't know of any other possible explanation."

Kevin replayed that conversation in his mind as he went to work, first stopping by the Cubs' clubhouse, where a bunch of players were gathered around Billy Slagle. When Slagle noticed him, he walked over and extended his hand and thanked him for the story in the newspaper.

He talked with Slagle for several minutes, diverting his attention from Tony Vitello and his money problems. Only when he left the clubhouse after Mike Callan had called a team meeting did his thoughts return to that topic.

"It's like he was taking that money to pay somebody off," he thought to himself. "But who, and for what?"

He thought about Tony, and how he didn't get the chance to do the interview with him and write the big profile about his years as the owner of the Cubs. He thought about his preparations for the interview, including his meeting with the retired reporter, Roy Singer.

Suddenly, his thoughts shifted to Melissa Vitello, Tony's first wife, and her mysterious death. Was somebody who had been involved in her death suddenly trying to blackmail Tony, or threatening to take that case to the cops? He remembered Singer's comments as he left their meeting – "I think the SOB killed his first wife."

Was that the possible connection to the missing money?

Kevin had to admit it made sense. Melissa's death was suspicious, and there is no statute of limitations on murder. If somebody had been involved in helping Tony push Melissa off that boat, maybe they suddenly wanted some more hush money to keep from going to the cops. It would explain why Tony had been so secretive about it – he certainly couldn't tell his second wife. The only person he possibly could have told was Donnelly, because that conversation would have been protected from the cops by the attorney-client relationship.

"The question is, how do I bring that up to T.J."

Donnelly welcomed T.J. into his office, the first time he could recall the two having met there. He offered T.J. coffee or soda, but T.J. declined.

"I know I have asked you before if you knew anything that was going on with my dad's finances, and you said you didn't," T.J. said. "I want to show you the latest information I have found out."

He proceeded to pull out the bank statements, and showed them to Donnelly one by one.

"Does anything stand out to you?" T.J. said when he was finished.

"Yeah, your dad was withdrawing a lot of money, from a lot of strange places. What does it mean?"

"That's what I'm here to ask you. You still don't remember my dad telling you anything that was going on. I don't want to hear about the attorney-client privilege bullshit, either. If you knew what was going on, I want to know about it now."

"How much do all these withdrawals add up to?" Donnelly asked.

"$125,000, in cash, between January and the first of July."

"And you don't have any idea where the money is, or what your dad did with it?"

"No. And so far nobody else I have talked to has any idea, either."

"Have you talked to your mother?"

"Not yet, but I am going to. I know she was in Europe for the last couple of months, but she was here when the withdrawals started. Her and dad didn't talk much about money or business – hell they didn't talk much about anything – so I doubt if she will be any help. But I'm going to try."

"Did Dad ever say anything about anybody trying to blackmail him, or anybody threatening him? That is the only reason I can think of why he was withdrawing the money this way, trying to hide it from the federal government, and not talking to anybody about it."

"Your dad and I talked about a lot of stuff, T.J., but he honestly never said one word to me about the withdrawals."

"What about when he talked to you to see if you could drop some hints that the club might be for sale in the near future? Did he say anything at all about needing money, or being short of money?"

"No, all he said, and don't take this personal because I'm just the messenger, was that he was tired of owning the club and didn't know if you could handle the responsibility. He wanted to see how much money the club could bring if he put it on the market, what that would mean in terms of the tax liability, etc. I told you we didn't get very far down that road. I talked to a couple of the larger investment banks and told them if they had any clients who were interested to let me know, but nobody has called."

"My dad actually said he didn't know if I could handle owning the club?"

"I told you not to be mad at me, those were his words, not mine. I think you're doing a great job, by the way, especially considering the circumstances."

T.J. was boiling. "If he wasn't already dead, I'd kill him! I can't believe he would rather sell the club than turn it over to me! Why had he decided he didn't want to own it any more? You said he had tired of it."

"Just all of the money. He just couldn't see having to pay every player more than a million dollars, it seemed, even the backups and the middle relievers. He thought the money was all out of whack. I think he was just physically tired and didn't want to put up with all the shit anymore. It just all was happening at the same time."

"And at the same time he was withdrawing all of this money, for what reason nobody has any idea."

"I wish he had told me about it, T.J. I would tell you if I knew. I am sure he had more on his mind and more things going on, but he never shared any of it with me. I hope he shared it with somebody, otherwise we may never know what he was doing."

"The only other people I can think of that there is even a slim chance he might have talked to was mom, and Tom Wilkinson at the bank. He has been dad's banker for years. I wonder if there is any way they could trace any of the money?"

"I doubt it. That was one of the reasons your dad probably kept moving from branch to branch and keeping the withdrawals under $10,000. If he was paying somebody in cash under the table, they are not all of a sudden going to bring all that cash to the bank and deposit it in their account. Even if they did, you would have to check every bank in the Chicago area and that would be next to impossible."

"I only hope Tom noticed the transactions and asked Dad about it during their regular meetings. Unless he can tell me anything, I really think we're screwed.

"If you do think of anything, or find anything in your notes that might be any kind of help, please let me know."

"You know I will, T.J. And if you find anything out please let me know. I agree with one thing you said – I don't like the way it looks."

Kevin did not see T.J. until the following day, when he almost bumped into him in the press dining room before the game.

"Hey, T.J., you got a minute?"

"Sure. That table over there OK?" said T.J., pointing to the table in the corner.

"Great."

After the two had sat down at the table, T.J. said, "I really liked your story on Slagle a couple of days ago, all the history stuff. I never knew some of that about Tinker to Evers to Chance. Good stuff."

"Don't give me the credit, it was all Slagle's info. I just cut the vein and let the blood flow all over the paper."

"Well, whoever deserves the credit, it was a good job. What's on your mind?"

"You may not know this, but before your dad died I was preparing to write a big profile about his years of owning the Cubs. We were supposed to do the interview in Los Angeles. I had done all of my prep work, including some background interviews and research."

T.J. knew there had to be a reason Kevin was bringing all this up now, so he motioned for him to continue.

"In the course of that preparation, I came across the story of the death of your dad's first wife, Melissa, in a boating accident on Lake Michigan, back in 1970."

"I don't know too much about that," T.J. said. "I know it was ruled an accident. If you need more on that I don't …"

"No, it was just this. I know your dad had made some comments about wanting to sell the club, and you asked me earlier if I knew why he would be doing that. The only real explanation I can give you is that he must have been having some money problems. And the only reason I can think of for that would be if his first wife's death was not an accident."

T.J. sat in stunned silence.

"You think my dad killed his first wife?" he finally said.

"I didn't say that," Kevin said. "All I said was if you are looking to explain a sudden change in behavior or finances, it sometimes helps to look in the past. You know a lot more about your dad's life than I do. The only really negative thing I could think of was Melissa's death. I don't know if the two are connected or not.

"But I could see how, if somebody else had been involved and it was not an accident, then suddenly he might have come forward and wanted some money to stay quiet or he would go to the cops. There is no statute of limitations on murder, you know."

T.J. didn't say a word.

"As long as you're going to hate me, there's one other piece of information I found out that you ought to know. I think your dad was having an affair with your mom before Melissa died."

"Who told you that?"

Kevin didn't reveal his source, but said the information had come up during the course of his research on Tony for the profile.

"I really don't want to get you upset, and I'm not making any accusations whatsoever," Kevin said. "I'm telling you this as a friend, looking for the answers to what was going on with your dad. None of this is going in the newspaper, OK? If we find out some facts, not just rumors or guesses, then that's another matter. So far it's just opinions and speculation."

T.J. didn't know what to say.

"I guess I appreciate the information," he finally said. "I know you have more of a background in trying to look into somebody's past life than I do, so I shouldn't be surprised you would have found out something. I'm still not sure what to do with it, but I guess one person I need to talk to is my mom."

He called his mom the next morning.

"Hey, Mom, you doing OK?" he said.

"Sure, T.J. How are you doing?"

"I'm OK. Hey, the hospital in Wyoming sent me a box with all of dad's personal belongings in it. You know, his wallet and watch and wedding ring, stuff like that. If you're going to be home later today I thought I would run by and drop it off."

"That would be great. How about if you come around 1? I will have Maria make us something for lunch."

T.J. agreed, and when he hung up, he picked up the phone again and called Tom Wilkinson at Bank One.

"Hi, T.J. I'm sorry I haven't had a chance to personally call and express my condolences," Wilkinson said. "Everything has been kind of a blur around here."

"That's OK, Tom, no apology is necessary. We've been kind of busy here, too. I did want to ask you something, though, about my dad's accounts if you have a minute."

"I do. What's the question?"

"Did you and he have any conversations about any of his financial matters the last six months or so?"

"Not that I can recall off the top of my head ... why?"

"Because I just found some transactions that were kind of strange, and when I went back through the statements for the last six months I found a lot of withdrawals that really bother me, because I have no idea what he was doing with the money."

"What kind of withdrawals?"

T.J. proceeded to fill Wilkinson in with what he knew. If Wilkinson had been involved in any way, he wasn't letting on.

"I honestly know nothing about it, and I guess that was an oversight on my part," Wilkinson said. "Your dad wanted me to be on the lookout for good deals for him, and let him know if something was going on with his accounts, but these slipped by me, I guess, because he knew enough to keep all of the transactions to less than $10,000. That really is strange."

"There's no way to trace where the money went?"

"Not if it was withdrawn in cash. Your dad had enough money in that account that it would not be suspicious."

"Even if he was not in his normal branch bank or the main office, and even if he was withdrawing it in cash?"

"No. All the teller would look at is to make sure he had the proper ID, and to make sure the amount he was requesting was in his account. He would just write a check to the bank to cash, and he would get the money."

"The teller wouldn't be able to tell that he had also withdrawn a sizable amount just a few days before that?"

"No, the history of an account doesn't come up for a simple teller transaction unless the teller requests it. If the money is in the account, there would be no reason for the teller to check that."

"I see."

"I wish I could give you a better answer. If he had written somebody a check, or made a transfer from his account to another account, even if it was in another bank, we would have a record of that. But since the withdrawal was in cash, I'm afraid there is no way to trace it.

"Have you put a block on the account now?"

"I think my mom did that as soon as she got back from Europe, but I will check. I'm meeting her for lunch."

T.J. thanked Wilkinson for his time, and tried to think of any other possible explanations for what was going on, other than Kevin's suggestion that Tony was being blackmailed by someone to keep quiet about Melissa's death.

"I just can't see it, but it's the only thing that makes sense," he said to himself.

❦

T.J. waited until after Maria served the chicken salad sandwiches before bringing up Tony's finances to his mom. The dining room table seemed a lot smaller than it had in the past. He could count on one hand the number of "family" dinners he had shared at this table. Far more common were the nights growing up when he had sat here and ate by himself, or maybe with Maria, who felt sorry for him that his parents were never home. This was the first time he had been at the house since the reception after Tony's funeral. He had talked with his Mom a couple of times on the phone, but she had always been so independent, especially in the last several years, and had so many friends that he knew she would get on with her life in due time.

"Mom, a couple of things have come up since I've taken over the club that have me a little concerned and I wanted to see if you knew anything about it."

"T.J., you know your dad hardly mentioned the Cubs to me because I really don't know anything about baseball, so I doubt …"

"It's not about the Cubs. It's about dad's accounts at the bank. Did you know he had been withdrawing a lot of money out of his checking account over the past six months?"

"I'm afraid your dad and I didn't communicate too much about money, either, dear. What was he doing with the money?"

"I don't know, that's why I'm concerned. Are you sure he never said anything to you about having problems, or somebody trying to blackmail him or anything? There has to be an explanation, but I have no idea what it is.

"Did he ever tell you he was thinking about selling the team?"

"No, he hadn't said anything to me at all. Why would he do that? He loved owning the team."

"I think he was having money problems. The only explanation I can possibly offer stems from Melissa's death."

"Melissa? What's her death got to do with this? That was an accident, a long time ago."

"I know that was what the police report said, but that doesn't mean that's what really happened. I'm not saying this is what happened but it might explain what was going on with dad the last few months. He must have needed money or he wouldn't have talked about selling the team.

"I know he was withdrawing a lot of money out of his account. If somebody was trying to blackmail him in order to keep quiet and not go to the cops, that could explain what was going on."

"I don't know anything about that. He never said a word to me about it."

"There's one other thing I have to ask you about: did you and dad start going out before Melissa died?"

"What? Who told you that?"

"It doesn't matter. I know you were working at dad's law firm and what I was told was that people believed you two were having an affair before Melissa died. You were married not too long after her death."

Katherine Vitello had a blank look on her face.

"I can't believe people said that," she said.

"Was it true?"

"Your dad was going to divorce her. He already had talked to a lawyer. He was going to file for a divorce the next week. He didn't kill her. It was an accident."

As T.J. drove back to the office, he didn't know whether to believe his mom or not.

※

Katherine Vitello stood at the front door of her mansion and waved as T.J. pulled out of the driveway. As she turned and closed the door, she was deep in thought.

Numerous times in the early years of their marriage she had tried to draw Tony into a conversation about what had happened on the boat that night. He had always refused to discuss it, saying only that he guessed Melissa had wandered to the deck of the boat and somehow fell overboard, an accident.

"I wonder if that is what really happened," Katherine said to herself.

※

T.J. drove away convinced that his dad had never told his mother the truth about what had happened on the boat, and that now the truth would likely never be known.

"Sometimes in life the best secrets are the ones that should never be told," he said out loud.

Chapter 18

Over the next week, Mike Callan saw some of his players do what he asked, playing more loose and relaxed and rising to their level of ability. The Cubs had fallen out of first place, trailing St. Louis by as many as three games, but he still wasn't worried. They had six games remaining with the Cardinals in September, plus the whole month of August to go.

One player Callan noticed who still seemed to have a bad attitude was Scott McKenzie, the left fielder picked up from Cleveland. He was not hustling, wasn't working hard in batting practice, and didn't seem to have any motivation, even when he came up to bat in a key situation. That had not been his reputation with the Indians, and those reports that he was such an energetic player were among the reasons Callan wanted him on his team.

After McKenzie struck out three times and grounded into a double play as the Cubs lost to the Phillies, Callan was in his office thinking about what he should do when he saw McKenzie walk by on his way back to his locker from the shower.

"Hey, Mac, after you get dressed, stop by back here for a moment would you? I've got something I want to talk to you about."

McKenzie didn't say anything, but nodded OK.

About 10 minutes later, he reappeared at Callan's door. "Yeah, Skip, what's up?"

Callan motioned for McKenzie to come in the office and have a seat on the couch. He stood up, walked behind him, and closed the door.

Callan saw McKenzie's worried look. "Don't worry, you're not going anywhere. I just want to talk to you. I want to find out what is going on with you. You had a great reputation in Cleveland for being an aggressive, hustling player. We haven't seen that side of you here. Is there something going on that I should know about? You had earned a spot in the All-Star game based on the way you played the first half of the season. You're not playing that way now. What's going on?"

"I don't know, Skip. I've just been kind of down ever since I came over here. You know I was really comfortable in Cleveland. I understand the situation here, and I appreciate the faith you have shown in me. But, well, I really wanted to play in the All-Star game."

"But the game got cancelled after the plane crash. They didn't play it. Why has that upset you so much?"

"Well, you know I gave up quite a bit of money when I signed that three-year deal with the Indians a couple of years ago. One of the ways they promised to make the difference up to me was with some bonus clauses. I was supposed to get $50,000 for making the All-Star team."

"So, you made the team. The clause didn't say anything about having to play in the game, did it?"

"No, but the Indians contended that since the game was cancelled, none of the All-Star selections were valid and they refused to pay the bonus. My agent and the Players' Association have filed a grievance, but I don't think they will have the hearing for a while. I had really counted on getting that money, and it's left me kind of short ever since then. I know I shouldn't let my financial problems affect the way I play, but I just can't seem to get it out of my mind."

"I can't believe the Indians wouldn't pay the bonus. Those cheapskates. I'll tell you what. Let me see if I can do anything. No promises, but let me look into it. In the meantime, you try to find your old self again. We really need you, OK?"

"I would appreciate anything you could do, Skip," McKenzie said. "I know it's not the Cubs' fault or any of your concern, but that is what has been bugging me. I just can't seem to snap out of it."

After McKenzie left, Callan finished getting dressed and went up to the front office, looking to see if T.J. was still there.

Callan found T.J. in his office. " T.J., you got a minute?"

"Sure, Mike. Tough game tonight. I thought we had a chance there in the ninth before McKenzie grounded into the double play. God, he had a bad game. What's going on with him, anyway?"

"That's what I wanted to talk to you about. He and I just had a short visit. I asked him the same question and you know what I found out is bugging him? The Indians shafted him of his All-Star bonus."

"You're kidding me? Why?"

"Because they said since the game was cancelled, none of the players made the All-Star team so they were not obligated to pay the bonus. He said he really needed the money. I'm thinking they saw a way out and hoped if they left him unprotected we would take him, and they wouldn't have to deal with not paying the bonus because he wouldn't be on their team."

"Those cheapskates," T.J. said. "Can't he do anything about it?"

"He said his agent and the Players' Association had filed a grievance, but you and I both know how long those things take. Apparently he is hurting for money for some reason and was really counting on getting that bonus. It isn't my call, and I don't know what our situation is, but if there is anyway we can include that bonus in his next check I know he would really appreciate it."

"I think it's probably OK, but I have to check with the financial guys to make sure," T.J. said. "I don't know any of those rules. It's not a money question. I know we can afford it, but let me see if it's legal for us to pay it."

"Thanks, T.J., I really appreciate it. I think it will make a difference in his play, and I know that will make a difference in our team's play."

Callan started to get up and leave, then sat back down.

"I've got one other idea I've been kicking around, about another player I am interested in. Let me sleep on it one more night and get all of my facts together and then I want to talk to you about it. Can we talk tomorrow afternoon about that?"

"Sure, and maybe I will have an answer about the bonus for McKenzie. Have a good night."

During Mike's first year managing at Triple A, in 1994, one of his star players was an up-and-coming slugger, Jason McGair, a 23-year-old outfielder who led all of Triple A with 33 homers.

The Cubs expected that he was going to be a star, but they were desperate for pitching. When the Texas Rangers offered two established pitchers and another good prospect for McGair after that season, the Cubs made the trade.

McGair became a star with the Rangers, and quickly advanced beyond their price range. After three years in Texas he was traded again, to the Yankees, where he became a perennial All-Star and one of the leading home run sluggers in the game. From 1998 through 2003, McGair averaged 53 home runs a year.

Callan was not surprised at McGair's success, and he also had to admit he was not surprised when it was revealed during the 2004 season that McGair had been taking steroids all of those years.

The news created a real firestorm in the media, especially because McGair was the big star of the Yankees. McGair was never the most communicative player in the world with the media, anyway, and the steroid reports made him even more of a recluse.

At the end of the 2005 season, McGair took advantage of an option clause to get out of his contract – and signed a six-year, $90 million contract to play with the Orix Buffaloes in Japan. At least over there, he had an excuse for not answering the questions, because he didn't speak Japanese.

That move had not worked out as well as either McGair or the Japanese team had hoped. The Orix Blue Wave had merged with the Kintetsu Buffaloes in 2005 to form the Orix Buffaloes, and thought signing McGair would be a public relations coup. Even though McGair challenged the Japanese home run record with 48 homers, the power display did not translate into victories.

The homers also did not translate into success at the box office. McGair had an attendance clause in his deal, giving him a percentage of every ticket sold that surpassed the team's attendance from 2005, and the attendance actually declined. He was still playing there, and still hitting more than 40 homers a season, but everybody involved thought the situation was bad and getting worse.

Callan had read all of this on the Internet, and how the Buffaloes were looking for a way to get out of the remainder of McGair's contract.

He knew McGair from their season together in Triple A, and he knew even if all of the steroid talk was true, that he was a good person and a good baseball player. He would fit in well with the Cubs. He made up his mind to see if he could talk T.J. and the front office into buying his contract and bringing him back from Japan.

When he got to Wrigley the next day, Callan went directly to T.J.'s office.

"Hey, Mike, I was hoping you would stop by before you went downstairs. I've got something for you."

T.J. handed Mike an envelope. When Mike gave him a quizzical look, T.J. explained, "It's the check for Scott McKenzie. The accounting folks said it would be simpler if they just wrote a separate check instead of adding it to his paycheck. We're also going to petition the Commissioner's office to make the Indians pay us back."

"Great, T.J. Thanks for being so prompt. I know he will really appreciate it and we will see the results.

"You remember last night I said I had one other idea I wanted to talk to you about – do you remember Jason McGair?"

"Remember him? Hell! Who could forget him, and all of that talk about steroids? He was on the front page of the paper every day a few years ago. Why are you bringing his name up?"

"Well, you may or may not remember he came up in the Cubs'

system. I had him on my Iowa team in 1994, the first year I was managing Triple A."

"You know I had kind of forgotten about that with everything that has happened to him since. That trade didn't work out too good, did it? What did everybody say, it was our generation's version of Brock for Broglio?"

"Yeah, well, we can't do anything to change that. But he was a good guy and a great player. I can't tell you whether he did or didn't take steroids, but I liked having him on my club. I wanted to know if you thought we could see if we could bring him back to the majors."

"He's in Japan now, right?"

"Yeah, he had an option to get out of his contract with the Yankees after the 2005 season and he signed a six-year deal in Japan. I have been reading up on him and his situation on the Internet, and it sounds like his team, the Orix Buffaloes, would love to move him and get out of his contract."

"What is his contract status in the majors, though? Is he still the property of the Yankees?" T.J. asked.

"I don't know for sure, but I think when he got out of his contact after 2005 he became a free agent. I would suspect that's still the case. I think if he can get out of his contract in Japan, he should be free to sign with any team."

"How old is he now?"

"He just turned 39, but he always kept himself in great shape. We don't have to sign him to a long-term deal, maybe just the rest of this year and next, and maybe give him an option year."

"Don't you think there would be a big media backlash because of all the steroid talk? Did he hit a lot of homers in Japan? Do you think he is still on the juice?"

"There would probably be some media dissent, but I think we could deal with it," Mike said. "I really believe even if he is guilty he deserves a second chance. We've kind of become a home for second chance guys, you know. I really think he would help us more than any negative publicity would hurt us. He still hit 48 homers over there last year, just seven off Tuffy Rhodes' record for a foreign player."

"Well, let me get Jack Reynolds to look into the contract situation and see what we can find out. The team's leaving right after the game tonight, right?"

"Yeah, a week in Atlanta and Florida, just where you want to go the first of August. Aren't you coming with us?"

"I'm going to try to join up with you somewhere during the trip. I've got a couple of things going on that need my attention here first. Get this game tonight and get them playing good. I'll let you know as soon as I find out anything about McGair."

Callan was actually whistling as he walked into the clubhouse and found McKenzie sitting on a chair in front of his locker. "Hey, Scott, I was hoping to catch you. Here, I've got something for you."

Callan reached in the back pocket of his slacks and pulled out the envelope. "T.J. just gave me this to give to you."

McKenzie opened the envelope, saw what it was, and immediately jumped up and wrapped his arms around Callan in a giant bear hug. "You are the best! I don't know what you told him to get this done, but you have no idea what it means to me. Oh, man, I can't believe it. I thought I was never going to see this money, or only after all of the hearings. I can't believe it. You are a man of your word. This changes everything. Thank you, thank you, thank you."

"Just remember your end of the deal," Callan said. "You said if we could get this taken care of, we would see the 'old' Scott McKenzie out on the field, and that's what I'm counting on. You don't have to hit six-run homers or steal five bases a game, but you know what I expect out of you, and I hope I start seeing it soon."

"You will, you definitely will. Just wait and see."

The re-energized McKenzie did spark the Cubs, who went on their longest winning streak since the "new team" was formed, five games, to move back into a first-place tie with the Cardinals. His aggressive play on both offense and defense seemed to rub off on his teammates, and as usual, winning games seemed to put everybody in a better mood.

Callan also thought his team benefited from playing on the road, away from Wrigley Field. There were just too many reminders around the park of the players who had been killed, and the fans seemed to be having a hard time connecting with the new players and forgetting about the past. On the road, the players were by themselves, and Callan was pleased to see that many of them seemed to be developing good relationships and the camaraderie that he had hoped would come was starting to build.

He smiled as he thought of the good-natured abuse that the new catcher, Luis Roman, was receiving from his teammates. Roman was a freak about germs and his health. There was no other way to put it. He was always washing his hands. He took about 16 different pills a day, convinced that each would prevent him from getting one fatal disease or another.

Maybe because he was also a Latin player, he was gullible and an easy victim for practical jokes. He had just fallen for the old rubber snake gag, and Callan was still laughing as he walked back into his office at the stadium in Miami. He was trying to find the early news on TV when T.J. walked into the office.

"Hey, I'm almost scared to come around because you've got these guys playing so well," T.J. said. "I needed to get out of the office for a few days, however, plus I've got some news for you about Jason McGair."

"What did you find out?"

"Jack Reynolds talked to the Commissioner's office and found out that he is a free agent as far as MLB is concerned. I won't lie to you, though, they didn't seem too pleased that we were inquiring about him. They asked a lot of questions, and Jack had to tell them the truth. It seemed they were secretly pleased when he fled to Japan because he took a lot of the steroid talk with him."

"But he is not under any sanctions or anything that means we can't sign him, if he can get out of the Japan deal, right?" Mike said.

"Correct. There would be nothing MLB can do to stop us if we decide to sign him."

"What else did Jack find out. Did he talk to the Japan people?"

"That's what took a couple of days. We had to reach McGair's agent, then find the right guy in Japan, and go through all the red tape over there, and then start the negotiations."

"So what's the deal?"

"He is owed about $30 million for the remainder of his contract, and the team will let him out of the deal for $10 million. Apparently they are having money problems; you were right about that. Of course, then we would have to sign him. The agent was trying to play hard ball, but I think we've finally got a tentative deal. We would give him a base salary of $2 million for the rest of this year, with some incentive bonuses, and a $10 million deal for next year. We also have an option for 2012 at $10 million, or a buyout of $3 million."

"You're the guy with all the money, T.J., can we afford it?"

"Yeah, the terms are fine, on one condition."

"What's that?"

"That McGair can still play and hit home runs. I know we are a little short on power, and that doesn't surprise me. All of the teams protected their home run threats. We have done really well trying to win games with pitching, speed, and defense, but especially at Wrigley, I know we need guys who can hit home runs."

"Don't we have a connection to a scout or somebody over there to let us know what they think? I can't promise you he can still play. I haven't talked to him in 13 years or seen him, except on television, and that was five years ago. All I can tell you is that he was a good guy when I had him in '94 and we had a good relationship. I think he would be thrilled to have another chance, but I can't promise you he would come over and hit 20 homers the rest of the year."

"We have had a couple of people watching him this week, and we have asked around to other people in Japan with connections over there. The consensus is that he can still play. If you still want him, we'll start the procedures to get all of the financial deals done. It will still take another week or so, and then he has to get here, so it probably will be about 10 days before we see him. I want to keep it out of the media until he is almost here."

"That sounds great to me."

"There's one more thing I wanted to mention to you," T.J. said. "Tim Jenkins and I have been talking. As we get closer to the end of the season and stay in the race, the media attention is going to start to build. There are going to be increased demands on our time with requests for interviews, appearances, etc. We need to start thinking about how we are going to handle it, and how we want to control the access to the players."

"We're not going to do anything different than we have been doing," Callan said. "These guys are grown men, they are in the major leagues, they can handle themselves. They don't need the manager or somebody from the front office telling them how to conduct themselves in interviews. The teams that try to control that are run by a manager who wants all of the attention for himself. I don't care about any of that and you know it. I want the players to be interviewed. I hope everybody in the media wants to talk to Billy Slagle and finds out what a great person he is.

"We don't have to 'control' the media, T.J. We want to welcome the media. We want the attention. I want my players to be the stars. These guys can handle it."

After T.J. left the office, Mike thought about their last exchange. T.J. seemed a little disappointed at what Mike had said. Why was that? Was T.J. wanting to be the star, the focus of all of the media attention? When he thought about it, Mike realized T.J.'s name was showing up a little more frequently in the newspaper, not only in the sports page but in the social highlights. He was seemingly on everybody's party invitation list, and looked and acted as if he were enjoying all of the attention.

He didn't seem to have a girlfriend and the more Mike thought about it, the more it seemed T.J. always was hanging around with a different guy. He was starting to dress up a lot more lately, too, wearing designer suits and Italian loafers. Mike knew he was spending $2,000 and more on the Italian suits, which he could not understand. Tony Vitello had always had a reputation for wearing the fanciest suits he could buy at the most exclusive stores in town, and it seemed as if T.J. was starting to inherit that habit.

Mike hoped T.J. realized that what was going to determine the Cubs' success or failure were the players, not the manager, and certainly not the owner, no matter how fancy a suit he was wearing.

Chapter 19

Adam Mathis knew what he was looking for. He just couldn't find it.

As the NTSB investigator closely examined the wreckage of the Cubs' plane, he knew he needed to find the source of the fuel contamination. Something had prevented the fuel from getting to the engines. The fuel boost pumps in each tank had overheated because they were trying so hard unsuccessfully to pump the fuel from the tank to the engine.

The results of the tests on what fuel residue they had found at the crash site and in the burned wreckage had been inconclusive. The only material that had shown up was some kind of silicon-like gel, and Mathis knew that material was not unusual and could have been used as a tank sealant or for some other repair purpose. It had burned in the fire, leaving a little residue, but Mathis knew there was no way that was the source of the contamination.

He and the rest of the investigation team had poured over the transcripts of the cockpit voice recorder and the information from the flight data recorder, none of which had provided them with any more clues about the source of the contamination.

"I'm convinced something happened to the fuel before the plane left Chicago," Mathis said to his investigators. "What or how I have no idea. But once the plane is in the air, with fully loaded tanks, there isn't anything that would suddenly make the boost pumps stop working. It if had simply been bad fuel, the pumps would have worked; the engines would have died because the fuel was bad, but this fuel was never getting to the engines."

The others nodded their heads in agreement, not sure if Mathis wanted them to speak or not.

"I think we've done all we can do here. I know we had people talk to the charter services company at O'Hare but I want to talk to them some more. I want to look at the maintenance records, and see when those fuel boost pumps had last been checked. There has got to be an answer somewhere about what happened."

🌿

Mathis flew to Chicago later that day, and at 9 a.m. the following morning, showed up at Charter Air Services to continue his investigation. Company officials were cooperative, providing him with copies of the maintenance records.

"I want to talk to everybody who was working here the night the plane left," Mathis said, "all of the people who had any contact with the plane."

"OK, we can arrange that, with one exception," the company president said. Mathis looked up. "What do you mean, with one exception?"

"Unfortunately, one of our employees, a man named Eddie Marshall, was shot and killed the night after the plane accident."

"He was killed?" Mathis said. "What happened?"

"The police said he apparently walked in on a robbery attempt at his apartment. There had been a rash of break-ins in his complex and in the surrounding area. He had been at work, stopped by the club as he almost always did, and got home about midnight. The robber was in the apartment, I guess, and shot Eddie just inside the front door. The cops said he died instantly, from a single gunshot to the head."

"That's terrible," Mathis said. "I'm really sorry to hear that. Did he have a family?"

"No, he was single. He was a good employee. We never had any problems or bad reports about him. He had worked as the fuel man here for about five years."

Mathis interrupted the president. "Eddie was the fuel man?" The boss nodded yes. "And he was working as the fuel man the night the plane left here and then crashed?" The boss nodded again.

"Damn. He was the most important guy I needed to talk to. He was probably the last person to look at the fuel before it went into the plane. I was hoping he could give us some answers about what happened."

"Well, I know the other investigators talked to him the day after the crash, before he was killed that night. I don't know what he told them because I wasn't in the room."

"I've got a copy of the interview right here," Mathis said. "He said nothing out of the ordinary happened, except the high pressure fueling wasn't working so they had to fuel the plane by gravity feed though the top of the wings. The report said that was a fairly common procedure."

"Yeah, I know that much is true," the president said. "We had been having problems with the high pressure fueling all that week. I don't know what they finally found out was wrong with it."

Mathis was quiet for a moment, lost in thought, and then asked, "Did Eddie have a locker here?"

"Yes, all of the employees here have a locker. Why?"

"I just wondered if I might look at it for a moment. I don't really know why, I just have a feeling I might find something that will help tell us what happened."

"Well, a couple of days after Eddie was killed we cleaned out his locker," the president said. "I really wasn't sure what to do, with him not having any immediate family. We put it all in a box to keep it until we figured that out. I guess it wouldn't hurt anybody to let you look at it. I'm not sure what was in there. I didn't clean out the locker. I don't know what you might find."

"I don't, either," Mathis said, "but right now I don't have any other great ideas."

One of the employees went to the storage area and brought back a small cardboard box, with "Eddie Marshall" printed on a piece of masking tape across the top.

Mathis sat the box on the desk and began to take items out of the box. An extra shirt. A pair of tennis shoes. A windbreaker. A cheap bottle of cologne. And a beeper.

Picking up the beeper, he looked at the other couple of employees who had gathered around him. "Eddie had a beeper? Does everyone here have a beeper?"

The employees shook their heads no. "Does anybody know why Eddie had a beeper?" Again the answer was no. "I never saw him with it and he never mentioned it," one said.

Mathis looked at the beeper. He pushed the review button and a number came up that Mathis of course didn't recognize, but wrote down on a piece of paper. He hit the review button again, and it produced another number. Mathis wrote it down. Those were the only two calls on the beeper.

Mathis went through both calls again and realized that in addition to the number, the beeper also recorded the time and date of the call. The most recent call had come in at 8:35 p.m. on Monday, July 24, from 773-404-2827.   The first call had been received at 4:45 p.m. on Sunday, July 4 – the date of the crash. It was a 312 number, also a local Chicago call.

Mathis scratched his head. He needed to call these two numbers and find out who had called, and why, but he needed to have a ready explanation about why he was checking out who had called this number. As he thought about it, he realized he probably needed to have a little talk with the police who were investigating Eddie's murder. Maybe these two events were not a coincidence.

Chapter 20

For as long as Mike Callan and anybody else in baseball could remember, the month of August was known as the "dog days" of the baseball season. Callan had no idea where the expression had originated, but he was sure it had to do with the heat of the summer and players becoming lazy, like dogs, as they had to force themselves to play with any degree of enthusiasm and interest.

This was especially true at Wrigley, which still featured more day games on the schedule than night games. Before the Cubs finally put up lights in 1988, the general belief among baseball types was that the Cubs would never win the pennant because their players became too worn out by having to play all of those day games in the summer while the other teams were playing at night.

Because these players had not gone through a Chicago summer, Callan decided to remind them that even though he never believed in the theory that the Cubs couldn't win because of all the day games, you did need to prepare differently mentally and physically for a day game than you did a night game.

"You guys are grown men," he said, "and I'm not going to tell you what to do. You may think you are indestructible, but if you screw around too much in August, it will come back to haunt you in September. I can guarantee it. Your body will be tired. You have a responsibility to yourselves and to your teammates and to this organization. Remember that, that's all I am saying. I'm not asking you to be priests, but don't do anything ridiculous, either."

Callan loved day games when he played, and he still loved them. He realized he was a throwback, when players actually enjoyed riding trains from Chicago to Philadelphia and New York. He wasn't the type to hang out at bars until 3 a.m. and sleep past noon. He liked having the games in the afternoon, then going out to eat a good meal in a nice restaurant, take in a movie and be in bed by 11 p.m. That was a perfect day. It was during a couple of those nights, when he was back alone in his hotel room as he was getting ready for bed, that he thought about Chelsea. He still hadn't called her, and she had not called him. He felt bad that their marriage had ended, and he knew deep in his heart he still loved her. Maybe when the season was over he would make an effort to get together. Now he didn't want anything interfering with his focus on the team.

As near as he could tell, he had a lot of players who were like him on this team. Of course, he wasn't waiting in the hotel lobby at 3 a.m. to see who came wandering in at that hour, and he didn't have a curfew and wasn't knocking on doors at midnight to see which players were in their rooms, preferably alone.

No, his evaluations came from watching the players in action, seeing how they went about their business, on and off the field. With only a couple of exceptions, he was impressed by all of these guys. Once the initial shock of having to pack up and move had worn off, and once they had gotten better acquainted with some of their new teammates, this group of players had actually come together much more quickly and better than Callan could have anticipated. The result not only was visible with the effort and results on the field, but with the way the team interacted in the clubhouse and on the charter flights.

There was good-natured ribbing, and practical jokes, and Callan enjoyed those actions as much as any of his players. They were a part of the game's history and lore. Callan was pleased to see that one of the players who had become one of the club's leaders, and leading jokesters, was Billy Slagle. One of the reasons he was glad of that was Callan had seen enough of Slagle to know that when the time came to be serious, he was all business.

There was no joking around with Slagle on the field, and Callan knew that was what won him the respect and admiration of his teammates, even those older and with much more major-league experience. He could have been ridiculed and abused for his love of the history of the game, and of the Cubs' franchise, but his teammates actually seemed to embrace it.

Slagle picked his spots when he could educate his teammates. Such an opportunity had come up today, when the team's bus got stuck in traffic on the way to the ball park in New York.

It is a long ride from the team hotel in midtown Manhattan to the baseball stadium in Queens. Many of the players take the subway in the early afternoon, knowing it will get them there faster. Today, however, it had been raining all day so there was a good chance the game was going to be postponed or delayed, which was why almost all of the players waited and took the team bus when it left the hotel at 3 p.m.

As the bus made its way out of Manhattan, it passed a man standing on the sidewalk walking a goat. It was an honest-to-God goat, walking down 2nd Street in Manhattan on the end of a leash, just like a dog. Callan couldn't believe his eyes. Neither could the players. All were pointing and laughing, and talking about how nobody kept a goat as a pet.

All except Slagle, who immediately launched into the story about perhaps the most famous goat in baseball history, which, coincidentally, was connected to the "curse" of why the Cubs had not won a World Series since 1908.

"It was in 1945," Slagle began, "and many of the best players in the game were away fighting in World War II. The Cubs won the pennant by three games over the Cardinals, who had lost Stan Musial to military duty. Otherwise, the Cardinals probably would have won five consecutive pennants. The win put the Cubs back in the World Series for the seventh time since that 1908 series. They had lost their last six appearances.

"The Cubs were playing the Tigers, and won two of the first three games, which were all played in Detroit. A man named William Sianis, a Greek immigrant, owned a popular tavern on Michigan Avenue in Chicago and he had a pet goat. He had two box seat tickets for game four at Wrigley and he decided to take his goat, named Sonovia, to the game."

Some of the players laughed, or looked at Slagle like he was nuts, but he ignored them and kept telling his story.

"The ushers tried to keep Sianis and his goat out of the ball park, but they made it inside, anyway. He actually made it down to the field, and was walking the goat around on the field before the ushers and Sianis got into a big argument. He had pinned a sign on the goat that said, 'We Got Detroit's Goat'. The ushers eventually agreed to let them take their seats. They actually were sitting right next to Warren Giles, who for a long time was the president of the National League. Sometime during the game, however, Philip Wrigley, the Cubs' owner, found out what was going on and had Sianis and his goat ejected from the stadium. Apparently, the smell of the goat made it up to the owners' box.

"Before he left the stadium, Sianis reportedly put a curse on the Cubs that the franchise would never win another pennant or play in another World Series. The Tigers won the game and went on to win the Series in seven games. After that loss, Sianis supposedly sent a telegram to Wrigley that read, 'Who smells now?'

"As we all know, the Cubs have not won the pennant or appeared in a World Series since."

"Hey, Billy, you don't really believe that, do you?" came a shout from the back of the bus.

"I'm not saying I believe it or I don't," Slagle said. "I'm just telling you the history of what happened. Enough people have apparently believed it over the years that they have tried a couple of times to see if they could break the curse."

"What'd they do?" somebody asked.

"On opening day in 1984, they had Sianis' nephew, Sam, bring a goat out onto the field at Wrigley before the game. It actually looked like that was going to break the curse when the team won the division and met San Diego for the NL pennant. They won the first two games at Wrigley and needed to win just one of three possible games in San Diego to win the pennant and a spot in the World Series.

"And we all know what happened. They lost all three and San Diego won and played Detroit in the Series. The Cubs actually led the fifth and deciding game 3-0 going into the bottom of the sixth inning, 12 outs away from winning, before the Padres rallied – thanks in large part to Tim Flannery's grounder going through Leon Durham's legs at first base in the seventh. Before the game, Ryne Sandberg had accidentally knocked over a Gatorade cooler, soaking Durham's glove. Don Zimmer was a coach then and he told Durham not to change gloves, that maybe it was good luck. It didn't turn out that way.

"As they say, you can't make this stuff up. Truth really is stranger than fiction.

"Ten years later, in 1994, the Cubs lost their first 12 home games of the year. The manager was Tom Trebelhorn, and he came up with the idea of trying again to break the curse. He arranged for Sianis and Ernie Banks to join a group of chanting monks for an exorcism procession around the outfield walls. They won that game, but not much else."

The players sat on the bus and shook their heads, not disputing Slagle's history lesson but questioning how people actually could believe "the curse" would keep the Cubs from ever winning again.

"What are they going to say when we win?" said catcher Luis Roman. "That will be the end of the goat. We eat goats where I come from. I will cook a goat for everybody."

"God, you're sick," said pitcher Steve Watson. "I never will forget when the Braves went to Mexico for a spring training series a couple of years ago. We played in Monterrey, and they actually were barbequing goats in the parking lot – right there on the grill, just like it was chicken.

"And that wasn't the worst of it. The next morning they took us to this fancy breakfast and just as we were finishing eating, the Mexicans brought these two live chickens in and they starting fighting each other. It was an honest-to-God cock fight. It was hilarious watching all of the suits from the Commissioner's office trying to figure out what to do. They wanted to get us out of there, but they didn't want to embarrass the Mexicans, either. It was a real case of international détente."

"Don't tell me about it tasting like chicken, either," Jim Baker said to Roman. "No matter what kind of exotic meat you see cooking – deer, rabbit, ostrich, whatever – you ask the guy cooking it what it tastes like and he says 'like chicken.' That's bullshit. Nothing tastes like chicken except chicken."

Callan sure hoped chicken was not on the post-game spread tonight.

The bus finally made it to the ball park and the game started about an hour late. Watson pitched a five-hitter, McKenzie hit a three-run homer, and the Cubs won, 5-1. The Cardinals lost to the Nationals in Washington, and Chicago had a two-game lead.

❧

After the reporters had left his office, Callan turned on his cell phone and saw that he had two messages. The first was from T.J. with the news that they had reached an agreement with Jason McGair's agent. He asked Mike to call him back after the game so they could work out the timing of the news conference and when McGair would join the team.

The second call was from Bobby Scott, the third baseman for the Cubs who was one of the two players to survive the plane crash. After spending several weeks at the hospital in Cheyenne, Scott had been transferred to a hospital in Chicago. Callan returned that call first.

"Bobby, it's Mike Callan. I hope I'm not calling too late."

"No, it's fine. I just got done watching the game. You guys are playing great."

"Thanks. I appreciate that. How are you feeling?"

"Getting better. The doctors said I might be able to go home in a couple more weeks. They said I was really lucky, and I know that's true. It took me about a month just to realize everything that happened. I still can't really believe it. It's like a really bad nightmare, but when you wake up, it's still there.

"Anyway, that's not the reason I called. I just wanted to let you know that I'm rooting for you. I don't know when or if I will ever play again, but this isn't about me. The Cubs have got to win to put an end to this shit about the curse. I read something else about it in the newspaper today. It's driving me nuts. People say the plane crash is just the latest example of how this franchise is cursed. You guys have got to win to end that talk. You have to do it for the fans, you have to do it for all the former players, you have to do it for yourselves. Whatever it takes. You've got to win."

"Bobby, I appreciate that. I really do. Everybody here knows we are in a tough spot, and I've told this team since our first meeting that the best tribute we can give to everybody on that plane is to continue what you guys started, and that's to bring home a pennant and a World Championship. That is exactly what we are trying to do, and we won't rest until that task is completed. You have my word."

Callan told Scott to call again whenever he wanted, and as soon as he felt like coming to a game, to be sure to let him know. If he ever wanted to come and talk to the team, he had an open invitation.

After getting on the bus headed back to the hotel, Callan called T.J. back. He told him about Bobby Scott's call and how he intended to mention it to the team tomorrow. "Now, what do you want to do about McGair?" he asked.

"We've got another game in New York and I kind of think it would be a good idea if we waited to announce the signing until after we leave town. You know, since he was on the Yankees and all, and with all of the normal New York media craze, I think it would be calmer if we do it when we get to Washington."

"You're probably right," Mike said. "When will he be able to play?"

"He's been playing all year, as you know, so he is in shape. He is ready to leave Japan as soon as we figure out the timing from our end. His agent felt, and I agreed, that it would look bad if he went ahead and left Japan before we made our announcement because then somebody would think something was up. If we make the announcement in Washington, he can be here and join the team when we come home on Friday."

"That sounds good to me," Mike said. "It won't hurt the gate this weekend, either, to have him in the lineup."

"I sure hope this works," T.J. said. "You know I don't really like making major changes when things are going pretty well, but I do agree with you that we need some power in the middle."

"Trust me," Mike said, "if Jason is healthy he will be a major addition for our team. Are we still agreed that we are going to put Richie Edwards on the DL? He's still got that bad hamstring and hasn't been 100 percent for a while. We can keep him there until September 1 and then bring him back. Then we won't have to make a decision on the roster until we get to the postseason."

T.J. agreed with that plan, wished Callan a good night, and hung up.

⚜

The news that the Cubs had signed Jason McGair and were bringing him back from Japan exploded through the media. As expected, there were out-cries that this was more evidence the Cubs didn't know what they were doing, and how could they give a druggie like McGair another chance? There also were positive columns that recognized the Cubs' need for power, that the Chicago brass admitted they were taking a chance, how they hoped it worked out, etc.

Since it had been so long since Callan had seen or talked with McGair, he really didn't know what to expect when he arrived at Wrigley about 10 a.m. on Friday, five hours before the game against the Pirates, and found McGair already in the locker room.

McGair saw him come through the door. "Hey, Mike! God, you do look like an old fart! Good to see you," he said as he walked toward Callan, extending his right hand. "It's been a long time. How are you?"

"I'm good, Jason. Good to see you. It has been a long time. You look good. I hope you are as happy to be here as we are to have you."

"Absolutely. I couldn't believe it when my agent called and told me what was going on. I thought I was doing the right thing when I went over there, for a couple of reasons, but I … "

Callan held up his hand to interrupt him. "Come on in the office, we can sit and talk there."

After grabbing a cup of coffee, Callan sat behind his desk and McGair took the opposite chair.

"So tell me everything about yourself since 1994 that I haven't read in the newspapers," Mike said.

"My life has pretty much been an open book since then, you know that. There really isn't much to tell. I made a few bad choices, but I don't really have any regrets. It wasn't like I was the only one doing what I was doing. I liked hitting all those home runs, it made me feel good, and obviously I liked the money and the attention, too. But after a while, especially in New York, it just got to be too much. I had to get out."

"That's why you went as far away as you could, to Japan."

"Yeah, I really wanted to become a recluse, but I couldn't give up on the game. It was my agent's idea. You know how agents are. It's all about the money. The more he talked about it, though, the more I decided he might be right, at least it was worth a shot. I didn't think anybody in the big leagues would touch me because of all the steroids talk, so I thought it was pretty much go there or retire. And I wasn't ready to retire.

"I can't thank you enough for giving me this opportunity. I really enjoyed playing for you in Des Moines. I thought for sure you were going to be managing in the big leagues in a few years. What the hell happened to you anyway?"

"Kind of like you, Jason, I made a bad decision and it cost me. There were a lot of side issues involved, and I was kind of pushed aside. I won't say I was totally innocent, but I was blamed for a lot of things I didn't do. I got a second chance. A lot of guys here are getting another chance, and I thought you deserved one, too."

"Do these guys understand and appreciate what a great guy you are?" McGair asked.

Callan laughed and shook his head. "If you asked most of them a month ago they would have put me before a firing squad or worse," Callan said. "They thought I was still coaching a high school team. They are a good group, though. I think you will fit in well with them."

"To be honest with you, I haven't really kept up too much on what has been going on. I heard about the plane crash and all, but until my agent called I hadn't even looked at the standings over here. Do you think we've got a chance to win?"

"I think we've got a great chance, especially with you here. We need a little power boost in the middle of the lineup. What do you think? You ready to give it a go today?"

"Absolutely. I'm here, I'm ready. Thank you. I won't disappoint you."

McGair sidestepped most of the hard questions during a 20-minute press conference, saying mostly how grateful he was to the Cubs for bringing him back to the big leagues, how he hoped to help the team win the pennant, and how sorry he was to hear the news of the plane crash.

Kevin Andrews stood in the back, taking notes, but trying to read between the lines while McGair was talking. He believed the Cubs were right – if McGair could still play, he could help lift this team to the pennant.

How unbelievable would this story be? Andrews thought he had already written the biggest stories of his life, covering the plane crash, but a Cubs' World Series victory, especially coming about in such a manner, would be better than any movie script or novel could ever be. Nobody would believe it. He would have to believe it, because he would be there watching the story unfold.

Part of the reason for this team's success, he was coming to realize, was the relationships that were building between Mike Callan and the players. The addition of McGair was just another example. He was a link to Callan's past, and he was offering the same compliments to Callan that his current players were starting to mention to Kevin.

Usually when a player comes up to a reporter, he wants to vent about something. He has a gripe, a complaint, or a question about a rumor he has heard, probably involving a trade. Most of the bitching is about the manager, how he isn't being fair, isn't giving me a chance, can you put something in the paper about how I am getting screwed ...

Kevin had noticed that lately, especially in the last two weeks, he was getting players coming up to him on a frequent basis asking about Mike, and offering compliments about their manager. Kevin could never remember that happening in his career.

He had asked Baker, who he remembered was one of the players complaining the most when he joined the Cubs, what was going on.

"You know, I have to give the guy credit," Baker said. " I was one of the ones who was bitching about what he was doing, how he was treating us like a high school team. I thought he was over his head, that he didn't have a clue about what he was doing. And you know what? I was dead wrong. I might have been more wrong about him than I have ever been about anything in my life.

"He is everything you could want in a manager. I think it took me and the other guys a little while to see it, and I think he did have to come to know us a little better, but I can understand that. He has taken this group of castoffs, brought us together in the middle of the season under incredibly terrible circumstances, and made us a team. I can't really believe it is happening. I thought this was going to be the worst three months of my life, and instead it is turning out to be the best.

"This guy has the ability to criticize us without getting mad, without getting upset and raising his voice. He lets us know that he is in charge, and nobody has a problem with that. I think I can safely speak for every player on this team when I say we would run through the brick wall in centerfield if he asked us to. He is the best manager I have ever played for. I haven't felt that way about any of my managers since I was in high school. Every manager in the major leagues could learn from him. He doesn't have an ego. He lets the players play and have fun. He doesn't have ridiculous rules. During the games he is calm and collected but you can tell his brain is always working. He knows what is happening. He has the best baseball mind of anybody I have ever met. What the hell he was doing coaching a high school team for the last 10 years instead of managing in the majors is one thing I will never understand. He is simply the best, and you can put that in the newspaper."

Kevin did, writing a glowing story about the blooming relationship between Mike Callan and his players and how it was one of the biggest reasons behind the Cubs' success. Mike was embarrassed by the story, but even some of the players that Kevin had not talked to or quoted in the story made it a point to come up to him and tell him how the story had been right on target.

September was only a week away, and the Cubs were in first place. Back in June, Kevin would have had no trouble believing that. With everything that had happened since, however, he found himself shocked, and he knew he wasn't the only person in baseball who felt that way.

Chapter 21

T.J. Vitello read Kevin's story about the players giving the credit for the Cubs' success to Mike Callan. He took the sports section, wadded it up, and threw it in the trash. He was as happy as anybody that the team was in first place, but he wasn't quite ready to anoint Callan as the biggest reason.

Missing in the story, for example, was any mention of how T.J. had been the one to reach out and hire Callan when he had been blackballed from pro baseball for 13 years. The story did not give T.J. any credit for taking over the team in the wake of his father's death and putting together the front office staff that had evaluated and drafted these players.

T.J. realized that all of the praise for Callan was coming from the players, and nowhere in the story did Callan take the credit himself. Still, he also had not said anything good about T.J.'s role in bringing this team together.

The national press, T.J. knew, would pick up on the story. The attention from the networks and the magazines already was starting to build. *Sports Illustrated* was going to have a writer spend the week with the team for the next issue's cover story. *USA Today* had a reporter at Wrigley all weekend. ESPN had added a couple of the games in the next week as national broadcasts. The Cubs, and Mike Callan, were hot, and they were going to be everywhere.

T.J. picked up the phone and punched in the extension for Tim Jenkins in the PR office. He answered on the first ring.

"Hey, T.J., what's up? Andrews wrote a hell of a story on Callan and the guys didn't he? That's the kind of PR we need. I just talked to Josie in the ticket office and she said the phones have been ringing off the hook. People already were excited about us getting McGair, and now this. We could have sellouts the rest of the season. Can you believe it? Amazing."

"Tim, I wanted to talk to you about all of the increased media that is going to be coming to town and traveling with us. I know *Sports Illustrated* is here, *USA Today,* ESPN and I'm sure there are going to be more. Is there any way to get them to spend some time with me? I would be happy to talk to all of those guys, tell them how this whole deal came together, you know, from my perspective."

Jenkins was quiet for a moment, trying to think how to react that would not piss off his boss and get him in trouble. He had known of owners who were publicity freaks, like Steinbrenner, and he had talked with his PR buddies about how hard it was to work for them. Suddenly he found himself in that same position.

"Well, I can certainly make that available to them if you want me to," Jenkins said. "You know those guys often have their own agenda about the angles they want to pursue, and sometimes don't listen to what we have to say. I will be happy to mention that you are available."

"Good. Do that, Tim, if you don't mind. I mean, don't take it wrong, I want the players to be the focus, but I just think I could help the reporters put everything that has happened into better context, you know, so they understand the big picture. I'm going to be traveling with the team full-time in September so if anybody needs me, I'll be available, you just let me know."

Jenkins said he would do just that and hung up the phone. He waited for a moment, then exhaled. He knew exactly what was going on. He had an owner who was jealous of the manager and the players. He was lying through his teeth when he said he wanted the focus of the upcoming national stories to be on the players. Bullshit. T.J. wanted the stories to be all about him, and what a great job he had done, and how he was the one who had put this first-place team together.

Jenkins had heard some talk around the office that T.J. was starting to get a little hung up on himself and his sudden rise to fame and fortune, but he had tended to discount that as normal office politics. Now he had to reassess that stance because, based on this phone call, it certainly looked like that was the case.

When he thought about it, Jenkins also realized he had seen T.J. hanging out a lot more in the clubhouse and on the field during batting practice. There was one time on the last road trip he actually saw him wearing a uniform, shagging fly balls in the outfield. He knew the players were starting to make fun of him behind his back, and he heard a couple of players talking in the training room that he was becoming a nuisance. Somebody had even given him the nickname "Sweetboy." Jenkins realized he also had never seen T.J. with a girlfriend.

If anybody knew about this phone call, and how T.J. wanted more media attention, the negative feelings toward T.J. would only increase.

❦

T.J. hung up the phone in his office, and he was still steaming. He felt trapped sitting behind this desk, he needed to get out of here, but he didn't really have anyplace to go. It was too early to go down and hang out in the clubhouse because nobody would be there yet. He got up, told Nikki he was going out for a while, and left the office.

He almost went out to the field, to sit in the sun-drenched seats behind home plate, but instead went out the front door onto the sidewalk where he saw dozens of people lined up at the ticket windows buying tickets for today's game as well as future games.

T.J. walked across the street to McDonalds and bought a drink. He sipped the soda as he began a leisurely stroll around the area known as Wrigleyville, the four streets that surround the ballpark – Addison, Clark, Sheffield, and Waveland.

This was where he had grown up and had spent virtually all of his life, ever since his dad had bought the Cubs. It had never gotten old to him, just as it never got old to the fans he now found himself watching.

For some reason he couldn't explain, T.J. found himself thinking about his dad. His mind wandered to the strange bank withdrawals, and to the mysterious phone number on the yellow Post-It note he had found in his dad's wallet. As he watched all of the fans milling around, waiting to enter the park for the game, T.J. thought about his dad's vague comments about wanting to sell the team.

None of it made any sense. He knew there had to be an explanation, logical or illogical, and somehow it had to all be connected. He thought about Kevin's comments that maybe somebody had been blackmailing his dad because he knew something about Melissa's death and was making Tony pay to keep him from going to the cops. If that was the case, why had it suddenly come up this year? Where had that man, or woman, been since 1970?

A strange thought hit T.J. Maybe this didn't just start this year. Maybe the blackmail had been going on for a long time. He had only checked the bank records back to January. He wondered if his dad kept the old records in his office. If not, he knew he could get copies from Tom Wilkinson at the bank.

He started back toward the office when he heard somebody calling his name. He stopped and looked across the street, where the shout had come from. He saw an overweight man he didn't recognize who looked about 50, wearing a Cubs T-shirt and baseball hat, coming toward him.

"T.J., T.J. Vitello right? I knew it was you. I'm Joe Madison, the biggest Cubs' fan in Peoria. We've got the family up here for the weekend. Things certainly are getting exciting, aren't they?"

T.J. mumbled "yeah" then said, "I hope you enjoy the games. I've got to get back to the office."

"Oh, I didn't mean to bother you, I just got all excited when I saw you. I recognized your face from the pictures in the newspaper. I never had a chance to talk to the owner of the Cubs before. It's a real thrill. Congratulations on everything. I hope this is finally our year."

"Thanks," T.J. said, "I hope it is, too."

T.J. had no idea where to look for the old bank statements, so before he made a mess of the office, he asked Nikki if she knew anything about where his dad kept those kinds of files.

Nikki, as efficient as always, went directly to a file cabinet and pulled open the second drawer. "All of his information from last year should be in here," she said. "If you can't find what you are looking for, let me know."

T.J. had no trouble finding it once he was looking in the right place. He took out the Bank One statements from last year and carried them over to the desk. He noticed his hands were shaking. He shouldn't be this nervous, but he was, believing he was closing in on an answer about what had been going on.

As quickly as he thought that, however, it vanished. There was nothing unusual or out of the ordinary on any of his dad's bank statements. All showed normal activity, withdrawals, deposits, checks being written, but nothing that T.J. could identify as matching the large withdrawals for the six months of this year.

"Damn. I don't know if that's good or bad."

The explanation for the withdrawals now seemed obvious to T.J. His dad's first wife, Melissa, had died in 1970. The police had recorded her death as accidental. Obviously, that was not the case. Somebody knew that, and after nearly 40 years of keeping quiet, had started to blackmail Tony to keep him from going to the police and implicating Tony. T.J. could see why Tony would have paid the blackmailer. If it came out that he had killed his first wife, not only would he go to jail, his life would be over.

The obvious question was why now, why come forward after so many years? Why remain silent for that long? Nothing had changed in Tony's life within the last year. The blackmailer should have known where he was all that time, and should have been holding out for money for years. Unless he couldn't – because he was some place where he couldn't threaten Tony or get to him, like in prison.

That was it. That had to be the explanation. It all made sense. Whoever was involved in helping Tony kill Melissa had somehow got sent to prison for another crime, most likely soon after the 1970 killing. While he was in prison, Tony was safe. Nobody would believe the word of an inmate whose only intention in ratting on Tony would be to get himself out of jail. The courts would see through that.

Once he had been released from prison, however, he would have been free to threaten Tony and say he would go to the cops and tell what he knew unless Tony paid him off. Tony could have gone to the cops himself, but the reason he didn't, and the reason he didn't tell Donnelly about the blackmail, was because he was guilty. He knew if the case was reopened, he could be found guilty. It was easier just to pay the man to keep quiet.

Easier except for the fact that Tony didn't know how long this guy was going to continue to demand this kind of money, and Tony's cash wasn't going to last forever. That had to be why he had suggested that Donnelly see if he could find somebody interested in buying the team. He then would have enough money to continue paying the blackmailer for the rest of his life and he would keep his freedom.

Another thought suddenly hit T.J.

Maybe "Eddie" was the blackmailer. That would make sense. "Eddie" and his dad probably had a system worked out. Whenever it was time for the next drop, Tony probably was to call that number, which most likely was a beeper. They probably had a time and place arranged in advance, and they would meet and Tony would give him the money. It seemed like a flawless setup, until Tony was killed. Now there was nobody left for Eddie to blackmail.

T.J. took the yellow Post-It note out of his desk and stared at the number. When he had called it a few weeks ago, he had panicked and hung up without punching in a number. As he stared at the number, he debated whether to call it again and leave his number and see what happened. He couldn't make up his mind what to do.

Maybe Eddie had also been the person making the strange phone calls that Nikki had mentioned. He was no doubt worried that his money source was now gone.

"I wonder if there is a way to trace this number?" he thought to himself. "All phone numbers can be traced, even if they are unlisted. Fax machines, too. Somebody at the phone company should be able to track down who had been issued this number."

The more he thought, however, the more T.J. realized he didn't care if his dad was being blackmailed. That was over. There was nothing else Eddie could do to him. There was no way he could get any more of his money. And even if he found Eddie, there was no way he was going to admit what he had been doing and suddenly give T.J. back the money. No, this was one thing he didn't have to worry about anymore. He had solved the case of the missing money. He just couldn't tell Donnelly, Wilkinson, or anybody else. The secret would be shared only by Tony, T.J., and Eddie. "I hope he hasn't blown all the money," T.J. thought. "It's going to have to last him." T.J. took the note, wadded it into a little ball, and tossed it in the trash.

⚓

The beeper that had belonged to Eddie Marshall was the main item on Adam Mathis' mind, as well.

He had talked to the police officers who had investigated Eddie's murder. There had been no arrests, but they were certain it was connected to the string of break-ins that had occurred in the area for a couple of weeks prior to Marshall's death.

What had them slightly concerned, however, was that no more robberies had been reported in the area since Marshall was shot. "I'm guessing the guy got spooked and took off," one cop said. "I think we have seen the last of him."

"How are you going to solve the murder?" Mathis said. "We probably won't," the officer admitted. "You know how it is. He wasn't married. He had no immediate relatives. He was a nobody. There isn't going to be anybody bringing any heat down on us to solve it, so it almost certainly won't be. That's the sad truth, but it is the truth.

"You're the first person that has come around even asking questions about it, and when was it, a couple of months ago almost? Why do you care who shot Eddie Marshall, anyway?"

Mathis proceeded to explain his role in investigating the plane crash, and how Marshall might have been the one person who could have answered the question of how the fuel had become contaminated.

"I can see you're kind of stuck there," the officer said. "I wish I could help you."

"Did you look around his apartment at all, find anything that seemed out of the ordinary?" Mathis asked.

"I know we did, but I don't remember anything unusual. Let me see what we said in the report. Yeah, here it is."

After scanning the report, the officer looked up at Mathis. "Nothing really. The only things we noted were that the apartment looked like it had been ransacked, which is normal in a robbery. The crook or crooks usually are looking for drugs or money or something they can sell real easy. Nobody steals TVs or stereos anymore. Nobody will buy them and they are too clumsy. People might see you carrying it down the street or into the parking lot. Naturally, we couldn't tell if anything had been taken or not."

Mathis explained about Marshall having a beeper, and the two calls that it had received. With the officers' help, the two numbers were traced to a downtown restaurant and to the Chicago Cubs.

"The Cubs? Are you sure?" Mathis asked.

"Yeah, that's their main number. It could have come from any phone in the ball park, though, so I don't know how you would ever figure out who had called. Could just have been a wrong number, too. I get wrong numbers all the time on my beeper. Really ticks me off, because I have to call them back and it is really a pain."

The officers had not provided Mathis with much help, except for tracking down the phone numbers, but he thanked them for their time and left.

He needed to see if anybody at the restaurant or the Cubs could remember calling this number at the date and time the call came in. He was more concerned about the first call, even though the call from the Cubs' office was intriguing, because the first call had come when Eddie was still alive, and hours before the plane crashed.

❦

Kevin and Nikki had gone out to lunch several times, but their schedules had been so busy they had not been able to go out much in the evening. Kevin was either working all the time, or out of town with the team. When Nikki was off, when the team was out of town on the weekends, Kevin was gone. They talked several times a day on the phone, and both had to admit they were developing a deeper relationship than merely being friends.

When Kevin called this morning, Nikki couldn't keep what Tim Jenkins had told her in confidence to herself.

"Guess what?" she said. "T.J. called Tim Jenkins to campaign for Tim to encourage the national press and TV people to do stories about him. Tim says he was really ticked off by your story this morning when the players gave all of the credit for the team's success to Mike Callan. It seems T.J. thought some of the credit should have come his way."

"You're kiddin' me," Kevin said.

"No, that's exactly what Tim told me. I knew T.J. was stomping around here this morning, all pissed off, but I didn't know why. Now it makes sense. Tim also told me that a lot of the players are starting to get ticked off at how much time T.J. is spending hanging around the locker room, acting like he's a player."

"A couple of the guys told me that, too," Kevin said. "He was even shagging flies during batting practice last week on the road. He had Yosh give him a locker and an extra uniform. I almost put a note in the paper about it, but finally decided not to. ... Where is the boy wonder now, anyway?"

"I don't know. He left a little while ago, just said he was going out. He didn't say when he would be back."

"Is he still worried about what was going on with his dad's money? Did he ever figure out what was going on?"

"I know he talked to a lot of people about it but I don't think he ever came to any conclusion. Why, did you find out something?"

"No, you know how busy I've been, I really haven't had time to look into it. I did have our police reporter get the public information officer to dig out the case file from the investigation into Melissa's death for me. He just sent it to me in the mail, but I haven't even had a chance to open it. I thought I would take it with me on the road next week. I should have a chance to read it then. I don't think anything is going to change about a 40-year-old case in a week."

"No, you're probably right about that. By the way, I liked the story even if T.J. didn't. It's nice to hear people say good things about somebody instead of ripping them."

"Thanks. I thought it turned out well. I can't believe T.J. is that worried about publicity that he called Tim to try to set up some interviews for him. How bold is that?"

"I think he is starting to like all of the attention he is getting, not only for being the owner of the Cubs, but for the Cubs' success," Nikki said. "His dad was like that in a way. He didn't want the publicity, but he wanted people to know who he was and that he owned the Cubs. He liked the social credit, if not the media kind. T.J. seems to want both."

"Well, he isn't going to get it from me. I know he stepped into a tough situation and all and I give him credit for that, but this team is not winning because of the owner. It is winning because Mike Callan is getting these guys to play their butts off. I have never been around a team like it. It is the best clubhouse and the best group of players I have ever seen. It's almost like it's a high school team. It's been a lot of fun.

"Speaking of fun, I know we haven't had much time to spend together. I've got to go to the game today, but I don't have to write. What would you think about maybe getting something to eat after the game, then going back to either my place or yours?"

"Mister, you've got yourself a date. Maybe we should leave here separately though, you know, we don't want my boss or anybody else getting the idea that something is going on between us."

"I agree. The game should be over by 6 or 6:30. How about I make a reservation at Eli's for 7:30."

"Sounds great. See you then."

Both Kevin and Nikki were smiling as they hung up their phones.

McGair hit a three-run homer in the sixth, Watson held the Pirates to two hits over five innings, and the Cubs won, 4-1. The victory increased the division lead over the Cardinals, who lost to the Phillies, to five games. It also guaranteed that the Cubs would be in first place on September 1, just four days away.

Kevin and Nikki spent a few minutes talking about the game, enjoying a drink, before they ordered dinner. Kevin ordered a filet; Nikki went for the pork chop.

"Did T.J. ever calm down after his little tirade this morning?" Kevin asked.

"You know, he might have been in the best mood this afternoon that I have seen. I have no idea what happened. It seemed like a big weight had been lifted off his shoulders. He was smiling, he was laughing, he was honest-to-God whistling. I couldn't believe it."

"I guess he took a happy pill," Kevin said.

Both laughed, then Kevin changed the subject. "All day I've been thinking about everything that has gone on this year, from the plane crash to the questions about Tony's first wife and how she died, to all of the questions about Tony being blackmailed. I wish I knew the whole story. All we know are pieces, and none of them seem to add up."

"I can't believe Tony would kill or help somebody kill his wife," Nikki said. "I mean, I know I didn't know him back then, or ever meet her, but in the few years I worked for him he never impressed me as somebody who was capable of murder. What would have been his motive? He wasn't as successful or rich back then as he was later, but he wasn't down and out, either."

"I think it had to do with him wanting to be with Katherine, and he couldn't figure out any other way to do it, if I had to guess. I wonder if he had much of a life insurance policy on Melissa."

"You think he killed her for money?"

"I don't know, I'm just speculating. You know what they say about finding the truth to any story – follow the money."

"Well, shouldn't that be easy enough to find out?"

"I don't know enough about how to research that. I'm going to have to check with some of our business desk types who know more about tracking down that kind of information than I do. I think I might give Roy Singer a call, the old reporter I talked to in June, to see what else he might remember. He told me, don't forget, that he thought Tony killed her, even though he couldn't prove it."

Kevin and Nikki were so involved in their own conversation, and their dinner, that they didn't notice a middle-aged man, dressed in a white shirt, blue tie, and black sport coat, walk into the restaurant and ask to speak to the manager.

Adam Mathis knew he was fighting long odds, but if he could find somebody who remembered making the phone call to Eddie Marshall's beeper the afternoon of the plane crash, he might finally start to find some of the answers he was looking for.

The manager came out to the hostess stand, and Mathis introduced himself. When he explained what he was looking for, the manager took Mathis back to his office and invited him to sit down.

"So you are looking to find out who at this restaurant might have placed a call to this beeper number at 4:45 p.m. on Sunday, the Fourth of July," the manager said. "I'm afraid that will be next to impossible. We have several phones, and all of them would register with the same main number. There is a phone here in my office, there is a phone at the hostess stand, there is a phone behind the bar, there is a phone in the chef's office, there is another phone in the kitchen, and one in the dish room. The call could have come from any of them.

"And, it could have come from an employee or it could have come from a customer. It doesn't happen as often now, because of cell phones, but we still get people asking to use the phone all the time. Either they forgot their cell or it isn't working. No, I'm sorry, but I don't think I'm going to be able to help you.

"You know, the other possibility, is it could have been a wrong number. Our phone number here is only one digit off the phone for the downtown YMCA. We get their calls all the time. It really is a pain in the ass. I understand you are just doing your job, but we aren't going to be of any help."

With nothing else to do, Mathis took a seat at the bar, and nursing a vodka tonic, he came to the conclusion that the beeper investigation was going to be a dead end. Eli's manager was right. Just knowing where the call came from would prove nothing. He would have to know who had made the call and why. He could ask for the employee records, see who was working that shift that day, and see if anybody had any connection or any reason to call Eddie's beeper. He would have to interview all of them and that could take weeks. At the end, he might be no further along than when he started.

Even if a waiter or bartender remembered a customer making a call about that time, they likely wouldn't remember the man, or woman's, name. He would have to research all of the receipts for that day and track down all of the customers, and he could only find the ones who had paid with a credit card. There was no way to track anybody who had paid cash.

No, the more he thought about it, this was a lost cause. Mathis knew the plane had crashed because of some kind of fuel contamination problem, but as he started on his second drink, he knew the exact cause would never be known. This was one accident that would always remain a mystery.

⚜

Later that night, as Kevin and Nikki were finally becoming much closer acquainted back at Nikki's apartment, she started laughing and couldn't control herself. Kevin didn't know what could possibly be this funny to interrupt their cuddling and necking.

"I'm sorry, it's just that I can't get T.J.'s comment about hoping I was not dating a reporter out of my mind," she said. "He would die if he knew where I was and who I was with and what we were doing right now."

"Well he isn't, I am, and forget about him and think about me," Kevin said. "You may think T.J. wants a lot of attention, but this is all about me right now. Come here."

⚜

On the morning of Friday, September 3, the Cubs found themselves alone in first place, three games ahead of the Cardinals, who were coming to Wrigley for what could be a make-or-break series.

Callan had his pitching staff lined up just the way he wanted, with his big three of Watson, Charlie Wolford, and Dave Cochran ready to go. A Cubs' sweep would give them a six-game lead with 30 games to play, counting the games they had to make up at the end of the season for the postponements in July.

Even if the Cubs won only two of three, they would be four games ahead, and even a single victory in the series would keep them alone in first by two games. For the Cardinals to make up any real ground, they had to sweep the series.

Looking over the team's statistics, Callan was pleased to see how well McGair had responded. In his 10 games, he had four homers and 14 RBI, and more importantly, the Cubs had won seven of the 10. He had provided the power burst Callan knew the club needed, and he was making the rest of the lineup more effective at the same time.

Callan had been thinking about whether he needed to call a pre-game meeting before the series opener, to talk about not becoming overconfident and to recall the Cubs' September collapse in 1969, but his friends in the media and Slagle had taken care of that.

The media had caught on to the fact that Slagle was a history buff, a baseball history buff, and even more specifically, a Cubs' history buff. Anytime there was a reason to talk to him about something in Cubs history, they were doing it, which was why his memories of the 1969 collapse were all over the back page of the *Sun-Times* and the *Arlington Heights Daily Herald*.

Really, Slagle had explained, the talk about the Cubs' collapse overlooked the great play of the New York Mets that month. Even though the Cubs had a 9 ½ game lead over the Mets on August 13th, Slagle pointed out they would have had to have been up by 13 or 14 games to hold off New York. The Miracle Mets, as they came to be known, won 38 of their final 49 games. The Cubs were 84-52 on September 2, but would have had to win 16 of their final 24 games just to tie the Mets. The Cubs knew they were in trouble on September 9, in a game at New York. Ron Santo was on deck, and a black cat approached him and then walked around him. The cat then walked into the dugout. Santo made an out, and the Cubs lost as Tom

Seaver beat Ferguson Jenkins. It was the Cubs' sixth loss during what became an eight-game losing streak.

The Cubs had finished with a 92-70 record, and most people put the blame on manager Leo Durocher for the poor finish, saying he played his regulars into the ground. The Cubs' excuse was that they couldn't find any adequate backup players to give their starters some rest because nobody in the league liked Durocher and wanted to help him in any way. The team had continued to win in August because of great starting pitching, but the offense already was collapsing.

Even though Ernie Banks was 38 years old, with two bad knees, he still started 153 games that season.

"The funniest thing that happened was in August of that year," Slagle was quoted by the *Sun-Times* as saying. "The writers came in to interview Durocher after an 8-2 loss to the Astros on August 22 and somebody asked him if he planned to make any changes, to give anybody a rest.

"Durocher was in the middle of shaving, and he put down his razor, stormed out into the clubhouse, and yelled for all of the players to get out of the shower and come into the locker room. When everybody was there, he turned to the reporter and said, 'Now ask them what you asked me.'

"The writer did, and surprise, nobody said they were tired. Leo went back into his bathroom and finished shaving."

Slagle went on to say that there were some allegations, never proven, that Durocher was betting on games, perhaps even betting on the Cubs to lose. Commissioner Bowie Kuhn launched an investigation, but not enough information was ever found to build a case against Durocher.

Callan could not imagine any manager ever betting against his own team. At least when Pete Rose was betting while managing the Reds, he was betting on them to win.

Callan would never gamble like that. But as he sat in his office, with a month to go in the season, he knew if he was going to bet on any team to win this season, it would be the Cubs. You might not have been able to say that very many times in history, but they really were looking more and more like the real deal.

Chapter 22

Mike Callan had been involved in enough Cardinals-Cubs series during his playing career to know that no matter what the team's records were, the competition was going to be intense. When you added the pressure of the pennant race, the bar was raised an extra notch.

He always thought the best game he ever saw, or played in, was that day in June of 1984 when Ryne Sandberg hit two home runs off Bruce Sutter. It came on the NBC Game of the Week and really propelled Sandberg to the MVP award that year. Willie McGee of the Cardinals hit for the cycle and nobody knew it.

For the first time since the early games after the crash, Callan could sense his players were nervous and a little on edge for the series. Callan had known players who didn't think they were ready to play until they threw up because of their nerves, but he thought that was carrying things to an extreme. He wanted his players to be intense, and focused, but it had not been his experience that players performed better when they were so nervous that they got sick.

The one exception, Callan noticed as the Cubs completed batting practice before the opening game, was Jason McGair. Callan always thought the three greatest batting practice hitters he had ever seen were Bo Jackson, Jack Clark, and Mark McGwire. When Jackson was with the Kansas City Royals, he regularly hit balls into the water fountain beyond the outfield fences, and Callan was there with his dad one time when he hit a ball off the scoreboard in dead center field at what then was known as Royals Stadium.

When Clark was with the Cardinals and they came into Wrigley in the mid 1980s, Callan always tried to make sure he was hanging around on the field or was sitting in the dugout when Clark took batting practice. He blistered the ball into the bleachers and onto Waveland Avenue. He might have hit the ball harder, if not farther, than any hitter Callan had ever seen.

McGwire, of course, was known for launching balls into the upper deck at Busch Stadium during his home-run breaking days with the Cardinals. Callan only got to see him a couple of times, but he had to admit it was a marvelous show.

As Callan stood behind the cage at Wrigley, watching McGair splatter the ball to the far reaches of the ballpark, he thought he might need to add another name to his BP honor roll. McGair hit four would-be homers in a row onto Waveland, over the left field bleachers. Each one brought a bigger roar from the sold-out crowd, which was almost equally divided between Cubs' fans and Cardinals' boosters.

Callan was admiring the latest shot when Kevin Andrews approached. Mike turned his head in a silent greeting.

"That guy has been something, hasn't he," Kevin said.

"You know, I always thought he was going to be a good player when I had him at Des Moines, but I never thought he would be this good. I was just thinking I might have to add him to my list of the greatest BP hitters I have ever seen."

"He's done pretty well in the games for you, too," Kevin added.

"I don't think he's the only reason we're in first place, but he certainly has been a factor. Just as important to me is how well he has fit in with the other guys on the team. I was a little worried about how the other guys would react, but they took him in without a problem."

"Why were you worried? Because of the steroids stuff?"

"I guess kind of, I didn't specifically know. I mean the other guys had been together for six weeks or so and were developing good chemistry and a bond between them. You always worry as a manager when you add a high-profile player to your mix because you are never certain it is going to work."

"Was he taking steroids at Des Moines?"

"Are we on or off the record here?" Mike said. "Are you just asking because you want to know, or are you working on something that you are going to put in the newspaper?"

"Is your answer going to be different depending on my answer?" Kevin said. "I was thinking of doing a story on Jason, seeing what he would tell me about his steroid use. He never testified at the BALCO hearings a few years ago, and his name was not included in the testimony of the other guys, but it was universally known that he had been using the juice at least since his days in Texas. I was really surprised Canseco didn't put him in his book, either. If he hadn't been in Japan, I think Congress would have subpoenaed him, too."

"I don't know anything about that," Mike said. "I had not seen Jason or talked to him from the final day of the 1994 playoffs at Des Moines until he showed up here a couple of weeks ago. I don't know anything about what he was or wasn't doing during those intervening years."

"But what about when he was playing at Des Moines? He had a good year there."

"Yes, he did. To be perfectly honest with you, there was some talk in our clubhouse about steroids that year. Guys knew there were major league players who were using the stuff, and there was no question it made guys bigger and stronger and let them hit more homers. Players, especially those who are on the fringe of the major leagues, are going to be interested in anything that will give them that little extra boost they think they need to get to the next level. If that meant taking steroids, I think a lot of them would have done it.

"None of my players ever asked me about it. If they had, I would have told them they would be making a mistake. Some of my high school kids asked me about it the last few years. I actually caught one kid shooting up. Did I really jump his ass! It turned out his parents bought him the stuff, thinking it would help him get a college scholarship. I couldn't believe it. The biggest problem with steroids is nobody knows what the long-term effects are going to be. You see a big strong guy like Lyle Alzado fade away to nothing and blame it on steroids and it really makes you wonder. I hope that doesn't happen with any of the baseball guys, but only time will tell."

Kevin looked up from where he had been taking notes. "That didn't really answer my question about whether Jason was using steroids then."

"You will have to get that information from him," Mike said. "That isn't a question that I am in a position to answer, and I am not going to lie to you."

That was about as honest an answer as Kevin could have gotten. He appreciated that about Mike. Unlike many of the managers he had dealt with, with the Cubs and other teams, Mike respected the job that Kevin had to do. As long as he was fair and objective, Mike never had a problem with anything Kevin wrote. Maybe it made a difference that Kevin had actually played the game. He understood the pressures and demands on the players, even if he had not reached the majors. He knew what it felt like to win, and to lose, and you could see that knowledge reflected in his reporting.

Some players expect reporters to be homers for their team, leading the cheers up in the press box and directing the hero worship of the players. In the 1980s and 1990s, the press had gone 180 degrees the other way, becoming critics and cynics about the team they covered. Both Mike and Kevin knew the proper way to cover a team was to keep yourself somewhere in the middle – being able to praise the players when they did well, but also being able to criticize and analyze when the situation called for it. Again, it required the reporter to be fair and objective. That was really all any player or manager could expect.

Writing a balanced story about whether or not a player had taken steroids, without the player actually admitting it, was not going to be an easy task. Yet Kevin knew it was a story that had to be written, because it was on the mind of every Cubs' fan as they watched McGair continue to hit long-distance homer after homer.

People could look at McGair and realize that he had tree trunks for arms, and was incredibly strong. He didn't look like Barry Bonds, whose head had seemed to grow bigger over the years, but it just didn't seem possible that a person could get that big and strong simply by spending hours in the weight room and by taking nutritional supplements.

Kevin hoped McGair would open up to him, relaxed by his solid performance and the Cubs' success, but he didn't know what he was going to say when he approached him with his interview request. He decided to wait until after the game, or maybe after this series, and hope to catch him when he and the club were both riding high.

He had to wait. The Cubs lost the opener despite Watson's strong pitching, 3-1. In the second game, McGair's ninth-inning homer tied the game, but the Cardinals won in the 12th.

When the Cardinals completed the sweep, 6-4, in the third game, the two teams were tied for first place. Another loss, in the opener of a series against Milwaukee, extended the losing streak to four, the longest since the resumption of the season. Callan refused to panic, even though some people, including T.J., were openly upset. He was talking about making trades and coming up with other stupid ideas, and Callan just ignored him. Callan even asked T.J. not to hang around the clubhouse so much if he was going to be negative all the time.

Two players who had emerged as team leaders, McKenzie and Baker, called a players' only meeting the next afternoon. It gave everybody a chance to express what was on their mind, and it was a healthy exchange. Whether it was because of the meeting or not, the Cubs snapped the losing streak that night with a win over the Brewers behind Watson. When the Cardinals lost, the two teams were tied again.

McGair's walkoff homer the following afternoon gave the Cubs a 3-2 victory, and another Cardinals' loss to the Pirates put the Cubs back in first place by themselves.

The locker room was almost as animated as a winning locker room in a postseason series, except the lockers weren't covered with plastic and nobody was spraying champagne everywhere. Since it was a day game, Kevin had more time than usual to spend in the locker room before he had to go back up to the press box and write his story.

McGair did interviews with the TV and radio media and held court with the print media for several minutes before retreating to the lunch room and then the shower. By the time he returned to his locker, nearly an hour after the game, Kevin was the only reporter left in the clubhouse. Almost all of the other players were gone.

"Hey, I'm sorry I didn't know you were waiting for me," McGair said as he approached Kevin. "I thought everybody was gone."

"No problem. Luckily, I've got more time than usual today or I wouldn't have been able to wait."

As McGair started getting dressed, Kevin began asking him a couple of easy questions about the momentum moving in the Cubs' direction, if he had been surprised by anything since he had joined the Cubs, about the fans' reaction with his curtain-call today after the homer, questions designed to get McGair in a positive and upbeat mood.

Now was the time.

"I was just wondering, with things going so good and all, if it might be a good time to write a major profile about your career, you know, how you started in the minors, found success in Texas, all of the New York stuff, the reasons why you went to Japan, what's happening now, just kind of let your life spill out all over the newspaper."

McGair was quiet for a moment.

"I've read your stuff, and I think you do a good and fair job. I know what you are getting at – you want me to talk about steroids. I've always thought I would do that some day, probably in a book. I don't want to libel anybody but I would like to explain what happened to me. I'm just not sure now is the right time. Things are going so well both for me and the team and the last thing I want to do is screw anything up. You're going to be here tomorrow, right? Let me sleep on it and we can talk tomorrow, if that's OK."

"Sure, take your time. I'm not trying to rush you into anything and I want you to feel comfortable doing the interview and the story.

I know it is not an easy subject. I'll find you tomorrow during BP."

They shook hands and Kevin returned to the press box, whipped through his 18-inch game story and similar-length notes sidebar, hit the send button on his laptop and looked at his watch – 6:05. He had made reservations at Ditka's for dinner with Nikki at 7 p.m. He had just enough time to pick her up and make it to the restaurant.

Later that night, as he and Nikki were watching TV in her living room, Kevin relayed his conversation with McGair. "You really think he would admit publicly that he took steroids?" she said. "I think that's wishful thinking. You've gotten awful lucky with people kind of spilling their guts out to you and you just being there to catch it and put it all in the newspaper, if you ask me. There isn't any way on earth that I would do that kind of story with you. Nothing personal, of course."

"You mean I'm not going to find out all of your deep and dark secrets unless I go under cover?" Kevin said. "I would be willing to do that, you know."

"Not so fast, lover boy, we've got to wait for that. If you don't behave I will have to send you home."

✬

The Cubs were only one game ahead with 24 games to play, but the *Tribune* insisted on starting the magic number countdown in the next morning's newspaper, even though Kevin tried to talk his boss out of it, saying it was too early.

Kevin didn't really lobby too hard, however, because he was more excited that McGair had agreed to talk to him for the story. They had arranged to meet for lunch the following day at the restaurant in the hotel were McGair was living for the rest of the season.

Of course, just agreeing to the interview did not mean McGair was going to give Kevin the complete, unedited version of everything that had happened in his life. He was hoping he would at least open up some about his steroid use, because he knew that would be the story everybody would want to read.

"I guess I decided to talk now because I am tired of having to try to hide everything," McGair started out. "I know people talk behind my back. I know people say 'did he or didn't he?' I don't want to live like that anymore. I want to take all of the guessing and doubts out of people's minds. I want them to know the truth."

McGair proceeded to spend the next hour and 15 minutes detailing how and when he started using steroids, how he bought them each winter when he vacationed at the swank Los Venitas resort in Cabo San Lucas, on the Mexican coast. He talked about what the steroids did for him, what he thought would have happened to his career had he not taken the drugs, about how he was able to get around drug testing, and about his worry for the future, when the effects of taking so many steroids for so many years would finally start to show up. He talked about why baseball needed tougher sanctions against steroids, saying he almost wished he had been caught so he would have been forced to stop juicing.

"I was hooked, there was no doubt about it," he said. "I didn't want to do without the stuff. My worth as a baseball player was directly linked in my mind to steroids. I thought without them I would be useless."

The only thing he wouldn't talk about was other players he knew were on steroids. "This isn't a tell-all about anybody except me," McGair said. "I'm not Canseco."

He said he had stopped using steroids when he went to Japan, partially because he never thought there was a possibility he would be returning to the major leagues and he had heard horror stories about what happened to Americans who were caught using drugs in foreign countries. When the Cubs had called his agent, it had come as a shock. He said playing as well as he had since he had arrived in Chicago, and not being on steroids, was the greatest feeling he had experienced in his baseball career.

It was a great story. The *Tribune* ran it across the top of the front page, under a banner headline. Kevin thought that was a little dramatic, but he knew it was done on purpose to try to sell newspapers, the ultimate name of the game. It was picked up by all of the wire services and national networks. Kevin did more interviews the next couple of days than he could count, with all of the major network stars. He was on with *Larry King* and *Geraldo,* and even *Nancy Grace. The Best Damn Sports Show* filmed an interview with him, as did Catherine Crier on *Court TV* and all of the morning shows, including the *Today Show* and *Regis and Kelly*. He was kind of surprised and disappointed Oprah didn't call, especially since she was right there in Chicago. He made the radio rounds, too, including interviews with Dan Patrick and James Brown and even Rush Limbaugh. He got calls from a couple of book agents, pitching him on doing a full biography of McGair, but he told them that would have to wait until the season was over.

Kevin and McGair had talked about how they hoped the story would not be a distraction for the team. They had timed it to come out on an off day, before the Cubs went to Pittsburgh, which is not exactly a media hotbed. Callan was clued in ahead of time, so none of it was a shock to him or the front office and PR staff. McGair had agreed to hold one news conference, before the next game in Pittsburgh, to do follow up interviews with other reporters and then the topic of steroids would be off limits for the rest of the season. Kevin knew other reporters were jealous of his scoop, and his new found national media attention, but he didn't really care. He was just glad it turned out well and that his bosses at the *Trib,* and McGair, were pleased.

Kevin knew his next big story was going to be if or when the Cubs clinched the division. They were running neck-and-neck with the Cardinals. When the Cubs took two of three from the Cardinals in St. Louis, they grabbed the edge, but it still looked as if the race was going to go down to the final few games.

On the next to last day of the season, it happened. The Cubs beat the Astros and the Cardinals lost to the Pirates. The Cubs had a two-game lead with only one game to play. Luckily, it was a day game at Wrigley, so Kevin had plenty of time to work the locker room and get all of the quotes and reaction he needed about the Cubs' clinching the divisional race.

It really was an unbelievable story, and no matter what happened in the playoffs, the fact these Cubs had come together in such a manner and won the division was remarkable. Callan was being praised as the likely winner of the Manager of the Year award, and people were giving the Cubs a good chance to win the pennant and advance to the World Series.

The Cubs would play the Phillies in the first round while the Giants had won the Western Division and were set to play St. Louis, the wild card entry.

The city of Chicago, always in love with a winner, was going crazy over the Cubs. The team was dominating all the sports talk programs and the newspapers, and playoff tickets were being scalped at record prices. Everyone, it seemed, was in a great mood all over town.

Everyone, that is, except T.J. Vitello. He was putting on a smiling face anytime he was in public, but was moping and upset when he was alone in his office.

Several hours after the Cubs had clinched and celebrated, Nikki was telling Kevin about that, and neither could figure out why he was acting that way.

"I think it all comes back to him wanting the credit, and everybody is giving it to Callan and the players instead," Nikki said. "He is acting like a baby."

"I've noticed he still is trying to cozy up to the players as much as he can," Kevin said. "Jim Baker told me the other day the players are really ticked off about it and getting tired of him trying to act like he is a player. He told me a couple of the veteran guys had gone to Callan and complained about it. Mike told them he had asked T.J. not to hang around as much, but since he's the owner there really isn't anything he can do to stop it."

"I wonder what he's going to do if the team actually wins the pennant and then the World Series," Nikki said. "It should be the happiest time of his life, although he should be sad and missing his father, but I actually don't think he will be able to enjoy it. I think he is building up so much resentment against Mike and the players that he might be hoping they lose."

"You can't mean that."

"I do! He seems to be more ticked off everyday. I can't wait for the team to go on the road so he will be out of the office and I won't have to deal with him except on the phone. The down side to that is you're out of town, too, though, and I don't like that."

"Maybe I need to have a talk with him. I could write a story and see if he opens up a little and lets some of his feelings out," Kevin said. "It might be a good Sunday piece, a little different angle."

When Kevin called the following day to see if T.J. would agree to the interview, the reaction was exactly as he had imagined. T.J. was so desperate for publicity, and what he hoped would be credit, that he couldn't agree to see Kevin soon enough. They agreed to meet that afternoon.

Kevin had not really decided how he was going to pursue the story. He finally thought it best to just throw out names and topics and see what direction T.J. ran in, if he would try to deflect the credit for the team's success or try to minimize the contributions of others and praise his own involvement.

It turned out to be a little of both, which initially surprised Kevin, but in retrospect should have been expected. T.J. was smart, he knew how the game was played, and he knew if he took all of the credit, the fans, players, media, everybody, would jump down his throat. So he had to be soft in how much credit he took, and try to offer backhanded compliments to others that really only reinforced what he thought of himself.

For example, in praising Callan's job as the manager, he said, "I always knew he would do a great job. That was why I wanted to hire him when nobody else would give him a chance."

In evaluating how the Cubs were able to put together such a quality team in the dispersal draft so quickly, he said, "One of the first things I decided as soon as I learned about the crash was that we had to establish a front-office team that could work through this tragedy and find the players who would make the new Cubs a team to remember. I knew both Paul Wendel and Jack Reynolds could do the job."

Kevin had to keep from gagging a couple of times during the interview, and hoped he was able to hide the fact that he thought T.J. was full of it. It was a hard story to write, trying to let T.J. hang himself without Kevin doing it intentionally, but it came off pretty well. For those people who knew the true inside story, they could see through the quotes and knew exactly what was going on. More than one player came up to Kevin to say they got a big kick out of it.

Team unity is a wonderful thing in sports, and Kevin knew these Cubs had it. They were united in their opinion about both the owner and the manager, different opinions to be sure, and they were confident in their abilities without being condescending to the Phillies or their other possible playoff opponents.

The Phillies had won the pennant the past two seasons, and were trying to become the first National League team to win three years in a row since the Cardinals did it in 1942-44, a streak that was broken by the Cubs – the last time the Cubs had won the pennant. The first round was still a best-of-five format, with the Cubs hosting the first two games at Wrigley, which Kevin thought gave them a huge advantage.

He was right, as the Cubs won the opener, 5-1, and the second game, 9-3, as McGair hit two homers. Billy Slagle made a great defensive play, almost running face first into the ivy-covered brick wall in left center to take an extra-base hit away from Ryan Howard and kill a rally in the sixth.

The Cubs flew to Philadelphia ready to wrap up the series, and they did so in the third game, winning 6-4. Meanwhile, the Cardinals took care of the Giants in four games, and for the first time in the storied history of the two franchises, the Cubs and Cardinals were going to meet to decide the National League pennant and a spot in the World Series.

Kevin sensed a little more nervousness among the Cubs' players before game one, but Callan seemed relaxed as he shot the breeze with the media in his office. He was so different from the Cardinals' manager, Tony La Russa, who always looked like he was about to chop somebody's head off. He managed games in June like they were the seventh game of the World Series.

The Cubs, of course, had been in this position before, on the verge of winning the pennant and advancing to the World Series, only to fall short for one reason or another. Mike had been on the 1984 team, but was left off the postseason roster when the Cubs played the Padres. He had been at the first two games at Wrigley, and felt sure he would be there for the World Series in a few days. The Padres' rally kept that from happening.

In 1989, the Cubs played the Giants in the National League Championship Series and couldn't figure out a way to stop Will Clark. He hit .650 with two homers and San Francisco won the series in five games. The Cubs lost to the Braves in the division series in 1998, then made it back to the playoffs in 2003, only to lose to the Florida Marlins in in seven games.

Slagle didn't have to give the players much of a history lesson about that series because almost all of his teammates were familiar with the outcome. Some might not have been able to remember Steve Bartman's name, but they certainly remembered a fan being blamed for trying to catch a foul ball that Moises Alou might have been able to reach in game six. Nobody will ever know if that play might have cost the Cubs the pennant.

"The key word is 'might'," Slagle said. "Guys, what we have to do is make sure we don't put ourselves in that position. We want to take all of the 'might' out of the equation.

"Did you see how Harry Caray's restaurant bought that baseball for more than $100,000, then came up with some kind of design on how to blow it up in some kind of chamber? It was unbelievable. And then they actually took the pieces of the ball that were left over and tried to turn them into a sauce as a way to raise money for charity. It gave new meaning to the old expression of 'eating the baseball.'"

"People actually did that?" McGair asked.

"Yeah, I guess so, at least they paid for the food. It was in some kind of pasta sauce. I don't know if anybody actually ate the stuff or not."

"That's almost as bad as barbequing those goats down in Mexico. I saw some weird food in Japan, but nothing like that."

Callan was glad to see Slagle keeping his teammates relaxed as the players waited for the pre-game introductions before the opener. One of the reasons players get so nervous in the postseason is that all they want to do is play the game, and there are so many ceremonies and formalities to take care of that playing the game almost seems secondary.

It wasn't secondary to Callan, however, and he didn't think it was secondary to his players. He sensed a real feeling of determination in the way these guys were going about their business, and he knew they were going to do everything they could to try to win. That was all he, or any manager, could ask.

The Cubs and Cardinals were pretty evenly matched. The Cardinals had an edge in experience, and certainly an edge in players with postseason experience, but Callan liked his pitching staff a little better, especially the bullpen.

Watson had been terrific since joining the Cubs, and he was just as good in the opener against the Cardinals. After allowing a two-out homer to Albert Pujols in the top of the first, he stopped the Cardinals on six hits through the seventh inning, and Tom Tippett came out of the bullpen to close out the 4-1 win.

One attribute of this ball club that Callan really admired was its understanding of situations. Which was why, when T.J. showed up in the clubhouse after the game, slapping backs and trying to exchange high fives with the players, they all beat a hasty exit to the lunch room and told T.J. to stay out, that it was a players' only meeting.

They weren't really meeting, of course, just trying to stay the hell away from T.J. and his premature victory celebration.

That was proven the next night, when the Cardinals pulled out a 3-2 victory to even the series at one win apiece. Callan still was proud of his team, however. The Cubs were down 3-0 going into the bottom of the ninth but scored twice and had the tying run on third and the winning run on second with two outs before Ryan Franklin got Slagle to fly out to center to end the game.

Just as the players had been calm after the game one victory, they remained focused and upbeat after the loss, knowing the series still had a long way to go.

Slagle had to wait through the travel and workout day as the series moved to the new Busch Stadium to get another chance, and this time he came through. His two-run double in the sixth inning broke a 1-1 tie and sent the Cubs to a 4-3 victory.

He wasn't done, either. In game four, Slagle hit a two-run homer and started two other rallies with a single and stolen base as the Cubs broke out in a 6-1 victory. They were now just one win away from the World Series.

Callan would have understood if the locker room had been a little more festive than usual after the game, but it appeared exactly the same as through the early games of the series. After making his required appearance in the interview room and doing all of the stand-up interviews with ESPN, CNN, and the other networks, Slagle came back into the locker room after most of his teammates had showered and dressed.

Callan was just coming out of his office when Slagle came out of the shower, and he pulled up a chair and sat next to the outfielder as he was getting dressed.

"Pretty exciting stuff, huh," Callan said.

"Oh man, Mike, I've got to tell you, I still pinch myself every day when I wake up just to make sure I'm not dreaming. These last four months have been the most exciting time of my life. Can you believe it? We've got to win one more game and we are going to the World Series."

"That sounds simple, but you and I both know we can't take anything for granted yet," Callan said. "After all, we are still the Cubs."

"I'll tell you one thing I know, Mike," Slagle said. "This isn't my grandfather's Cubs. This is a great team. I have never been with a greater group of guys in my life. I would go to war with these guys, and for you. One of the reasons I want to keep winning is so this season doesn't end. You can't make this stuff up. I know you took a chance on bringing me up from Iowa, and I know you had other choices. I just want to say thanks again. I appreciate everything you've done for me."

"You've done it. All I did was write your name on the lineup card. You were the one who got the hits, stole the bases, and made great plays on defense. That was all you. Just like the rest of the guys. I agree with you – it is a great group, and I also don't want this season to end. Or at least when it does end, I want to be holding that trophy.

"Are your folks going to be here for the game tomorrow?"

"No, unless we win it tomorrow, they are going to come to Chicago. They had already made their plans and couldn't change them. My dad took vacation time so he could be there for the end of this series and, hopefully, all of the World Series. He said he wouldn't miss it for the world."

"Well, I hope he knows what a great kid he has. Get some rest and go get 'em tomorrow."

"Thanks, Mike. I'll do just that."

For a few innings, it looked like the Cubs might complete the series in five games and deny their home fans a chance to witness history, but the Cardinals rallied to tie the game and send it to extra innings. In the 11th, Matt Holliday ruined the Cubs' hopes, at least for a night, with a walkoff homer.

"When you've waited 65 years to get back to the World Series," Kevin Andrews wrote in the next day's *Tribune,* "what's two more days?" He also noted that winning the final game at Wrigley would be even sweeter for the Cubs, allowing their fans to pour into Wrigleyville and onto Rush Street in a celebration almost certainly unmatched in the city's history.

To a man, the Cubs wished there was not another off day between the fifth and sixth games. Supposedly it was for travel, and rest, but nobody needed it at this point in the series. All it meant was a long, boring day, trying to find a way to fill the hours until it was time to go to the ball park.

When Callan arrived at noon for game six, which was scheduled to start at 7:05 p.m., he was not surprised to see half his team already in the locker room, just hanging out. He had a good feeling about this game, and he hoped tonight would be the night.

The game started well. The Cubs jumped in front, 2-0, in the third, and inning by inning, the volume at Wrigley was building. It died down when the Cardinals tied it three innings later, but increased again when McGair's two-run homer put the Cubs up, 4-2, in the seventh. Callan thought about the history of the Cubs as the fans were going crazy, remembering that day in 1983 when then-manager Lee Elia flipped out, saying "85 percent of the people in this country work. The other 15 percent come out here and boo my players." Nobody was booing now.

Callan then had an uncomfortable pair of flashbacks, for some reason thinking about Leon Durham and Steve Bartman. He wiped his face with his hands, trying to erase that bad picture. It was replaced with a different bad picture, however, when Pujols tied the game with a two-run homer in the top of the eighth.

The game was still tied when the Cubs came to bat in the bottom of the ninth. A walk put the winning run on first, but Lee Thomas grounded into a double play. Junior Peterson came up to pinch-hit and delivered a single. A wild pitch moved him to second. The crowd was on its feet, everyone screaming at the top of their lungs as Slagle came up to bat.

Callan smiled. How fitting it would be if this kid was the hero, the man who lifted the Cubs into the World Series.

At least in this at-bat, however, it wasn't meant to be. Slagle grounded out to second and the game headed to the 10th.

Both teams had chances in the 10th and 11th but couldn't score. The Cardinals finally broke through in the top of the 12th, and when McGair flied out to the warning track in left for the third out in the bottom of the inning, the series was tied, three games apiece.

The pennant, and the spot in the World Series, would be decided in a seventh game.

Callan knew his players were disappointed, but he decided not to say anything in the locker room after the game. He wanted them to forget about this game as quickly as possible and focus their intensity on game seven. He would save his speech for tomorrow.

About 15 minutes before the team was scheduled to be on the field for stretching, Callan had the clubhouse attendants bring everybody together in the middle of the room.

"Guys, this will be short. I just had a couple of things I wanted to say. First of all, it goes without saying how incredibly proud I am of all of you. You were presented with an almost impossible task back in July and here we are on the brink of going to the World Series. You have defied the odds. You have made it happen. You have shown the

entire baseball world the kind of players you are, but more importantly to me, you have shown what kind of people you are. You deserve
to be here. This is not a fluke. You earned the right to be here.

"If I had told you when we came together for that first flight to
Houston back in July that you would be here tonight, getting ready
to play the seventh game of the NL Championship Series, you would
have had me locked up. I know a lot of you thought I was crazy
anyway back then, but not that crazy. But that is exactly where we
find ourselves. One more win, and we are going to the World Series.
It is an incredible story, and I know none of you are ready for the final
chapter.

"I want you to do two things tonight. I want you to keep giving
the same effort and the same performance that you have given me
and all of the Cubs' fans since we came together. And I also want you
to have fun. This is a game. Remember that. You have been playing
baseball all of your lives. Everybody in baseball would gladly trade
places with you tonight. You should feel honored and privileged to be
here. I am honored and privileged to be your manager. OK, that's it,
let's go."

The game was tight early, with both teams showing signs of
nervousness. The score was tied, 2-2, when the Cubs came to bat in
the bottom of the sixth, with the top of the order due up.

The leadoff hitter, Chico Gonzalez, worked the count to 3-2,
fouled off three pitches, and finally drew a walk.

Conventional strategy would have had Callan signaling for Billy
Slagle to bunt, sacrificing the runner to second. He did think about it,
but decided to give Slagle a couple of chances to hit away. He knew
the first and third basemen would be charging, the second baseman
would be moving to cover first, and the shortstop would be headed
for second. With all of the infielders on the move, Callan thought
Slagle had a better than average chance of getting the ball through the
infield. Callan also knew that with his speed, the only chance Slagle
had of hitting into a double play was if he happened to hit the ball
right at one of the infielders. It was a chance he was willing to take.

It was one of those kinds of managerial decisions, which if it had not worked, would have been second-guessed forever.

When Slagle didn't square around to bunt on the first pitch, T.J. Vitello, in the owner's box, was screaming louder than any of the other fans at Wrigley.

"Callan, what the hell are you doing! Where's the bunt?" he yelled. "We need this run! Come on!"

T.J.'s objection was overruled on the next pitch, when Slagle slammed a one-hop grounder just to the right of second base. The ball normally would have been an automatic double play, but the second baseman had left his position to cover first on the anticipated bunt attempt. When he stopped and tried to dive back toward the ball, he came up about two feet short and the ball bounced untouched into right center.

The Cubs now had runners on first and second with no outs, and their big hitters, Jim Baker, Jason McGair, and Keith Orlando, coming up. It was so loud Callan couldn't hear himself think.

He thought about having Baker bunt, but then he knew La Russa would walk McGair intentionally, and he didn't want to take the bat out of his hands. Even if Baker hit into a double play, he still would have the go-ahead run on third and McGair up. It was an easy decision.

Baker fell behind in the count by fouling off two fastballs, but then showed his patience and great eye by working the count to 3-2. After two more fouls, he took a curve that dropped just out of the strike zone for ball four. The bases were loaded, with McGair coming to the plate.

Now there were no decisions for Callan to make. All he could do was stand and watch, along with the 40,000 screaming maniacs in the stands. Callan actually wondered for a moment how far away the noise could be heard. It was so loud you couldn't even hear the person standing next to you. Callan thought about how McGair had wanted to get away from all of the attention and become a recluse, and here he was, right in the middle of this mob, the man of the hour.

Callan began to yell, along with everybody else, as soon as McGair's bat made contact with the ball. From that exact moment, there was no doubt where it was headed. Within seconds, somebody in the throng on Waveland Avenue had a very famous souvenir.

McGair was mobbed as he reached home plate, his grand slam having suddenly put the Cubs ahead, 6-2. Psychologically, they were even further ahead, and now both the Cubs and the Cardinals knew it was only a case of making the result official.

The final out came in the top of the ninth, when catcher Yadier Molina flied out to Slagle in center field. Callan knew it was real, that it had actually happened, but there still was some small part of his brain that was refusing to let the knowledge sink in.

The Cubs had won the pennant. They were headed to the World Series, and a matchup against the New York Yankees.

An hour later, after the trophy presentation and all of the interviews, after T.J. had made a fool of himself on national television, after all of the champagne had been sprayed and drunk, Callan found himself watching Slagle embrace his father with the biggest bear hug he had ever seen. Both men were crying.

"Can you believe it?" the elder Slagle said, to no one in particular. "My son is going to the World Series."

That was the moment Callan began to cry. This was a moment for fathers and sons to share, and he couldn't spend it with his father. He knew he was crying not only for himself, but for all the thousands and perhaps millions of Cubs fans who had wanted to share this moment with their fathers, only to never have that chance.

As he tried to wipe away his tears and look around the room, Callan saw that he and the Slagles were not the only ones crying. Nobody was making an attempt to hide it, nobody was embarrassed. It was a time of sheer emotion, a time to realize what had just happened.

As Callan began to compose himself, he realized there was something he needed to say to his team, and it needed to be said right now. He climbed onto the table in the middle of the room, and waved his arms and whistled, trying to get everybody's attention to quiet down. About 30 seconds later, the locker room was completely still. Callan didn't care which relatives or reporters were still in the room. He wanted the world, and his team, to hear what he had to say.

"Everybody said the Cubs were cursed," Callan said. "They said we couldn't win the pennant, but we did."

The room erupted into cheers, but Callan motioned for quiet so he could continue.

"I just want everybody on this team to realize one thing. The curse doesn't end here. The curse ends only when we win the World Series."

With that, the room was engulfed again in cheers and yells, and Callan was pulled off the table and immediately mobbed by his players. He had never been so happy in his life. He wished his dad could share this moment. He began to cry again.

Chapter 23

In all his years of cheering for the Cubs, Dr. Milton Hansbrough could not remember a more exciting time. Having been born and raised on the city's North Side, Dr. Hansbrough had suffered through the Cubs' collapse in 1969, the disappointing playoff loss in 1984, and the unfortunate foul ball interference by Steve Bartman in 2003.

This year, it didn't seem like anything could stop the Cubs. Dr. Hansbrough's only regret was that his long-time friend, Tony Vitello, had not lived to see the team's success.

Hansbrough and Tony Vitello had become friends back in the 1960s, when Vitello was representing a woman who had filed a lawsuit against the drug company where Hansbrough was working as the lead chemist. That company, Marx Pharmaceuticals, had developed a pill designed to lower a person's blood pressure. Even though it had been approved by the FDA, this woman, Sarah Ramsey, and others claimed they suffered from internal bleeding in the stomach after taking the pill. The pill had to be taken off the market, and the company was being sued for actual and punitive damages.

Since the pill was developed in Hansbrough's department, he was one of the people called to testify in the case. Vitello had grilled him about the tests the company had run on the pill before it was released to the public. Since it was a civil case and not a criminal trial, Hansbrough never had to worry about going to jail. But when the jury returned an award of $30 million to the victim, somebody had to be the scapegoat, and he was fired by the company.

Vitello felt sorry for Hansbrough, even though he was only doing what he was supposed to do as a lawyer, working on behalf of his client. Vitello thought the company had taken the easy way out in firing Hansbrough, and that was why he had used some of his influence at the University of Chicago to get Hansbrough a teaching position in the chemistry department.

Hansbrough never forgot how Vitello had helped him get the job, which he thoroughly enjoyed. After becoming the owner of the Cubs, Vitello had also given him tickets to games any time he asked, box seats right behind the Cubs' dugout, and had never asked for anything in return – until he called back in January and asked if they could get together for lunch.

Over steak sandwiches, Vitello said he had a business proposition for Hansbrough. He needed to find a chemist who could make a silicone-type gel in the form of a small bead, like the bath beads they sell in bottles in the fancy department stores. The catch was it had to be able to dissolve in jet fuel instead of water, with the thickness of the walls of the gel determining how long it would take to dissolve.

Vitello did not tell him why he needed the substance. He only asked if he thought it was possible, and Hansbrough agreed that it could be done. Vitello said he needed enough beads to fill a canister the size of a tennis ball container, and that the walls should be thick enough that they would dissolve in approximately an hour and a half to two hours after they were exposed to the fuel.

What made Hansbrough really pay attention, however, was when Vitello said he would pay him $50,000 cash for the work. He even gave him a $5,000 down payment, in cash, in a large manila envelope, 50 new $100 bills.

When he thought about it later, Hansbrough questioned why Vitello needed that product, and what he intended to do with it. He also knew, however, that what Tony was asking was not a hard assignment, and he really needed the money because of some bad investments he had made over the years, so he went ahead and did it.

Vitello seemed excited when Hansbrough delivered the beads to him in April, dropping them off when he went to the Cubs' home opener. Tony handed him the remaining $45,000, in cash, in a small black backpack. One of the conditions Tony had set in their first meeting was that Hansbrough could not ask him any questions about what Tony intended to do with the beads.

So even though Hansbrough had the thought that Vitello might have something illegal in mind, he knew it was better not to ask questions.

He never thought much more about it until that terrible morning in July when he woke up to the news that the Cubs' charter plane had crashed, killing almost everybody on board, including Tony Vitello.

Hansbrough watched the television coverage for hours, and days later attended the memorial service at Wrigley. He wondered for a moment what Tony had done with the beads, and when he heard that the suspected cause of the plane crash was fuel contamination, the thought crossed his mind that the beads might have been involved.

As soon as he thought that, however, he quickly dismissed it. Tony was on the plane. Why would he do something that would kill himself along with almost his entire team? It made no sense.

As the crash investigation continued, Hansbrough read the stories in the newspapers and the news magazines. The more it became obvious that something had contaminated the fuel of the plane, the more Hansbrough questioned whether it could have been the beads.

Like every Cubs' fan, Hansbrough got caught up in the excitement of winning the division and beating the Phillies in the first round of the playoffs. He had tickets to all of the NLCS games at Wrigley against the Cardinals, and had ridden the emotional roller-coaster through the wins and losses in the first six games with the rest of the fans.

It was only today, the morning of game seven, when he opened the *Tribune* and saw the front-page story that the NTSB had concluded its investigation and determined that the cause of the crash of the Cubs' plane would likely never be known, that he again thought of the beads.

Hansbrough went back to the records he had kept of how he had made the beads so that they would dissolve in jet fuel. He had run tests as he developed the beads because he didn't know how thick to make the walls so they would dissolve in the amount of time Vitello wanted. He had kept some of the beads, and a small bottle of the jet fuel Vitello had brought him for the tests.

What he remembered after looking at his notes was that after the beads dissolved, they turned into a silicone kind of jelly. He still couldn't see how that would have contaminated the fuel.

Hansbrough took the leftover beads and the remaining jet fuel and put them in a solid metal container in the lab in the basement of his home. For his own mental well-being, he had to know if the beads he had developed could have played a role in causing the crash.

An hour later, he looked at the container and saw that the beads had dissolved, leaving the silicone type jelly that was contained in the beads. It was when he attempted to drain the fuel into another container, so he could safely throw it away, that he finally understood what had happened.

The silicone jelly did not contaminate the fuel, but it prevented it from going anywhere. There was a small hole in the bottom of the container, like the capped drain on the bottom of a cooler. When you unscrew the cap, the water flows out of the drain. But as Hansbrough opened the drain, the fuel did not come out. The silicone had covered the drain, and blocked the fuel from spilling out.

Hansbrough felt sick. He knew why the NTSB investigation had failed to reveal the cause of the crash. When the silicone dissolved, it not only had leaked into the fuel pumps, causing them to clog, it had covered the opening where the hose connected to the tank, carrying the fuel from the tank to the engine. When no fuel was able to get to the engine, the engines had stalled out. That's why the plane had crashed.

The fuel gauges would not have revealed the problem, because the plane still had plenty of fuel. It just was blocked from moving from the tanks to the engines. There was no way to test the fuel that had been left in the tanks because it had all burned in the fire after the crash.

Hansbrough also knew that even if the investigators had found the silicone gel in the fuel tanks, they would not have suspected it as the cause of the contamination. The fuel wasn't really contaminated – it had just been blocked from moving to the engines.

Somehow, and Hansbrough suspected Vitello had paid some- body like he had paid him, the canister of beads that Hansbrough had given Tony had been dumped into the fuel tank before the plane left Chicago. When they dissolved to the point that no fuel could get to the engines, the plane crashed. It was pretty simple, and actually was a brilliant plan.

As he sat on the couch in his family room, convinced that he was right, two questions competed for space in Hansbrough's brain. The first was why would Tony want the plane to crash, and even if he could come up with the answer to that question, then why would he want the plane to crash when he was on it? The second, and more important to him, was what should he do with the information that he was certain was correct?

He couldn't go to the NTSB or the police, unless he wanted to go to jail as an accomplice to murder. If he was correct, the crash was no accident. The only other person he could implicate was Tony, and he was dead, so nothing else could happen to him.

Hansbrough considered his options. He could say and do nothing, which was the immediate favorite. Telling anybody what had happened would require him to confess his role in the plot. He wasn't certain he could do that. Yet he also wasn't certain he could live with the guilt knowing what he had done had caused the deaths of so many innocent people.

Since he had already committed a crime, another choice was to see how much his information might be worth, or to see how much somebody – like Tony's son, T.J. Vitello, would pay to keep him quiet. He had never met T.J. but he had been reading about him in the newspaper and watching him on the interview shows. He knew it would be disastrous publicity for T.J. and the Cubs if Hansbrough were to go public with his information right as the Cubs were on the verge of reaching the World Series.

That was the other factor involved – Hansbrough's love for the Cubs. The last thing he wanted to do was say or do something that would impact the Cubs' chances of winning the World Series for the first time in his lifetime.

He wished there was somebody he could trust, somebody he could talk to, but he was alone. His wife had died in a car accident eight years ago. The couple had never had children. The students that he taught at the university had been his children, but he was semi-retired, teaching only one class a semester, and there was nobody there in whom he could confide.

The more he thought about it, the more he decided the person it made the most sense to talk to was T.J. He knew T.J. would not want to implicate his father by revealing Tony's involvement in the crash, even if nobody knew why he would plan it when he was on the plane. Maybe T.J. already knew something about what happened. Maybe he would know why his dad wanted the plane to crash.

If T.J. didn't know any more about it, maybe Hansbrough could convince him the information was worth some money. He didn't have to tell T.J. that his dad had paid him to make the beads. He could simply say he had figured out the cause of the crash. No, he realized, that wouldn't work. T.J. would tell him to go to the cops, unless he knew that his dad was involved.

Hansbrough realized he had to tell T.J. the truth, what Tony had asked him to do, and how he had done it. If his reason for not remaining quiet was to clear his conscience, he couldn't go around telling more lies and trying to bribe people. Telling T.J. was the right thing to do.

The problem came with trying to convince T.J. why he needed to see him. "Hi, T.J. I was a friend of your dad's, and I know why the plane crashed." T.J. would dismiss him as a fruitcake. He needed a better plan.

He knew T.J. was very busy, considering the Cubs and Cardinals were playing game seven of the NLCS at 7 o'clock tonight. Now that he was convinced he was right, however, Hansbrough did not want to sit on this information for long. He needed to tell T.J., and he wanted to do it today.

He got out the phone book, found the number for the Cubs' main office and, after letting out a deep breath, dialed the number. He was on hold for several minutes, as he expected, before the switchboard operator answered.

"Mr. Vitello's office, please," he said.

"One moment please."

After two rings, another woman answered.

"Mr. Vitello's office."

"Hi, my name is Milton Hansbrough. I was a friend of Mr. Vitello's father, and I was wondering if he might have a few minutes in his schedule today that I could see him. I have a very important matter to discuss with him that concerns his father."

Hansbrough was going to continue, apologizing for calling on a day like today, but the secretary interrupted him.

"I'm afraid he is completely booked for today, Mr. Hansbrough, and I really can't set up any future appointments until we know whether we are going to be playing in the World Series or not. Are you sure this matter concerns Mr. Vitello, and that you need to talk to him about it?"

"Yes, I am, and I really do. I know his time is very limited, but this information has just come to my attention today and I need to pass it on to him. I'm sorry I can't be more descriptive on the phone, but if he could just give me 10 minutes today I am sure he would believe it was worth his time."

Nikki could tell she was not going to get rid of Hansbrough easily. She asked him to hold on, then went into T.J.'s office. He really wasn't as busy as she had said he was, but she knew how he felt about talking with people he didn't know.

"Sorry to bother you T.J., but there is a man on the phone who says he was a friend of your father. His name is Milton Hansbrough, and he says he has some information concerning your father that he wants to talk to you about. He wants to come in and see you this afternoon."

"This afternoon? On game seven of the playoffs? Is he serious? What is it about, did he say? And why can't it wait for a couple of weeks?"

"Those were all questions I tried to ask him, but he was insistent. I did look at your schedule, and it looks open for an hour or so right after lunch. Maybe if we let him come down and see you, you can get it over with and not have to worry about it when the Series is going on."

"Yeah, you're probably right. If he isn't going to go away, it would be better to see what he wants and get it over with rather than have him continuing to bug us. Did he say how he knew my dad or tell you what this was about? I hope he isn't going to say my dad owed him money. If he did, he sure waited a long time to show up.

"Tell him I can squeeze him in for about 10 minutes around 1:30, but that's all."

Nikki returned to her desk and relayed that information to a happy Milton Hansbrough. He thanked her and promised he would be on time.

Even though they didn't speak about it, both Nikki and T.J. thought about the mysterious call from Milton Hansbrough. The voice did not sound familiar to Nikki, but she could not be sure if he had been one of the strange callers who kept bugging her in the days immediately after the plane crash.

T.J. searched his memory to see if he could place Milton Hansbrough's name. He came up empty. If he had been a friend of his dad's, he could never remember his dad mentioning him and he could never remember him coming to the house for dinner or anything. No, he simply would have to wait until he met Mr. Hansbrough to find out what was going on.

Hansbrough arrived at the Cubs' main office about 1:25 p.m., and the receptionist took his information and relayed it to Nikki. She checked with T.J., who said he was ready for the meeting. She walked out to the lobby to escort Hansbrough to T.J.'s office.

"Mr. Hansbrough? Nikki Williamson. T.J. is ready for your meeting, if you will please come with me?"

Hansbrough was tall and trim. He had short white hair and wore black glasses. He was wearing a white shirt and checkered tie and dark gray trousers and black shoes.

"Are you going to the game tonight?" she asked.

"Yes, I'm going home to change and coming back for the game. I wouldn't miss it for the world. I hope tonight is the night."

"We all do," Nikki said as they reached her office.

She knocked on T.J.'s door, and when he said, "come in," she opened it and had Hansbrough follow her. "T.J., this is Milton Hansbrough. Mr. Hansbrough, T.J. Vitello."

The two men shook hands as Nikki left and closed the door behind her.

"How about having a seat on the couch, Mr. Hansbrough, and tell me how I can help. You said you were a friend of my father's, I believe, and wanted to discuss a matter that concerned him."

"That's correct, and I really appreciate you seeing me on such an important day. I will get directly to the point."

By the time Hansbrough had filled in T.J. about how he had first become friends with Tony, and about everything he knew about making the beads, except how much money Tony had paid him, T.J. was visibly upset. He was almost shaking. He had stood up and was walking around in circles, making Hansbrough repeat pieces of the information he had revealed.

"And you're sure of this?" T.J. said.

"Yes, I am sure. The only things I can't figure out, as I told you, was why Tony would want to intentionally make the plane crash, and why he would do it when he was on board."

"I agree with you on that," T.J. said. "I think my dad is the only one who knows those answers, and we aren't going to get that information from him."

"You can see why I didn't want to take this information to the police or the NTSB," Hansbrough said. "I would go to jail as an accomplice to a murder. I liked your dad. He was good to me. Without his help in getting me the teaching job I don't know what I would have done. This was the first favor he asked me to return, and I just didn't think I could say no. I wish I had asked him more about what he wanted the beads for, but that was one of the conditions he set on our agreement – I couldn't ask any questions.

"The last thing I want to do is ruin your dad's image and reputation. I believe I am the only person who knows what happened, even though there are things I don't know, either. I don't know how the beads ended up in the fuel tanks, but I assume your dad found somebody to put them there. The plane crash was not an accident, and I just couldn't live with myself if I kept silent, knowing I played a role in killing those innocent people."

"Other than trying to clear your conscience, why are you telling me this?" T.J. asked. "Do you want more money to keep quiet?"

"No," Hansbrough said, shaking his head. "I just had to tell somebody what happened and you were the only logical person I could think of."

T.J. was silent for a minute.

"I can understand why you feel that way, and I sincerely thank you for coming down here and telling me everything," T.J. said. "Let me do this. Give me your phone number, and knowing what I know now, let me see if I can solve any other pieces of this puzzle. I promise if I figure something more out, you will be the first person I call."

"Thanks, T.J., I'm really glad you are taking this so well. I didn't know how you would react, because I have no idea what I would think or do if I were in your shoes. The only other thing I can tell you is that I'm sorry, I'm so sorry."

Chapter 24

After Hansbrough left the office, T.J. walked to his desk, sat down in the black leather chair, and buried his face in his hands.

He couldn't believe his dad was responsible for the plane crash, that it was not an accident. Even if Tony had wanted the plane to crash for some un-Godly reason, what could the reason possibly be? And why would he want to kill himself at the same time? It made no sense.

"I've got to think," T.J. said. "There have got to be answers, and I've got to find them. I've got to piece this thing together."

He had just closed his eyes and leaned back in his chair when there was a knock on the door. As he sat up in his chair and started to speak, the door opened and in walked his mother, Katherine.

T.J. knew she had not been at the ball park since his dad had died, and he could count on one hand the times she had been there in the previous five years. What she was doing here now, of all days?

"Mom, what a surprise, why didn't you tell me you were coming?" T.J. said as he came out around the desk and gave her a peck on the cheek. "Don't tell me you're caught up in Cub fever and had to come watch the game, too?"

Katherine smiled, "No, you know I don't know anything about baseball and really don't know anything about what's going on. All I know is that Senator Durbin's secretary phoned this morning and said the Senator was hosting a big reception here tonight before the game and that he would be honored if I would attend. I don't like to say no to a Senator, you know."

Now T.J. understood why she was here, but he really hoped she was not expecting him to entertain her until the party began upstairs. He was certainly in no mood for happy talk, especially saddled with the news he had just received from Dr. Hansbrough.

"So why did you get here so early?" he said. "Are you meeting somebody else before the party?"

"No, I just wanted to avoid the traffic, and I wanted to spend a couple of minutes with you. Even though I don't follow baseball, I know enough from what my friends and their husbands have told me to know that you have done a wonderful job. I am really proud of you, and I know your father would be very proud of you."

T.J. didn't know how to react. She had no idea what her late husband had planned before he died, and she had no idea what her son was going through trying to decide what to do with that information. "She knows nothing about either of us," T.J. thought.

He mumbled, "Thanks."

"Mom, I hope you don't mind, but I didn't know you were coming and I've got some things I need to do before the game, so I am going to need to get going. You are welcome to stay here until you go upstairs. I'm going to stop by the party, so I will see you up there."

He gave her another peck on the cheek, then left the office, heading down the hallway, looking for a place he could sit and think in private.

Everywhere he went, however, he found people waiting to shake his hand and congratulate him and wish him luck in the game, as if he were in the starting lineup. T.J. knew, of course, why everyone was so excited. A win would accomplish the almost unthinkable, putting the Cubs into the World Series.

Later, when he finally reached the party, Hansbrough's visit and his message had been moved to the back of T.J.'s mind. He had another mission now: to impress his new-found political friends and all of the big business honchos who wanted to make sure they were included on the A list of invitees for the World Series parties. They wanted the power of saying they were friends with the Cubs' owner just as badly as T.J. wanted the satisfaction of having them suck up to him. It was a win-win situation for all involved.

There wouldn't really be time to think about the implications of what Dr. Hansbrough had said for a while longer, if the Cubs won. Because this series had gone the full seven games, there would be only one day off before the opening game of the World Series. Since the Commissioner had canceled the All-Star game after the accident, home field advantage for the Series had been decided by a coin flip, and the NL had won.

Between the parties, hosting the dignitaries who came in for the Series, and actually watching the games, T.J. knew this was one problem that would just have to wait. After all, it wasn't going anywhere and nothing was going to change what had happened. He was convinced Hansbrough wasn't going to go to the NTSB or the cops, or to the media, or he would not have come to him. T.J. would deal with it when the Cubs' season was over, hopefully after the World Championship parade down Michigan Avenue.

T.J. was leading the cheers as the Cubs finished off the Cardinals to win the pennant, and then made his way to the victorious locker room to accept the championship trophy. So much had happened in the last four months, he still was having trouble digesting it all. It didn't seem real, but he knew he was not dreaming.

T.J. made the rounds in the clubhouse, congratulating the players and coaches, accommodating the photographers and other media, and joining in the spraying of champagne.

Kevin Andrews stood in the corner, trying to avoid getting sprayed, but trying to take in the whole scene. Before the crash, he could have imagined he would be in this position. After the plane went down, however, he would have bet everything he owned that there was no way the Cubs would be playing in the World Series.

He felt happy for the players, who had worked their butts off in an incredibly difficult situation. They were partying harder than any locker room celebration Kevin had ever seen, and rightfully so. Their only allegiance to those who had died in July was that they were wearing the same uniforms. They never asked to be put in this position, but once they were, they had done more than anybody could have imagined.

Kevin also was happy for Mike Callan. He really thought Callan had gotten a raw deal when he was fired as the Triple A manager and then couldn't get a job in pro ball for 13 years. He had proved over the last four months that he was the equal of every other major league manager, and better than most. He was the best Kevin had seen at any level, including all of the managers he had played for, in communicating with his players. He was not the only one to notice how Mike was crying like a baby during the celebration and how the players, to a man, made it a point to come by where he was standing and exchange heartfelt hugs. You could tell how deeply they cared about a man they not only had never met, but had never heard of, only four months ago.

As he watched T.J., the emotion Kevin felt was different. It was hard to describe, Kevin told Nikki later that night. He felt sorry for him, because he had suffered the most personal loss from the crash of anybody in the room. His father had been killed. Yet Kevin, not only tonight but almost from the first time he met T.J., had never seen him display any sign of sadness. He still found that strange, even knowing what he knew about the relationship between T.J. and his father.

Kevin had liked T.J. initially, but – based on what he had heard about him from the players and from Nikki – had formed a different opinion over the past month. That was another reason he felt sorry for him. He knew other people who had changed when they suddenly became rich or famous, or both, and he thought that was what had happened to T.J. Kevin could tell he was enjoying his moment in the spotlight too much, and for what Kevin thought were the wrong reasons.

He returned to the press box to write his game story and locker room sidebar, stories he knew would be read by all of Chicago the next day and by Cubs' fans around the world, thanks to the Internet. These were newspapers that would be saved and passed down to the next generation of Cubs' fans, not used to line the kitty litter box the next day, where his stories often ended up.

The Cubs were in the World Series. He had to keep repeating it to himself to make it seem real.

The entire city, or so it seemed, was swept up in World Series fever. People Kevin hardly knew were calling, asking for advice about how to get tickets, a question he was unable to answer.

Not only was this the first time the Cubs had been in the World Series in 65 years, but it was only the second World Series in Chicago since 1959, when the "Go-Go" White Sox won the American League pennant but lost the Series to the Dodgers. The White Sox made it back to the Series, and won it, in 2005, but there still was a large percentage of Chicago residents that really didn't care. Normally, the White Sox fans and the Cubs fans wanted nothing to do with each other and that had been the case again that season. But everyone in Chicago was now a fan of the Cubs.

All the talk on the radio shows, and in offices and stores throughout the area, was how the Cubs had finally ended the curse. Kevin knew that wasn't the way the Cubs felt – he had heard Mike Callan's emotional remarks in the locker room last night that the curse would not be lifted until the Cubs won the World Series. That was what Kevin wrote as his main story previewing the opening game against the Yankees.

The only player Kevin had really talked with about the curse was Billy Slagle. Kevin didn't believe in a curse, just as he didn't think there had been a curse against the Red Sox. They simply had experienced bad luck, or good pitching, when they had had chances in the past to win the World Series. Slagle didn't believe in the curse, either, and he said he was going to try to pass some more knowledge onto the players at some point during the Series.

"People talk about the curse, but you know the Cubs had never won a World Series at Wrigley even before Sianis supposedly put the curse on the team in 1945," Slagle said.

Kevin was reluctant to admit that he didn't know that, so he merely nodded at Slagle to continue.

"Wrigley Field wasn't built until 1914. A man named Charles Weeghman built it for $250,000 to be the home park for a team he was forming in the Federal League, the Chicago Whales. Not surprisingly, he called it Weeghman Park. I'll bet you didn't know the site he picked out, where the park still stands, had been occupied by the Chicago Lutheran Theological Seminary."

Kevin looked up. "That means … "

"Yep, the park was built on hallowed ground that had absolutely nothing to do with baseball.

"Anyway, the Whales played here for two years before the Federal League folded. Weeghman still loved baseball, so he bought the Cubs and moved the team here. The Cubs have been in Wrigley since 1916. He finally sold the team to the Wrigley family in 1920 and the name was changed to Cubs Park. It didn't become Wrigley Field until 1926."

"So when the Cubs won the series in 1908, where did they play?" Kevin asked.

"At a place called West Side Grounds, which of course is no longer there. It was on the corner of Polk and Lincoln streets. Lincoln has since changed its name to Wolcott. I went by there a few weeks ago because I was curious about it. The Illinois State Hospital and Medical School is now at that site."

"What do you know about that park?"

"I know I wouldn't have wanted to play center field there, I can tell you that. It was 560 feet to the fence."

"560 feet? You're kidding me."

"No, I can't imagine my great-great grandpa Jimmy having to run all that way. Of course, I doubt many balls ever went over his head. He could have been playing 400 feet deep and it still would have looked like he was playing shallow."

"Was the rest of the outfield that deep?"

"No, left field was 340 down the line, and right field 316. I've seen pictures, it was a strange looking place."

"Sounds like it."

"It was while the team was playing there that it became known as the Cubs, you know."

"They weren't always the Cubs?"

"No, they had a lot of different names in the late 1800s. When Cap Anson managed the team it was known as the Colts, but when he left they were nicknamed the Orphans for a couple of years, referring to Anson not being there. A sportswriter for the *Chicago Daily News* started calling them the Cubs around 1900 because so many players were very young. The name stuck, and was officially adopted as the nickname in 1907."

"You are amazing," Kevin said.

"If I only knew this much about stuff that really mattered I might agree with you," Slagle said. "All my family bugged me for years about trying out for *Jeopardy!* or *Who Wants to be a Millionaire,* but I knew I would embarrass myself because they would ask questions about art or Shakespeare or something and I would be totally lost.

"I know I got into this because of my great-great grandfather, but it really interested me. Look at this."

Slagle reached in his locker and pulled out a microfilm copy of an old newspaper.

"This is the front page of the *Chicago Daily News* the day after the first game of the 1906 World Series between the Cubs and White Sox. I don't know why you can't write like that."

The headline read in part, "Partisan Feeling Runs High in Vast Throng of Exultant Fans, Whose Heated Arguments Counter Icy Blasts at West Side Park."

"If I wrote something like that I would be busted back to copyboy," Kevin said.

"Yeah, I know, times are different," Slagle said. "I think the most interesting thing is that the Cubs have never won a World Series at Wrigley. I hope that changes in the next week."

※

Mike Callan did not believe he needed to make any big speeches before the Series opener. He had gone over the scouting reports with the team, and he believed the pitchers and his catcher, Luis Roman, understood the strategy they wanted to use against the Yankee hitters. McGair had been a big help, filling in gaps in the reports with his personal knowledge of the New York players who were still on the team from his days as a Yankee.

The only thing that worried Callan was the possibility of a letdown, because he knew it had happened on other teams. Teams worked so hard just to get to the World Series that when they finally got there, they relaxed, whether intentionally or unintentionally, and then were not able to turn it back on in time to win the Series.

He had tried to guard against that, counting on all of the curse talk, and he had heard part of Billy Slagle's lecture to the team about how they could be the first Cubs team to win the World Series at Wrigley. Callan hoped that, along with the players' own motivation, would be enough to help them win four more games.

Callan had never been the type of person who worried about the future or things he couldn't control. He knew in his heart that was one of the reasons he hadn't gone crazy when he couldn't get a job in pro ball for all those years and had settled into the teaching and coaching job in Mound City. It was also why he was at peace his own mind, no matter what happened. He had slept well last night and felt relaxed as he watched his team complete the pre-game warm-ups.

Callan had never heard a louder ovation in his life than when he ran out and shook hands with Joe Girardi, the Yankees' manager, as the starting lineups were introduced. He had goose bumps and chills, and he knew his players must have the same butterflies. He honestly was glad he didn't have to swing a bat or throw a ball because he didn't know if he could do it.

The Yankees, of course, had much more October experience than anybody on the Cubs so it wasn't surprising they jumped out to a 3-0 lead in the third inning. Callan was disappointed the Cubs didn't mount any serious threats and they dropped the opener, 4-1.

Still, he considered it a good day because now the jitters and butterflies should be out of the way and the team could come out relaxed for the second game. Callan didn't believe in so-called "must win" games, unless your team was facing elimination, but he knew in his heart the Cubs had to win the second game if they were going to have a realistic chance of winning the Series.

The game was tied in the eighth, when McGair came back to haunt his former team with a solo homer into the bleachers in left. Tippett retired the side in order in the ninth, and the Cubs had the win that tied the series at one game each.

The Series now shifted to Yankee Stadium in the Bronx. Even though the team had moved to a new stadium in 2009, Monument Park still stood as a tribute to all of the late Yankee greats.

Callan stood in Monument Park, almost reverently, as he paid tribute to Babe Ruth, Lou Gehrig, Joe DiMaggio, and the other honored Yankees. When he heard a noise behind him, he turned around and was not surprised to see Slagle standing there.

"This place is almost creepy," Slagle said.

"Why do you say that?"

"Because it seems like there are a lot of ghosts around, all of these dead players."

"These guys aren't really buried here, you know. These stones are just tributes to them," Callan said.

"I know that, but still you think about all of them and it almost seems like they come alive. Everybody knows so much about them, and about Yankee Stadium."

"Well, the only thing I don't want to see the next three days are the current Yankees jumping up and down on the field. We've got to get this series back to Wrigley."

"We will, Skip. Don't worry."

Callan was a little worried when the Yankees won the third game, 6-4. They had beaten his best pitcher, Steve Watson, and now led the series two games to one. He had barely sat down the next night, however, when Slagle came to bat with one out in the top of the first and lofted a ball that just reached the stands in left for a home run to put the Cubs ahead.

The homer ignited a four-run inning, and Callan relaxed as the Cubs coasted to a 9-3 win. Slagle followed his homer with two more hits, including a two-run double.

Callan now knew that no matter what happened in the fifth game, the series would be going back to Wrigley.

The fifth game was the best played of the series so far, and the game was tied after nine innings. Neither team scored in the 10th, and the Cubs got a runner to second in the top of the 11th before McGair grounded out to end the threat. A hit, a stolen base, and a bunt put the winning run on third in the bottom of the inning, and Derek Jeter came through with a fly ball to center that was deep enough to score the winning run and give the Yankees the victory and the series edge, three games to two.

The plane flight back to Chicago was quiet, as Callan expected, but it was far from somber. The players were tired, as they had a right to be. Callan only needed them to play two more games, and he had the confidence that they could win those games. If they could win game six, with Dave Cochran on the mound, Watson would be ready for game seven, and Callan knew Watson would not let him down.

As Callan tried to catch a nap, he noticed T.J. a couple of rows in front of him on the charter flight. T.J. had been mysteriously absent from the locker room and the field so far during this series, and for that Callan was grateful. He was still having a difficult time coming to grips with his feelings for T.J. and how their relationship had changed since July.

Callan had thought about it a lot, and had come to the conclusion that it was T.J. who had changed, not himself. He knew he could not be 100 percent objective, but he tried to look at it as honestly as he could. "If it is me who has changed, I need to know why," Callan had told himself.

In his conversations with others in the front office, and with Kevin Andrews and other reporters, Callan learned he was not the only one who thought that way about T.J., which helped convince him that he was right.

As Callan looked at T.J. now, he saw that he was on the phone. Many of the airlines had dropped the plane phones in the last couple of years because nobody used them anymore. The novelty had worn off, and the calls were expensive. But T.J. was definitely talking on the phone, sitting alone in his row, and it looked and sounded to Callan like he was getting upset.

Callan glanced at his watch – 2:45 a.m. eastern time, which meant it was 1:45 a.m. Chicago time. There must be something awfully important going on for T.J. to be on the phone at this hour of the night. Callan didn't want to seem obvious, but he was curious, so he unbuckled his seat belt and leaned forward, trying to hear what T.J. was talking about. T.J. was adamant about whatever it was he was saying.

Callan couldn't hear everything, but he heard words and phrases. He thought he heard the words "insurance" and "settlement" but he couldn't hear enough to figure out what was going on or who T.J. might be talking to.

About 10 minutes later, T.J. hung up the phone and stood up. He started down the aisle past Callan, no doubt heading for the bathroom. Callan couldn't help but notice that the color had drained out of T.J.'s face. It looked for all the world like he was going to throw up, even before he made it to the bathroom.

"T.J., are you all right? Do you need some help?" Callan said as he started to stand up and reach his arm out to steady T.J.

"I'm, OK, really, I must have just eaten something at the post-game party that didn't agree with me. As soon as I go to the bathroom and splash some water on my face I will be fine."

By this time one of the flight attendants had come forward and was offering her assistance. The two of them helped T.J. make it to the bathroom, waited, and then helped him back to his seat.

"Are you sure you're OK?" Callan said.

Somebody had awakened the trainer, and he joined the group by T.J.'s seat.

He took T.J.'s pulse and blood pressure, but didn't indicate that either was a cause for concern.

One of the flight attendants had soaked a towel in cold water, and the trainer placed it on T.J.'s forehead. He loosened T.J.'s tie, and opened his shirt collar, Callan was worried for T.J., but he also was worried that he might be coming down with the flu or something. He really didn't need his team being exposed to that with two games left in the season.

As Callan stood in the aisle, watching T.J., he noticed a notebook lying open on the empty seat next to him. He had always had great eyesight, and working 13 years as a high school teacher had enabled him to read upside down and from a distance away. He saw T.J. had written down a bunch of numbers. The largest number, and it had been circled at the bottom of the page, was $382M.

What the hell did that mean?

Callan thought whatever that number meant it had something to do with T.J. suddenly becoming ill. He had seemed fine on the bus to the airport, and for the first 15 minutes of the flight, until he got on the phone. Callan wished T.J. had used his cell phone, because he could easily check the call log to see who T.J. had called. He couldn't get that kind of record from the air phone.

He finally went back and sat down in his seat, and took out a pad from his briefcase and wrote down the number – $382M. All he had to do was figure out who T.J. had called and what that number meant.

By the time the plane landed at O'Hare, some of the color had returned to T.J.'s face. He was able to walk off the plane without assistance, and insisted he was OK to drive himself home. Callan wasn't so sure about that, but there was nothing he could do.

※

The cool breeze as he stepped off the plane hit T.J. and helped bring him around. He reset his watch to central time, 3:35 a.m., as he got in his car. Instead of going home, however, he headed straight to Wrigley. There was no way he could go to sleep, not knowing what he had found out while on the plane.

The security guard was dozing as T.J. pulled the blue Mercedes S65 into the team's parking lot. The car was only a week old, T.J.'s gift to himself for the team winning the pennant. He didn't mind that the $169,720 check was the largest check he had ever written in his life. This car was worth it, and he could afford it. Because it was so new, the guard didn't recognize the car, but he stopped as soon as he recognized T.J.

"Good evening, Mr. Vitello. Tough game last night. Guess you couldn't sleep, huh?"

"Yeah, it was tough. I napped a little on the plane, but just decided to go ahead and come on over here. I may snooze a little more on the couch. Quiet night, isn't it?"

"Yes, sir, nothing going on," the guard said as T.J. entered the office and the guard returned to his post.

T.J. flipped on the hall light so he could see his way to his office, then opened the outer door and closed and locked it. He went into his office, turned on the light, locked that door as well, and finally dropped his briefcase on the floor and sat down at his desk.

"Well, Dad, I don't know everything, but I know the basics of what you were doing, you old son of a bitch," T.J. said out loud.

He took his pen and a piece of paper and again wrote down the numbers Phil Donnelly had told him over the phone while he was on the plane. Donnelly had called before the game yesterday saying he had an urgent matter to discuss, and for him to call when he could, no matter how late. T.J. had not had a chance to return the call until he was on the plane.

Donnelly had called to tell T.J. that he had received a phone call that afternoon from the club's insurance provider, Illinois General. Donnelly reminded T.J. that the club had taken out insurance policies to cover the costs of the contracts in the event a player was killed or injured to the extent that he couldn't play.

Yes, T.J. said, he remembered that. What was so important about that now?

Well, the team's agent had called to let him know that since the NTSB had now officially ruled that the cause of the plane crash could not be determined for certain, the company was ready to discuss the settlement of the policies the team carried.

Donnelly said he had no knowledge that there were any other policies, but the agent just laughed. "Mr. Vitello, I guess because of his years as a defense lawyer, insisted on handling these policies personally," the agent said. "We just signed the documents back in February."

It was that information that Donnelly had shared with T.J. during the phone call from the plane. The numbers were staggering:

In addition to the insurance covering the costs for the remaining money due the players under their existing contracts, Vitello had taken out a policy "to protect the value of the franchise." What that meant, the agent told Donnelly, who relayed the information to T.J., was that he had added extra protection to the policy covering the costs of the contracts. If a player was killed, for example, the policy not only paid off the remainder of the contract, but an additional payment was due to the club.

The total of that "extra protection," added up to $150 million.

In addition, Vitello had taken out what the agent called "catastrophic plan" coverage. What that meant was that if seven or more players were killed in a common accident, the coverage would pay the team $5 million per player. There was an additional payment due the club of $1 million for each of the other 22 people who were killed in the crash. The total payout on that policy was going to be $132 million.

If T.J. had been standing, he would have been staggered by the news. It was a good thing he was sitting, although he still felt lightheaded.

"There's more," Donnelly had said.

Because the Cubs owned their own plane, they also had $100 million of insurance coverage in the event of an accidental plane crash. That protection also had been in place whenever another team or college had flown on the Cubs' plane, the agent said, and was required by the federal government of all charter and commercial airline providers.

The total amount of insurance coverage due the Cubs was $382 million.

T.J. was staggered by the figure, as was Donnelly.

"I had no idea your dad had taken out that kind of coverage on the team," Donnelly had said. "He never said a word to me about it. All I knew about was the insurance to cover the costs of the contracts, which we had been doing for years. I remember him bitching to me about it the past couple of years, about how he didn't think that was necessary and not wanting to pay the premium, but I told him we had to have it. He finally agreed. I don't know why he took out all of these other policies, but your club is suddenly worth a lot more money."

As T.J. sat at the desk in the middle of the night, he knew what Donnelly didn't know. He still had some questions in his mind, but he also had a lot of answers.

In the locker room before game six, Callan could sense his team was on edge. This was only the second time since they had come together that the Cubs faced a game where they either won or they would be going home, the first having come in game seven against the Cardinals.

Callan had a hard time with the idea that the season might be over in a matter of hours. It had seemed so far off he hadn't given any thought to what he would do, whether he would stay in Chicago or go back home. He had nothing he had to do, he had a contract for next year, so he had no worries or concerns of any kind. It was the first time in his life that he found himself in that position.

Still, Callan didn't want to be in that position just yet. After tomorrow, he could deal with it, but right now his attention was focused on getting this series to a game seven.

The crowd was on edge, as Callan expected, and the emotions of both teams were running high. Callan had always respected Girardi as a manager, from a distance, but having the chance to watch him during this series from the opposing dugout gave him a new perspective. How could he sit there and act so calm? He looked as if he were watching high school kids during a regular-season game.

Indeed, Callan had been in that exact position only months earlier and he had seen a lot of managers get a lot more worked up at that level than Girardi was now.

His respect for Girardi didn't change the fact that Callan wanted to beat him, especially tonight. The Cubs broke out to a 2-0 lead in the third, only to see the Yankees tie it in the fourth. Both teams added a run in the sixth, and the game was tied going into the seventh.

The seventh inning always was an exciting time at Wrigley, dating back to when Harry Caray got the fans excited by leading them in "Take Me Out to the Ballgame" during the seventh inning stretch. When Caray died, the Cubs continued the tradition by having a guest conductor lead the song. Some of the people who did it were very good, even professional singers, but others, especially the politicians and coaches from other sports, were downright awful. The worst, Callan had been told, was "singer" Ozzy Osbourne's attempt to "sing" the song in 2004. Osbourne had mumbled a lot more than he sang.

During the playoffs and World Series, the Cubs had used former players to lead the crowd, including some of the team's all-time greats like Banks, Williams, Santo, and Sandberg. Tonight, however, was a surprise. Only Tim Jenkins knew who the guest conductor was going to be, which was why, as the teams traded places in the middle of the inning, every face was looking up to the WGN broadcast booth.

Callan saw two young looking men, wearing Cubs' hats, but he didn't immediately recognize them. They both looked too young to be retired. The crowd, already on its feet, was going wild, cheering as if the Cubs had already won the World Series.

Wayne Messmer's voice came through the loudspeakers. "And now, to lead us in 'Take Me Out to the Ballgame,' please welcome back to Wrigley Field, Bobby Scott and Sam Johnson."

"I'll be damned," Callan said.

As soon as they started to sing, Callan recognized Scott's voice from their phone conversation a few weeks earlier. He had never met the man, however, and stood with the rest of the crowd watching Scott and Johnson belt out the song.

When it was over, Callan picked up the dugout phone and called Jenkins in the press box.

"Tim, if we win this game, I would like for you to bring Scott down to my office if you can. I would like to talk to him," he said.

"Sure, Skip, I'm sure that won't be a problem. I think Bobby would like that, and we all know none of us is going anywhere fast after this game. The traffic is going to be awful."

"Well, we need to go win this thing first," Callan said. "I would like to meet Sam, too, if he wants to come."

Callan had just hung up the phone when the crowd erupted again as Chico Gonzalez smacked a fastball into leftfield for a leadoff single.

As Slagle came to the plate, Callan was faced with the same decision from game seven of the series against the Cardinals. Conventional wisdom called for Slagle to bunt, but then he knew the Yankees would walk McGair, hitting third against the left-hander, to set up the double play and bring Jim Baker to the plate.

He had gambled in that game that Slagle would not hit into a double play and it had worked out. Slagle had gotten a hit, Baker had walked, and McGair had hit a grand slam.

Not that he didn't think a similar thing might happen this time, but Callan signaled the third base coach, Alex Thompson, to give Slagle the bunt sign. Slagle gave the return sign, indicating he had the sign, and then stepped in the batter's box.

One of Callan's strengths, at least in his own mind, was that once he made a decision in a game, he never second-guessed himself. If it didn't work out, a lot of others second-guessed him, but if he knew he had made the right decision, he never questioned himself. He knew, of course, that if this move backfired he would never hear the end of it, but he thought it was the right decision.

Slagle took the first pitch high for ball one. The Yankees were expecting the bunt. Callan thought for a second about switching off, but didn't. He flashed the bunt sign again.

The pitch, a curveball, came in belt high before beginning its drop toward the ground. Slagle timed the break just right and dropped down a perfect bunt between the charging first baseman and the pitcher. The only play was to first.

The boos started almost as soon as McGair stepped in to hit and Yankees catcher Jorge Posada stepped to his right, holding his glove out, signaling for the intentional walk. Callan knew that was going to happen. As long as Baker came through, everything would be fine.

After the fourth intentional ball, McGair trotted toward first and Girardi came out of the dugout to have a word with his pitcher. Two relievers were warming up in the bullpen, but Girardi elected to stay with his starter.

Baker was glad Callan had shown confidence in him by having Slagle bunt, knowing the Yankees would walk McGair. He thought back to the early days in Chicago, and how Callan had made a couple of moves that had not worked out, but the players knew what he was doing. It was part of the reason the players had completely changed their opinion about Callan.

As Baker stepped in, he wanted to get a hit now more than he had ever wanted anything in his life. With Gonzalez' speed, a hit anywhere in the outfield, except a one-hopper directly to the leftfielder, would let Gonzalez score easily. Baker wanted this hit for himself, but he also wanted it for Callan.

He worked the count to 2-2 before fouling off two pitches. Finally, he got the pitch he had been waiting for. It was a fastball, just off the plate, and even though Baker thought it would be a ball, he jumped on it. The cheers started as soon as the bat made contact with the ball and it took off toward left center, headed for either the gap, or perhaps, the bleachers.

The Cubs' players on the bench leaped to the dugout steps and then came out in front of the dugout, erupting along with the frenzied crowd as the ball sailed into the bleachers for a three-run homer.

Callan had never heard a louder crowd in his life. The din continued in the eighth, as the Cubs got another run, and as Tippett came in to record the final three outs in the top of the ninth for a 7-3 Chicago win. Callan had got his wish for the day. There would be a game seven.

※

As hard as T.J. Vitello tried to concentrate on the game, he felt his mind continuing to wander, back to the phone call from Donnelly, back to the conclusions he had made about what his dad had set in motion when he had gone to visit Milton Hansbrough.

The Cubs' victory sent the whole stadium into a wild celebration, and T.J. was taken along for the ride with all of the well-wishers, business leaders, and politicians who had crammed their way into his private box. He didn't think he had ever been slapped on the back so many times in one day in his life, maybe not in his entire life added together.

"I'm only sorry your dad isn't here to enjoy this moment," one man said. "He would have been so excited. He wanted this for so long."

T.J. acknowledged the comment as gracefully as he could, and tried to get out of the box and back to the privacy and security of his office as quickly as possible.

When he reached his office, he noticed the blinking light on his private line, indicating he had a voice mail.

T.J. picked up the phone, punched in the code, listened, and literally dropped the phone on his desk.

"Hello, Mr. Vitello, this is Frankie Cusamano," he heard the caller say. "You may not know me, but I'm an old friend and associate of your father's. We did some business together."

The voice sent a chill through T.J. Maybe he was going to get an answer to one of his remaining questions.

"Your dad and I had an arrangement, and I took care of a little situation for him, let's just say. Does the name Eddie Marshall mean anything to you?"

Cusamano paused for a moment, to let the name sink in, then continued. "I doubt it, but you might want to check it out, then you will understand why I am calling. I found a little bonus in Eddie's apartment, but I think your father, God rest his soul, still under-estimated the value of my participation in this project. As his son and successor, I believe you will want to take care of this matter in a confidential and satisfactory manner. The fee for my services is now $1 million. I will contact you again tomorrow to complete the necessary arrangements.

"I know you will not want to draw extra attention to yourself, especially on such a big night for the Cubs, so let me just say this. If you make the wrong choice, and don't do exactly as I say, you won't know if the Cubs win or lose the World Series tomorrow night because you won't be there to see it. "

T.J. heard the click as the phone disconnected, and Frankie hung up. T.J. stood there, with the receiver in his hands, staring at the phone.

He replayed the message three times, each with the same, chilling result. He had jotted down the name of Eddie Marshall, but in his current confused state, the name meant nothing to him.

As he stared at the name, however, it hit him. Eddie was the name his dad had written on the Post-It note, with the beeper number. He had not included a last name. T.J. was convinced Eddie had been blackmailing his dad to buy his silence about the death of Melissa, his first wife.

How could Frankie, whoever he was, be connected to that? Why wasn't it Eddie who had called?

Frankie had said that T.J. might want to check out the name if it didn't mean anything to him. He powered up his computer and waited, then went to Google News and typed in the name "Eddie Marshall."

The computer spat out a couple of noises, then the screen changed and the search results appeared. T.J. had to scroll down no farther than the first entry. He didn't even need to go past the one-paragraph abstract of the story from the *Chicago Tribune* of Wednesday, July 7, but he clicked on it anyway to pull up the complete story.

"Local Man Killed in Break-In Attempt" was the headline, and the story detailed how Eddie Marshall, 46, was shot and killed when he apparently interrupted a robbery at his apartment in Schiller Park shortly after midnight Tuesday. T.J. kept reading, looking for how this story could possibly be connected to his dad.

It was obvious this was the Eddie Marshall that Frankie had referred to, and it was just as obvious to T.J. that Frankie had been the person who had shot him. Still, he couldn't see the relevance of how this could be connected to his father, until he reached the last paragraph of the story.

"Police said Marshall had stopped at a local nightclub after finishing his shift at Charter Air Services at O'Hare, where he worked as a fuel man, before going home. He was shot just inside the front door, where he apparently had interrupted the robbery. Police said there had been a string of break-ins in apartments in the area recently, but none of the victims had been home at the time of the incidents."

T.J.'s hands felt clammy. His heart was beating faster than it had ever beat in his life. He was worried for a moment that he was having a heart attack. Now he knew the connection, and now he knew almost everything his dad had been doing.

There had been no blackmail. This had nothing to do with Melissa's death. This was part of a master plan his father had created to pull himself out of whatever financial trouble he was in. T.J. still didn't know the depths of those problems, but he made a mental note to confront Donnelly one more time tomorrow. Donnelly might not have known everything his dad was doing, but T.J. was still convinced he knew more than he had told him. This time, he was going to demand answers.

Everything else fit. The cash withdrawals had been to pay the chemist to develop the beads that would block the fuel from getting to the plane's engine; to pay Eddie Marshall to dump the beads into the fuel tank; and to pay Frankie Cusamano to kill Eddie and make it look like a robbery, so Eddie wouldn't get cold feet and decide to go to the police.

His dad had been convinced that neither Milton Hansbrough nor Frankie Cusamano would take their information to the cops because doing so would incriminate themselves.

T.J. turned back to his computer, cleared the Google search screen, and typed in the name "Frankie Cusamano." A few seconds later, the results popped up. This time, T.J. found what he was looking for on the second page, a *Sun-Times* clip from September 1999 about the sentencing of a Chicago man, Frankie Cusamano, to 10 years in prison for attempted murder.

If he had served the complete sentence, Cusamano would have been released in September. As he read the story on the computer screen, beads of sweat rolled off T.J.'s face. His hands were shaking.

Chapter 25

T.J. didn't want to go home, but he didn't want to spend the night in his office, either. He had never been so scared in his life. He finally left the office, got in his car, and drove to his condo in Highland Park. He kept looking in his rearview mirror to see if anybody was following him. It seemed he was alone.

T.J. pulled into his parking space, locked his car, and quickly let himself in his front door. Remembering how Eddie Marshall had been shot as soon as he entered the front door, he took a couple of cautious steps as he turned on the lights in the living room. His heart was beating faster than it had during P.E. class in high school as he quickly went through his entire condo, turning on every light, cautiously opening every closet door, and even looking behind the shower curtain in the bathroom.

Finally convinced that he was alone, T.J. double-checked the locks on all of the doors and windows as he turned off some of the extra lights. His heart rate had calmed down as he walked into the kitchen and took a beer out of the refrigerator.

He sat at the kitchen table, opened the beer, and just sat in silence, not knowing what to think or do, for a good five minutes.

"OK," he finally said to himself. "I'm going to see if I can make some sense out this. I've got to figure out what I know and what I don't know, and which of those lists puts me in the most danger."

T.J. got up from the table and walked over to his desk, grabbing a yellow legal pad. He sat back down at the kitchen table and began to write.

He started with the chemist, Dr. Hansbrough. He worked through Eddie, and Frankie, and all of the cash withdrawals. For the moment, he concluded that Melissa's death, whether it was accidental or murder, was not involved in this latest activity.

He moved on to what Donnelly had told him about the extra insurance money that was due the club because of the accident. It was now obvious to T.J. that his dad had created this master plan to purposely sabotage the team's plane so it would crash. All of the extra money, $382 million, was more than enough to wipe out whatever financial problems his dad had been having.

Tony Vitello had never been a sentimental fellow, and he always liked money a lot more than baseball.

As he stared at the notes he had written, T.J. had to give his dad credit. In order to collect the insurance money, there had to be no question that the crash was an accident. If there was any suspicion by the NTSB that the plane had been sabotaged, the insurance companies would have refused to pay.

T.J. was amazed that his dad had been able to pull off this plot without any of the closest people around him knowing anything about it. Donnelly wasn't lying – he really didn't know what was going on. The only thing T.J. felt Donnelly knew, but hadn't told him, was how come his dad was losing money. He needed to know how he was losing money, and how much he had lost. Donnelly knew about the insurance money, but that was all. He would not have even known about that if Tony had not died in the crash.

The unanswered questions boiled down to two – if Tony had developed this plot to have the plane crash, then collect the insurance money, why was he also planting the idea that he might sell the team? Wouldn't the extra insurance money have been enough to solve his financial problems?

The second question, and the one that haunted T.J. the most, was this – if he was right about Tony's role in developing this plot, why had the plane crashed when Tony was onboard? The only way for Tony to benefit from this plot was if he had lived. He would not have gone to all of this illegal activity just so the money would be paid to the club. Tony would want the money.

He thought back to his conversation with Donnelly. He had known nothing about the coverage until the insurance agent had called him. The agent said Tony had worked out the coverage himself. That meant that if Tony had not died, the agent's conversation about the payout would have been with Tony. The money would have been paid to the club, and since Tony was the 100 percent owner, he could have done with it whatever he pleased, most likely immediately deposit it in his own account.

Nobody, other than the insurance company and Tony, would have known anything about it. None of the finance people with the club would have known to look for any suspicious activity, because they wouldn't have known the money was coming. If they didn't know it was there, why would they miss it?

T.J. went to the refrigerator and took out another beer.

"OK, so now what do I do?" he said as he sat back down at the kitchen table.

It seemed to T.J. that he had several choices. He listed them on the paper, not in any particular order:

He could pay Frankie the $1 million and hope he never heard from him again.

He could arrange to pay Frankie the money, then call the police, and tell them he was the victim of an extortion attempt and have the cops arrest him.

He could pay Frankie the money, call the cops and tell them everything he knew, and then have them go arrest Frankie and Dr. Hansbrough.

He stared out the window as he thought about the choices, then went to take a shower before getting dressed and heading back to the office.

It was about 10 minutes before noon when T.J.'s private line rang. He let it ring twice, then picked up the receiver.

"Mr. Vitello, it's Frankie. I trust you had a good night's sleep."

"Yeah," T.J. mumbled.

"Well I hope you have had time to make the necessary arrangements to complete the agreement I mentioned to you last night."

"Yes, everything is taken care of. Tell me what you want me to do."

"Good, very good. I was hoping you would say that. Here is what I want you to do. I want the package divided into very small items, you understand what I mean?"

"Yes."

"OK, I want you to take those items and place them in a large black backpack, the kind the college kids lug around."

"I know the type."

"I want you to keep the backpack with you at all times during the game. You don't want it falling into the wrong hands, you know."

"No, we wouldn't want that."

"In the top of the seventh inning, I want you to leave your private box and walk down to the seats behind the Cubs dugout. You must be in place before the seventh inning stretch, got it?"

"Where exactly am I going?"

"Section 213, row A, seat 1. The seat will be open. When you get there, take off the backpack and place it under the seat. As soon as 'Take Me Out to the Ballgame' is over, leave and head back to your box. Leave the backpack under the seat. Under no circumstance are you to turn around after you leave. If you do, I'm afraid our agreement will be broken, if you know what I mean.

"Also, if anybody looks as if they are watching the backpack, or if you put any kind of monitoring device on the backpack, our agreement will be broken, and you won't like the consequences. You won't have a pitcher, a catcher, or an infield anymore."

"I understand. I will be alone, and nobody will be watching."

"Good, thank you. It's been a pleasure doing business with you."

⚜

Frankie might have had the most chilling voice T.J. had ever heard. He had just threatened to kill T.J. and his pitcher, catcher, and infielders. And T.J. had no doubt that he would do exactly that.

He told Nikki that he was leaving for lunch, but instead got in his car and drove to the closest discount store, where he bought the backpack Frankie had described. Next he went to the Bank One branch and picked up the money he had requested earlier on the phone. He had spoken to a vice president he knew pretty well, using the excuse that he wanted the money in cash so he could award all of his loyal employees bonuses before the game tonight. He joked about how odd a request it was, but he liked giving people cash instead of a check. It was less work for the team's accounting folks, for one thing, and he didn't have to match the employee with the name on the check since he didn't know where all of the employees worked.

He also told the bank officer there was something special about handing an usher or a maintenance worker $100 in cash, that they didn't have to report on their taxes, and the officer knew T.J. was right. He placed the money in the two empty briefcases he had carried into the bank.

Back in the privacy of his office, T.J. transferred the money from the briefcases to the backpack and hid the backpack under his desk. He looked at the clock on the wall – 2:45 p.m., four hours and 50 minutes until game time.

⚜

In his office, Mike Callan was also looking at the clock. Nerves were getting the best of him, too, but for a much different reason.

Waiting for the game to start was always the hardest part, far more difficult than actually playing. It had been that way when he was a player, and even as a high school coach. He always found himself staring at the clock, determining how long it was until game time.

He hated road games the most. At home he always had something to do to stay busy, but on the road, it seemed like your choices were limited to sleeping, eating, watching television, or walking around the downtowns of strange cities. None of those options appealed to Mike Callan.

That was one of the reasons so many players became good at cards. They would wake up, get something to eat, and head to the ballpark, where they played cards in their underwear all afternoon. Oh, the glamorous life of a major leaguer.

Nobody was playing cards today, even though all of the players were already in the locker room, most of them in uniform. Callan looked at the clock again, knowing it was about time for his special guest to arrive.

When he talked to Bobby Scott after the game last night, he asked Scott if he would like to come to the locker room and speak to the team before tonight's game. Scott had quickly agreed. No matter what he said, Callan knew it would be far more inspirational and motivating to the players than whatever he would have said. He had asked Scott to be there at 3:30 so he could speak before the team took the field for batting practice.

The doctors had said it looked like Scott was going to make a full recovery from his injuries and should be able to join the team in time for spring training next year. Callan knew Scott had had a rough time since the crash, mentally questioning why he and Sam Johnson had been the only two players to survive. Maybe one of the reasons, Callan thought, was about to be revealed tonight in Scott's speech. Scott had told him he did think one of the reasons was evident when Johnson told him he had become a Christian since the accident.

Scott had not said anything to Callan about what he planned to say. Still, Callan was more than a bit shocked when Scott knocked on his door – wearing his complete Cubs uniform.

"Hey, Skip," he said, "I hope you don't mind me getting dressed out. It just felt like the right thing to do. I asked Jack Reynolds about it and he cleared it with the Commissioner's office. If it's OK with you, I'd like to sit on the bench tonight."

"Bobby, I'm only sorry I didn't think about it. I want you there, right next to me. You ready to talk to the team?"

"You bet."

The players who had come from the National League immediately recognized Scott when he and Callan walked out of the manager's office. Mike whistled to get everyone's attention.

"Hey, everybody, come here a minute. This won't be long, but we have a special guest who would like to say something to you. I think you all know Bobby Scott."

The applause was genuine, as were the slaps on the back and the exchange of hugs. After a few minutes, the players grew quiet and Scott began to talk.

"Guys, I can't begin to tell you how proud I am of what you have done this season, and I know I speak for all of my former teammates who have been watching you from a better place. You have paid those players the ultimate tribute with the way you have conducted yourselves, on and off the field, since you came here in July.

"I have questioned many times why I was one of only two players who was not killed in the accident. I have asked God why, and I have never received what I thought was the right answer. People have called me lucky, and said 'I guess it wasn't your time.' All I know is that God didn't want me yet. He had something else He wanted me to do, before He thought I was ready to go to Heaven.

"I think I know now at least one of the things God wanted me to do. He wanted me here, so I could be in this locker room tonight, talking to you. You guys have only been members of the Cubs since July. I played here for six years, and God willing, I will be back on the field with you next year. A lot of the players who were killed had been here a lot longer than I had. They wore this uniform with pride, they wore it with honor. It meant something to them. They never realized their dream, their goal, of winning the World Series while wearing this uniform.

"I figured it up this morning. Since the Cubs last won the World Series in 1908, 1,539 different players have worn your uniform for at least one game. You have the chance to do something tonight that none of those players accomplished. You have the chance to win the World Series.

"I want to see you guys go out there and beat the Yankees and claim that World Series not only for yourselves, not only for the city of Chicago, not only for the great Cubs fans, not only for the players who died in that plane crash in July, but for every player who has ever worn this uniform and didn't have the chance to do what you can do tonight. That's what I want you to do, and I know you can do it."

Callan smiled. He couldn't have said it better himself.

※

There is always a debate among sports fans, and the media, about what is the greatest or most dramatic game in sports. Some people believe it is the Super Bowl, a one-game showdown for the championship of the NFL. Others vote for the seventh game of hockey's Stanley Cup Finals.

But for most, the answer is the seventh game of the World Series. Since Commissioner Landis officially adopted the best-of-seven format in 1922, 33 series had gone to a seventh and deciding game.

Only three times since then had the seventh game gone into extra innings, in 1924 when the Washington Senators beat the New York Giants in 12 innings; in 1991, when the Minnesota Twins edged the Atlanta Braves in 10 innings; and in 1997, when the Florida Marlins topped the Cleveland Indians in 11 innings. Widely considered the most dramatic seventh game in history was the 1960 game between the Pittsburgh Pirates and the Yankees, when Bill Mazeroski's homer in the bottom of the ninth gave the Pirates a 10-9 victory and the World Championship.

Callan was expecting that kind of game today. He knew Steve Watson would turn in a great pitching performance, and he knew the Yankees' ace, C.C. Sabathia, would be up to the task, as well.

The game settled into a pitching duel. Sabathia allowed only two scratch hits and a walk through the first four innings, and Watson was matching him almost pitch for pitch, allowing only three harmless singles. In the top of the fifth, Watson made the first mistake, leaving a fastball over the middle of the plate. Derek Jeter did not miss it, slamming it into the left field bleachers.

Fortunately, there was nobody on base, and Watson got out of the inning without further damage. Callan heard himself saying the motivating plea to his team that he had used in Legion ball, and even with younger kids. "That's all right guys, we'll get it back. We weren't going to win unless we scored, anyway."

The Cubs did get it back, plus a bonus run, an inning later. With two outs in the sixth, Slagle and McGair singled and Baker followed with a double to the gap in right center that scored both runners. The Cubs led, 2-1, and after Keith Orlando grounded out for the third out, they were just nine outs away from the World Championship.

Up in the press box, Kevin Andrews was nervous. He had done some preliminary stories, ready to go in the newspaper if the Cubs won or if they lost, but now he was getting ready to start writing the framework of the game story that would lead tomorrow's paper.

Kevin had always worked better when he was under a tight deadline, letting his fingers fly over the computer keyboard, in effect letting the story write itself. He knew that would have to be the case tonight, because if he let himself think about it, he would be overwhelmed and unable to write.

Kevin had had more than the Cubs on his mind lately. He kept thinking about Nikki, and the more he thought about her, the bigger his smile grew. He knew he was falling in love. He was looking forward to spending as much time with her as possible this winter, and he was becoming convinced that at some point in the near future he was going to ask her to marry him.

The people who were with T.J. Vitello in the owner's box were aware of how much he was sweating as the game progressed. They empathized with him, knowing how badly he wanted his team to win.

T.J., of course, was sweating for another reason that only he and Frankie Cusamano knew. As the crowd went wild when the Cubs took the lead in the bottom of the sixth, T.J. quietly picked up the backpack and slipped out of his box and began the walk down the ramp toward the lower deck.

He knew, of course, that he was being watched. He had no idea how Frankie would be able to guarantee that seat 1 in row A of section 213 would be unoccupied at this exact moment, but there was no doubt in his mind it would be. Every seat in Wrigley, as it turned out, was open because all the fans were on their feet, screaming and yelling as loud as their lungs allowed.

Would Frankie be in the row behind him? Or sitting next to him? T.J. had no way of knowing, and he knew if he tried to look around and identify him, it would be the last thing he would ever do.

T.J. reached the designated seat just as the first Yankee batter was retired in the top of the seventh on a ground ball to short. The seat was, indeed, vacant. As T.J. placed the backpack under the seat and sat down, out of the corner of his eye he thought a couple of people might have recognized him. He whispered to himself, "Don't do it, don't say anything, just watch the game."

Everybody's eyes quickly were drawn back to the field when Alex Rodriguez lofted a long fly toward center that looked like it might leave the park. Slagle kept going back, reaching the warning track, then the wall, before he jumped. He timed it perfectly, catching the ball at the apex of his jump just as it was about to drop over the wall.

Watson got the final out, and the Cubs were only six outs away from the win. As T.J. and everyone else looked toward the press box, to see who would be singing "Take Me Out to the Ballgame," T.J. realized he didn't even know who it was going to be. Tim Jenkins had told him before the game he wanted it to be a surprise.

As he looked toward the home radio booth, he now saw who it was, and it was more than just one person. It was a quartet, the four greatest living Cubs, all Hall of Famers – Ernie Banks, Billy Williams, Ferguson Jenkins, and Ryne Sandberg. T.J. had seen them earlier, in the press box, but he thought they were just here to watch the game. The crowd reached a new decibel level.

When the song was over, T.J. slipped unnoticed from his seat, leaving the backpack behind. He almost expected somebody to come running after him as he walked away and tap him on the shoulder. "Sir, you forgot this." But nobody seemed to notice him or the backpack.

Entering his box, he saw Phil Donnelly for the first time. He must have been in the seats behind the dugout and had come up to the box during the last inning.

"Phil," he called out, "I've been trying to reach you all day. We have to talk."

"Now?" Donnelly said. "Can't it wait?"

"No, it's waited long enough. It won't take long. We can still watch what happens."

The two men moved into the front row of seats and sat down, just as the Cubs finished going down one-two-three, sending the game to the eighth.

"Phil, I've been going over everything and I just have got to get answers to some questions about my dad's finances. You have to know more than you have told me, and I am afraid I must insist that if you want to continue working for me, and the Cubs, you have to tell me everything you know."

"Are you threatening to fire me?"

"If that's what it takes. Tell me why my dad was so bad off. Why was he going to sell the team? What happened to all his money?"

"OK," Donnelly sighed, "I'll tell you, even though your dad swore me to secrecy. There's really not a whole lot of mystery to it. You know your dad always was interested in making a quick buck. Back in the 1960s, he found out about this oil company that was digging a lot of new wells and was looking for investors. He got in at the ground level and made a killing, something like $60 million in just 10 years or so.

"That was great, but he didn't get out when he should have, and when the market bellied out in the 1970s, he lost more money than that. Still, he didn't learn his lesson and stayed in the oil market, even expanding his shares, and his fortune steadily began to grow again in the 1980s. He made back all of the money he had lost, and quite a bit more.

"The last few years, the bottom fell out again and he was losing his shirt, more money than he had ever lost before. He was so desperate for money I was afraid he might do something drastic. I was actually relieved when he told me he was thinking about selling the club, and wanted me to find out what he could get for it.

"I think he was tired of some of the bullshit in baseball, but I think he was more tired of making and losing money. He wanted to make one last big hit, the biggest score of his life, selling the team, then be able to walk away. He just never got the chance. Just think, he took out all of that extra insurance when I know he thought it was a waste of money. I bet he would be laughing right now if he was here."

T.J. absorbed the information, thinking more about what Donnelly had said than what was happening on the field, where the Yankees had used a single, a bunt, and another single to score the tying run.

"Oh, my dad would be laughing all right. You're right, he was going to make the biggest score of his life," T.J. thought.

"One more question, and then we can get back to the game," T.J. said. "Why did my dad change his plans to go on that trip? He almost never went on the road with the team. Did he tell you why he decided to go?"

Donnelly shook his head no. "Nothing specific. He just said it had been a long time since he had been on a road trip and he wanted to take one last trip. I remember him using those exact words 'one last trip.' I know he didn't have any premonitions of disaster, but that was the first thing I thought about when I heard about the crash. It was indeed his 'one last trip.'"

T.J. rested his chin on his left thumb.

"It's one of those questions we will never be able to answer," Donnelly said.

❧

The Cubs had managed to get out of the inning with the game tied. They failed to score in the bottom of the eighth, however, leaving the Yankees the chance to go ahead in the top of the ninth.

Callan brought in Tippett, his closer, and the right-hander responded as he had since joining the Cubs, blowing away the Yankees in order. The stage was set for the bottom of the ninth.

Callan had made a double-switch when he brought in Tippett, since the pitcher's spot was due to bat second in the inning. The catcher, Luis Roman, led off the inning by drawing a walk from the Yankees' closer, Mariano Rivera. The crowd was roaring on every pitch.

Callan called time and sent in a pinch-runner, Matt Kennedy, for Roman. Scott McKenzie was the batter, and he laid down a perfect sacrifice bunt that moved Kennedy to second. Chico Gonzalez was up, and Callan thought the Yankees might walk him to set up the double play.

Instead, Girardi had Rivera pitch to Gonzalez and the Cubs' shortstop swung and missed at a ball in the dirt for strike three and the second out.

As Slagle walked toward the plate, Callan's eyes were glued on Girardi in the Yankees' dugout. He could not believe the Yankees' manager would risk walking Slagle, bringing his former slugger, McGair, to the plate. He knew he would take his chances with Slagle, and he was certain Girardi would, too.

The first pitch was low for ball one. Slagle swung too early on the next pitch from Rivera and fouled it off to the right side. One and one. Slagle called time and stepped out of the batter's box, moving his shoulders up and down to try to stay loose. Stepping back in, he was ready.

Rivera delivered the pitch, and Slagle recognized the break of the curve and this time his swing was perfect. The bat connected squarely with the ball and it took off about six feet over the shortstop Jeter's head. With two outs, Kennedy was off and running as soon as Slagle's bat made contact. He picked up the signal from Alex Thompson, the third base coach, who was frantically waving him home.

Slagle was watching, too. He knew he had to get to first base – he didn't want to be his generation's Fred Merkle – but he reached the base with his head turned back toward home. Kennedy slid, just as the throw reached catcher Jorge Posada. Umpire Ron Kulpa was in perfect position, peering through the dust, and his arms went straight out in the universal safe sign.

The Cubs had won the World Series.

Pandemonium. The security guards and Chicago police tried to keep the fans from pouring onto the field, but they were severely outnumbered. The Cubs players were just as animated as the fans, finally reaching the safety of their clubhouse.

Callan was crying, and he was not the only one. Slagle was in tears, even before his father made it through the crowd and into the locker room. When Slagle saw his father, the tears flowed faster as the two men exchanged a giant embrace. No words were necessary.

From the corner of his eye, as he watched Slagle and his father, Callan thought he saw a woman that he recognized. He turned his head to get a better look and almost did a double take, considering it had been 13 years since he had seen his ex-wife. She had her arm around the shoulders of a young boy, whom he immediately recognized from the last picture she had sent him in the spring. His son, Charlie, was wearing a Cubs' jersey.

"Hey," Chelsea said as she and Charlie walked toward him. "Congratulations. You did it."

Callan didn't know what to say. "I didn't know you were here. How did … Did you … Is this … Where are … "

Chelsea put her finger up to her lips to quiet Mike. "Shh. Don't worry," she said, "I've got the answers to all of your questions, and I'm going to give you plenty of time to ask them. I know it's been a long time. But now we will have time to see what the future holds. You're going to need some time to get to know your son."

Mike was still looking at the smile on Chelsea's face and the gleam in her eyes, something he had been longing for and hadn't seen in 13 years, and thinking about how to respond when somebody tapped him on the shoulder. Turning around, he found Sam Lawson staring him straight in the face.

"Oh great," he thought, "I go from a great moment to having to talk to this jerk a second later."

"Mike, congratulations," Lawson said as he offered his right hand to Callan. "But I've got something more important to say to you. I'm sorry. I owe you the largest apology I can offer. I made a mistake 13 years ago, and I didn't know how bad a mistake it was until last night.

"My wife told me everything that happened with the team in Des Moines. She told me how you were the one she wanted to sleep with, but you kept telling her no. She started sleeping with one of your players, hoping to make you mad. When I found out something was going on and confronted her, she said she was having an affair with you. That's why I fired you. I just needed the excuse of the fight in Omaha to convince the rest of the front office. That was why I sent out the memo to all of the teams after I moved to the Commissioner's office telling them not to hire you. I was still mad that you had been with my wife. As soon as I found out last night what actually happened back then, I found Chelsea and explained it all to her and asked her and Charlie to come to the game tonight as my guests. I knew one of the reasons she had divorced you was the rumored affair. I told her you were completely innocent.

"I don't know what else to tell you. I was wrong about you. You did a hell of a job this season, and you should be awfully proud."

Commissioner White and T.J. had finally reached the stage, set up in the middle of the tiny locker room, and were ready for the presentation of the World Championship Trophy.

The ceremony was brief, T.J. thanked the Commissioner, thanked his players, thanked Callan, and thanked the fans. He thrust the trophy high in the air, then turned and handed it to Callan.

While the celebration roared, in the locker room, in the ballpark, throughout Wrigleyville, on Rush Street, and through the entire city of Chicago, T.J. walked, unnoticed and alone, back to the silence of his office.

Chapter 26

T.J. didn't know how long he had sat in his office, staring at nothing, thinking about nothing and everything at the same time, before he finally stood up, took a beer out of the small refrigerator in the corner, and sat back in his dad's old leather chair.

He twisted the top off and took a long drink. Setting the cold beer on his desk, he interlocked his fingers and placed them behind his head as he leaned back and gazed at the ceiling.

"OK," he said out loud, "What am I going to do?"

T.J. now had all of the answers he was going to get. The only remaining question, which he knew would never be answered since it involved only two people and they were both dead, was what had gone wrong in the communications between his father and Eddie Marshall.

The two had no doubt set up a plan to have his dad call Eddie on the beeper, a signal that he was to go ahead and dump the canister of beads into the fuel tanks of the plane. T.J. suspected that his dad had purchased the beeper for Eddie and was the only person who knew the number. That had to be the number that was on the yellow Post-It note folded into his wallet.

His dad would never have called to signal Eddie to go ahead and dump the canister into the fuel tanks if he was going to be on the plane. Somehow the beeper had gone off that Sunday afternoon and since the team was leaving that night, Eddie thought that was Tony calling with the signal. Eddie would have had no idea Tony was going to be on the plane. The only explanation T.J. could think of was that the call had been a wrong number, a total accident. Somebody had reached that number by mistake.

T.J. knew his dad had taken out the extra insurance to more than make up for all of the money he had lost the last several years through his bad oil investments. And, putting that information together with what Donnelly had told him, he knew his dad was going to go one step farther after the plane crashed. He would have announced that he was too distraught to continue owning the club and was placing it up for sale, collecting another $700 million or so on top of the $382 million he was going to get in the extra insurance payoffs.

Even if half of the money for the sale of the team went to taxes, Tony still stood to gain almost $600 million from his scheme. It was, T.J. had to admit, brilliant.

Tony had made those decisions on his own, without consulting anybody. Now it was time for T.J. to make decisions.

If he went to the NTSB and the cops and told them everything he knew about the chemist, and Eddie, and Frankie, Dr. Hansbrough and Frankie would be arrested and sent to prison. If the insurance company found out the crash was not an accident, however, they would refuse to pay off on the policies.

T.J. could keep quiet, as he was sure Hansbrough and Frankie would do, accept the insurance money and then decide if he wanted to carry out the final part of his dad's plan and sell the team, or keep it. Donnelly was the only other person who knew about the insurance money, and he would have no reason to think T.J. was anything other than a very lucky son of a wise man.

The curse on the Cubs was over. The team had won the World Series. T.J., however, was not free.

He had not broken the curse that traps someone when they are driven by the desire for power and money. He had not broken the curse of sin, passed down from generation to generation. The sins of the father had been passed on to his son. That was a far greater curse than anything that had haunted the Cubs.

He hadn't noticed it before, but T.J. suddenly realized the Muzak system was still playing inside the Cubs' offices. Harry Chapin was singing "The Cat's in the Cradle." T.J. heard the final line of the song.

"He'd grown up just like me, my boy was just like me."

As he heard the final words of the song, and the last chords of the guitar disappeared in silence, T.J.'s gaze landed on a picture on the rich, paneled wall. It was a photo taken at a reunion of past Cubs' greats, Hall of Famers all. They were all there, smiling, rejoicing, remembering the pride they felt in wearing a Cubs' uniform.

T.J. stood up and walked closer to the photo. He looked into the eyes of Billy Williams and Ernie Banks and Ferguson Jenkins and Ryne Sandberg, their arms stretching across each other's shoulders. As he moved his focus from player to player, T.J. could almost feel their eyes boring a hole deep into him.

T.J. started to shake. He turned to steady himself on the corner of his desk, afraid he was going to fall. As the tears began to come, slowly at first, then faster, he made it back to the chair and collapsed. He buried his face in his hands, his elbows resting on the desk.

He didn't know how long he had been crying, when slowly, the tears stopped. T.J. reached into his back pocket and pulled out a handkerchief and blew his nose and wiped away the final few tears.

"I can't do it," he said, to an audience of one.

"When I was a boy, the only goal I had in life was to see the Cubs win the World Series," he said. "I wanted that more than anything. I prayed, asking God to let it happen. We came so close, but in the end, each time, something went wrong.

"Here I am, the owner of the Cubs, and we have finally won the World Series. The whole city is celebrating. The whole country is celebrating. I am the only person in the world not going crazy. I can't take it. I've got to stop this."

T.J. turned toward another wall, where a photo of Tony Vitello was prominently displayed. It had been taken on the day his dad bought the Cubs from the Wrigley family.

"I'm sorry, Dad, but owning the Cubs was the best thing that ever happened to you in your life, and you never realized it. It was always about the money. That was all you cared about. I almost fell into your trap, but tomorrow I am going to do something about it."

T.J. noticed that day's *Tribune,* discarded in the trash can next to his desk. He knew at that moment Kevin Andrews was probably still up in the press box, working on what he thought was the biggest story he would ever write in his life, about the Cubs winning the World Series.

"Kevin, ol' buddy, I'm going to let you get a few hours of sleep and then you are going to find out you were wrong. I've got a story to tell you."

T.J. stood up, took a Cuban cigar out of the humidor behind the desk, lit it, and smiled as he walked out of his office, ready to join the party.

The End

Acknowledgements

This book would not have been possible without the help and assistance of numerous people, foremost the two most important women in our lives, Lauri Van Slyke and Sally Rains.

The authors are indebted to pilots Dave Kloth and Jeff Jacober for their assistance with the technical details of flying an airplane, and the procedures used in the event of an actual emergency. Airline mechanic Mike Hanser also answered many of our questions and provided additional information on technical issues.

All of the people we have encountered in baseball over the years during our careers also played a role in formulating this book, either intentionally or unintentionally. Several key people who offered assistance and advice included former general managers Kevin Malone and Lee Thomas, front office executive Brad Wood of the St. Louis Cardinals and agent Jim Turner.

Thanks to Sharon Bedgood for providing details about the very real town of Mound City, Kansas. Britt Casteel, an American baseball fan living in Japan, provided assistance with details about Japanese baseball, and friends Curt Smith, Ken Samelson, Mike Barnes and Rick and Ann Horton also provided advice and encouragement for which we are very grateful.

Andy Van Slyke and Rob Rains
March 2010

Authors

Andy Van Slyke played in the major leagues for 13 years. He won five Gold Gloves and was a three-time All-Star selection. He was almost as well known for his quick wit as he was for his baseball ability. He spent four baseball seasons as a coach with the Detroit Tigers. Van Slyke provides the inside knowledge that makes this book stand out from other baseball novels.

Van Slyke was the co-author of *Tigers Confidential, The Untold Inside Story of the 2008 Season.*

Rob Rains is the author of 28 non-fiction books, most on baseball, including autobiographies or biographies of Tony La Russa, Mark McGwire, Ozzie Smith, Jack Buck, Red Schoendienst, and Dave Phillips. He currently is the sports editor of *St. Louis Globe-Democrat.com,* an online daily newspaper, and an adjunct professor in the school of communications at Webster University.